# THE MATH TUTOR

# THE
# MATH TUTOR

A NOVEL

## ROBERT LAURENCE

SUNSTONE
PRESS

SANTA FE

Sunstone books may be purchased for educational, business, or sales promotional use.
For information please write: Special Markets Department, Sunstone Press,
P.O. Box 2321, Santa Fe, New Mexico 87504-2321.

Book and cover design › Vicki Ahl
Body typeface › Minion Pro
Printed on acid-free paper
∞
eBook 978-1-61139-367-5

---

Library of Congress Cataloging-in-Publication Data

Laurence, Robert, 1945 September 19-
  The math tutor : a novel / by Robert Laurence.
     pages ; cm
  ISBN 978-1-63293-053-8 (softcover : acid-free paper)
  1. Interpersonal relations--Fiction. 2. Teenagers--Fiction. 3. Physicists--Fiction.
4. Widowers--Fiction. I. Title.
  PS3612.A9442278M38 2015
  813'.6--dc23
                                2015002715

---

**WWW.SUNSTONEPRESS.COM**
SUNSTONE PRESS / POST OFFICE BOX 2321 / SANTA FE, NM 87504-2321 /USA
(505) 988-4418 / ORDERS ONLY (800) 243-5644 / FAX (505) 988-1025

For Ferdinand, by Nijinsky II, out of Banja Luka, by Double Jay, who won the Kentucky Derby only to feel the butcher's knife. *Sic transit equorum mundus.*

## Author's Note

Similarities to living persons, real places and actual events are acknowledged. Readers are reminded, though, that this is a work of fiction. All events, descriptions and snatches of dialogue should be considered to have been made up by someone who doesn't know what he's talking about, and neither actually to be, nor intended to be, reflections of reality.

Except for this: Horses, Thoroughbreds particularly, Thoroughbreds running at lower-rung tracks even more particularly, can lead very precarious existences. Their lives are long, their careers short, and their off-the-track futures uncertain. Some are abused; more are neglected. Too many are slaughtered for their meat. Readers are encouraged to pick a Thoroughbred retirement charity and be generous thereto. The horses will be better for it, and grateful in their own way.

—RL
Hindsville, Arkansas
January 2015

# 1

**The Second Tuesday.**

Horses divide the things around them into two groups: horses and other things. Among other things, there are things that move and things that don't move. Things that move should be run from. Things that don't move are either good to eat, or not good to eat. Things that don't move and aren't good to eat may be ignored, except for prickly things, like blackberry bushes and electric fences. Prickly things should be avoided. Human beings present a quandary. On the one hand (so to speak), they are not horses and they move, and so they should be run from. And often are. On the other hand, they bring food and open gates and can generally be handy to have around.

Just One Look, a five-year-old bay Thoroughbred gelding, recently retired from the track at Claremore, stood in his round pen early one November morning and watched as the day came upon him with its usual orderliness. The sky turned from black to gray; the lights went on in the house on the hillside; the school bus went by; a human walked down the hillside and approached his round pen. There were two humans at this place: this one and the other one. Just One Look did not himself deal in names; he merely knew them as *this one* and *the other one*. This one walked down the hill soon after the lights went on in the house. This one would have something sweet in his pocket, with hay and grain to follow. This one smelled musty and old; the other one smelled young and pretty. There had been many humans around the backside in Claremore, too many for Just One Look to keep track of, and not all of whom had treated him kindly, but here in this place there were only two: this one and the other one, who would come to see him later.

The human that Just One Look awaited with what passed for equine patience was Sam Butler, sixty-eight years old, retired, widowed and only half-awake. He wore jeans, work boots and a worn, torn, faded-red hooded sweatshirt, whose inscription, whatever it might once have said, was now washed into illegibility. He had the hood up, and under it was a sweat-stained US Forest Service ball cap. Ragged, graying, thin, unwashed-today-or-yesterday hair under the cap. Reading glasses in plastic frames on a cord around his neck. A five-day-old beard, more white than gray. Tall, with a thin, aging build. He held a plastic bottle of Coca-Cola Classic, room temperature and a third down. Hopping along beside him was a three-legged black and tan squirrel-dog he called Teena, short for Fifteen Dollars, that being what Sam had paid the owner of the dog's mother in order to keep the pup, who was the runt of the litter, from being shot. Sam knew for a fact that she had turned out to be a better hunter than any of her sibs, but she had lost her right front three years previously to a copperhead bite, and her squirrel-chasing days were over. She still got around pretty well, considering, but Sam hoped that her next confrontation with *A. contortrix contortrix* would kill her, because she couldn't afford to lose another leg, and he didn't want to have to be the one to put her down. She was his complete pal.

Sam tucked the Coke bottle into the hip pocket of his jeans, rubbed his hands together against the morning chill, opened the gate to the paddock around the stalls and looked over the morning scene. Fifteen Dollars, wary, as always, of the horses, hung back.

There were five stalls that made up the stable, backing up against the creek, which gurgled with the autumn's rains. They were closed on the back, that is to say the north side, and on the west, but open to the east and south. A gate separated the westernmost two stalls from the easternmost three, and a round pen was attached to the two, which allowed him to keep the new horse up overnight. Eventually the new horse would join the others in the night pasture, but for now Just One Look, whom Sam called The Looker and who just six weeks ago had been running for a thousand dollar claiming tag at Claremore, for now he seemed more comfortable being confined overnight, used as he was to spending twenty-two hours a day in a cement-block stall. Sam hadn't needed a fifth horse, but a farrier he knew at Claremore had called and said that this horse was one more off-the-board finish away from having his haunch ground up and served as pâté in Antwerp. Claremore was the bottom of the race-track barrel, and a gelding claimer over there—even one who was winning—had three hooves in the goddamn slaughterhouse anyway, so Sam had driven over with the trailer and brought him home. Sally would have been pleased.

Just now, The Looker stood at the gate of the round pen, bobbing his head up and down, wanting his hay and grain. "Good morning, buddy," Sam greeted him, and rubbed his blaze, which was crooked, pointing toward his left nostril. "Oh, you are a handsome boy." He let the horse nibble the carrot stub out of his hand, enjoying the feel of the rough lips on his palm. Evening Smoke, the twenty-year-old lead mare, had kept The Looker company standing outside the round pen all night, a duty she didn't enjoy and which she would take out on the other three later in the morning when she rejoined them in the east, or day, pasture. "Good morning, Princess." He scratched behind her left ear. "Yes, you're handsome, too." She shook her head and walked away, letting him know how she felt about having to spend the night here with this boy.

The other three—two geldings and a mare, all Thoroughbreds and all rescued by his wife after failed careers at the track—were officially named Dreadnaught, Miss Run Run and Restive, though Ellie called them Naughty, Daisy (after the star on her forehead) and Mister. They had wandered down to the stable from the night pasture and were now on the other side of the gate, ready for their morning feed. Restive and the mare had put themselves into their proper stalls, while Dreadnaught, as was his practice, stood at the gate, pawing the ground, trying to hurry Sam along on the morning's business.

"Dee! Stop that. Be patient." Dreadnaught ignored him. Sam cleared his throat, spat, took a swallow of Coke and spoke again. "Stop that." The pawing went on, as it always did. Sam put the cap back on his Coke and opened the feed room door. First he put out food for Teena, who checked both ways for horses, then hopped up the step and into the feed room. Then he gathered up three flakes of Bermuda grass hay, two for The Looker and one for Evening Smoke, stepped out, closed the feed room door behind him, and carried the hay in his arms out to their two stalls.

The accident seemed to happen, as such things often do, in slow motion. Dreadnaught, seeing the hay, continued pawing, now at the gate itself, and his right front hoof found its way between the middle slat of the gate and the diagonal support board. It then slid to his right—Sam's left—jamming the horse's fetlock into the small angle between the two boards. Lifting a front hoof up and moving it forward and to the outside, which was what was needed now to release Dreadnaught, is not a natural movement for a horse unless he's moving forward at the same time. So instead, the horse pulled back, doing himself no good, but only rattling the wooden gate, which increased his frustration and jammed the fetlock tighter into the angle where it was stuck.

"Hold on, Dee. I'll help." Sam put the hay back into the feed room, which caused The Looker to increase his head bobbing, and Evening Smoke to begin pacing around in a circle in her stall. "Hold on, hold on. God damn it, would everyone just relax and settle down? Smokey. Stop it." Fifteen Dollars, finished with her meal, began to bark from inside the feed room at the commotion. "Teena, shut up. God, I can't hear myself think." Sam headed for the gate to extricate the trapped leg.

And then, for whatever reason, Dreadnaught lost his balance, his hindquarters went over and he fell down heavily on his left side, his right front leg still trapped in the angle of the gate, and now levering the middle rail away from him and the diagonal brace toward him. He began to snort and struggle in earnest, approaching the panicky stage that can be dangerous. Not liking the sound of the struggle, The Looker ran out of his stall, into the round pen, and began to whinny and paw himself, which in turn caused Evening Smoke to run out of her stall and begin bucking and kicking at nothing in particular. The dog continued to bark, now standing at the feed room door with her hackles raised, and the two other horses, who had been waiting patiently for their hay, began nervously whinnying.

Sam stood with his hands in the pouch in the front of his sweatshirt and watched. There is nothing much you can do with a struggling horse other than get yourself hurt. And this situation was well beyond the point where calming words would do any good, so he just stood and watched. It was going to be a close contest between the strength of the slats in the gate—a true inch thickness of rough-sawn sycamore, tougher than pine, but softer than oak—and the horse's cannon bone, about as strong, say, as a baseball bat. If there had been time to analyze the situation, which there wasn't, Sam would not have been able to guess which was going to win. Maybe the horse would just calm down, stop struggling and let himself be helped, but Sam wouldn't have bet on that possibility.

Finally—though the whole event could not have taken longer than a minute or two—finally, the wood gave way. The diagonal support board splintered, the middle slat broke in two places, and the leg came free. Dreadnaught heaved himself quickly to his feet, shook, blinked, snorted and then stood quietly.

Sam studied the scene. Dreadnaught was bleeding badly from the shank, but a horse can lose a lot of blood and still not be in danger. More important, he was putting his full weight on his right front, which meant it probably wasn't broken. So he didn't need to hook up the trailer for an emergency trip to the vet, which wouldn't have done much good anyway, if the leg had been broken. The gate was smashed and dangerous. The other horses were beginning to calm down, now that the fuss was over, and Teena had gone to lie down in safety, now that the situation no longer required her direct supervision. So: first get everyone safely in his or her stall, munching hay. Then stop the bleeding and check for other damage that might need doctoring. Then grain. Then dismantle the gate. Then re-bandage the shank. Then send them all up to the east pasture, clean up the stalls and rebuild the gate. Somewhere in there breakfast for himself would be nice.

Sam Butler enjoyed having his morning scheduled out for him. Ellie would be by at around ten.

Melissa and Stuart Wyckoff, Ellen Quincy's maternal grandparents, were hippies. They found their way to the Ozark Highlands during the back-to-the-Earth movement of the Seventies, and bought into a beautifully situated, if aggressively primitive commune near the headwaters of the Kings River, in southern Madison County, Arkansas, not the Ozarks at all, strictly speaking, but the Boston Mountains. The buy-in was cheap and the commune was friendly, commodious, and compatible with their own strongly held, if loosely defined, anti-corporate, anti-war, New Age sensibilities. At the commune, they went by the names Blue Drift and Prince Rupert.

And so it was that, on a warm autumn afternoon in 1983, when she was twenty-eight years old, Blue Drift, f/k/a Melissa Wyckoff, delivered her first and only child in the large tipi that served as the commune's meeting lodge, lying naked on a worn Persian rug in the center of a circle of allegedly sacred stones, her red hair in plaits and damp with the sweat of her efforts. She was attended to by an informally trained midwife, by Prince Rupert, the proud father-to-be, and by a dozen or so other members of the commune, who had invited themselves to the event, along with an assorted handful of their children. Two pet dogs, who hung out most afternoons in the tipi, would have stayed, but were banished by the midwife. The labor was neither prolonged nor difficult, so the occasion was played festively, marijuana smoke mixing with East Indian incense in the tipi's air, and reggae music playing on a boom box off to the side. Near the end, already as naked as Blue Drift was, their ardor increased by her exertion, and their discretion decreased in equal measure by a cocktail of controlled and uncontrolled substances, two members of the audience who went by the names of Sky and Harmonia began what was plainly foreplay. Blue Drift was oblivious, the midwife did not approve, but many members of the audience, also (if not equally) stoned, hooted their encouragement. As this play became rather less fore- and more during-, Harmonia's usual partner suggested somewhat sourly that Sky might find a more suitable place to complete the job, and the couple complied to the extent of exiting themselves from the tipi. The privacy afforded them by their departure, however, was more visual than auditory, and so, in the end, one woman crowned while the other climaxed, and the girl baby slipped into the midwife's waiting hands to the accompaniment of the synchronized wails of Blue Drift and Harmonia, to which she added her own lusty squall.

Given the melodious expressions of agony and ecstasy that greeted her birth, it was a complete bloody miracle that the baby wasn't called Michelangelica, but Blue Drift was in one of her bird periods, so the child was named Cardinal. When the midwife observed that a last name was customary, Blue Drift and Prince Rupert admitted that they were in fact married and used the same last name, asking for midwiffic confidentiality, because both of these items would have been subjected to loud, if good-natured, communal derision. The midwife said she understood, and the birth certificate was made to read Cardinal (no middle name) Wyckoff. Christening, as we shall see, was to come considerably later. For the time being, the blessings of Isis and Xochiquetzal, along with some obscure and mispronounced Druidic chants were thought sufficient.

Cardinal's upbringing at the commune was unstructured, undisciplined, and largely unclothed. Her schooling was spotty. She learned to read quickly and easily, but there were few books for children, so, except for trips to the county library in Huntsville, she was mainly left with New Age tracts and science fiction that was too old for her. However, Blue Drift enjoyed reading Dickens and the Brontës aloud to her daughter, and before long she began to recognize the words above her mother's forefinger as it traced across the page: "Chapter One. I am born." Her education in music and art was, as one might expect, eclectic, and Prince Rupert told her about history, albeit with a certain Trotskyite slant, but for math or science neither of her parents cared much. Overall, it would be fair to say that Cardinal enjoyed her early childhood, missed few meals, and was loved by her parents and the extended family that was the commune. She never knew her grandparents.

By 9:45 when the dog began barking at the car that she, but not Sam, heard coming along the road, the horses had been fed, looked after, and sent up to the day pasture, except for Dreadnaught, who was in his stall for observation, having been washed, wrapped and administered a gram of bute against pain and inflammation, and 10 cc IM of penicillin against infection. Sam had managed to fit in a slice of raisin bread, an apple and another Coke for breakfast, though Dreadnaught had gotten more than half of the apple and Teena about a quarter of the raisin bread. The broken gate lay off its hinges and on the ground, and Sam was dismantling the pieces when the dog began barking. The dirt county road that ran along in front of Sam's house was little enough used so that it had a grassy strip down the center of its only lane. It went nowhere, really, and was traveled by hardly anyone who did not live in one of the five farms along its three-mile length, except for the Huntsville school bus twice a day and the postman once. Since the amputation, Teena had developed a discerning ear for the sound of the cars that needed chasing and those she could trust to depart on their own, so most of the day she'd lie and watch the passing traffic, such as it was, with a mere woof or two to remind the cars to keep going.

This one, though, which Sam could now see coming down the hill from the west, she didn't recognize, and she set up a howl and took off to meet it at a truly astonishing three-legged clip. Sam went back to studying how he could salvage enough of the broken diagonal to rebuild the gate. Perhaps he could eliminate the diagonal altogether and put a vertical support here in the middle. He had enough wood for that. But what, then, would keep the damn thing square? He marked the board just above where Dreadnaught had busted it.

The car, contrary to Teena's unambiguous instructions, did not drive past, but pulled in and parked behind the larger of Sam's two pickups, the one he used to pull the trailer. He didn't recognize the car, but then Sam, unlike most of his neighbors, was not particularly good at identifying people by their vehicles. A still-unrecognizable man got out of the car, and Teena, as was typical, immediately stopped demanding that the intruder leave, and instead began whining for all the attention she could get. The man, Sam noted with approval, took the time to greet the dog and scratch her, first behind the ears and then on that spot above her tail that was impossible to get to.

"Back here." Sam raised his voice and waved, then laid the board he was working on across the saw horses, picked up the Skil saw and whacked off the end, two-thirds of his attention on not cutting off his thumb, and half of what was left on the man walking toward him. A suit, with an unbuttoned overcoat. Dress shoes. Jehovah's Witness? Alone?

Then the man waved. "Sam."

Ah. It was R. Johnson Reynolds, former colleague, one-time dean of the law school, now the holder of the Muckity Muck Endowed Professorship of This and That, blah, blah, blah. Nice guy, if a little full of himself. Fifteen years younger than Sam, and eight inches shorter, bald, but well-bearded. Sam put down the saw and wiped his right hand on his jeans.

"John." They shook hands. "Nice to see you. Welcome to Hindsville."

"This is Hindsville?" Reynolds asked, looking around at the woods and pastures.

"Greater Hindsville. Downtown is that way." He pointed to the east.

"Downtown?"

"Post office, bank, café and A.T. Smith's Mercantile."

In the fall of 1993, as she had just turned ten, and in what was to be the first step in the family's eventual departure from the commune, Cardinal was sent to the nearest public elementary school, located, perhaps prophetically, in the town of St. Paul. She initially tested into the third grade, mostly because she had never seen a multiple choice question in her life, and filled in the little circles so as to create an interesting pattern. Before the first grading period, however, she was moved up to the fourth grade, and again into the fifth before Christmas. There, she was found by her teachers to be bright, but incorrigible. She read voraciously, well above her grade level, though she calculated somewhat below it. She played unselfishly with the other children, much practice at which she had received at the commune, but she seemed to follow her teacher's instructions, or not, largely at random. When she moved on from the sixth grade, the staff at St. Paul Elementary was largely glad to see her go.

Junior high school in Huntsville was a long morning's bus ride from the commune, to avoid which the family rented a small house in town, returning to the commune on the weekends. At junior high, Cardinal was found by the staff to be bright, but promiscuous. One place her education had not been lacking at the commune was in the matter of sex, and she had watched many sex acts—both conventional and less so—being performed, and she unselfconsciously shared her knowledge with her classmates of both genders, sometimes to the point of penetration. Her intimate little lessons were valuable in their own way, as they freed up the time needed for the Huntsville Junior High staff's aggressive pursuit of an Abstinence Only curriculum. At the age of fourteen, she and her mother, who by now had reverted to being called Melissa, had a very tardy discussion about birth control on the drive home from the Fayetteville Women's Clinic, the only abortion provider for a hundred miles. Cardinal then proceeded to surprise her mother by choosing the principle of abstinence over the mechanics of contraception. Sex was not all that important to her, and, with her early-teen partners, not all that interesting either, and she gave it up without apparent effort or regret.

In high school, Cardinal was found to be bright and studious. She worked hard and did well, avoided math and science when she could, and placed herself near the top of her class. She began to think of a career as an English teacher, or, when she let herself dream, as a professor of literature. But, in the end, she reverted to her old habits sufficiently so as to be three days pregnant at commencement, where she gave an earnest valedictory address, and received a Rotary scholarship to attend the U of A in Fayetteville. But when the pregnancy became manifest that summer, she shelved her plans and her dreams, and, against her mother's advice, forwent another trip to the Women's Clinic, and married her boyfriend, a good-looking if rather listless young man named James Austin, two years her senior, who had never finished high school, did odd jobs and cut firewood out of the hardwood forests of Madison County, and grew a little marijuana on the side, though any potential profit from that crop, he and Cardinal mostly smoked away. They rented a used trailer that sat off the highway between Hindsville and Clifty, and settled in to await the baby in a state of near poverty that is common in Madison County, Arkansas.

Cardinal's baby, unlike Cardinal herself, was delivered by Medicaid dollars in the non-exotic environment of the Springdale Hospital's maternity unit, and was given the very ordinary name of Ellen Christine Austin.

"What happened here?" Johnson Reynolds said, looking at the gate on the ground.

"A horse, that one over there, decided to bust the hell out of it this morning. Did a nice job of it, too."

"Pissed off, was he?"

"Tangled up. He's a lucky son of a bitch not to be standing over there with his leg broken, waiting for the vet to come by and put out the big light."

"Which explains why you've got blood all over you?"

"Exactly. It was a little crazy around here this morning."

"Looks under control now."

"Pretty much."

Reynolds turned on his well-clad heel and looked around. "It's nice out here. I'd forgotten. Beautiful day."

"You've been here before?"

"For the memorial service."

"Oh. Of course."

"How long's it been?"

"Three years. A little more."

"Is Sally's grave out here? I remember how nice the ceremony was. Service, I mean."

"No. She was an only child who predeceased her parents, and I thought she should be buried in the family plot back east. Philadelphia. Her folks appreciated the gesture." Sam looked off toward the hollow where he and Sally used to walk while she picked mushrooms. She'd always teased him because he didn't trust her enough to eat what she picked, until she tried them first. "Very few people ever die from eating mushrooms," she had told him. And she hadn't.

Reynolds paused to give him a minute. Then, "How's retirement?"

Sam shook loose from the memory. "You mean except for the not-being-paid part?"

Reynolds laughed. "Except for that."

"Nice. Couldn't be better. Totally cool." His voice was flat.

"How do you stay busy?"

"Want to see my things-to-do list?"

"Not really. I meant how do you stay, I don't know, challenged?"

"Hanging a gate by oneself is harder than anything I ever did at the university. Which, now that you mention it, is why I'm not totally dismayed to see you."

"Can we talk for a few minutes?"

"You mean you didn't drive half-way into Madison County to ask me how I like retired life?"

"Word has it that the dean offered you a chance to come back when Sandy Olsen's unexpected departure left us one Contracts teacher short."

"She was very generous."

"But you said 'no.'"

"I said 'no.'"

"Why?"

"I'm past my best-by date."

"Oh, hell, Sam, we're all past our best-by dates. You were a goddam legend in the classroom."

"A legend. Huh. It's always better to be well-remembered than to be remembered well."

"A legend."

"What a massively ridiculous thing for anyone to say about anyone."

"You could still do it. We've got colleagues still teaching who are older than you." Sam said nothing but looked at Reynolds over the tops of his reading glasses. "Okay, forget that point. But still, why not? You know what they say: if you want to stay young, never retire."

"Who wants to stay young? I've been young; I didn't care for it."
"You're impossible to argue with."

The dissolution of the Kings River commune need not be dwelt upon at length, other than to note that it shared characteristics with events happening across the country in the Eighties and Nineties, events sufficiently similar to have led to any number of thoughtful and carefully footnoted scholarly articles produced by the next generation of academic sociologists seeking tenure. As previously noted, the Wyckoffs had become only part-time residents when Cardinal entered junior high, soon after which Stuart began rather successfully to sell used cars (and only a bit less successfully to speak Spanish) at a buy-here-pay-here lot in Huntsville. In 1999, when the membership became, for their tastes, rather too obsessed with preparations for Y2K, they surrendered their share back to the commune for ten cents on the dollar. The entire parcel eventually ended up in the hands of one member, who initially appeared to be savvy in the ways of land speculation, until he borrowed heavily in order to subdivide the parcel, lost everything, and took bankruptcy, before returning to Michigan to marry his high school sweetheart. He now manages a Payless shoe store in Saginaw.

After Cardinal graduated from Huntsville High and married James Austin, Stuart and Melissa moved to Fayetteville, and Stuart, who possessed a pre-commune BA in History from Penn State, gave up car selling and enrolled in the university, seeking an MA in communications. Melissa took a job as a check-out clerk at the local food coop, and babysat Ellie, giving Cardinal the opportunity to wait tables at the Crossbow in Huntsville. Melissa enjoyed both pieces of work and they were able to scrape by on her pay and Stuart's assistantship, which increased when he half-heartedly entered the PhD program in the fall of '03.

Providence intervened one day in the spring of 2005, when, walking back from lunch on Dickson Street, Stuart wandered into the Fayetteville Center of Ouachita Baptist University, a satellite facility remote from OBU's main campus in Arkadelphia. He began to hang out there, first studying in the quiet library, then chewing the fat with the students, finally seeking faculty advice about his future. Within two months he received his Calling: he was to preach the Gospel, first on the radio, then on television. He was to bring the Word to the listening and watching public. Praise the Lord.

Stuart was good at it. He made some demo tapes and was quickly given an early morning slot on the local Christian AM station. Then the morning drive. Then he was picked up regionally. The step to TV came via the local public access station, then to local cable, then to regional cable. Melissa, who knew a cool gig when she saw one, came on board, learning the production and bookkeeping sides of the business, so that eighteen months after Stuart had walked into OBU, the Wyckoffs had a thriving electronic ministry going—radio, TV, live streaming, podcasting, you name it—and, if they weren't exactly getting rich at it, they were doing all right.

If there were those cynical enough to see Stuart's conversion to Christianity as a career move, and Melissa's as Another New Thing, in a lifetime full of New Things, no one doubted the sincerity of their daughter's conversion. Cardinal fell for Jesus and she fell hard. She came to see her life as an unending series of sinful, self-indulgent acts, and she repented. Included in this repentance was her confession to James that she was not entirely certain that he was Ellie's father. In fact, due to one particular evening during graduation week, an evening when she had sort of let things get out of hand, she was precisely twenty percent certain that he was Ellie's father.

The divorce quickly followed, and when a DNA test showed that the dice had not fallen James's way, he surrendered all parental rights to the girl, provided, as he told the chancellor, that he didn't have to support the little bastard. He testified in open court that he had never, in fact, established a father-daughter relationship with Ellie, which was not so very far short of the truth. Ellie's opinion was not sought in the matter, and the divorce was granted, setting James free. The chancellor told her husband that night that never had she severed parental rights with so few reservations.

James celebrated his freedom with a three-day bender in Tulsa, which ended, as did his life, when he fell asleep with his truck straddling the Kansas City Southern shortline tracks in Siloam Springs on his way back to Clifty to claim what was owed him, to wit one last piece of ass from the bitch. Cardinal, who had recently discovered that God did not traffic in divorces, considered herself to be a widow, a widowhood she endured gracefully, and she and Ellie prayed every night at bedtime for James Austin's eternal soul.

"Anyway," Sam shrugged, "whomever you got to take Sandy's place is three months into the semester. Which means that that's not why you drove out dressed like you've got to be in class in ten minutes."

Reynolds checked his watch. "Class is in two hours and twenty-five minutes. No, it's something else. I'm chair of COPT..." The Committee on Promotion and Tenure.

"How the hell did you let that happen?"

"It was my turn."

"Small enough reason."

"Anyway, I've been instructed by the Committee to make you a proposal. Basically, Sam, the university needs you."

Sam studied the gate lying between them for a moment. "Cleveland."

"What?"

"I grew up in Cleveland, not Cincinnati. There was a good long period of my early childhood when I thought that Cincinnati was the end of the Earth. The literal end. A cliff. The river. Then nothing. I had a rather Ohio-centric upbringing. My parents finally took me down to see that it wasn't, and we drove back and forth across the Ohio River bridge six times. That was before there were interstates. It was quite a trip."

"I'm sure it was, but what does that have to do with anything?"

"Don't you know who Cincinnatus was?"

"No."

"Well, never mind then."

"Tell me."

"Hell no, the elegance of the point having been lost."

Reynolds rolled his eyes. "So, can I make my proposal?"

"If you hold up that end of the gate so I can reattach the hinges, you can propose any damn thing you want."

Reynolds took off his overcoat and jacket, hung them over The Looker's stall gate and rolled up his sleeves, as the morning had warmed nicely. "Okay, tell me what to do."

Sam lifted the top of the gate so it stood vertical to the ground. He grabbed the end with the hinges hanging loose, and spoke to Reynolds. "Lift your end. Higher. Not that high. Down an inch. There, hold it there." Holding his end of the gate with one hand, Sam pulled a lag screw out of his right front pocket, and a ratchet out of his right rear, and quickly put a screw through the hinge and into the post that held the gate. Then he squatted to address the lower hinge. "Up a bit. More. More. Stop." He put a screw in the bottom.

"How would you have done that if I hadn't been here?"

"Probably with the tractor," Sam said, as he ratcheted the remainder of the screws in. "Okay. Let go." The gate sagged. "Well, damn it." He opened the gate and walked through, to look at it from Reynolds' side. He studied the gate, saying nothing for a moment. Then, "You may begin proposing."

"Isn't there any place to sit down around here?"

"On that table right there, though you'll get hay all over your nice suit."

"I was thinking of up at the house."

"We're not done here. It sags. Propose, while I think."

"Well, okay. What the hell." Reynolds lifted himself up and sat on the work table between the stalls. "Did you ever meet Jonathan Wheeler?"

"Don't think so."

"Assistant Professor. Three years in. Good in the classroom, but has written nothing."

"How not unique. So, he gets denied tenure and cleans out his office. Why is that my problem?" Sam walked over to the end of the gate and lifted it against the sag, studying the way the top corner moved. "It's happened before. To what's her name? Rebecca something."

"Thornhill. This one is different. The provost, you'll remember, has a program to encourage the hiring of couples, on the theory that one department will occasionally get better than it deserves if another department hires the spouse."

"As in the Williamsons."

"Right, as in the Williamsons. We got Emily, the star, and History got Ralph, a decent hire."

"Whatever happened to them?"

"They're still here. It worked out well. History, I'm told, is as pleased as we are, and the Williamsons love it here. They have two kids now."

"How nice."

"So, this time, the shoe was on the other foot. Dr. Stratford—Gwendolyn—is some kind of brilliant Physics type—Stanford, then Cal Tech PhD, MIT post-doc. MacArthur Genius potential. The complete package."

"Not your typical U of A Physics Department hire, I'm guessing."

"You'd be guessing right. But she's married to Jonathan Wheeler, top third of his class at UCLA law, LLM from BU, small-firm practice in some LA suburb. No law review. No clerkship. An ordinary résumé, with nothing that would have caught the Hiring Committee's eye. But they both wanted to teach, and most places that she's interested in won't touch him, and *vice versa*. Physics heard of their fix and went drooling over Stratford to the provost, who put considerable pressure on the law faculty to hire Wheeler."

"Turnabout from the Williamsons being fair play, and all."

"Exactly. Except that some of your former colleagues were not entirely good sports about it."

"Shocking."

They were interrupted by the sound of a four-wheeled ATV coming down the county road from the direction Reynolds had come. "He's driving fast," Reynolds observed.

"She. That will be Ellie; she's a little late."

"Who's Ellie?"

"Little neighbor girl. Her folks have a chicken farm on the other side of the highway."

They watched as the ATV driver expertly fish-tailed around the back of Reynolds' parked car, and between Sam's pickups and into the front paddock. She killed the engine, grabbed her backpack, greeted the dog and began to run up to the house.

"Back here, Ellie," Sam yelled, and she changed her direction and ran, all elbows and knees, back toward where they stood.

"Why isn't she in school?"

"Home-schooled. I help her with math."

"Home-schooled. So her parents are either Christian or New Age."

"The former. Watch your language."

Cardinal found a steadiness in Scripture. She thought it remarkable, in fact, that someone had taken the time to write down any standards of human behavior at all. Her life so far had been lived largely without rules or restraints, and she found the authority of the Bible comforting, and its penalties for misbehavior reasonable. She gave up the trailer house and moved herself and Ellie back in with her parents, while she, with their guidance, restructured her life along biblical principles. She thought for a while about tracking down Ellie's other four paternal candidates, confessing her sins and offering the girl up for daughterhood, but she was counseled by her mother to give up the whole thing as a bad job and move on.

Instead of searching for a husband, she sought a church to attend. Stuart and Melissa's electronic ministry was not sufficient because it did not involve live Sunday or Wednesday services, Cardinal having determined to become a twice-a-week churchgoer. Her parents themselves attended the First Baptist Church of Fayetteville, the mainstream SBC church in town, but that church was too straight-laced for Cardinal's tastes, and, so she set about on some considerable looking around. There were many to choose from—Church of Christ, Missionary Baptist, Freewill Baptist, Cooperative Baptist, Regular United Baptist, Apostolic, Adventist, Disciples of Christ, Christian Union, Pentecostal, Assembly of God, Sheppard's Flock, Living Water and so forth—and Cardinal applied to the task a determination that she had rarely shown since her spell of studiousness in high school. She gave each church a good six-week trial, talked doctrine with the preacher—they were all male of course, 1 Timothy 2:11-12—and talked community with the members. In the end, she decided on a Church of Christ in Wesley, a small congregation in a small town, led by Brother David Quincy, and it was there, fourteen months after her divorce, and at the age of twenty-four, that she was finally christened. Brother David himself immersed her, clad in a plain white frock that she would never wear again, proclaimed her to be Cardinal Evangelina, and ushered her into the body of Christ. Ellie watched, seated with her grandparents who, if they harbored any mixed emotions, didn't show it. Brother David was not adverse to baptizing youngsters, but cautioned against it regarding Ellie, as he suspected her commitment to Jesus was not yet ripe.

A year and three weeks later, Cardinal married Brother David Quincy, in a ceremony performed by her father at the church in Wesley. Melissa's misgivings, if not Stuart's, were now evident, though she held her peace at the ceremony, and afterwards she hugged Brother David, who was closer to her age than Cardinal's, over the cake and punch.

After the wedding, Cardinal and her husband, whom she now called simply David, had dinner at the Crossbow, where she showed off her ring and dress to her former employers, and then she and Ellie moved into David's double-wide trailer home next to his chicken houses near Hindsville. Cardinal had suggested, demurely, that Ellie could spend the night with her grandparents, but David said no, they were a family now, so the marriage was consummated that night rather more quietly than Cardinal had expected. David, a thirty-eight year old virgin, was clumsy and embarrassed, embarrassed not by his clumsiness but by the entire sex act, start to finish, and he had never imagined that there would be two separate acts of intercourse on the very same night.

Cardinal, of course, had considerably more experience in sexual matters than her husband, but she was more than willing to submit to his authority in this and other realms. David prayed at length regarding the practice of fellatio, deciding in the end that this, too, was according to God's plan, so long as his seed was not cast upon the Earth, a concern that Cardinal was content to accommodate. Nevertheless, he was insistent that sex be primarily for procreation. She had admitted to him the uncertainty of Ellie's paternity and the fact of her teenage abortion, both of which shocked David, who considered his new wife to be a murderer and a whore. A redeemed murderer and whore, to be sure, but all the same. And, as part of her redemption, he required that she should get pregnant and stay pregnant. Repetitively. And so it was that she produced three children in the first three and a half years of their marriage, whom they named Joshua, Isaiah and Esther. Ellie, David adopted as his own, an act more properly characterized, perhaps, as one of Christian charity than of love, but both Cardinal and Ellie appreciated the gesture, and she became Ellen Christine Quincy.

Ellie arrived. A black, long-sleeved Wyckoff Ministries International tee shirt. Jeans, threadbare at the knees. A black baseball cap with a red Razorback on the front; her hair, pulled as a ponytail through the back of the cap, a dark auburn. If she were a horse, she would have been chestnut. Skinny and girlish, growing too fast for her body to keep up. Freckles. Chewed finger nails. Thrift-shop sneakers.

"Ellen Quincy, this is John Reynolds. He teaches at the university."

"Pleased to meet you, Mr. Reynolds."

"Oh, call me John."

Ellie looked uncomfortably back and forth from Sam to Reynolds.

"You've put her in a bit of a fix, John. Ellie has been taught to refer to her elders by their last names. But she's also been taught to defer to adults. So, she doesn't know what to do." Turning to Ellie, Sam said, "You should call him 'Mr. Reynolds,' like you did."

"Pleased to meet you, Mr. Reynolds."

"Pleased to meet you, Ellie."

"Hey," she said, now that the formalities were over, "where are the horses? How come Naughty is still in his stall?"

"I sent them up, except for Dee. He had a little accident this morning."

"What kind of accident?"

"Well…" Sam said, looking at the remaining pieces of the gate, still lying on the ground.

"He did *that*? He *is* a naughty boy, aren't you?" She walked over to greet the horse, and stepped in a pool of his drying blood. She looked at her shoe, then at the bandage on the horse's leg, which, by this time was beginning to leak through. She turned back to Sam. "He's bleeding."

"I think he's going to be okay."

"But he's *bleeding*." She spread her hands, her eyes rounding.

"Ellie." Sam looked at her. "Settle down."

"But he's bleeding."

"I was here. He lost about half a liter."

"But…"

"Settle down." He spoke softly. "How much blood can a horse lose before he's in trouble?"

She thought for a second. "Two gallons, you told me."

"Right. Now, what part of two gallons is a half a liter?"

"I don't know." She glanced nervously back toward the stall, her eyes on the horse's leg. Reynolds folded his arms across his chest, enjoying the exchange.

"Yes, you do," Sam said. "Slow down and think. Look here."

This time she paused, then looked up at Sam. "No, I don't."

"Yes, you do. How much is a liter?"

She answered quickly. "A thousand milliliters."

"Right. In English units?"

"I don't remember."

"About."

"Uh, about a quart?"

"Right. Now, how many quarts in a gallon?"

"Four."

"Right. So?"

"Eight quarts makes two gallons."

"So, a half a liter is about...?"

"A sixteenth?"

"Right. Now, is that a lot or a little?"

"A little?"

"How tall is The Looker?"

"Sixteen hands?"

"Sixteen-two, actually, but let's say sixteen to make it even. So how far up his leg is one-sixteenth of his height?"

"One hand?"

"Right. How high up is that?"

She looked at her own hand. "Half way up his hoof?"

"Well, it's my hands, not yours," he held out his own, "so I'm guessing up to his coronet band."

"Not very far."

"Not very far. Always remember when a horse is bleeding to calm down and keep your wits about you. They've got a lot of blood in there."

"But *still*..."

"Why don't you put a halter on him and a lead line and take him out in front so we can see how he's walking. Later on, we'll change the bandage. Go on, Ellie, take him for a walk. Mr. Reynolds and I have some more talking to do. Better take him around behind; he'll not want to come near this gate for a while."

"How did it happen?"

"He got tangled up in the gate, and then fell down. Go on, now."

Ellie went into the horse's stall and began fussing with him, scolding him, in a tone of voice that no horse would ever believe, and telling him what a bad boy he had been, but that she still loved him and was sorry about his wound. As Ellie walked the horse away, Sam kept an eye on how off he was on his right front.

"She calls him Naughty, I heard," said Reynolds. "A bit of a malapropism from 'Dreadnought,' no? I guess she's allowed; she's a kid."

"Less than you think. The first owners spelled the horse's name on his registration papers N-A-U not N-O-U. The Jockey Club accepted it. Where were we?"

"You're past your prime as a teacher, that's for sure."

"What?" Reynolds gestured toward Ellie with his head. "Oh. That was mostly to distract her. Besides, teaching a ten-year-old about fractions is different from teaching first-year law students about the implied seeking of forbearance as consideration for a contract."

"Why math?"

"I was an undergrad math major, you forget."

"I did, yes."

"*Where* were we?"

"The hiring of Jonathan Wheeler. In the end, the provost gave us a new line and funded it herself for six years, and the deal was done. Two offers. Two acceptances. Someone dubbed them 'The Streelers.'"

"Clever."

"Overly."

"Except that he can't write."

"Right. Well, *doesn't*, anyway. And so Jonathan started off with some of his colleagues not liking the deal to begin with and looking for an excuse to say so. He produces nothing except excellent student evaluations and general good colleagueship for three years, and COPT votes two weeks ago not to renew his contract. The provost has a stroke, the dean is ready to vomit, Physics is lobbing WMD at the law building, and the chancellor is tearing his hair out over a profile of Stratford that is set to appear early next year in *The New York Times Magazine. The New York Times Magazine,* for Christ's sake. *February.*"

"Careful." Sam nodded toward Ellie. "She's out of earshot, but using the Lord's name in vain is something she takes quite seriously. So COPT reconvenes to reconsider, right?" Reynolds nodded. "What's the lay of the land?"

"COPT has seventeen members, and it takes two-thirds to reappoint."

"So, twelve-five and he wins."

"How did you do that so fast?"

"He needs twice as many *yeses* as *noes*."

"Okay, so twelve-five, in favor of reappointment and he wins. Eleven-six, he loses. The initial vote was ten-seven, in favor."

"Ouch."

"Yes, except that three of the seven agreed to a compromise: Wheeler gets reappointed and stays on tenure track, Physics gets to keep various Stratford-generated, megabuck NSF grants, the chancellor gets to continue flaunting the impressive Dr. Stratford, the provost again casts an approving eye on the law school and the dean gets off the COPT chair's back, if..."

"If ?"

"If Emeritus Professor Samuel C. Butler—*comma* Legend *comma*—agrees to mentor Jonathan in the whole how-to-be-a-scholar thing."

"Mentor. It's not a verb."

"Whatever."

Sam again lifted the sagging gate. "How in the hell can this stay square without a diagonal brace? Here," he picked up his measuring tape. "Put the end of it on that corner up there." Sam looked at the length of the diagonal. "Now on that one down there." He measured the other diagonal. "Three inches out of square. Let go." He let the tape retract. "Who fingered me?"

"The deliberations of COPT are confidential, as you well know."

"Meaning you suggested it."

"Meaning the deliberations of COPT are confidential. I must say the suggestion makes sense to me. A timely extension of the legend."

"Listen, the supposed legend related to teaching, not scholarship. Students don't give a lick about what we write. Writing is what professors do with their doors shut when students want to talk about the exam."

"Aw, hell, Sam. You wrote. And you made it seem so effortless. It was like turning on the goddam..."—Reynolds caught himself—"the darn tap with you."

"There must be someone else to do it. Someone less busy. Less retired."

"The compromise brokered by the dean and agreed to by the three *no* votes is personal to you, Professor. It's not supposed to be all that logical. What compromise is? That was the deal. You. Sam Butler. Otherwise the *noes* stay firm and Wheeler cleans out his office."

"What are the expectations?"

"None, explicitly. But—I'm guessing here—a year from now, one article published, another submitted for publication."

"Unrealistic."

"Why?"

"You know how the system works. With most reviews, if he had an article accepted today, it might not appear in print until a year from now. And if he had one accepted today, you wouldn't have driven out into the country."

"So, what should the expectations be?"

"Two acceptances? One, plus another submitted and under consideration."

"Not here?"

"Not here."

"So, you'll do it?"

"I have to decide by when?"

"COPT meets Friday afternoon."

"I'll phone you Thursday."

"I'm not sure whether to be encouraged that you haven't asked about the pay."

"I get paid?"

"The dean's got fifteen grand for the job."

Sam picked up a short piece of broken board and held it at the corner of the sagging gate. "I think two diagonal pieces here and over there will square it up, don't you?" He paused, waiting for Reynolds to say something. When he didn't, "There are people within five miles of here who don't make fifteen thousand in a year." He looked off across the paddock to where Ellie was now circling Dreadnaught at the end of a twenty-foot line, at the trot. He was showing no sign of lameness, but Sam wouldn't know for sure until the bute wore off, but it was certain that the leg was not broken, he thought. "Tell the dean I'm flattered to have been asked." He raised his voice. "Okay, Ellie, bring him into you and walk him over here."

"What?"

Louder: "Bring him into you and walk him over here."

They watched as the little girl pulled the line to her belly and bent to exaggerate her look at the horse's butt. On cue, he stopped and turned to face her, then he walked toward her as she coiled up the line. When he was close enough to be touched, he stopped and she reached up to rub his blaze, and he then followed along as she walked back toward the two adults.

"It's extraordinary, don't you think?" Sam said. "That horse weighs ten or fifteen times what she weighs and is probably a hundred times stronger. A thousand, maybe. But he follows her around like that. Extraordinary. So, what do you think?" This last to Ellie, who now stood before them, holding the lead line loosely in her hand.

She shrugged her shoulders and smiled, shy in front of the stranger. "I don't know."

"I think," said Sam, his hand on the bill of her ball cap, "that he's going to be all right. And I think that bandage doesn't need to be changed until this afternoon. Walk him back to the day pasture and let him go. Keep an eye on him. I'll be along in a minute. Say goodbye to Mr. Reynolds. He'll be gone when you get back here."

"Bye," she said. "It was nice to meet you."

"Same for me, Ellie. Bye."

And off she walked, speaking quietly to the horse she called Naughty.

"Until Thursday, then." Sam held out his hand. "But I'm inclined to decline."

"'Inclined to decline.'" He emphasized the first syllables. "Why?"

Sam spread his hands to his sides. "Because I don't have any advice to give. And I don't have the time to give it."

"Isn't that a little contradictory?"

"A privilege of the elderly."

"More money?"

"You insult me. Google Cincinnatus and see if he haggled over the fee."

"But you'll think about it? I can tell the dean you didn't refuse?"

"No, I didn't refuse."

"Good enough. Thanks. Okay." They shook. "Talk to you soon."

Reynolds dusted the hay off of his suit pants, picked up his two coats and walked, under Teena's escort, to his car. Sam watched him go, thinking about the job he'd been offered, about how he didn't need the money and didn't want to do it. The whole deal came perilously close to campus politics, which he tried desperately to avoid, even when he was working. He almost called after Reynolds to decline right there and then, before deciding to wait until Thursday, which would do no one any harm. Then he quickly sawed the two corner pieces for the gate, and screwed them in, reducing, but not eliminating the sag, and then walked back to watch the horses with Ellie. Dreadnaught had re-joined his pasture mates and was now nibbling some grass about a hundred feet away from them, as if nothing had happened.

"The chickens are still up."

Sam glanced over his shoulder and saw her peering into the hen house. "Oops. I forgot them in the morning's drama. Let them out and put down some scratch for them, why don't you?" He turned back to gaze across the pasture again. The low temperatures had turned the Bermuda grass dormant, but the rye, oats and other cool-weather grasses were still green, in spots a nice blanket of green, but mostly the green blades reached up through the red-brown of the winter Bermuda. The first frost had come early this year, back in October, so most of the leaves had turned and were now on the ground, blown into piles in the corners and dips and against the sides of the out-buildings. Except for the black oaks, which held onto many of their dead leaves until the spring. The leaves wouldn't all be back until the first of May, six months, the cherries the first to leaf out, the walnuts the last. A transparent moon hung high in the blue sky, and somewhere off aways calves were being weaned and the cows were objecting. Nearby, two crows were fussing, but otherwise it was quiet, the breeze rustling the remaining leaves.

"I think the black one is setting," Ellie called from inside the hen house.

"Well, kick her off and pick up the eggs. We don't need any more chickens."

"I'm afraid she'll peck me."

Sam walked over and ducked his head into the hen house. "No one who drives a four-wheeler like you do should be afraid of being pecked by a setting hen." She smiled up at him from where she was squatting in the wood chips, next to the row of nests. "Put your right hand over her head, quickly now."

The hen ruffled her feathers and pecked at Ellie's hand. "Ouch!"

"Here, I'll show you." He squatted down next to her. "See?" Without hesitation, he cupped his right hand over the hen's head, causing her to hiss and squawk. "She's like a horse—she can't hurt you if you're right in close to her." He released the hen, who settled back on the eggs, which were probably not, in fact, hers anyway, but she guarded them as if they were. "Now you do it."

This time, Ellie got her hand over the hen's head without trouble.

"Now, put your left hand under her tail and throw her out the door."

"Throw her?"

"Out the door. She'll be fine. She can fly, remember." Ellie evicted the hen from the nest in one movement. Outside, the hen sputtered and strutted in protest of the indignity of the treatment, before she left to begin scratching around the coop. The eviction revealed six eggs of various colors and sizes. "I must have forgotten to check for a couple of days. Make a basket out of your shirt and carry them up to the house and put them in the sink for me to wash. Is Cardinal coming over today?"

"I'm not for sure. The baby has the colic."

"Well, there's another dozen up there for her in the fridge. You go on up and get your homework organized. I'll be up as soon as I put the sawhorses and tools away."

In addition to being the sacred receptacle of his seed, David decreed that Cardinal was to become, beginning with Ellie, the children's primary teacher. He considered the secular public schools, if not exactly instruments of the Devil, then at the very least complicit in the Devil's business, even the public schools of Madison County, where, for example, the subject of evolution was handled, how shall I say it?, delicately. Public schools, David sagely noted, had not existed in biblical times, and God's plan was for the mother, supervised by her husband, to school the children at home, though David considered it possible that the Lord made special arrangements when it came to talented football players, about which he had certain expectations regarding Joshua, who had become a strapping toddler.

Cardinal was happy to submit to this assignment, not only because life had offered her nothing better so far, but because she had always dreamed of becoming a teacher anyway. Home-schooling was better than waiting tables for tips and besides her husband required it, so where was the objection? She visited several libraries and talked to several pastors, seeking the best home-school materials, at least the best that were affordable to them, as some of the programs were pricey. Finally she settled on the Sonlight curriculum. Ellie was withdrawn from the fourth grade, and the home-schooling began. Ellie missed her friends at school, but she came to enjoy the flexibility of school at home, where she had to spend many fewer hours a day at her lessons.

Cardinal quickly came to recognize—quickly, but still about two weeks after Ellie had recognized it—that she was woefully unprepared to teach the mathematics portion of the curriculum. She shared her failing with David and received, much to her relieved surprise, his sympathy. They determined to find a math tutor for the little girl, and began to ask around until finally, through the friend of a one of David's parishioners they learned that Sam Butler, a retired professor of some kind, who lived quite near them in Hindsville, had helped the friend's son with his algebra, and that had worked out well. David in fact knew Sam, having hired out to help him clear some timber off of a pasture-in-the-making some years ago, where he had found him to be a persnickety boss, but one who worked alongside the crew, and who paid well. He had no idea that he was either a retired professor or a math tutor, but he knew him to be a Northerner, over-educated and too liberal. Likely a non-believer. A nice enough guy, maybe, but word was a Jew, and David didn't trust him. Far from the ideal math tutor from David's perspective, but what other choice was there?, and so David consented to discussing the hiring of Sam to help Ellie with her math.

Sam, it turned out, was willing to do it, and didn't want to be paid. But he wanted the lessons to be at his house, not across the highway at the Quincy chicken farm, and he said that what he called the tuition would be that Ellie was to brush his horses before each lesson. There were four of them, and would take about an hour, total. David agreed, but required, without telling Sam, that Cardinal accompany Ellie to her lessons, ostensibly to see for herself how the math was taught, for the good of the babies that were to follow, but actually to see what the atmosphere was like at Sam Butler's place.

Up in the kitchen of the house, Ellie was finishing off the last of her homework problems, while Sam washed up the few breakfast dishes and, when that was done, the shells of the eggs they had collected from under the setting black hen. These he placed in a used egg carton, added six more from the fridge and then placed the carton, and another full carton, on the table near her backpack.

"Don't forget to take these when you go." One of the multitudinous rules that came under the contract governing the growing of chickens for Tyson's by David and Cardinal was that they were not permitted to have any other live poultry on their farm, so he shared his eggs with them. "Do you want something to drink?" he asked, opening another Coke for himself.

"Can I have a Coke, too, please?"

"You may not. But you may have a glass of milk. Or orange juice."

"Milk, please. You're having a Coke."

"My teeth are old and yellow. Yours are new and white."

Ellie smiled, confirming his description. "David says I can get braces next year. Grandpa is going to pay, but I'm not supposed to know. I heard them talking."

He poured her a glass of milk, and put a peanut butter cookie from Rick's in Fayetteville on a little plate and set both in front of her on the table. "Braces. That'll be nice." In Sam's day, braces had been a teenage embarrassment, one he had avoided, but now they were being installed earlier, and had become a pre-teen fashion statement and rite of passage. "Almost done?"

"Yes!" she said, putting her pencil down. "I think I got them all right. I have to use the bathroom, please."

"Go." Sam sat down in the chair that she had been using and picked up her papers. He checked the clock on the wall. Almost eleven.

Ellie walked up the stairs to use the toilet. There were three rooms upstairs: the bathroom, a bedroom, and a small room that Mr. Butler used as a library and study. She had discovered once that when she stood at the entrance to the bathroom and looked across the little hallway into the room with all of the books in it, she was able to see on the next shelf to the top, in the middle bookshelf, a copy of the Holy Bible. It always comforted her to see it there, as she worried about Mr. Butler, whom David said was a heathen and would be going to hell when he died. She didn't see how that could possibly be true if there was a copy of the Holy Bible right there in his study.

She used the toilet, but did not flush. The rules were different here from at home: she had to take off her shoes when she came inside, and she wasn't to flush the toilet when she just peed, but it was okay to flush if you pooped. Something about the septic tank. And she had to put down the lid on the toilet when she was finished, something that no one did at home. She washed her hands, dried them on the towel, replaced the towel on the rack and walked back downstairs.

"Did you like Mr. Reynolds?" Sam was sitting holding her homework, but not looking at it.

"He seemed nice. Why was he here?" She sat down in the other chair at the kitchen table—there were only two—took a bite of her cookie and sipped her milk.

"He wants me to help out one of the other teachers at the university."

"Did you use to wear a suit to work?"

"Every day."

Ellie giggled, covering her mouth. "You'd look funny in a suit!"

"Hey." He looked at her. "What makes you say a thing like that?"

"You just would. I've never seen you in anything except jeans. You wouldn't seem natural in a suit."

"Well," he said, "that's because I used to shave every morning. And keep my hair trimmed. And I'd take a shower every morning, too, and use perfumed after-shave lotion and deodorant." He wiggled his fingers at her. "And I'd keep my nails clean. The whole routine."

"I still think you'd look funny."

"So maybe I'll get all slicked up, put on a suit and let you see. Where could we go?"

"The Indoor Nationals?"

"We're going to do that for sure, but no one wears a suit to the Indoor Nationals."

"You could come to church with us some Sunday. I'd like that."

"Would you, kiddo?"

"I *really* would."

"More than going to the Indoor Nationals?"

"Yes, more."

"Well, we'll see. Do all the men wear suits and ties at your church?"

She giggled again. "No. Only David. The rest just come as farmers. Would you come? Sometime?"

"We'll see."

"Are you going to help that other teacher?"

"What do you think? Should I?"

"I think you should. It would be a nice to help him. You helped Naughty."

"But he's a horse. He needed help; he couldn't bandage his own leg, could he?"

"You help me, and I'm a person."

"You're special. But I don't even know this man."

"Well," she took another bite, "maybe he'll be special, too? Once you get to know him? It would be nice to help him, wouldn't it? I think you should."

"Maybe I will. You are a wise girl, Ellen Quincy." He smiled and handed her school work back. "But number seven is wrong."

Her face fell, as she took the papers. "Number seven? Why?"

"You tell me." And the math lesson began.

**The Following Thursday.**

The law building at the University of Arkansas had grown almost organically over the years. It had originally been a straight-line, unlovely, three-story building facing Maple Street, built to reflect, on the cheap, the lines of the art building across the Quad, the latter having been designed by Edward Durell Stone and hence all straight lines, flat roof and square corners, with lots of glass. Each building presented a glass wall of windows to the other, allowing the artists and lawyers to see each other in the distance, which is about as close as the two departments ever came to communicating.

In the Seventies, however, the law building turned a corner and headed south, with a stucco'd, windowless hulk of an addition that was mostly library and classrooms. Thus it was when Sam Butler arrived in the Eighties, settling into an office on the third floor along the main corridor linking the administrative suite with the classrooms. Then, after Sam retired in the Aughts, the building headed to the west, then turned north, completing the circle, so to speak, actually now more of a square donut, presenting a rather elegant face to the unchanged art building across the way. (The last-stage architect had discovered rather late in the game that the finished building was in fact three degrees out of square, but it takes a careful eye to see the angle.) The square donut hole contained the Atkinson Memorial garden which, depending on the season was a green, leafy, flowering place, or a cold (or hot) cement and glass box.

It was through that garden that Sam now walked on a day when little was leafy or blooming, but it was a sunny day, warm for November, and the Garden was a pleasant place to sit, and was speckled with students talking or studying. Jesus Moroles, the architect of the place, had worked in granite; Sam would have preferred local limestone, but it was long past the time to wonder about that choice. He suspected that Atkinson himself, once Sam's best friend among his colleagues, who had died much too young, would have liked the granite.

Now inside the building, Sam went first to collect the local newspaper, given away free by the university to the students, in a largely fruitless attempt to make them into newspaper readers. He picked up the *Democrat-Gazette*, along with the campus paper, *The Traveler*, then headed down to the office of his former secretary to find out where Jonathan Wheeler hung his hat, and what his class schedule was.

"He has Contracts at ten; better hurry." It was now nine-forty-five.

"What's his office number?"

"Three-sixty."

"Where's that?" Sam knew his way only poorly around the new part of the building.

"West side, third floor."

"Right. Thanks, Donna."

Sam headed for the stairs, in no hurry really as he wanted there to be not much time for chit-chat: an introduction, a request and gone. Five minutes would be plenty.

Room 360 lay in a small cul-de-sac, with three other faculty offices, a seminar room and a small waiting area. Sam sat down, looked at his watch and glanced at the front page of the *Dem-Gaz*. The door to Wheeler's office was open and Sam could see a group of students sitting and talking, apparently to their professor, who was out of Sam's line of sight, to the right. Three students, a male and two females, one of whom sat on the floor, as there were only two chairs, and with her shoes off. Two had laptops open while the third had an iPad; they were a study group, was Sam's guess, here to get their questions answered, a little unusual just before class, but not unheard of. The students were relaxed and, though Sam could only see half of the conversation, and hear even less of it, it was clear that there was an easy camaraderie between the students and their teacher. When Wheeler spoke—a forceful baritone—they listened and typed, but they seemed comfortable interrupting with a question or to refine a point. All-in-all, Sam liked what he watched.

After about ten minutes, the meeting ended, the students packed up and filed out to where Sam sat. He nodded hello and they returned the greeting, even though they did not know him. Sam stood up and approached the open door, then rapped quietly with his left hand. Wheeler had his back to the door, packing up his own books to head off to class.

"Jonathan Wheeler?"

He turned around. "Yes?" He looked very much the southern Californian: stylishly shaggy sandy hair, bright blue eyes, tall, with a good build. Shirt and tie, but no jacket, khakis and tasseled loafers. Good looking. Perfect teeth. "I, uh, have to be in class in about five minutes."

"I'm Sam Butler." Sam stuck out his hand and Jonathan took it.

"Uh... Yes. Well, of course. Professor Butler. It's nice to meet you. I've heard a lot. But..." he looked at his watch, clearly in a quandary presented by this so-called mentor and the demands of his class.

Sam broke in. "This will only take one of your five minutes." He walked over to the edge of Jonathan's desk and laid down a piece of white paper. "Here's a map to my place out in the country. And..." he laid two bills on top of the map, "... here's thirty bucks. Buy us some take-out—anything you want, except not from a chain. Shall we say about six on Sunday?"

"Well, uh, sure. What should I bring?"

"Just the food."

"Nothing for you to read?"

"If you like, but mostly we'll just talk."

"Should I bring my wife?"

"Is she having trouble getting tenure?"

Jonathan laughed. "That's almost funny. But no, she isn't."

"Okay then. Just you and me." Sam turned to go. "Sunday night then. Don't be late for your class."

**Same Day, Minutes Later.**

"gwenie—met my babysitter. call me."

"mtg. cant talk. wha ze like?"

"said 10 words. wrking dinner sunday 6. yr not invited!"

"jerk. myb Ill srprz him. qck lunch union?"

"busy. c u home"

"details at 7. out."


**Same Day, More Minutes Later.**

For the next half-hour or so, Sam wandered the halls of the law school, poking his head into the new classrooms and stopping by the dean's office for a short meeting about why he was here and what her expectations regarding Jonathan Wheeler were. He knew none of the students, of course, and most of his former colleagues greeted him with a wave, a "howdy, stranger," or a "how's retirement?" or a "what're ya up to?" Or "what's the word, Sam?" And then they were gone, off to more important things.

Exiting the building, he wandered aimlessly around campus for a while, enjoying the fall morning and thinking that the coeds got younger, cuter and taller every year. He walked off campus to the east and up Dickson Street, the center of campustown, and the link between the university and downtown Fayetteville. When Sam had first arrived back in the Eighties, Dickson Street had a funky, seedy, biker feel to it, but over the years it had become more upscale and trendy (as had the bikes and bikers themselves), except for a few holdouts (likewise). There were about equal numbers of bars and restaurants, and tonight, and even though ninety percent of the students were too young to drink legally, the street's bars and sidewalks would be hopping. Thursday night drinking had become popular during the decade before Sam retired, a development of which he did not approve. He used to hang a poster on his office door: "*THURSDAY NIGHT DRINKING—BAD FOR YOUR LIVER; BAD FOR YOUR GRADES,*" not that it did any good. It made him feel tremendously old, just to think about going out on a Thursday night.

One holdover from the old days was the Dickson Street Bookshop, one of the Seven Literary Wonders of the World. Ask anyone. It rambled through a warren of rooms in a couple of connected old buildings at the corner of Dickson Street and School Avenue and contained a truly unimaginable number of used and rare books. Tens and tens and tens of thousands. No one knew how many, likely not even the owners. Books on the shelves, lining the aisles, stacked on chairs and along the floor, books bought from customers, but still in boxes and grocery sacks. Paperbacks and hardbacks, old magazines, books in Turkish and Malayan and Greek, art books, trade books, how-to books, self-help books. Cook books, dog books, presumably dog-cooking books, perhaps cooking-dog books, philosophy books, romance novels. And aisles and aisles of literature, shelves from floor to ceiling, with ladders to reach the top. Sam browsed for an hour and left with numbers by Wodehouse, le Carré and Amos Oz.

Outside, he continued his walk, now turning south on School Street to the Fayetteville Public Library. There he browsed the new-novels display, but found nothing that caught his fancy. Now near downtown, he decided to drop in on a former student whose office was on the square, and that led to a nice chat, then for Mexican back down on Dickson Street. By the time he got back to his pickup, it was after two o'clock, and nearly three before he was home.

Pulling into the gate, Sam saw Ellie's four-wheeler parked in the front and saw her backpack on the table by the feed room. He walked on back to the rear of the property, where the chicken coop stood, and a gate led to the day pasture. She was leaning with her arms folded on the middle rail of the fence, staring through to where the horses were grazing on the north-facing hillside. The dog noticed Sam before Ellie did.

"Hey. Didn't you get my message? No math class today." He walked over to Teena, who had rolled over to present her belly, with her one front leg pawing the air for attention. "I had to go to town." Now he stood up and moved next to the girl, his stance duplicating hers, one rail higher. "Wha'cha looking at?"

"Mom told me she got the message, but I didn't have anything to do and wanted to come over and see if Naughty was okay. But I didn't want to go into the field without you. I've just been watching."

"How long?" She shrugged her shoulders but didn't answer. "I think he could use a brush. Run and get his halter..." she turned to leave, "...and a lead line."

A few minutes later she was back, her arms full of halter, rope and brushes. "Did you bring a hoof pick?" he asked.

"You didn't say a hoof pick."

"Didn't I?"

"No."

"Well, how are we going to clean his teeth without a hoof pick?"

"Whaaaa? You're teasing."

"So I am. Well, go get him."

"Aren't you coming?"

"I can see from here. Go get him." Sam stood at the fence while she headed out across the pasture after Dreadnaught. All five horses watched her with interest as she approached, and when it became clear to all of them which one she was coming after the other four lost interest and went back to grazing. Dreadnaught decided that he saw no advantage to being haltered, so he turned and walked away from her, just a few steps, but enough so she couldn't reach his head with the halter. She'd step; he'd step. She'd stop; he'd stop. She'd step; he'd step.

Sam climbed through the fence rails and trotted the twenty-five yards to where she was. "Going to follow him all around the pasture?" Dreadnaught's attention was on the two of them as he nibbled at some short grass.

"He walks away."

"I can see that. What are you going to do?"

"I'm not sure." She thought for a moment, then took another step toward the horse, who took another step away.

"Well, I suppose you could just keep walking towards his butt, but then that doesn't seem to be getting you anywhere."

"Hide your hiney?"

"Exactly. Take two steps out this way, so you're not directly behind him." She did. "Okay, now...?" She twirled the free end of the lead line around and slapped it on the ground, causing the horse to lift his head and look back at her. "Again. And scold him."

She snapped the rope against the ground again, lowered her eyebrows and spoke. "*Naughty!*" This time the horse took a half step to turn his forequarters toward her.

"Again. Stamp your foot. Tell him what you want."

"*Naughty! Hide your hiney.*" And sure enough, the horse put his butt behind him and turned his head to face her.

"Take two steps back to the left and this time do it without speaking." She moved to the left, then bent at the waist and scowled at the horse's butt. He took a hind step to his left, once again obscuring his butt from her stern gaze. "Right, now walk forward, rub his ears and put the halter on. Then lead him back to the gate. Take it slow; I'll meet you there."

At the gate, Sam said, "I think we should look under his bandage, so walk him all the way back to the stable." He picked up the brushes she had dropped and followed along behind the girl and the horse. Back at the stable, he said, "Tie him up. Remember how?"

"I'm not for sure."

"Like this." He showed her how to tie the quick-release-in-case-of-emergency knot, then he cut off the old bandage and they both knelt to look at Dreadnaught's wound from his battle with the gate, now two days ago.

"Eee-uuu. It looks yucky."

"Some soap and water would help," and together they washed the wound, treated it with some HEW antibiotic ointment and re-wrapped it. "Let him have a sniff of the cotton; he's interested. Remember, now, there's got to be cotton all the way around his shank or the wrap will pull too tight and cut off his circulation. Hold the cotton right there. With your other hand. Right. Now, I get this roll started and up, down, and back up again. How do you like the yellow?"

"It's pretty. Do you think the cut hurts him?"

"Hard to know. Horses don't tell you much unless they're *really* sore. They're pretty stoic, do you know that word? Strong but quiet. They don't show much. As long as he's not off, is perky and has an appetite, and isn't running a fever, I think he'll be okay. We'll just have to watch him. Okay, feel that bandage." She put her two hands around the horse's wrapped leg. "Feel how tight it is? But squeeze it...and you can feel the cotton give under your hands. There...now I think he'd like a treat. Grab a handful of oats out of the feed room, and then you can brush him down."

The brushing took a while, because Dreadnaught's mane had become tangled, and they talked while Sam worked the tangle and Ellie brushed his tail.

"What do you do when Cardinal combs the tangles out of your hair?"

"It hurts."

"What do you do? Cry?"

"Complain."

"What do you say?"

"Mom!"

"But Dee says nothing. Why do you think?"

"He's a horse?"

"But he could complain, couldn't he?"

"I guess."

"But he's *stoic*, see? He puts up with it without complaining, even though it hurts."

Ellie looked around the horse's hindquarters to his head. "Good boy."

"I met the man you wanted me to help at the university today. His name is Mr. Wheeler."

"Is he nice?"

"We didn't talk for long, but yes, I think so. He and his wife are from California."

"Why's he need your help?"

"Good question. I'm guessing you're not the only one wondering. See, teachers at the university have to do more than just teach. They also have to write articles..."

"For the newspaper?"

"No. More like what your mother calls reports. Very brainy discussions of something the professor knows about, but the rest of us don't."

"Did you write reports when you were a professor?"

"I did, yes. So, Mr. Wheeler is a good teacher but he's having a hard time getting started on his report. Sound familiar?"

She smiled. "Like me. But he's a professor..."

"Exactly. So his boss, the dean, thought maybe I could give him some help." Sam switched sides, as Dreadnaught has a mane the back third of which falls naturally to the right.

"My mom wanted to be a professor once. My grandma told me."

"Is that right? I didn't know that. When did she tell you that?"

"Once when we were talking about you."

"Me?"

"We talk about you all the time, partly about math, but mostly just about what we do over here, the horses and stuff."

"Stuff?"

"You know, the horses and the hens and everything."

"So why didn't Cardinal become a professor?"

"I guess I got borned and she had to take care of me."

"*Born*. You were *born*, not *borned*."

"Got born. Then my dad died—my first dad I mean—and then she married David and so now she looks after the babies. I don't think moms can be professors, can they?"

"Well, sure they can."

"But who looks after the babies?"

"I don't know, babysitters, I guess, until the children go to school."

"I wish I went to school."

"Why?"

"I don't know. I just do."

"Why?"

"It was more fun with all the kids and I miss my girlfriends and I liked my teacher."

"But here you are, brushing Dreadnaught's tail in the middle of the afternoon. I think Dee likes it this way, don't you boy?" The horse, now dozing under the comfort of the brushes, ignored him.

"What does dreadnaught mean?"

"Afraid of nothing."

"Afraid of Nothing. I like that. It's better than Naughty."

"You could call him Afraid of Nothing. I guess he wouldn't mind."

"And what's Mister's real name?"

"Restive."

"What's that mean?"

"Well, that's interesting. When I was about your age, I was taught it meant balky, at rest, like a horse that's stuck and won't get started. But these days it's come to mean restless. Squirmy. Can't sit still. Like you sometimes during math class. Since no one would name a race horse Balky, I assume his first owners thought he was squirmy. All over the place. Restless."

"I get that way sometimes in church, too."

"It's not uncommon."

"But I think it's wrong to get that way in church. You should pay attention."

"Some of it, I suppose, is aimed at the adults, not the kids. It's hard to sit still when someone is talking over your head."

"Over my head?"

"That means using words or talking about topics that are too old for you."

She considered this for a bit, still brushing. "Still. I think it's wrong to get squirmy in church."

"Or in math class."

"You said it was not uncommon."

"I did."

"Why not just say common?"

"That's the way lawyers talk sometimes."

"How can a word change what it means?"

"Like restive?"

"Yeah, how?"

"Well, there's three hundred million Americans, most of whom speak English. It would be surprising, I guess, if we all used the same words in the same way. What you call a milkshake, people in Boston call a frappe. And when David says it's the evening, it's what I'd call the afternoon."

"I think words are more interesting than numbers."

"That's okay. Maybe I do, too."

"Then why do I have to take math?"

"Because Cardinal and David want you to be a smart, well-rounded girl. It's too soon for you to become a word specialist. Besides, almost all jobs these days require you to know both words and numbers."

"If I went to school, couldn't I still come over and see the horses?"

"Sure, but the school bus with the other kids doesn't go by here until nearly five o'clock."

"I don't think David will let me go to school. He always prays in the morning for the Lord to help the kids that go to school, and show them the truth of Jesus. I also don't think that he would say that moms could be professors. He thinks they should stay home and do the housework and mind the babies. I heard him talk about that at church once."

"Well, maybe when you're big, he'll change his mind. People change their minds all the time."

"Do you?"

"Sure. Like five years ago, I would have panicked when Dreadnaught got hurt and I'd have run him to the vet's. But see? You learn to slow down and watch and see and sometimes horses just get better all by themselves. It takes a while to learn that."

Their conversation lapsed as Ellie thought that lesson over and then whispered quietly to the horse, while Sam found himself remembering one vet emergency when Sally had been in no shape to help and he'd had to manage the horse alone, and how angry she had been, angry both that he could manage without her, and that he had had to. When Sam snapped out of the memory and looked at the clock on the stable wall, twenty minutes had gone by without either of them speaking.

"Look at the time. You should probably go."

"Can I help put the hay out?"

"Tell you what. Do you have your cell phone? Call Cardinal and ask her if you can stay to help feed and to have supper with me. I'll grill you a hamburger, but you'll have to eat it without ketchup."

"That's okay."

"By the time we're finished, it'll be dark, but I'll run you home and come back for you tomorrow. You can leave your four-wheeler here."

"It's okay if I ride in the dark."

"Not with me it isn't. Go ahead and call. I'll put this these things away, and if Cardinal says it's okay then we'll put the hay out."

**The Next Sunday Night.**

"How do you like Arkansas?"

Sam Butler and Jonathan Wheeler were seated at Sam's kitchen table over the take-out Thai that Jonathan had brought. He'd been conservative about the heat, so Sam had a collection of small bottles of hot sauce laid out—more New Orleans and Albuquerque than Bangkok—and a beer for each of them. Jonathan had offered chopsticks, which he himself used rather dexterously, but Sam had declined.

"It's nice."

"Nice?"

"Quiet. Small. Outdoorsy. My wife says it reminds her of Portland."

"Maine?"

"Oregon."

"There's one of those comparisons you never expect to hear. You know, like my friend Joe paints and his work kind of reminds me of Rembrandt."

Jonathan laughed. "Yeah. Like this painting here of an abandoned pickup behind a chicken house suggests *Night Watch*, doesn't it?"

Sam took a drink of his beer. "So why Portland?"

"You'll have to ask Gwen. It's not the whole city of Portland, you see. Where did she say? Southeast Portland? I think. Less pretentious than the northeast, a little down on its heels, but more interesting than some of the more fashionable parts. Like Fayetteville."

"With, of course, The World's Largest Retailer up the road in Bentonville."

"Of course. There is that. I hear they hire lots of our grads."

"They do. Especially in their real estate division. Walmart owns more land than the US Army. And then there's The World's Largest Producer of Protein in Springdale."

"I haven't heard that one. Who's that?"

"Tyson's. Did you know that a million chickens a day are killed in Washington County, Arkansas? Well, Washington and Benton Counties, in order to take in the processing plant in Rogers."

"A million *a day*?"

"Correct."

Jonathan whistled, then scooped up another chopstick load of pad thai. "That's a lot of birds."

"Quite a few."

"Makes me kind of glad I didn't bring the chicken *prew-wan*."

"Seen the Buffalo?"

"Yes. We've kayaked it a half-dozen times. Most recently, last month. Beautiful."

"You kayak."

"Seriously. White water. Last summer we did the Tsaina in south-central Alaska. East of Anchorage."

"Sounds nice."

"Heart-stopping."

"The kayaking or the scenery?"

"Both. But I meant the rapids. Seven miles of Class Five. Stunningly difficult. Gwen is very good; much better than me. She could have been an

Olympian, if she hadn't decided to become a brilliant physicist. Training at that level's a full-time job, and she wasn't willing to give up her photons. I could cover the expenses, I guess, but it really wasn't a matter of finances. So..." he took a sip of beer, "...yes, we've done the Buffalo and enjoyed the time on the water. Less adrenalin than the Tsaina, but easier on my shoulders. And, here we are..."

"Some say the best trout fishing in the country is over at Cotter. That's the White River. Below the Bull Shoals dam."

"I don't fish, actually."

"I used to, before I retired."

"That seems backwards."

"Much about retirement is."

Sam had finished eating and pushed his chair back from the table, then tipped back on the rear legs. "Still and all..."

Jonathan looked at him. "Still and all?"

"It's not LA."

Jonathan gave a short laugh. "No, it's not LA."

"Don't you miss it? The big city, I mean."

"I actually don't know LA all that well. I grew up in Escondido..." Sam shook his head. "Near San Diego. And went to college at Cal Poly, in SLO." Another shake. "San Luis Obispo."

"Okay. Cal Poly. They had a big-time track program back in, what would it be?, the Seventies and Eighties."

"You're a track fan?"

"A dedicated one."

"Arkansas is pretty good, no?"

"Forty national championships. Not counting the two they took away from us."

"Because?"

"Oh, we sent a limo to pick up Tyson Gay at the airport or something like that. When we were recruiting him."

"A limo, and you lose a national championship?"

"Two. Okay, so maybe it was more like a mobile fellatio parlor. Anyway, they took away the points he scored at two national meets and that dropped us out of the championship. Forty's a nice round number, though. And they should be in the running next year, at the Indoor Nationals, anyway. But, like I say, I seem to remember that Cal Poly was quite good years ago."

"Before my time."

"Good school?"

"Underrated."

"What did you study?"

"IT. Programming. Machine language. Artificial intelligence, that kind of thing. Then I worked in the Valley for a couple of years."

"Which valley?"

"Silicone. With a start-up that stalled, then died. Too bad; they had a good idea. And it was fun. But I managed to meet Gwen and when she got into Cal Tech for her PhD, we got married and I tagged along, went to UCLA law, practiced a couple of years while Gwen finished up, then a year in Cambridge, and..." he spread his hands, "...here I am in Fayetteville."

"You like your job?"

"Love it. Think you can help me keep it?"

"Maybe. What's in the box?" Sam looked at the cardboard box Jonathan had carried up from the car and which now sat near the front door.

"Law review articles and cases, mostly. I thought you'd like to see what I've done. Mostly, I'll admit, it's things my RA has run off for me."

"About?"

"Constitutional issues regarding web privacy. Whether the Fourth Amendment protects passwords from government seizure, to be more specific. I figured I should dig into something that relates back to my IT background; there's a lot being written. I can get you copies of everything—in fact, I can leave that box here with you."

Sam stood up and started clearing the dishes from the table. "I haven't read a case since I retired, and I don't think I'll start now. And I'm guessing I couldn't follow the articles even if I tried, which I'm not inclined to do. I don't know much about the Fourth Amendment. Well, nothing really. Except that it comes between the Third and the Fifth."

"So, what are we to do? You'll read what I write, or what?"

"I'll read anything you write, but don't expect me to know much about the law."

"Then?"

"Strategy, mostly. How to get started. How not to end up with a box full of cases and law review articles that are too much for anyone to read."

"Instead?"

"I have three pieces of advice. First..."

"Wait, let me get my tablet." Jonathan made a move to get up.

"Sit still; it's not that complicated. First," Sam counted off one finger, "think small. Second," a second finger, "avoid the Constitution. And third," he made three fingers with his thumb, index and middle fingers, " third, your first article should come straight out of your class notes." Jonathan sat, waiting and thinking. "That's it. I'm guessing what's in the box breaks all three of my rules."

"It does. Why avoid the Constitution?"

"It's too hard to begin with. It has too few words, with too many words written about it by judges and professors, most of whom are not particularly good writers. Save your own constitutional insights for later."

"And think small? I guess avoiding the Constitution is a corollary to thinking small. But I thought I had to think large in order to impress my colleagues."

"Some, you do, but we're ignoring them for the present."

"I'm not with you."

"Look. Your vote was ten to seven, in favor of reappointment, with three of the seven willing to vote *yes* if we work together, right?"

"So I was told. Do you know who the three are?"

"No, and I never will. Nor will you for that matter. COPT deliberations are confidential. And by the way: it's considered bad manners to ask around. So, we've got two goals here—one, not to piss off any of the ten *yeses* and two, to satisfy the three soft *noes*. That leaves the four firm *noes*, and you've got the rest of your career to bring them around. Maybe you never will. So, first, don't offend the ten *yeses*."

"How would I do that, especially since I don't know who they are?"

"By asking around to try and identify them. Or plagiarism would do it. Or submitting your article in draft form to COPT in a notebook with Mickey Mouse on the cover. Or by turning in continuing ed materials as an article. None of which you are going to do. So, don't seek them out and they'll stay *yeses*. Which leaves the three swing votes. Satisfy their expectations and you're home free."

"And those expectations are...?"

"We don't know precisely."

"Well, Christ." Jonathan's face became red. "This is like trying to hit a fucking moving target. Maybe I..."

"No, no. You've got it backwards. We *want* their expectations to be indefinite. In fact, the dean wanted to put everything down in writing, but I resisted."

"Because...?"

"So that you can produce what you want to produce, and then we convince them that that's just what they wanted. I don't want the three, or the dean, to think too carefully about what their precise minimum requirements are, because the more they think the higher the minimum gets ratcheted up. And I don't want to get hung up on some detail, either, like your production deadline is July First and you didn't get the acceptance until the Eighth. The more flexible the target, the better. The worst thing of all would be for them to give us a list of certain law reviews for you to appear in. That takes control away from us and gives it to someone else."

"You seem to have thought a lot about this."

"Actually, it just came to me during the drive in on Thursday. I hope I'm right. But then, what the hell? It's your career, not mine."

Sam said it in such a way that it made Jonathan laugh, and he lifted his beer bottle in toast. "It's my career."

Sam walked over to the table, picked up his bottle and clinked necks. "To your career."

"Mind if I ask you something? You've done this before?"

"Actually, no."

"So why now?"

"Because I was asked?"

"It's not common for someone to be in my position?"

"Rather common, really. Academic publication is not every lawyer's cup of tea."

"But this here..." Jonathan gestured around the kitchen, "...takeaway Thai in your home—this isn't S.O.P.?"

"No."

"Why me? My limitless potential? My winning charm?"

"I get the impression it has to do with your wife. And some article in *The New York Times*."

"The *Magazine*."

"The *Magazine*. Right. It is perceived, I think, that if you get the not-published boot, she'll pack up her tools and move on."

"Which she will at some point anyway, of course."

"But not before the *Times* article."

"We haven't talked about it directly, but I imagine there is some truth to that worry. Against all odds, she seems to like me enough..."

"Enough?"

"Enough to come to Arkansas from Cal Tech."

"And to leave Arkansas if we don't do right by you."

"We?"

"Old habit. They."

Jonathan was quiet for a bit. Then, "Okay, that explains why you were asked. Why did you agree to do it? You don't seem the type who takes on a job that doesn't interest you for the money..."

"Thank you."

"...And the word around the corridor is that you haven't exactly kept your hand in since retirement."

"True enough."

"So?"

"I was advised to do it. Encouraged. By a friend of mine named Ellen Quincy."

"I guess I should thank her for her winning arguments."

"As I recall, her entire so-called argument was along the lines of 'It would be a nice thing to do, wouldn't it?'"

"Nice?"

"She's ten, eleven in January. Her standards of niceness are more finely calibrated than most people's, including mine. One of her favorite horses had hurt himself that morning. Not her very favorite, but one of them. She was worried about him and approved of my concern, and my treatment of the wound. She said that if I was nice enough to help the horse, I should also help the person. You."

"Good for her. She'd make a good prosecutor."

"John Reynolds came by with the dean's proposal shortly after the accident and met Ellie. She asked me what was going on, I told her and she said it would be nice to do it. Like I had helped Dreadnaught. To be honest, I was very much disinclined to get involved, until she shamed me into it."

"Shamed? How flattering."

"Okay, then. Persuaded me. For whatever it's worth, I plan to use the dean's money to set up a little trust fund for her." He let the thought settle, realizing that the idea for the trust fund had occurred to him only moments before he had said it.

"So, where were we? Rule three: something out of my class notes. That's thinking small, I'll give you that. Which class?"

"You tell me. Give me an example of some topic from one of your classes that you had to work real hard to get the students to understand."

"I don't get it. Why? What's the connection?"

"Writing a scholarly article is not so very different from getting ready for class, remember that. In both cases, you've figured out something that your audience hasn't. You'll explain it. Different audiences, different formats, but the same idea. So, give me an example."

Jonathan thought for a bit, scratched his chin and ran his fingers through his hair. "Okay, maybe requirements contracts, from second semester Contracts class."

"Talk to me. You won't mind if I do the dishes while you talk?"

"Where do you want me to start? The case in the textbook presents the issue that the students..."

"No," Sam interrupted, now with his back turned while he organized the dishes in the sink.

"You don't have a dishwasher?"

"For one person? Besides, my wife thought they were wasteful."

"You were married?"

"A widower. No, start from the beginning: what's a requirements contract?"

Jonathan ignored Sam's direction. "How did you and your wife get to Arkansas?"

Sam turned back to face Jonathan. "Independently. I practiced for four years out of law school. Up in Kansas City. Then got into teaching and climbed on the university carrousel. After bits of time here and there, I ended up at the U of A in the mid-Eighties. A few years later, just out of college, Sally was a Vista volunteer, and spent two years working in a health clinic down in Franklin County. She went back east for her teaching degree, but decided this is where she wanted to work. So she came back and got on at Huntsville Elementary. We met at a Huntsville High basketball game. I was smitten. I felt light headed, like I was one of the teenagers at the game. I still remember the score: Eagles fifty-two; Mountain Home forty-five." Sam paused, lost in the thought.

"It sounds heartwarming: new-found love."

"Yes. Of course, there were two long-term relationships that had to be terminated, with all of that messiness. And in my case, with the added indignity of having to divorce an entirely decent woman."

"And a pissed-off one?"

"That would have made it easier, wouldn't it?"

Jonathan shook his head. "Probably not."

"No, probably not."

"Children?"

"No." Sam turned back to the dishes in the sink. "Now, what's a requirements contract?"

"I thought you used to teach Contracts."

"I've forgotten. Remind me."

"This is silly."

"Indulge me."

"Okay, a requirements contract is one where the quantity term is set indefinitely by the buyer's requirements for the product."

"So?"

"Well, it's the quantity term, which is—or may be, anyway—the most important term in the contract."

"More important than the price?"

"Yes, because if the price term is omitted we can fill it in with the market price. But there's no such thing as a market quantity. The students have a hard time with that, having been consumers most of their lives."

"I remember. Go on."

"So, the Code loosens up the necessity of a specific quantity, and allows the contract to depend on the buyer's needs."

"Restrictions on the buyer?"

"He can't shop around. He has to buy all his product from the seller he's contracted with. With whom blah blah blah." Jonathan paused. "Want me to dry?"

Sam ignored him. "An example?"

"The case in the text book deals with a bakery company that's decided to convert all its delivery trucks from gasoline to propane and contracts to buy all of its conversation kits from the gas company. Plus all the propane to run them. Empire Gas, to be precise."

"Of which I was once a customer."

"Really? Small world."

"And so the problem is...?"

"What happens if the buyer doesn't want any?"

"You skipped a step."

"I did?"

"Disproportionate over-orders."

"I thought you'd forgotten everything."

"My recollection is spotty."

"Okay, so the buyer can't demand a quantity disproportionately larger than what he's ordered in the past."

"And if he does?"

"Seller's option. He can, of course, fill the large order, or he can decline to cover the overage, and not be in breach."

"Giving the buyer...?"

"The right to shop elsewhere for the excess that he needs."

"Okay, now, the problem is...?

"What about disproportionate under-orders, about which the statute is vaguer. As in the gas case, where the bakery decides not to convert after all, thereby needing no conversion kits and no propane."

"And that's where it gets complicated."

"Right. Want me to go on?"

"No. What I want is for you to write that up."

"Which?"

"What you just told me. That's Part Two of the article."

"Part Two?"

"Part One: Introduction. Two pages, max. Write that last. Part Two: Requirements Contracts in General. What you just told me. Part Three: The Problem of Disproportionate Under-orders. Part Four: Recommendations for Reform. Part Five: Conclusion. You just spoke Part Two aloud, so write it up."

"After I research it, you mean."

"Before. You know enough to write the text of Part Two, as you just related it to me. Formalize it a bit, write the text, then go back in and fill in the footnotes, changing the text as you learn quirks and refinements. Oh, and fire your RA. Do your own searching; you'll learn things while skimming cases that your RA would never think to print."

"Just like that? Write Part Two?"

"Just like that. Might take a day or two, given that you just spoke it. Then a couple of weeks to footnote it. That puts us near Christmas break, but you'll have exams to grade. So, say before classes start in January, you'll have Part Two drafted and footnoted. I'll read it if you like."

"You make it sound too easy."

"Look. We're trying to get you tenure. We're not trying to get you into the damn Harvard Law Review, to be cited to—or by—the damn US Supreme Court. The material in that box over there is designed for those worthy goals. I hope you're not insulted if I say I have no confidence that the material in the box will ever get written up. Maybe it will, but do this first. To a large extent, you have an audience of three. They'll be satisfied, I think, if you write something intelligible and get it published in a respectable journal. That's a nice wide target to aim at for now. After the next vote, you can write any damn thing you want to, and I can go back to being retired, and thinking about what I should be thinking about."

"Like?"

"Pastern dermatitis. Least common denominators. The sophomore pole vaulter from Slovenia. Be mundane for now; save your brilliance for later. Deal?"

"I can do mundane."

"Good. Call me if you want to talk. I don't do email much."

"Life without email? Similar to life without Cheetos. How do you resist?"

"I actually have a gmail address, but there's no computer here at the house, so I have to go to town and visit the library. It's usually not worth the trip."

"No computer? That's a little aggressively retro, isn't it?"

"Less so than you'd think. It's two miles thataway…," Sam pointed out the front door, "… to the nearest fiber-optic cable. Welcome to the far side of the Digital Divide."

"Area wi-fi?"

"Blocked by a hill to the west."

"Cell service?"

"Iffy. You're sitting down in a holler. What signal does yours show?"

Jonathan pulled out his phone. "Two bars. One. Two. Probably enough to give you access to the web, holler or not."

"Actually, I have a smart phone, a gift from my little sister. I don't use it much, though, unless I'm in town. I'm told that even a small data plan could send my retiree finances into a tail-spin."

"So, what's the best way to get in touch with you?"

"The number's on the map. It's to that land line right there." Sam nodded toward the wall phone.

"How 'bout I just post my queries on your Facebook page?"

"I think we're going to get along just fine," Sam said. "Finish your beer; I've got to go put some hay out for the horses. I'll be back up in, say, fifteen minutes."

But before Sam could complete that chore, Jonathan had packed up his things, hailed "Goodbye" and driven off to the west, leaving a note on top of the box: "Recycle."

# 2

## DECEMBER

**The First Thursday.**

Horses do not deal in the future tense. Their memories are keen, if not sharp in a grammatical, past-tense way, but they live in a Zen-like present. (It might be more accurate for me to say that Buddhist monks strive for a horse-like present.) Their memories are not fond, nor fearful nor anguished; nor do they brood over what the future may bring. They do not regret; they do not reflect in embarrassment. They do not anticipate; they have neither remorse nor expectations. They are very much in the now.

This combination of memory and presence, without the bother of what-is-to-come, makes routine important to them. This is especially true of horses at the track, whose lives outside their stalls are minimal. They work, they race, they cool down. Other than that, they stand in cement-block stalls, and they eat, they are medicated, and they sleep. Thus it becomes important to them that their grain arrives on time, as the routine requires. They are not always patient.

Just One Look had adjusted to the new routine at Sam Butler's place within a few weeks of his arrival. As noted, he did not compare it to the very different routine at the track in Claremore, appreciate the differences nor stew over their causes. He was comfortable and content with the new one, much of which occurred outside his presence. At around four o'clock p.m., Sam would begin to make his own dinner, tonight left-over pasta made into a cold salad with sardines and scallions, with some steamed greens on the side. *All Things Considered* on the kitchen radio, as Sam, what is called these days an "appointment listener," had to catch the four o'clock hour or not at all. He had decided preferences when it came to *ATC* hosts, and tonight it was Melissa Block alone, his favorite combination—or non-combination, actually. Out the kitchen window he could see the five horses off to the east in their day pasture.

At five, he would head down the hill to the stable, while the horses, knowing the routine, would drift themselves to stand by the pasture gate, fussing at each other, ears back, the occasional nip on the hindquarters or warning kick as the two dominant ones kept order. Sam would put out their hay and grain, then walk back to let them through the gate, each heading for his or her own stall, always in the same order: Smokey, The Looker, Restive, Daisy and Dreadnaught. Now, in December, the chickens would have already gone to roost in their hen house, needing only to be closed up by Sam against raccoons and other critters of the night.

Sam would then walk back up the hill to the house for his own meal, the salad, greens, a thick slice of French bread, warmed in the oven, and tonight, a half-glass of claret, and the dinner book he was reading, *The Student Conductor*, by Robert Ford, a local writer whom he slightly knew. At seven, and by now, in December, full dark, he would walk back down to the stable, with a carrot for each, food for the dog, and three horses to the night pasture, Smokey and The Looker still to stay around the stable. Clean up the stalls, which were lighted, then back up to the house to clean up his own kitchen.

So that now he lit the fire in the living room hearth, the fire he had laid earlier in the day, settled himself in a chair before the fireplace, and opened his evening read. He had come upon Wodehouse late in life and was reading his third *Wooster & Jeeves* novel, finding himself chuckling aloud on occasion. Fifteen Dollars lay curled up near the hearth with her nose under her tail, now and then having to get up and rotate a half-circle, as one side got too hot from the fire. It was just after eight o'clock.

Teena lifted her head, perked up her ears, and gave a quiet woof.

"It's just a car, Teena." Sam could see lights moving along the road from west to east. "Go to sleep."

Instead the dog roused herself, and hopped to the kitchen door, now barking more sharply. Sam heard footsteps on the porch and a rap on the storm door. He marked his place in the Wodehouse, walked to the door and snapped on the porch light. He was expecting no one. Standing in the light was a young, dark-haired woman. A hooded sweatshirt and puff-vest. Jeans and day-glo red running shoes. Teena seemed to approve, as the end of her tail was twitching. Sam opened the inside door and the storm door a large crack.

"You're lost," more an observation than a question. "Where're ya trying to get?"

"Here, I think," the woman said, holding up a piece of paper and, with her other hand, opening the storm door the rest of the way. Teena was immediately outside, presenting her butt to be scratched. Ignoring the invitation, the women walked inside and stuck out her hand. "I'm Lynda Stratford." Sam took the hand, but said nothing, not recognizing the name. "Jonathan Wheeler's wife."

"Oh, right. Dr. Stratford. Where's Jonathan?"

"*Lynda*. With a *y*. At his office, doing the homework you gave him." She stepped farther into the kitchen, took off her vest and looked around. "I thought it was time we met."

Sam got the dog back inside and sent her to lie down near the fire. "I don't give him homework."

"He calls it homework, though he does it at his office. I like your house." She tossed her vest onto the rocking chair, then pulled off her sweatshirt and did the same with it. Underneath, she wore a long-sleeved, fine-knit black sweater, maybe cashmere. "How old is it?"

"About a century. Well, can I get you something to drink? I'm not really set up for, you know, drop-ins."

"Nothing special needed."

"There's an open bottle of a passable red wine, a couple of room-temperature beers. Tea, black tea. Instant coffee."

"Tea, thanks." She walked around the kitchen like she was at home, looking at the furniture, rubbing her palm across the surface of the kitchen table, while he began making tea. "Nice."

He looked over his shoulder. "What's that?"

"The kitchen table. Nice."

"It's pine. A scrub-top table, it's called."

"Old?"

"Fairly."

"You have a rocking chair in the kitchen."

"My wife's insistence."

She walked over and peered into the refrigerator. "Boring. Do you eat?"

"Most days, yes." Her forwardness was remarkable, and puzzling to him. Now she picked up his book from the table. "You read Wodehouse."

"I was late to discover him. I laugh out loud."

"It's the perfect cover." She showed it to him. "Bertram Wooster as elegant, charming and entirely vacuous."

Sam looked at the cover while she held the book. "I hadn't really noticed, but you're right."

"Too bad about the Nazi thing, though," she said, now looking into the living room.

"Oh, no. What Nazi thing?" The kettle began to whistle, so he turned off the gas burner and placed two mugs with tea bags on the table. "Milk or sugar? Honey?"

"Yes, dear," Lynda said to his back as he walked to the cupboard and pulled out a jar. "And lemon, if you've got it."

"Sure. What Nazi thing?" he asked as he pulled a lemon from the fridge and cut off a slice on the counter.

"He was either naïve or a collaborator. Probably something in between." Lynda picked the kettle up, tucking her hand in the sleeve of the sweater, using the sleeve as a hot pad. She poured both cups full. "What's the copyright on that one?"

Sam picked the book up and looked in the front pages. "Odd. There's no copyright date at all. Only 'First published in the UK in forty-seven.'"

She helped herself to the honey and lemon, and then walked into the living room and sat down on the stone hearth. "Thereby disguising the fact that he wrote it while enjoying the hospitality of Herr dr. Gœbbels." She raised her voice to be heard.

"Your German pronunciation is impeccable." He followed her in and sat in his chair by the fire. "I'm sorry to hear that. I must say he has an admirable facility with the English language. Wouldn't you like a chair? The fire screws up the thermostat, making the rest of the house chilly. Not very efficient, but I do like having something to back up to."

"Or to stare into?"

"One of life's pleasures. I thought your name was Gwendolyn."

"Gwendolynda, precisely. But I jettisoned the Gwendo- in middle school."

"Doesn't Jonathan call you Gwen?"

"To irritate me."

"What's wrong with Gwen?"

"Middle school. It made me feel like a pixie. Short, cute, haircut like a boy. *Gwen*. I wanted to puke."

"You're a physicist, right?" She nodded. "Theoretical or experimental?"

"Experimental."

"And on what do you experiment?"

"It's really pretty hard to explain."

"You could try."

"I'd rather not," she said, reaching with the poker to stir the fire on her own. "Reduced to its simplest terms, it would take me fifteen minutes to explain, and the only word you would understand in those fifteen minutes would be 'laser,' not counting 'and' and 'the.'"

"I'm not so sure I even know what a laser is."

"Ah. The world's last honest man. Congratulations."

"Okay, then, how did you find your way out here? Oh, well, I suppose Jonathan... But he's only been here once."

"He showed me your map. He thought it was quaint."

"Quaint?"

"Quaintly twentieth century. Everyone with a phone these days has a GPS device to lead the way."

"I forget. And I like drawing maps."

"Typical, apparently."

"Typical of what?"

"You. Your generation, maybe. Like that you sit here at night with the dog and the fire, laughing over Wodehouse, instead of watching lesbians make out on the web, or downloading *The Hangover* from Netflix."

"Her name is Fifteen Dollars. The dog. Teena for short."

"How did she lose her leg?"

"Snake bite."

"Do you play?" she asked, nodding toward the old upright piano, standing against the west wall, next to the window.

"Not a note. It was my wife's, a family heirloom actually, from Great Aunt Martha, as I recall. It's a little embarrassing to say these days, but I think the white keys might actually be ivory."

She put her cup down on the hearth, patted the dog on the head, and walked over to the piano, first seeming to inspect it merely as a piece of furniture. "It looks like it should be sitting in Fellowship Hall at a Methodist Church in Nebraska. I suspect that Wodehouse was just one of those guys to whom everything is a joke, up to and including the Nazis. They annoy the hell out of me. Joan Rivers is another one."

She then sat on the piano stool and ran her fingers over the keys.

"I'm not sure it's in tune. It hasn't been played since..."

"Since?"

"For a long time. I'm trying not to be surprised that you didn't ask permission."

"Do I seem like someone who asks permission?" She began playing scales, then chords. "The tuning is pretty good, actually."

"You have perfect pitch?"

"Yes, but that's the wrong question to ask. You don't need perfect pitch to tune a piano. You mostly have to listen for the wolf intervals. A whole number of perfect fifths just can't fit into the whole number of octaves on the keyboard, so all you can do is try to make them sort of fit in the most pleasant way. Tuning a piano is an exercise in compromise, not perfection."

"Like life itself..."

"Speak for yourself." She played several right hand chords repeatedly, narrowing her inquiry, with her head turned to the left as she listened, and tipped down, her right ear close to the upright's strings, her black hair hanging straight down, almost to the keys, then she played one chord three times running. "There. It's not quite right. Right there." She hit the chord again. "But it will do." She began playing a melody with her right hand, then picked up the bass part with her left.

"What's that?"

"Oh, just a little thing I composed when I was an undergrad." She played on, filling the room with music.

"It's lovely. Did you really write it?"

"It's Brahms, you dope." She stopped playing and swiveled on the stool to face him. "Is that her?" She gestured with her head toward a photograph, a five-by-seven black and white, set in a silver frame on the top of the piano.

"Yes."

"Her name?"

"Sally."

"I like her looks." The photograph showed a young woman with light, but not blond hair, parted on the side. The wind blew the side away from the part across her face and into her smile, several strands catching on her lips. Sunglasses were perched on top of her head, and she looked up and off to the left of the camera lens.

"She was about your age then. Mid-thirties, I'm guessing."

"Close." Lynda turned back to the piano and began playing again, this time something soft and quietly jazzy. "What got her?"

Sam stood up to stir the fire, then returned to his chair. "She taught second grade at Huntsville Elementary, so parents who wouldn't read to their kids. Drought. Racetrack vets. George Bush."

She continued playing. "I said what *got* her, not what got *to* her."

"I heard what you said, but I barely know you. I can't think right now of a good reason why I should tell you."

"Well, you're a constant humiliation to my husband. That should count for something." She quit playing again and turned to meet his eyes.

He stood up from his chair and moved to stand by the couch against the far wall. "It's too hot by the fire." He sat down. "It was a drunk-driving accident."

"Shit. I hope the guy is rotting in jail." She turned and began to play the jazz again, but when he said nothing, she looked over her shoulder at Sam, who was staring into the fire.

"It was a one-car accident." He spoke softly.

"What? How...?" She paused. Then, "Oh." She turned back towards him. "Look at me." She waited until he did. "How are you with that? Don't look away." She held his eyes with hers. "How *are* you?"

"Ah, yes. The stages of grief when an alcoholic loved one dies. Stage one: relief that her struggle is over. Stage two: guilt at the relief felt in stage one. Stage three: self-forgiveness of the guilt felt in stage two. Stage four: resolution and recollection of the times that were good."

"Where are you?"

"Stage one."

"Relief?"

"Yes."

"How long's it been?"

"Three years. Three and a half."

She turned back to the keyboard and played, now a slowed-down ballad.

"*Love is a Rose*," he said. "Neil Young. How appropriate."

She finished the song, then stood up and walked to stand in front of him at the couch, leaned down and put her arms around his shoulders, her right hand touching the back of his neck. "Samuel, I'm so sorry." She held the embrace and, not knowing what to do with his hands, he put his right one on her left shoulder. "For whatever it's worth, I think you should skip two and three and go directly to four."

"No one actually calls me Samuel." She straightened up, put her hand on the top of his head, then sat down right next to him on the couch, putting her head on his shoulder. Her scent was strong, more soap than perfume, with the soapy smell wearing off at the end of the day, losing the battle to an earthy skin-smell beneath. The scent from her hair on his shoulder was different yet again, a yeasty smell, like unbaked bread.

"Samuel Butler," she said. "Who can resist that? What? Were your parents fans of *The Way of All Flesh*?"

He stood up. "Samuel *Coleridge* Butler. I'll get you some more hot water?"

"Is that wine bottle still on offer?"

He walked into the kitchen, talking over his shoulder. "My sister is Emily Dickinson Butler, now Komota. Our parents had literary careers in mind for us."

"How did that work out?"

He returned to the living room with the bottle and two glasses. "She's a thoracic surgeon. And I ended up writing law review articles about indirect preferences in bankruptcy."

"What are they?"

"You don't want to know. I hardly remember myself." He handed her a glass and poured.

"Thanks. You're having some, too? Is it too hard after talking about Sally?"

He took a sip and sat back down in his chair, crossing his legs. She moved from the couch back to the hearth. "We went to a counselor once who suggested that I quit drinking. She thought it might help Sally to quit."

"And did it?"

"It made it worse. It wasn't fair that I could quit so easily and she couldn't. There's nothing much logical about life with an alcoholic."

They let the thought linger for a while, both watching the fire. Lynda then got up and began walking around the living room, looking at the books on the shelves, the art on the walls, the furniture, all dark and antique-y. "What's upstairs?"

"Bathroom, bedroom, study."

"Which George Bush?"

"Beg pardon?"

"Which George Bush got to her?"

"Both. All of them. The whole damn family, actually, starting with Prescott, and extending to generations yet unborn."

"That's not really fair, is it?"

"Which?"

"Condemning the unborn."

"The sins of the fathers are visited upon the sons..."

"Who said that?"

"God, I guess. It's in Genesis somewhere."

"You said 'god' as if it were capitalized."

"Isn't it?"

"Only if you also capitalize antimatter."

"Antimatter? Who would capitalize that?"

"Exactly. You read the bible?"

"No. Sally did. Step two, you know."

"Step two?"

"Of twelve. 'A power greater than ourselves can restore us to sanity.' She read the Bible every day, rain or shine. It's still upstairs where she placed it the night before she died."

"You know what I'm wondering."

"Hardly."

"Rain or shine?"

"Rain or shine."

"Drunk or sober?"

"Drunk or sober."

"Did it help?"

"Not enough."

"Are these your children?" She was looking at a picture on the bookshelf.

"Niece and nephews."

"Oh, right. Half-Japanese. Emily Dickinson Komora, right?"

"Komota."

"You and Sally?"

"None. Five horses, though," He spread his hand. "Thoroughbreds, retired from the track. They'll live into their thirties, needing to be looked after, and they won't grow up and go away to college."

"Hence all the horsey little knick-knacks I see?" She picked up a small figurine.

"Causing our friends to roll their eyes and make comments about childless couples of a certain age and their animals."

"Fuck 'em."

He ignored the profanity. "Are you and Jonathan going to have children?"

"Yes." She didn't amplify.

"They are remarkable animals, though. You know the one job that people thought where the horse would never be replaced?"

"Tell me," she said, continuing to snoop around.

"Milk delivery. See, the horse would learn the route."

"Learn the route?" she asked.

"Right. See, the milkman would disembark the milk wagon, carrying in his rack the deliveries for, say, his next six customers, all on one side of the street—quarts, pints, milk, cream, butter, and so forth. He'd set off to make the deliveries and the horse would pull the wagon up to the next stop, just where the milkman would have to return to the wagon to drop off the empties and pick up for the next six customers. The horse would then take off for the next stop. Neat, eh?"

"The driver-less cars that are being designed would be able to do that."

"Great. So twenty-first century technology can make a machine as smart as a horse. Congratulations."

"Except nobody gets milk delivered at home anymore."

"A shame. Just like no one draws maps anymore. Would you play some more of that Brahms?"

She sat on the stool, rubbed her palms together and put her hands on the keys. Then, nodding at Sally's portrait, she began to play. Teena settled down, Sam sat back in his chair, sipping his wine and staring into the fire, lost in thought.

When she stopped playing, she spoke, "The End. Are you awake?"

"What was that?"

"Two intermezzos. Opus one-seventeen, numbers one and two."

"You play very well. Better than Sally."

"Thank you." She swiveled around to look at him. "I should go."

"And Teena and I have to check on the animals. Want to come down to the stable with us?"

"Not this time." She picked up her glass and walked into the kitchen, where she put on her sweatshirt and vest. "Thanks for the wine and the tea."

"I don't mean to humiliate Jonathan, you know."

"I didn't say you humiliate him. I said you were his constant humiliation. There's a difference. Everyone around the law school knows that you're holding his hand, you know that don't you? It's hard for him to live with."

"I'm sorry."

"Don't be. It's his own fault."

She walked to the door and he followed. "So goodnight," he said. "Thanks for the music. Next time, call ahead and I'll have something nicer planned."

"Do I seem like someone who calls ahead? Come here." She pulled him into an embrace. "Bend down." He did, and she planted a kiss on his lips. "Good night, Samuel. It was nice to meet you." And she was gone. Sam watched her tail lights disappear up the hill for the drive back to town.

**Later That Night.**

Lynda arrived home to a dark house, the cat begging for food and Jonathan asleep in bed. She fed the cat, showered and climbed into bed, naked, intending to wake Jonathan, which she did. They then had energetic and sometimes noisy sex for about an hour, after which Jonathan fell back asleep. Lynda rolled out of bed, cleaned herself up in the bathroom, put on a bathrobe and now sat in the study with her iPad, a cold glass of Boutaris white, and a sore, roughly-treated left nipple.

Google search: *Sally Butler*. Too many to count. *Sally Butler Hindsville*. No help. *Sally Butler Huntsville Elementary School*. Nothing. Duh. Maybe her name wasn't Butler. *Sally Huntsville Elementary*. Too many Huntsvilles. *Sally Huntsville Elementary Arkansas*. Bingo. Sanderson, from the caption to a picture in the local paper. She was identified in the picture, with her class of small children on a field trip, apparently to a park somewhere, older and somewhat fuller in the face than the picture on the piano, but clearly it was she. *Sally Sanderson obituary*. A dozen entries. *Sally Sanderson Hindsville obituary*. Nothing. So Sally is short for, what? Sarah, maybe. *Sarah Sanderson obituary*. There, from the *Philadelphia Inquirer*. Lynda whistled softly. It was not one of those paid-for, oddly-fonted obits, but the real thing, right there on the *Inquirer*'s website. She was a Main Liner. BA Swarthmore, MAT Syracuse. Her grandparents' names were mentioned. Her mother was on the Board of Trustees of Penn. Her father of several hospitals. Date of death May 12, 2009, no details given. Survived by her mother, father and husband, Samuel C. Butler of Hindsville, Arkansas. No off-spring. No siblings. Search: *Sally Sanderson accident May 12, 2009*. Bingo. Articles from the *Northwest Arkansas Times*, the *Madison County Record* and the *Arkansas Democrat-Gazette*.

"Jesus." Lynda spoke aloud. There had been a child in the car with her. A boy, unnamed. He had been airlifted to Children's Hospital in Little Rock, where his condition was listed as serious but stable. The driver, Sally Sanderson, had died. There was no follow-up story that Lynda could find and, after trying for a while, she gave it up. She powered down the iPad, put it on the charger, treated her left breast, which had been badly scraped by Jonathan's unshaven cheek, to some lotion, and climbed into bed, this time quietly. It was after one, and the alarm was set for five, to get her to the lab by six-thirty, as was her routine.

**The Following Tuesday.**

Sam sat at the kitchen table, dressed in suit and tie, and watched Ellie walk from where her four-wheeler was parked up to the house. Her backpack, heavy with her math book, was over her shoulder and she walked quickly, Teena hopping along at her side. She thought she was late, though Sam knew she wasn't. He stood up to open the door for her.

"Hey, do you look nice." She did. Her hair was pulled back with a black ribbon that was a nice contrast to the chestnut, and she wore a shirt with a collar, under her fall jacket. Clean, unpatched jeans, ironed even, and sneakers.

"Mom said I had to put this stuff on."

"Stuff?"

"Yes, sir. This shirt and clean pants. And she combed my hair all out. Why are you all dressed up?"

"Because I asked your mother if I could take you to lunch in town."

"Really? Why?"

"We need to buy our tickets to the track meets before they sell out."

"The Indoor Nationals?"

"Yes, and the Tyson, and the outdoor SEC meet. It should be a good season. Did you see in the paper that the Razorback men are pre-season number one?"

"Yes, and the girls are number four!"

"So, anyway, we'll go into campus and buy the tickets and maybe we can nose around the track center, and then we'll have lunch. I'll look over your homework tonight and we'll do the next lesson tomorrow. We're ahead of schedule anyway. We deserve a break, don't you think?"

"Where will we have lunch? McDonald's?"

"*Not* McDonald's. At a place called Hugo's, just off the square downtown. Leave your backpack here, but keep your jacket on. Ready?"

It was all a contrivance, really—track meets never sold out and there were always tickets available the day of. Additionally, their favorite seats were on the unreserved side, near the pole vault runway, and those tickets always sold last anyway. He could have waited two months to buy. However, contrived or not, it was a nice outing. They rode in the small pickup into Fayetteville, where he first made a stop at the grocery for a few things he needed—milk and dish soap—and then drove to campus. Sam's emeritus status came with a free parking sticker, so they pulled into the Fac/Staff lot near the football stadium and walked up the long hill, through the Union and, skirting the Quad, to the law building.

He had wanted to hit the law building as classes were passing, and his timing was just about perfect. So he sat her down on one of the couches in the entrance lounge amidst all the hubbub—ramped-up hubbub as exam week was about to begin on Thursday—while he left, ostensibly to check his mail, of which there was none, then joined her as the crowd was thinning out. They stopped by the dean's office for a short chat, Sam making a point of asking her how her son was, while Ellie sat, saying nothing but looking at everything. He then introduced her to Donna, his former secretary, and they walked upstairs to see if Jonathan Wheeler was in. He was, talking to a student, but Sam interrupted and introduced Ellie to Jonathan and the student, a female. Jonathan was charming and he treated Ellie as if she were twice her age. He then handed Sam an envelope, saying, "You'll be interested in this," then excused himself and returned to the student. Sam glanced inside the envelope, saw that it was Jonathan's Part Two, and said, "I'll call you."

"Exams," said Jonathan, and the student groaned. "Make it after Christmas."

Sam and Ellie exited the law building, past the Six Pioneers Room, named for the first six black law students, admitted without litigation back in the late Forties, making the University of Arkansas the first integrated state university in the South. Sam noted the significance of the room, but otherwise said nothing about the little tour.

From the law building, they walked south, back across the Quad and downhill to the new outdoor track facility, which was open and where there were a few runners working out. Ellie took a picture with her phone of the scoreboard with its notice: "40 National Championships." However, what he had expected to find in the facility—a ticket window—was closed and when he inquired he was told that they'd have to go to the main ticket office, down by the baseball stadium. That would be too far for them to walk, so they went back to the pickup and drove to the office farther south, where he bought them two unreserved seats for the three track meets, total price $120.

Now it was nearly noon—his schedule was meshing like clockwork—and he drove them downtown, where they parked on the square and walked one block down Block Street to Hugo's, a classic below-street-level bistro, dark, crowded, noisy, good food and beer. It was busy at the lunch hour, in fact there were a few couples on the stairs down into the restaurant waiting for tables, but Sam cut line, with Ellie in tow, and inside, in the gloom, he looked around. And yes, there was one of his former colleagues waving her hand, seated with another ex-colleague, and saving two seats for them. Herding Ellie ahead of him, Sam weaved their way between tables. Introductions were made and like magic the waitperson appeared to take their orders. Ellie studied the menu, Sam told her to order anything she wanted, one of the ex-colleagues said the trout was good, and that's what she had.

**Christmas Eve.**

It was not until nearly ten o'clock on Christmas Eve that Sam settled himself before the fire, Teena curled in her spot, without a book—Sam, that is—and with Ellie's present to him lying in his lap. He wasn't sure that he had given up on Wodehouse entirely, but he was giving him a rest for now. Lynda had run off a couple of articles from various British newspaper websites and had, like a smart aleck, mailed them to him *Poste Restante,* Hindsville, and, while he doubted that Phyllis understood the French term, she, of course, knew Sam and got the envelope into his box. The articles had not exactly exonerated Wodehouse, but they were mostly forgiving. Still and all, Sam was giving him a rest, not anxious to read the exploits of the fools of upper-class Britain, composed while the author was sitting out the war in Berlin, nominally a non-combatant prisoner, but by all accounts living quite comfortably amongst the fascists.

Sam sat, bookless and holding Ellie's present, rather later than was his custom. Restive, the middle gelding, had shown up at the stable lame on the left front, head-bobbing lame, as he jerked his head upwards with every other front step, trying to keep his weight off the sore one. It was surely an abscess, Sam thought, a pressurized pocket of infection in the hoof that needed to drain or be drained. He had decided to wait and see if the infection would blow out at the hair line above the hoof in the morning; if not he'd have to dig it out from the bottom. So he soaked the hoof in hot water and gave the horse a gram of bute to keep him stepping on the bad foot, which might cause it to drain on its own, and had put Restive up in a stall for the night, and all of this had taken an hour or more, causing Sam to be late settling down before the fire, bookless and holding Ellie's present, listening as Restive whinnied into the night, answered by Dreadnaught and Daisy, all complaining about the unusual separation. Eventually, he thought, they would all settle down and accept the departure from routine.

When Sam retired, he had expected to be as unsettled as Restive was that night, until he adjusted to the new routine, but instead he had been surprised to find how little changed. Sally was still working, so they got up at the same time and ate at the same time, though Sam took over most of the cooking. He had enjoyed every day of his career, or nearly, teaching, reading and writing, but when he quit he found he missed none of it. Sally observed that he was either kidding himself about having liked it, or now about not missing it, but Sam himself was more inclined to think not.

"That was then," he told her, "and this is now."

"Whatever," she said, shrugging her shoulders and not believing him.

The fact was that life on the farm divided itself into projects and chores. Rebuilding a fence line or siliconing the trailer's roof where it leaked, or changing the oil in the tractor, those were projects. Treating a horse's lameness, or cleaning up the stalls or mowing the pastures, those were chores. And, as he settled into retired life, he came to realize that work at the university, too, had divided itself into projects and chores. Writing an article was a project; getting ready for class a chore. The difference was smaller than he had ever imagined it would be, nor did the idea of chores have the usual negative connation for him, then or now. He had enjoyed the chore of preparing for class, and he now enjoyed the chore of cleaning up the stalls. He was comfortable and content.

Then came the accident, followed by months of chaos. On essentially no notice, his neighbors agreed to look after the animals while Sam accompanied Sally's body back to Pennsylvania for the funeral and burial. The Sandersons were inconsolable; parents should never have to see their children die, especially an only child. There was, for them, no stage one relief; their grief was immediate and infinitely deep, and they clung to each other for their lives. There was no room in that embrace for Sam, and he soon flew home to Arkansas.

Back here, there was the memorial service to organize, though mostly that was done by their friends, and the lingering madness that was the aftermath of the accident. And there were the animals to look after. If the horses noticed Sally's absence, he couldn't tell, but to Sam she was everywhere, or her shadow was. But, after a few weeks he found himself no longer raising his voice for her to bring something out of the tack room for him, and he learned to make the equine medical decisions on his own. School restarted, most of their friends went back to their lives, and Sam settled into the life of a retired widower, still occupied with projects and chores. There was always plenty to do; there was never nothing to do.

But what he noticed right away was that the structure of time was gone. Because they had both of them been teachers, their years had been framed by semesters, and now that was gone. Month flowed into month, season into season, without bright, discernible lines. Even more dramatically, the week had no frame to it, and Sam began to forget what day it was. When the clerk at the grocery or the teller at the bank would wish him a nice weekend, he would realize that another Friday had snuck up on him without his noticing it. He battled back in small ways: he ate off of the nice dishes on the weekend; he drove into town and treated himself to a *New York Times* on Fridays for the movie reviews; and every morning after waking he would say aloud to the mirror in the bathroom, "Good morning, it's..." whatever day it was.

At which point Ellie arrived in his life. She always knew what day it was and, even though home-schooled, she always knew when the weekend or especially the breaks were coming, for Cardinal roughly followed the Huntsville school schedule. They made a math game of it, and he'd ask her "What day of the year is this?" And she'd say "The one-hundred-seventeenth," or whatever. And, though her science education was not his responsibility, he got her to pay attention to the phases of the moon, and drew a diagram to show her why the phases happened. And when the diagram didn't work, he went over to the Quincys one night and they played around in the darkened living room with a bare light bulb as the sun, a basketball as the Earth and a baseball as the moon. Ellie was fascinated with the demonstration and was soon darting in and out, looking at what the moon would look like from the Earth, then holding the basketball and spinning as if she were the Earth. Cardinal sat, bemused, on the couch with the younger children, while David stood in the doorway, vaguely uncomfortable with the entire exercise. Later, David would wonder aloud to Cardinal, "Science class without the Bible?"

Holidays were difficult for Sam, not difficult to get through, but difficult to see coming. This was especially true for moveable feast-days like Thanksgiving and Easter, and meaningless ones like Presidents' Day or Columbus Day, but it remained true even for the more predictable days like the Fourth of July or Memorial Day, which had a way of arriving into his conscious unnoticed. Of course, he knew that it was now around Christmastime, who didn't?, but he could not have told you what day of the week was to be Christmas Day. And then on the Thursday before Christmas, Cardinal and Ellie had arrived unexpectedly in the afternoon intending, they said, to decorate his tree. At which point Ellie, jumping up and down with excitement, said, "We have one for you!" And sure enough out of the back of their pickup came a rather scrawny-looking cedar tree, probably cut off the Quincy property, a box of homemade ornaments and one strand of colored mini-lights. Sam had been quite touched, as well as relieved that they had spent little money on the project either, for the family didn't have it to spare. They set up the tree in the corner away from the hearth and, while Ellie was putting the ornaments and the lights on the tree, Cardinal pulled Sam aside.

"She wants to set up a Nativity scene for you. I didn't know what to tell her. We don't... I mean I know..." she spread her hands in frustration, unable to put his potential objections into words.

"Cardinal, it's fine. I'll just make a place on this table here. I'd be pleased if she'd do it."

"But..."

He put his hand on her shoulder. "It's fine. Really. Right here." He moved a lamp and a ceramic pot to the back of the table to the left of the hearth. Ellie then unpacked the Nativity set with care: Mary, dressed in blue and white, and looking Norwegian; Joseph, more Semitic; the baby Jesus, too old for the occasion; the stable itself, three-sided, not unlike Sam's own; and then the animals, which Ellie arranged carefully around the people. Cow, sheep, goat, another cow, camel.

"What? No horse?" Sam exaggerated his surprise.

"No," Ellie said, moving the goat from one side to another.

"How can there be a stable without a horse? I never heard of such a thing!"

"This set doesn't have a horse." Her voice was quiet.

"Why not?"

"It just doesn't, that's all."

Sam was going to continue to razz her about an equineless Nativity when he caught a glimpse of Cardinal behind Ellie, shaking her head ever so slightly. This seemed to be a point better dropped, so Sam said, "It's very nice, but why not have the two cows standing together? There, that's very nice."

Ellie had seemed satisfied, and soon she and her mother departed, having asked Sam to join them for Christmas dinner, and he having declined, with thanks. That left Sam to discover, as he should have guessed, that Ellie had left behind a small, wrapped present under the decorated tree.

It was that present that he now held in his hands as he sat before the fire, late for him on Christmas Eve. He decided to open it tonight, instead of Christmas morning. Tomorrow promised to be a busy morning, Christmas or no, what with Restive's foot to doctor and all. It was the only present he had, though along the table behind the Nativity stood cards he had received from his niece and nephews, with smiling pictures and "Dear Uncle Sam" notes about their lives and loved ones. Tomorrow, he would talk to his sister on the phone, and she would complain that another year had gone by without his coming for a visit, and he would defend, as always, based on the needs of the animals. If the truth were to be told, he had no desire to be away. Besides, while he loved his little sister, she could be a pest.

Sam pulled at the bow on Ellie's present, hoping that it would not be expensive. He, after consulting with Cardinal and David, had bought Ellie a Seiko interval stopwatch for Christmas, a nice one and rather expensive, and he hadn't wanted to embarrass the Quincys by being too extravagant. This way, he had told them, she could keep track of the lap times when they watched the Razorbacks run, and all the work with numbers would be good for her math. They had agreed, and the watch in its box now sat under their tree, wrapped in satiny red paper, waiting for Christmas morning. He thought she'd like it.

The ribbon did not pull, so Sam had to slip the bow off of the present and then carefully unwrap the paper. Inside, a box, and in the box was the missing horse from the Nativity scene. "Ah, ha," he spoke aloud to the dog, "Teena, the mystery is solved, and the absent horse arrives. I'm guessing that Mary has been waiting." He stood to place the horse in the collection of figures, thinking that it was clever of her—or Cardinal, more likely—to have thought of how to give a gift without going to any extra expense. But it was only when he put the horse down in its place that he understood the true nature of the gift. He stepped back and put one hand to his mouth; he found that his eyes were misting over at the scene. For he could now see that she had found just the right paint and had hand painted the horse to match the markings of Daisy, her favorite. The dark chestnut—the match was very close and Cardinal might have helped her get it just right, probably at Hobby Lobby—with the white star on her forehead, which gave Daisy her nickname, and two white socks on her hind, one reaching a bit higher than the other. Mane, forelock and tail just a touch darker than her body, the little figurine was perfect, and it meant quite a lot to him what she had done to make it special.

He stepped back up to the table and adjusted Daisy's position slightly, giving her a certain, perhaps blasphemous, prominence in the scene. He smiled at the thought that an indifferently-bred, over-medicated, out-of-the-money racer with a bowed tendon would be attending the Birth. She had, though, the blood of Tim Tam, who almost won the Triple Crown, and of the great Nearco, while at the same time she had the disposition not to kick over the Crèche in a rush of female hormones. He had watched her last race, on the day they'd bought her, and had found videos of a few others on the web, and she had tried, he'd give her that. She had been a front-runner who was empty late, but still she was game down the stretch, even though badly beaten. Maybe she was just right and, yes, she deserved to be in a Nativity scene. Sam made one tiny readjustment and sat back down in his chair.

The fire was fading, and the only lights on in the room were the small table lamp lighting the Nativity scene and the string of colored lights on the tree. Sam decided not to add another log to the fire, and soon all the flames had flickered out, and he sat in the dark room watching the coals, smelling the smoke and listening to the crinkle of the dying fire. As he had expected, Restive became quiet in the stable down the hill and across the creek. The dog snored quietly and soon Sam, too, was asleep in the chair.

**The Wednesday between Christmas and New Year's Day.**

"Tell me about the boy."

"What boy?"

"The boy who was in the car with Sally."

"How do you know about him?"

"Google."

"Right. There are no secrets from Google."

They were sitting in the Valley Café in Hindsville, mid-afternoon, over excellent pie and bad coffee. Lynda had called him at around two, inviting him to afternoon dessert at the café, which she had heard had a reputation for pie. Sam had begged off, claiming that pie in the afternoon would spoil his dinner, to which she had merely snorted, said "Two-thirty," and hung up.

At the café, he had first demurred, but then agreed. Apple for him and coconut crème for her, though he noticed that she only picked at hers so he knew that the whole thing was a pretext, and now he knew for what. He took another bite of pie, which really was quite good, looked out the plate glass at the road in front, mostly deserted, now that the by-pass had been built. "Where should I begin?" She took the question, correctly, to be to himself, and said nothing. "His name was—*is*—Tommy. Tommy Greene. We knew his parents, Tom and Natalie, quite well. Sally and Natalie taught together. We were a good bit older than they were but we enjoyed each other's company. They knew of Sally's, uh, struggle and did whatever they could to help, which, of course, was not much. We were there at Tommy's baptism and might have been his godparents, except no one does that anymore."

He stalled for more than a minute, but Lynda knew enough to let him restart on his own.

"The previous day had been her two-hundred-fifty-fifth—such numbers become important, at least they did for us. I remember remarking at breakfast that today was an important milestone—two hundred fifty six: two to the eighth."

"Four to the fourth."

"Right. She had a meeting that night and I said that she should announce the milestone to the group. She had gone longer a couple of times in the past— three years once—but still, it was a nice long run and I was proud of her. She seemed subdued at breakfast, but said she'd think about it." Sam moved his fork from the right side of the pie plate to the left. "So, she took off for school after breakfast, and that was that. I never saw her again, not alive."

"You were still teaching?"

"No. I'd retired the previous year."

"Why?"

"We thought it might help, but it didn't. Or maybe it did. I don't know. Two-fifty-six is a long time. So, after school, Natalie got tied up in a meeting with some parents, and Tommy needed to be picked up from day care, and she asked Sally to please do it for her—she'd have to use Natalie's car because it had Tommy's car seat in the back. Sally took the keys, said 'sure,' picked up Tommy at the day care center and then disappeared for three hours. No one knows where to. At about six o'clock, she missed the turn at the twin bridges on forty-five—you drove over them to get here. She rolled the car over twice, the airbags failed, and she ended up nose down in the White River at the base of the second bridge, with the steering column nestled against her spine. There was a half-empty fifth of Jack Daniel's on the front seat floor. No one saw her go over so it was an hour before the ambulance arrived."

He paused, staring into her eyes, but it felt to Lynda more as if he were looking at the back of her skull. She did not speak.

"When I have nightmares," he continued, "I dream of Tommy, strapped in the back seat for an hour listening to Sally scream, while the river water washed over her lap, not high enough to drown her." He turned his gaze out the window again, seeming not to notice the state trooper speeding past, its lights flashing. Then he literally shook, shivering off the nightmare, and went on in an almost academic manner, as if he were talking about people he didn't actually know. "But you asked what became of Tommy. Sally died in the ambulance on the way to Washington Regional, but Tommy was helicoptered from the scene all the way to Little Rock. He was okay—shaken up, a mild concussion, incalculable infantile post-traumatic stress, but otherwise okay.

"The sad thing is that, while Tommy survived, his parents' marriage didn't. Tom wouldn't—*couldn't* maybe—forgive Natalie for entrusting Tommy to Sally. The kid was okay, but everything had changed between them. Well, I suppose there were other issues all along. Six months later, Tom sued for divorce and there was a terrible, terrible custody fight over Tommy. Tom's attorney called me to testify and it was agony for everyone. I made one of those 'don't blame Natalie, it was Sally's fault' statements from the witness stand, but of course it didn't do any good. There was no one else to blame.

"In the end, Tom got custody and immediately disappeared with Tommy, denying Natalie even the court-ordered visitation. I don't know where they went. Natalie went back to her parents' home in Texarkana and almost immediately remarried, but then divorced a year later. Her life is messed up; she must blame herself, too. I don't hear from her anymore." He paused, but wasn't quite finished.

"Then there was the insurance nonsense, over Tommy's medical expenses, which turned into a fight between the insurer of the car and the insurer of the driver. I never paid attention to how that came out." Now he leaned into the table between them and locked eyes with Lynda. "You know, I'm sorry Tommy was in the car, but that's the only reason I know for sure it wasn't a suicide."

"Is that important to you?"

"Yes." Sam watched as Lynda picked up her phone and looked at the screen. "Call?"

"No, the time."

"You have to go."

"Soon." But she made no move to get up, and picked around the edges of her slice of pie, moving the filling around but not eating. "You want to know what I think." It was not a question. "I think your stages of grief have it wrong. Not totally, but still seriously wrong." He said nothing, but was listening. "The first stage is relief that your own struggle is over, not just hers." He started to say something, but she quieted him. "Just listen. Stage two, then, is guilt for the relief felt in stage one, but that guilt is enhanced because the relief was dual. Plus you feel guilty because you think you caused her to drink. Be quiet. And you wonder if your innocent little comment about two-fifty-six being two to the eighth made her buy the Jack, which ramps up your guilt. So, if you thought she wrecked the car to kill herself, it would all be too much to bear."

"What I think is that you ought to stick to physics; I hear you're good at it. Psychology is not your calling." He pushed his chair back to leave.

"And while we're at it," she said, ignoring his statement, "I think you need to get laid. Right away."

Sam pulled his chair back up to the table. "Show some proper respect." He laughed. "At least that took the sting out of your previous psycho-babble. And I might say that my getting laid is an item high on the list of things that are not going to happen. Up around, say, top ten. Right in there with one of the horses sprouting wings and taking flight."

"Why?"

"Because I need a friend a good deal more than I need a lover."

"Fair enough. Choose well and you'll get both. I personally think it would do you good. Keep me posted. Leave a text message: 'Pegasus is aloft.'"

"I don't text. I'm content to have you come out to the house and play the piano for me."

"Anytime. Next Wednesday night."

And with a nod, they both got up to leave. Sam stopped at the cash register on the way out to pay, while Lynda continued through the door and out onto the quiet street. When Sam joined her, she said, "I need a tour of the town."

"Without moving." Sam pointed to the left, the east. "Bank." To the south. "Jim Vaughn's antique store." Katy-corner to the southwest. "A.T. Smith's Mercantile. A funky little store, camouflaging a very successful fertilizer business and A.T. himself, who owns half the land from here to Missouri." He hooked a thumb over his shoulder to the north. "Post office, behind the restaurant." He shrugged his shoulders. "That's it." Then, "Wait." Pointing across the street to the southeast. "Baptist Church."

"Money, antiques, fertilizer, pie and the mail. What else does one need in a town?"

"And God?" he asked.

"Pfffft."

"Walk me to my pickup; you can greet the dog while I check for mail. Don't you have time to stop by the house?"

"Really, I can't."

"I'll show you my Nativity scene."

She rolled her eyes. "Please."

"No, really. Ellie and Cardinal stopped by before Christmas and set it up. It was nice."

"Ellie the Cardinal?"

"Ellie *and* Cardinal. Ellen Quincy is the little girl I help home-school. Cardinal is her mother. I think they decided I'm a lonely old man who needs to be fussed over at Christmastime. They set up a tree and a Nativity set. I'll show you. Ellie painted the horse at the Crèche to look like her favorite mare. I was quite touched."

"Are you?"

"Am I what?"

"A lonely old man?"

"Pick two."

"You help home-school her?"

"Yeah, with her math. Cardinal struggles with math and science."

"Yet the girl is home-schooled?"

"Ellie. Yes."

"Because?" She raised her eyebrows. "What's wrong with the public schools, where the math teachers presumably know more math than you do?"

"Easy, now. Give me a break. I was a math major in college, before law school." They had reached their vehicles, parked side-by-side behind the café, next to the post office, and Lynda allowed Teena, in the back of Sam's pick-up, to make a fuss over her. "Do you have to go? Here's the quick version: Cardinal was born on a commune about thirty miles south of here. Her parents were back-to-the-Earth types and she was raised as a free spirit. She sowed some wild teenage oats, one of which sprouted into Ellie.

"But then—get this—the hippie grandparents came to Jesus and became religious broadcasters. Quite successful, I hear. Cardinal converted, too, and married a local chicken farmer named David Quincy, who is the part-time pastor at a small Church of Christ up in Wesley. Just a few miles up that way." He pointed south. "Cardinal has become quite religious, and Ellie is, too, in a little-girl sort of way." Lynda unlocked her car door, but did not open it, as Sam went on. "So," he shrugged his shoulders, "David doesn't believe in public schools and Cardinal home-schools Ellie and her sibs, except in math, which is where I come in. That's it. Go to work."

Lynda climbed into her car, then ran the window down. "I'm speechless," she said. "And you're part of this plan to keep the girl in the Dark Ages?" She shook her head. "Please tell me you're a mole, planting doubt, bringing enlightenment to the poor kid."

Sam put his hands on her car door and leaned down to talk to her. "I certainly am *not*. I teach her math. Together we look after the horses. We go to track meets. We watch the phases of the moon, the nesting birds. I'm not her father and her religious upbringing is none of my business. She's a nice kid, and I like Cardinal, too. I'm not going to spoil it because I disagree with David's view of evolution, or whatever."

She looked up at him. "Suit yourself, but I know what I'd do. I've got to get back." She leaned her head down and gave his left thumb a kiss, then patted his hand. "Thanks for the pie; it was fun. See you next Wednesday night, I'm not sure what time. Are you going to take my advice?"

"Which piece? Pegasus is aloft? Or god is a figment of your father's imagination?"

"Take your pick."

"Your choice?"

"Okay, forget the religious thing and think about the other. You won't be sorry."

And she drove off, waving her hand out the window, while he walked to check his post office box and then drove home, thinking that he wasn't going to be very hungry for dinner.

**Two or Three Days Later.**

Sam Butler considered the invention of caller ID to be one of the greatest techno-advances in human history. He reckoned as slim the chances of anything good resulting from a telephone call from a stranger, and with caller ID he did not answer the phone unless he knew the caller. Voice mail, on the other hand, was a techno-retreat, as it allowed complete strangers to leave you messages, almost certainly about something you wouldn't be interested in. It also destroyed plausible deniability; one could not say I would have loved to come to your thing—your party, your committee meeting, your reunion, your cousin's graduation, your wife's son's bar mitzvah—but I didn't know it was happening. So he didn't have it. His friends knew of the quirk and shook their heads, his phone rang rarely and he enjoyed the quiet.

Cell phones threatened his peace with their unknown numbers and their "WIRELESS CALLER" non-ID, but mostly he just ignored such calls, which became harder and harder to do as more and more people went wireless. And then came Lynda Stratford, who used a cell phone only, didn't care a whit for his peace and quiet, and enjoyed chatting with him. The first time she called he had ignored the unknown number WIRELESS CALLER call, and she had let the phone ring for four minutes before, in desperation, he had picked up. Not knowing who was calling and hence dripping angry sarcasm, he had said "This is an emergency, right?" but she had ignored him, declined to identify herself and began talking as if he'd picked up after the third ring, not after the one-hundred-and-third.

And so it was that he had learned to recognize her cell number when it showed up. And Jonathan's, as the two of them used each other's phones interchangeably. And when he picked up tonight it was Jonathan.

"You read it?"

"I did."

"And...?"

"It's just what I had in mind. You write well."

"Thank you. Getting started is the key, someone said. You, I think."

"That's what counts for wisdom these days. How's Part Three coming?"

"Well, I think. The structure you set up at your kitchen table made the thing seem to fall into place. And firing my RA was good advice, too. She was disappointed, though. Thought she'd fucked up. Plus, I think, the position looked good on her résumé."

"Keep her on. She can Blue Book the end result. Or look up things for your blog. Have her come to your Contracts class, take notes and tell you what she thinks at the end. Let her read Part Three and critique your writing style. Just you do the research."

"Yes, Boss. I let Wilson, Selvig and Pryor read Part Two, to see what they thought."

"And...?"

"Well, I just slid it into their mailboxes yesterday, so nothing yet."

"I would have waited for Part Three, but no harm done. Let me know what they think."

"Will do."

"Why them in particular?"

"Pretty random. People I know. I thought they might be helpful."

"Uh, huh. Well, let me know. Anything else?"

"You really have no comments on Part Two?"

"Nothing important. Some typos but it's just a draft. Maybe I'd add another paragraph on disproportionate over-orders, with a quick example. And maybe a paragraph at the end to transition to Part Three, but that can wait until I see how Part Three..."

"Hold a minute," Jonathan interrupted. "I've got a call coming in."

"We can talk later," Sam said to an empty line. He sighed aloud, cursed silently, and sat holding the phone, looking out the kitchen window where he could see The Looker, up for the night, standing in the round pen, staring into the dusk.

"Samuel." It was Lynda.

"Oh, hi. You're at home? Where did Jonathan go? I thought some call was coming in."

"That was me in-coming. I'm at the lab and called Jonathan, who said he had you on hold. Knowing how that thrills you, I asked to be patched in to sooth your no-doubt irked sensibilities."

"She's better at that than I am." It was Jonathan.

"You're both here?"

"We're conferencing."

"He did it on his phone."

"Where are you?"

"Who?"

"You."

"Me? I'm at the lab. I told you."

"No, Jonathan."

"At the office."

"You're at the office? I thought you were home."

"Nope. Working late."

"Who's going to feed the cat?"

"Do I really need to be a part of this?"

"*You* feed the cat."

"Me?"

"No. Samuel."

"What?"

"I was saying you should feed the cat."

"He doesn't have a cat."

"*Our* cat."

"I do, too, have a cat, or at least there's one that hangs around the stable. I'm not sure he's exactly *mine*."

"You feed our cat. I won't be home until after ten."

"Who?"

"Who what?"

"Who feeds your cat?"

"You."

"Me?"

"No, me."

"Right. Jonathan feeds our cat. I don't know who feeds yours."

"He's a stable cat. He feeds himself."

"A *stable* cat? So what's that make ours? Conflicted?"

"This conversation is driving me crazy. I'm leaving."

"Leaving? For where? You don't have to feed our cat. I was kidding."

"Hanging up."

"Don't go. I'm not sure we're done talking."

"About the cat?"

"About Part Two."

"We were talking about Part Three, not Two."

"But what about the cat?"

"*I'll* feed the cat. I should be home in a half-hour."

"Why are you still at the office, anyway?"

"Working on Part Three, presumably."

"Actually, I was preparing for that trip in January to...wherever."

"Where?"

"Nebraska."

"Topeka."

"Topeka's in Kansas."

"Washburn."

"I thought it was Nebraska."

"That's in March. Creighton."

"Creighton's in Iowa, not Nebraska."

"No, Creighton's in Nebraska. Drake's in Iowa. That was last semester."

"I'm leaving now. Tell me when you've got Part Three for me to read."

"Goodnight, Samuel. I'll see you soon."

"Goodnight, Sam. And I'll see you at home, Gwenie."

"Stop calling me Gwen. And feed the cat."

When Sam hung up, his head hurt.

**The Final Sunday.**

At eleven-fifteen, on the last Sunday morning of 2012, quiet settled over all of them.

Jonathan and Lynda were still in bed, after a late night out with some of their friends. Lynda had awakened around seven just long enough to read a text message from her post-doc—"6.58 Central. Status: nominal. Chang"—before drifting back to sleep until ten. They had made love twice, and would so again before rolling out of bed for good, but this was that quiet in-between time, with Jonathan drowsy, perhaps dozing, and Lynda with the foggy-brained feeling that Jonathan gave to her, the feeling that she disliked in the abstract, but which she adored while it was here, and which was memorable when it left.

Ellie and her extended family sat quietly, too, observing what the visiting preacher called "a time of silent meditation." The visitor was from India and the visit had been arranged by Wyckoff Ministries International, and the family was sitting in a pew at the First Baptist Church in Fayetteville, which Melissa and Stuart attended. Someone was subbing for David at the little Church of Christ in Wesley so that the family could attend, right to left across a pew: Melissa, Ellie, Cardinal holding the baby, David and Stuart. (The boys were in Sunday School, and were not at the moment quiet.) David sat nervously but quietly, generally uneasy with what he considered to be Stuart's progressive evangelical ways, and specifically uneasy about this Indian, with his hard-to-follow accent, his almost black complexion, his oily black hair, and his use of the word "meditation," which smacked to David of Eastern mysticism. Stuart's mind was itemizing the points he would make later in his on-line summary of Dr. Singh's message. Melissa was sorting through the visit's practical details of which she was in charge; she hadn't yet arranged for Dr. Singh's ride to the airport on Monday evening, which was New Year's Eve. Cardinal's mind was quietly blank, only conscious of Esther in her arms, approaching what Dr. Singh had in mind with the moment of silent meditation. Esther was asleep, dreaming what babies dream. And Ellie finished her prayers, which she assumed was what meditation was, and was now day-dreaming of brushing and fussing over Daisy, her favorite of all of Sam's horses.

And, at eleven-fifteen on that Sunday morning, Sam, too, was immersed in quiet, appropriately enough engaged in exactly the activity of which Ellie day-dreamt. He was brushing Miss Run Run—Ellie's Daisy—with the soft brush, the palm of the hand without the brush following along behind each stroke. The mare's winter coat was deep, full, and dark red. He had sent the others up to the day pasture, but had kept this one down, partly because it was good for her, he thought, to spend time alone, as she had a tendency to become buddy-sour, meaning difficult to control when deprived of equine company. Since one never knew when some emergency would require such a separation, it was good for her to spend some time alone.

She did not agree, and had not agreed from the beginning.

They were of two minds about the track. They enjoyed watching the horses run in circles, which was the last thing of interest to most of the other people in attendance, but there was little else about the racing scene that they liked, not the gambling, not the fashionable high-rollers, not the low-end losers, not the college kids, not the cowboys, not the veterinarians nor most of the trainers. And it was not good for Sally to be around all the drinking.

But once they had needed an expert Thoroughbred farrier to work on a horse who had come up lame, and this person knew that person, who knew someone else, and the trail led to Kenny Smith, who had done it all on the backside—owned, trained, exercised, jockeyed, doctored a bit and shod. All Thoroughbreds and only Thoroughbreds. They had become friends, the three of them, and when they had a horse that needed Kenny's special touch, they'd drag him or her over to the track at Claremore, where Kenny hung out, and they'd make a day of it, looking at the horses, watching the races and listening to Kenny's stories of the backside, from Churchill to Santa Anita to Fair Grounds, and now to here, where the pressure and money were less, the pace slower, and Kenny, part Indian himself, enjoyed living amongst the Cherokees. So once, and only because Kenny had said so, they returned to Arkansas not only with the horse they had brought over to be shod, but with the one in stall 54, too, just because Kenny said he needed a home. A dark bay gelding named Restive, so dark as to be almost black, though they say there are no true-black Thoroughbreds.

Kenny had phoned again in August of '08: "Saturday morning. Bring your trailer. And your checkbook." And, because it was Kenny and he had said so, they drove over with the trailer—US 412, across the state line at Siloam Springs, along the Cherokee turnpike to the Pryor exit and north to Claremore and the track.

Lower-rung Thoroughbred racetracks are not for the faint-hearted, and the track at Claremore, while not the worst, is typical. An unpretty cinder-block and steel-beam grandstand, with plastic seats, yellow and green, cigarette-burned and pigeon-shit-stained. Peeling signs on the tote board, ragged flags flying—American, Oklahoma and Cherokee Nation. A run-down backside and weedy infield, behind a white plastic fence. Flickering TVs for the simulcast gamblers, with a chintzy slot-machine casino behind. Many horses on the way down, a few on the way up. Dirty silks and saddle cloths, the horses running for the last few dollars in them, doing little more than playing the role of the ping pong balls at Saturday night bingo at the Knights of Columbus.

They pulled into the parking lot, half full with cars and pickups, and many horse trailers parked across the way near the backside, as owners or trainers would van a runner in for one race and save the price of boarding at the track. They walked the long way around to the backside, and found Kenny, who immediately said, "Too late. The horse you wanted got claimed in the second race and loaded up and drove off before I knew what happened. Sorry you wasted your trip."

So they sat around the stalls for a while, looked at a couple of horses, watched Kenny chain smoke and listened to his stories, until a trainer came by with a horse to be shod, when they wandered off to watch the races.

"Can I get you something from inside?"

"A Coke." He looked down at her. She nodded. "Just a Coke."

When he came back with one for each of them, she was watching the post parade for the sixth race. Sam liked to sit high up in the grandstand where he could watch the backstretch dynamics, but Sally was a railbird and wanted to be as close to the horses as possible, which at a track like the one at Claremore is close enough to hear and smell them, and almost close enough to touch.

"Number three."

"The winner?"

"No. She's mine."

He opened his program. "Sixth race. Number three. Miss Run Run. Dumb name. Six-year-old chestnut mare. By nobody; out of nobody. She's a maiden. Sixteen races; one second, two thirds. Won thirty-two hundred bucks. Here, Remington, Fair Meadows. Oklahoma bred." None of that mattered. Sally didn't care about names. Kenny said it was bad racing luck to change a horse's name, but nicknames were okay, and he called all the fillies he liked Gardenia, and the colts Oscar. And Sally knew little and cared less about pedigrees and breeding.

This mare was a maiden, meaning she'd never won, but Sally was not looking for winners, who were generally better off than the losers. "Nothing special," he summarized. "Why her?"

"She winked at me."

"We could claim her. Two thousand bucks."

"We're not registered in Oklahoma."

"Kenny is."

"Too late." They were at the post. "Safe trip, fillies," she whispered toward the starting gate.

Miss Run Run led through the clubhouse turn, but weakened on the backstretch and finished sixth out of eight. They walked over to the side of the track where she was being de-tacked, while the winner and her connections were getting their pictures taken in the winner's circle.

Sally spoke: "You the trainer?"

"And owner."

"Sell your horse?"

"Three thousand."

"She was running for a two-grand tag."

"So, claim her."

"I'll give you a thousand dollars, right now."

"Cash?"

"Check."

"How do I know it's good?"

"Keep her papers until it clears. Kenny Smith knows us."

"Two thousand."

"Fifteen hundred."

"Here." He handed Sally the lead line. "She's a slow piece of shit and she eats too much."

They walked her over to the backside and found Kenny, sitting, smoking, legs crossed. He looked at her and approved of what they had done. "She don't need to be running on that tendon again, do ya, Gardenia?" He took off her racing plates, put standard 2s on her front, and they loaded her up and headed home. It was near the end of August, 2008, they had retired a nice horse, and Sally had quit drinking for the last time. Miss Run Run fussed in the trailer the whole way home. She didn't like being alone.

The quiet ended. Jonathan stretched, turned on his side and wondered aloud if he should start the coffee machine first, but Lynda, worried that the fogginess would slip away, said "No," and rolled over onto her stomach, her face turned to him. "Finish me."

At the First Baptist Church, Dr. Singh stopped meditating and began to preach about coming to Christ as a sinful teenager in India, considering suicide, and David relaxed, as he knew exactly what the man was talking about. To Ellie, though, the man used words she didn't know, and strangely pronounced the ones she did, and so she continued to day-dream of being at the stable with Daisy, and wished the service would soon be over.

And at that very stable, Sam smacked that very horse on her rump and spoke aloud. "Well, go on then." He opened the stall door, Miss Run Run looked both ways and, ears pricked, nostrils flared, she whinnied to her mates. Some-one—probably Dreadnaught—whinnied back and she turned left and trotted up to the day pasture. Then the phone rang, and Sam picked up the extension in the tack room. It was his sister, wondering what he was doing for New Year's Eve. He lied—more of a fib, really—and said he was getting together with some ex-colleagues, when actually he was looking forward to sitting by the fire with Teena, Dawn Upshaw singing Górecki's Number Three, his New Year's tradition since Sally's accident. A shot or two of XO cognac, forty years old. Maybe he'd make it to midnight, maybe not. There would be ice to break in the stock tanks in the morning. They were saying it might snow.

# 3

## JANUARY 2013

**The Second Saturday.**

When a horse moves across the ground at the walk or trot, he moves symmetrically, that is to say that his right legs are doing the same thing that his left legs are doing, except at a different time. At the canter or gallop, however, the gait is asymmetric. On the right lead, the horse's right front reaches somewhat farther out than the left, and pulls back more strongly. On the track, a Thoroughbred is taught to be on the right lead on the straightaways, and on the left lead around the turns. At least in America. In Europe and Asia, they run the other way around the track, and everything is backwards.

Thus a horse has to be able to change from the right to the left lead on command, and back again. These are called, sensibly enough, lead changes, and, at full speed, flying lead changes. When done smoothly, they are a wonder to watch, akin to seeing a horse and rider in flight.

Sam Butler and Cardinal Quincy stood with their backs to the wooden fence line that enclosed the riding paddock on Sam's farm, and watched Ellie and Just One Look do flying lead changes around about five acres of smooth, flat, grassy pasture. She was riding him at a fast canter through large figure-eights, sixty yards long and twenty wide, with a cheater in the middle at the crossing point, that is to say, a piece of four-inch white PVC pipe, ten feet long, laid on the ground perpendicular to the figure-eight. When she came out of the left-turn loop on the left lead, and just as The Looker approached the cheater, Ellie would give him a tug on the right rein and tap his left flank with her left hand, and he would step over the cheater and change to the right lead, heading now into the right-turn loop. He didn't slow down a bit, and he didn't miss a step, and Ellie looked so at ease on his back that it was sometimes hard to tell where the girl ended and the horse began.

Sam and Cardinal watched without speaking. After five more trips, Sam intended to replace the cheater with a rope laid across the ground, and, after ten of those trips, to remove the rope and let her do the lead changes truly on the fly.

"God made them to be beautiful creatures, didn't He?" Cardinal said at last.

"Yes, He truly did," Sam said. "Wait." He looked across and down at her; her head came up to his shoulder. "Wait. Do you mean horses or little girls?"

"Horses."

"Oh, but look at her. At the way she sits him. How effortlessly she controls him. The look of concentrated peacefulness on her face. At the way her eyes are focused on a spot out ahead of them. The way her ponytail streams out the back exactly duplicative of his tail. It's a beautiful sight, and she's at least half of the beauty."

"I can't look at her without seeing my own sin."

Sam looked back toward the horse and girl. He paused. Then, "Shame on you," he said.

They stood and said nothing for several more trips around the figure-eight. The Looker was furry in his winter coat, and had put on some weight after his training days at the track, but it was still possible to see his muscles flow with the exercise. He was starting to lather up a bit, even on the cool January afternoon, whose low, watery sunlight was just strong enough to keep the temperature in the forties. Tonight it would drop into the twenties. The horse's nostrils were wide with the exercise, and he blew steam on the exhale.

"Forgive me," Sam said after a minute. "It was not my place to say that."

"It's okay."

"When I look at Ellie, I see a beautiful little girl, not some reflection of The Fall."

"I didn't mean The Fall," Cardinal said. "I mean that when I look at her, I see my own actual sin in her conception."

"It doesn't have to be..."

Turning toward Sam, Cardinal interrupted him by putting her hand on his forearm. "I don't know who her father is." She said it matter-of-factly, then turned back to watch the horse.

"Bring him over here, Ellie." Sam cupped his hands to his mouth and raised his voice to be heard. Ellie pulled The Looker down from his canter and into his long-legged Thoroughbred trot—head raised, ears pricked forward, his sheath squeaking—and steered him over to where her mother and Mr. Butler stood near the fence. She, like the horse, was breathing hard, and she was sweating under her doubled-up sweatshirts. Sam jogged past them into the middle of the paddock and replaced the PVC cheater with the rope that he had coiled in his hand. Then he walked back to re-join the girl, the woman and the horse, trying not to think about what Cardinal had said, but at the same time trying to figure out what he should say in return. Cardinal was holding The Looker's bridle, as he breathed deep and hard; Ellie drank from a plastic Evian water bottle.

"Go," he said, and Ellie tossed the water bottle to him, swung the horse around sharply on his hindquarters and took off across the paddock. Clods of earth flew up from his hooves into their faces and Sam ducked out of the way. Cardinal turned her back to the flying dirt, before turning back.

"It was one night my senior year," she said. "Graduation week. I had sex with four different boys in one of the rooms at the high school, one after another, then later that night with my boyfriend, too. The next thing I knew, I was pregnant."

"So?"

"So, I married my boyfriend, the only one we now know for sure was not her father. When he found out, he divorced me and gave her up." She paused, while they watched the first pass over the rope cheater, which went smoothly. "He's dead now."

"She's a natural rider," Sam said. "It's as if she can communicate directly with the horse, and she knows what to do instinctively. See the way her hands are getting lighter and lighter in his mouth as he gets used to the routine? Who taught her that? Not me. No one. See the way she looks out ahead of him, and not at his ears?" He turned to look at Cardinal. "None of that matters to me. Why should it to her? Or to you for that matter?"

"David would yell at me if he heard me say this, but I think what I did, and the way I lived then, was unforgiveable." She took a breath and shook her head. "Horribly, horribly unforgiveable. But as Christians, we are forgiven our sins. David says it compounds the sin to think it unforgiven, but I can't help myself."

"I forgive you, if that matters. I did worse. So did David, I'll bet."

Cardinal laughed quietly. "David was too afraid as a child to be sinful."

"Afraid of his parents?"

"Afraid of the Lord."

"Does being good count if you're afraid to sin? In any case, he was a teenage boy, so he had plenty of occasions to be sinful. I doubt he passed up all of them."

She laughed again, but said nothing for a minute, then another. "Don't you believe in The Fall of Man? Eve and the apple?"

He shrugged. "I don't really think one way or another about it." She looked at him skeptically, and he relented. "Okay. No, I don't believe in The Fall. When I look at the innocence of a young girl like Ellie, I can't imagine that she was born sinful, irrespective of the circumstances of her conception."

"David says that little kids lie, cheat and steal because of The Fall."

"Little kids lie, cheat and steal because they don't know the rules. Think how complex the concepts of property are: mine; yours; ours; his; the class's, but we all share; Mommy's, but it's okay with her if you play with it. Naturally, children have to be taught the rules before they know not to steal. She's a good kid, and she doesn't lie, cheat or steal, at least not around me."

"She's a good kid now, but David says the sin will come out in her with the blood and the hair." Sam said nothing. "If you don't believe in The Fall, then what do you think happens when we die, Sam?"

"Just a minute." He walked slowly out to where the end of the rope lay in the middle of the paddock. After the next time Ellie and the horse flew over it, he slowly pulled the rope to the side and walked back to where Cardinal waited. "Let's see what she does now." And they watched while the girl gave a minuscule tug on the right rein and touched the horse's left flank and he changed leads at the crossover point, without missing a beat. Sam cupped his hands again and called, "Next time around, keep both hands on the reins and don't touch his hip." To Cardinal: "She uses the touch as a crutch. I don't think she needs it." Ellie looked back at him as she turned the end of the figure-eight, cupping her hand to her ear. He yelled again, this time louder, "Don't touch his flank." And sure enough, the next time through the crossover the light tug on the rein was enough.

"Whoopee!" Ellie yelled, and pumped her right fist in the air.

"Nice job!" Sam hollered to her. "Okay," he said to Cardinal, "I'll tell you what I think. But two things first. One, I'm not trying to convince you of anything. And two, I would never have this conversation with Ellie. Not ever. Make sure both you and David understand that I never talk to her about religion, and never will."

"What do you two talk about? She loves it over here."

"Horses. Math. The Razorback track teams. How Wallace Spearman, Jr. is doing."

"Who?"

"Wallace Spearman, Jr. Our favorite former Razorback runner. We talk about the farm. Hens and eggs. The hawks that raised two fledglings in that oak tree over there last spring and whether they'll come back this spring. How dry the creek got last summer. Everything, really. But not religion. Okay?"

"Okay."

But he said nothing for a long wait, collecting his thoughts, and then, instead of answering Cardinal's question, he yelled out to Ellie, "Okay. That's enough. Bring him in." And when she looked, he gestured her to come in. Ellie trotted over to them. "That's enough for today."

"A few more times?"

"No, we don't want him to get too warm. The sun will be setting in an hour and he might take a chill. Take him back to his stall, de-tack him and give him a good rub-down. Don't let him drink until you've finished the rub-down. Then, once he's cooled off, put his blanket on."

"Then can I ride Daisy?"

"Ask your mother, but it will be getting dark by then."

Cardinal said, "We'll see. Now go do what Mr. Butler told you to do."

"Okay," she said, and she was off at a slow trot across the paddock, taking the long way back to the stable, so as to have the longest possible ride, while still staying in compliance with the instructions of the adults.

As Ellie headed back, Sam walked into the middle of the paddock, where the PVC pipe and the rope still lay in the grass, away from where The Looker had been running. He coiled up the rope, put the pipe on his shoulder and headed back to Cardinal, who was still standing by the fence. He lay the pipe along the fence line and put the coil of the rope over one of the posts, then turned to put his back to the fence again and looked out across the grass. The shadows were getting quite long now, and soon they would be in the shade and chilly. After a moment, he spoke. "I think it's like a fire in the fireplace. When you're alive, the flames are bright and yellow, and when you die, the flames go out. But the coals still glow and are quite hot, each coal being a memory that someone has of you. Maybe even an animal, like Teena or Smokey would remember me in their own kind of way. And then, one by one, the coals go out; the people and animals who remember you die or forget, the coals fade away and get cooler. When the last coal goes out, the last direct memory of you has gone away. For a while yet, though, the ashes are warm with the final thoughts of you still around. Maybe a picture of you that no one can identify any longer. Maybe something you've written, a diary or a letter or something, that no one remembers anymore who wrote it or to whom it was addressed. And finally, the ashes grow cold. Maybe the only thing that remembers you is the ground, the weight of your footsteps. And then, you're gone." He looked over and down at her. She was not looking at him, but out across the riding paddock. "That's what I think happens."

"Is that enough?"

"For me."

"I can't go there. So much of my life anymore is tied up with the opposite."

"What opposite?"

"Heaven, hell, eternity, damnation, forgiveness, redemption, the Savior, the Resurrection, the Rapture, the Second Coming, the New Jerusalem, everything. I think if I let go of one piece, everything will fall apart and I'll be back..." she paused, "...where I was."

"I'm not telling you to let go of anything. Remember that. You just asked me, and that's what I think. I might be right; I'm probably wrong. But I'm not trying to change your mind. Not."

"I believe you, Sam, I really do. But David is suspicious."

"Suspicious of *me*?"

"That you're making her question the Bible. That you're trying to subvert his authority as Ellie's father. Or step-father anyway."

"Never."

She looked up at him, her eyes clear and challenging. "The lunch at Hugo's before Christmas was a little obvious, don't you think? Even I wondered about it."

"That wasn't about religion."

"In David's worldview, *everything* is about religion."

Sam looked away, across the paddock. "It was just a lunch. A burger for me, trout for her."

"With two women law professors? And a meeting with the dean? Who just happens to have a son around her age?"

"She blabbed."

"You didn't think she'd tell us all about it? She couldn't talk of anything else at supper for days. The trip to the law building, the tour of the campus, buying the tickets, the restaurant, the fancy food, the waiter, the huge coffee machine..."

"And our lunch companions."

"Your companions."

"Some of my former colleagues."

"And the place swarming with women law students, she noticed."

"Cardinal, it wasn't some kind of anti-Christian feminist consciousness-raising exercise. Half the law students *are* women. More than half campus-wide. I wanted her to see that, and make what she would of it on her own. I didn't lecture her. Nor did my colleagues at lunch. The conversation at Hugo's did not touch on the errors of St. Paul, or on twenty-first-century career choices, or on liberated female law students. The postponement of child bearing didn't come up, nor did the difficulty of finding quality child care. They didn't talk about their multiple divorces, which they don't have, nor about their lesbian relationships, which, as best I can tell, they don't have either. Mostly they talked about their classes. Mostly I ate my burger. Mostly Ellie just listened. It wasn't like what you think. And it certainly was *not* like what David thinks."

"Then why take her along?"

"We were buying our track tickets. I asked you if it was okay."

"Yes, you did. And I said it was all right. And I'm not making a huge deal out of it. I can handle David. But just tell me: the lunch setup didn't just happen, did it?"

Sam stared a long time across the paddock, then turned and set his arms on the top of the fence, looking back to where Ellie was rubbing down Just One Look with a towel. "She told me that she didn't think moms could be professors. I didn't make a big deal out of it either, but I wanted to show her, that's all. Just show her." Cardinal said nothing. "She told me that you had wanted to be a professor, except, as she put it, she got borned." He gave her a minute to respond, but she still said nothing. "It's just very hard for me to hear a bright little girl say that she can't be a professor because she's a girl. I hope you and David don't expect me to just stand there and reinforce that idea."

Now she turned to look up at him. "I'm pretty sure that's exactly what David expects." Sam started to speak, but she stopped him. "But I don't. And like I said, I can take care of David. As long as you don't directly challenge his biblical teachings to her."

"I won't. I don't. I don't even want to."

"Just next time, make your reform agenda a little more subtle, okay? Now, let's go and see if we can pry my daughter away from that gorgeous animal." They started to walk back to the stable, when she stopped and said, "And thanks, too, for saying that I could have been a professor. Indirectly, anyway."

"Do you still dream of it?"

"Not really. But it's nice to be reminded that I did. Once."

**The Following Wednesday.**

Except for the quick stop-by he had made with Ellie, Sam had not seen Jonathan Wheeler for more than a month. He assumed, based on no particular evidence, that progress was being made on Part Three. On the other hand, most of December very well could be a scholarship vacuum: teaching the end-of-semester rush-to-cover, fielding student questions and quelling their tendency to panic, not to mention writing, administering and grading final exams. Plus everyone, including law teachers, Sam conceded, was entitled to some away-from-the-law time, and Jonathan, he knew, had taken a few days off to ski in Colorado.

He knew this from Lynda, whom he had not seen since the occasion of pie in the afternoon at the café in Hindsville. She had been a no-show on the Wednesday following the pie, a no-show without excuse or explanation, and when she had called him several days later, she had seemed ready to pass over the missed rendezvous entirely, until Sam had said "I missed you the other night," and immediately wished he hadn't. "I got tied up," she had said and nothing else, and they had chatted on pleasantly about this and that until she rang off, apparently having had no particular reason for calling.

She telephoned sporadically, without pattern or schedule, sometimes from home, sometimes from her car, sometimes from her lab, and once from a conference she was attending in Chicago. "What's the conference about," he had asked. But all she had said was "Light," and moved on to ask him about the horse who had come up lame on Christmas Eve. And it was during that phone conversation that she had mentioned that Jonathan had gone skiing in Colorado in December, without her because she couldn't leave the lab right then, though she could fit in this thirty-six-hour in-and-out to Chicago.

She moved at her own pace and in her own direction, that much was clear. "Headstrong" is the word you would use to describe such a horse. (Horses are generally indifferent to the fact that they influence the way humans speak.) And so it was of no particular surprise to Sam when she appeared unannounced late one afternoon some considerable time after she had stood him up. He was putting out some hay and water for the horses, who were still up in the day pasture, and mixing their feed, when he looked out the door of the feed room and there she was, sitting on the work table next to the third stall.

"Hello. I didn't even hear you drive in. Tenna is supposed to warn me when strangers approach."

"Who's a stranger? What's for dinner?"

"They actually call it supper out here. Dinner's in the middle of the day. What you'd call lunch."

"What's for supper?"

"But I still say dinner. It's my Midwestern up-bringing."

"What's for dinner?" She seemed to be enjoying this.

"Spaghetti. Linguini, actually. With broccoli and pesto sauce."

"Good, because I brought cannoli. From Rick's."

"Go on up; I'll be along in a minute." When she made no move to go, he said, "Or take that hose there and top off the stock tank around the corner." Still she didn't move, but just sat on the table, swinging her feet and sitting with her thighs on her hands. He shrugged his shoulders, exited the feed room, turned on the faucet himself and walked around the corner to fill the tank.

"Nice day," he heard her say from behind him.

"Nice day," he confirmed. "Are you going to play for me?"

"Does my invitation to supper come with a requirement that I play?"

"*Dinner.*"

"Does it?"

"I missed the 'you're invited' part."

"Does it?"

"No."

"Okay, then I'll come up with something. Maybe you'll like it."

"All right." He turned off the water and coiled the hose up. "This place is about to be full of five large mammals, all trying to get where their feed is, and not used to your otherwise delightful presence. Maybe you'd better stand over there out of the way. Stick with Teena; she's good at knowing where's safe." And Lynda stood aside while Sam walked up to the gate to let the horses through. They trotted down toward the stable in the usual order, then suddenly there were five horses stopped in their tracks, ten ears frozen up and forward, ten nostrils wide and seeking the scent of the stranger. "If you want to know where a horse's attention is focused," Sam said, "don't look at his eyes, which see front-to-back without moving. Watch his ears." Sam came walking up behind them, went to Evening Smoke who was in the lead, and said, "Relax." And with his hand on the side of her jaw away from him, he led her into her own stall, where she immediately began to eat her hay. Her relaxation was contagious, and within minutes the other four, too, had found their ways to their stalls and their feed.

"That will hold them; come on up."

They walked up to the house, Teena staying put around the stable, ready to clean up whatever feed the horses left safely behind. The linguini was prepared and consumed slowly and by candle light, with an Italian red and then coffee with the cannoli. Lynda had objected to Nescafé, and had brought her own grounds, a nice Guatemalan dark roast, so Sam actually brewed a pot, the first time he had used the machine in years. Mostly they talked about her trip to Chicago and how, on the flight up from XNA on United Express, both pilots had been female and the attendant male, and how Lynda figured that, if they'd taken a survey, there would have been way too many lefthanders among the passengers. And Sam told of how a few years ago, he had ridden a commuter jet from XNA to DFW and how when he got on the bus to ride into the terminal, a young woman had jumped up and offered him her seat.

At about seven o'clock, he headed back down to the stable to get things arranged for the night, and upon returning found that Lynda had cleared the table and done the dishes, and now sat at the piano in the living room, playing what appeared to be random, searching chords. "I didn't put the dishes away," she said over the notes, "knowing your generation's obsession with everything being in its proper place."

"It's an age obsession, not a generational one. At your age, I hardly cared at all. At Ellie's, I was a mess. Fire?"

"Please."

He set about laying one. "More wine?"

"I'll get it. You?"

"I'll get the wine. You'll play some Brahms?"

"I'm not in the mood for Brahms. You have to concentrate too hard over him, which means we can't talk."

"You have to concentrate? It seems so effortless. So what is that?"

She played on a bit, smooth, soothing. Light, but unidentifiable. "That is whatever comes out," she said.

The fire didn't draw at first, and smoke pulled out into the living room, but Sam tossed some cedar twigs on the top of the oak, and they caught and snapped hotly and soon the room was clear. Lynda played on while Sam went back to the kitchen for the bottle and two clean glasses, which he set on the hearth before saying, "I'll be down in a minute." Upstairs, he used the bathroom, washed up and walked downstairs, and sat down with the book he was reading. "Mind if I read while you play. Is that rude?"

"Semi, since I told you I wanted to talk while I was playing. What happened to Wodehouse? Get the hook?"

"Benched, but not yet released. This is le Carré. *The Little Drummer Girl.*"

"Let me see." She continued to play with her left hand in the middle of the keyboard, now clearly an improvisation, while she reached behind with her right. He handed her the book, which she glanced at, front and back, then handed it back to him. "Mm hmmm."

"What's that mean?"

She was back to playing again with two hands. "Nothing. Just mm hmmm." She changed keys.

"Ooo, what was that, what you did there? I like that."

"A modulation. Up a perfect fifth. Often thought of as up-lifting. Common in hymns and gospel music." She did it again. "Terrorist as fashion model?"

"Say again?"

"The cover. Terrorist as fashion model?"

Sam considered the cover, which showed a full-front silhouette of what was clearly a female, just as clearly dressed in fatigues, one hand on a womanly hip, cocked rather provocatively to the viewer's right, the other arm leaning on an AK-47. "Close, actually. More like the reverse."

"Fashion model as terrorist."

"Actress."

"As terrorist?"

"Pretending to be. Acting as if. The plot is pretty implausible, if you want to know the truth, but it's well written. The first fifteen pages or so approach fine literature. Look here: 'The international number one best seller.' So there."

She quickly and heavily played six chords, three two-hand pairs, then swiveled around on the stool and leaned back against the keyboard, her elbows and shoulder blades striking random keys. She stretched her legs straight out, her feet in socks spread the width of her shoulders on the hardwood floor. "How did Sally keep her job teaching little kids all those years?"

"Wow. A conversational modulation?"

"*Excellent.* Down a minor third. How?"

"She was what's known as..." he made air quotes, "a functioning alcoholic. She'd have an unwinder when she got home from school, then a couple glasses of wine with dinner. Afterwards, well it depended. Sometimes she'd get a little tipsy; sometimes I'd have to put her to bed. But either way, she'd pull herself together in the morning and go off to school."

"The weekends?"

"It varied. Cheerful, sometimes. Sometimes hazy, sometimes manic. Out of it, sometimes."

"Depending on what?" Sam shrugged. "It must have been hard on you."

"It was a good deal harder on her."

She turned back and began to play again. After a few dozen bars, "Maybe."

"Maybe what?"

"Maybe it was harder on her than on you, a point I am not yet ready to concede."

"Mozart?"

"Vivaldi. Concerto for two horns..." She played on a bit, "...sort of made to fit into one piano. One upright, not quite in tune, but rather handsome piano."

"Thank you."

"For?"

"The 'handsome.' This is the slow movement?"

"How could you tell?"

Sam picked up his book and began to read aloud, into the music. He began at the beginning, not picking up where he, himself, had left off the night before, but at the beginning, with the bombing of the Labour Attaché's house in Bonn. He read for several pages, and quit when the music ended.

"I think it's very nice the way he describes this scene, his language is so perfect whether the image is pastoral or mundane, then he quickly reminds you of the blast, but the next thing you know, you've left the violence again and you're back to a peaceful Bonn street scene."

"Mundane," she said, closing the cover over the keys and turning to face him as before. "It has become a fashionable word around our house. "Think small," Butler says.'"

"Jonathan told you that I told him to lower his sights?"

"About a hundred times."

"And you don't approve, do you?"

"I'm indifferent."

"I'll bet you never lowered your sights in your life."

"Maybe not. Once. A couple times. Have you?"

"Regularly."

She moved herself from the piano stool to the couch, where she pulled her feet up to sit cross-legged. "I don't make those kinds of comparisons between the two of us."

"Why not?"

"We're two rather different people." She leaned back in the couch and stretched both arms across the back. She did not amplify, and Sam rose to stir the fire, then walked to the porch for a new log, called Tenna in for the night, and waited while she hopped up the stairs and into the house. Back inside, he added the log to the fire, then settled himself back into his chair. Lynda had not moved, but looked at him rather forthrightly.

"You were quite a scholar in your day," she said. "I looked you up. An impressively long publication list, though I know nothing about the journals."

"I have quickly faded into well-deserved obscurity."

"Jonathan says you are spoken of with reverence around the law school."

"No students know me anymore, and my former colleagues can't be trusted in such regards."

"How would you appraise yourself?"

He thought for a moment. "I guess I would say that I passed without objection in the profession under the contract description."

"Meaning?"

"That was a rather clever allusion, thank you, to the area I used to teach. I was fit for the ordinary purposes for which such things are intended. Goods, in the actual statute. I was, in a word, *merchantable*. The musical equivalent would be the ability to carry a tune."

"Which is something that would be said only by a musician immersed in false modesty. Have you thought about my advice?"

"That I should take over the religious instruction of my young math student? I have thought about it not for an instant."

"The other piece of advice: that you should be having sex."

"Even less." He paused and sipped his wine, but she said nothing. "I told you that I'm more in need of a friend than a lover."

"And I told you 'why not both?'"

"I hold the advice dear, but no one comes to mind at the present."

"Don't be obtuse. I was talking about me." He said nothing, thinking she was teasing. But she didn't crack a smile, and held her cross-legged, arms-spread pose on the couch, finally raising her left eyebrow. "Well? No response?"

"I guess I should be flattered, but no. Assuming, against all odds, that you're serious. No."

"Oh, I'm serious. I'm on the look-out for a non-monogamous, friendly-sex partner. You win."

"No."

"Because?"

"Because when a man of my age has sex with a woman of your age, it's either ridiculous or it's disgusting. I have no curiosity regarding into which category we'd fit."

"You don't give me much credit for creative love-making."

"You have in mind a gymnastic workout?"

"No. What I have in mind is something face-to-face, eyes-to-eyes, intertwined in the missionary position. Slow. Quiet. Barely moving. Your thoughts wherever. You might cry. I might say 'there there.'"

"All nicely choreographed, I see."

"Surprise me."

"You make it sound like therapy."

"When is an act of love not therapy?"

"The answer is still 'no.'"

"Why?"

"Same reason."

"You mystify me, Samuel, totally aside from the fact that I'd like to have you between my legs. What are you going to do with your life? Is this it?" She gestured around the living room. "You sit here in your Sally shrine, with your crippled dog and a piano you don't play, managing the animal shelter down below, while you wait to die?"

"And the alternative to waiting to die is...?"

"I didn't mean it like that."

"Which is the first time I've ever heard you say that you misspoke."

"I didn't misspeak. You misread my meaning."

"The comfortable refuge of the misunderstood: blame the listener."

"Okay. I don't want you to die, I want you to live. A little."

"And one aspect of living is getting laid..."

"It's a start."

"...by you..."

"I'd be honored."

"...starting tonight, I presume."

"Upstairs, probably, though..." she pressed the cushion of the couch, "...here would be okay, in front of the fire. I might require you to put the dog out."

"When I was a child, I spake like a child..."

"Meaning?"

"I've put aside childish ways."

"Like putting the dog out?"

"Like having sex with juveniles."

"*Juveniles*? You bastard."

"The subsequent generation, then. Would it be too obvious of me to point out that you're young enough to be my daughter?"

"But the chances that I am are exceedingly remote. A possibility hardly worth considering. You *really* need to get beyond the age thing. And you will. No male has ever said he was too old for sex and meant it. I'll say this, though: You do me honor by not raising any of the other practical objections. No mention of your wife. Or my husband. Or the work you're doing with him. Or how many other such offers I may have outstanding. Or whether I'd expect you to be equipped with birth control devices. Or whether I'd go home and leave you here, or want to stay for breakfast."

"Breakfast?"

"Jonathan's in Topeka. Some conference at Creighton."

"Creighton's in Omaha. Washburn is in Topeka. Suppose he calls?"

"Try not to be so predictably old-fashioned. He'll call my cell."

"It's supposed to be nice, Topeka."

"He says it is nice. He'll be home Saturday night."

"He flew?"

"He drove."

"Nice drive?"

"Don't change the subject. I disagree with your appraisal of what it would be like, you and me, but at least you didn't embarrass me by raising those other issues. Thank you for that. Think about it. Let me know. It doesn't have to be tonight. Just think about it."

"I intend exactly *not* to think about it."

"Oh..." she said, still looking straight into his eyes, "...oh, I suspect you *will* think about it, probably tonight. Perhaps overly long, tonight. And here's my guess: you'd enjoy being in bed with me a lot more than you'll enjoy being in bed by yourself, thinking of being in bed with me."

"Will you continue to come here and play for me, and bring me cannoli, and evaluate my literary choices if I continue to say 'no'?"

"If I say I won't, will it cause you to accept my proposal?"

"No."

"Good, because if you'd said 'yes,' I'd have left."

"I wish you'd stay. But I'm worried about that hell-hath-no-fury thing."

"What?"

"You know: 'hell hath no fury like a woman scorned.'"

"Bullshit. What idiot said that?"

"Shakespeare."

"Additional evidence, if any were necessary, that Shakespeare did not know shit about women."

"For example?"

"*Romeo and Juliet.* No way does Juliet kill herself at the end."

"Oh? She does what, then?"

"She tracks down that ridiculous meddling priest and slips the dagger up between his ribs, not her own. O! Happy dagger, here is thy sheath. Taste cold steel, you child molester."

"And then?"

"*Romeo and Juliet, Season Two.* I don't know; the Capulets kick ass? No one with any sense ever believed that the kids' deaths would bury their parents' strife. Not bloody likely. It's even less likely that I'll be furious with you over anything. Yes, I'll be your friend. I'll also be your lover, if you'll have me. I suspect you'd be pleased."

Sam arose and said, "I'm not sure how this evening ends, except for two things: I've got to walk down to put some hay out in the so-called animal shelter, and..."

"And?"

"And it will not end with you either upstairs or on the couch."

"But, you see, I *am* on the couch."

"I'm walking down to the stable. Will you be here when I get back?"

"You bet."

And she was. She did not renew her proposal, but she didn't have to, for it floated through the air like her scent and settled onto the furniture like dust. It was present like the smell of the fire; it awaited his attention the way a small piece of something in the corner of the kitchen by the stove waits for a mouse's attention. It curled to the ceiling like the tail of the candles when he blew them out. She kissed him good night as she had before, on the lips, but passionless, and when he went upstairs to bed later there was a note in her hand on his pillow: "Sweet dreams, you stinker. XXX, L."

**The Next Morning.**

Perhaps it was Lynda's characterization of the house as Sam's "Sally shrine" that led him to discover the post office box key, but likely he would have come across it eventually anyway even without her comment. The next morning, he awoke not thinking at all of her fantastic proposal. This failure would have been more of an affront to her, had she known of it, than his declining of the proposal itself. She had hardly bothered to veil her suggestion that he would fantasize about the two of them having sex, and her understandable assumption was that he would obsess over her and her proposal, turning over and over in his mind its making, if not its consummation. Instead, he awoke thinking the words "Sally shrine." He looked from his bed at the room surrounding him, lit only by the small reading light on the bedside table.

Her clothes were gone, off to the Goodwill within a respectable time of the accident. It had seemed even to Sam too much of a cliché to keep her clothes in the closet. Sure, that meant that there were three empty drawers in the bureau, but he didn't need them for his things anyway. And the bathroom closet had been cleaned out of her pill bottles, tampons and liners (for she, younger than Sam, had not yet reached menopause), and what makeup she wore, which was little, except that she liked polishing her nails bright red.

So there was the study, the kitchen and the living room, about which Lynda had made her observation. The kitchen, he thought while brushing his teeth, was not part of the so-called shrine. Sure enough, there was the rocking chair, which had become a fixture of their kitchens, as soon as they had a kitchen big enough to accommodate one. The present kitchen, close to being the largest room in the house, was plenty big enough, and the rocker they had in it was one that Sally had found at the War Eagle fair and had restored. It was lovely, he sat in it often, with a coffee cup and the paper, and saw no reason to deprive himself of that pleasure. Which left the study. (The living room he would leave for last, thereby, he guessed, confirming Lynda's appraisal.) He'd start with the study, right after feeding, breakfast, and the chores, and before Ellie's lesson.

He almost put off starting until after lunch, but then decided to start first, then break for the lesson and lunch; once again he could picture Lynda smiling smugly. So, around nine-thirty, he sat at their desk and surveyed the scene. There were the bookshelves, with her Bible in its place, next shelf from the top, middle section, but their tastes in reading were similar enough that many of those books were not really part of the so-called shrine. He'd thin the books out, taking some of his and some of hers to the used bookstore on Dickson Street. There were a couple dozen DVDs, and it would be easy enough separating her favorites from his. Likewise the CDs. The single bed, which made the study a guest room when it was needed, was innocuous, not part of the so-called shrine. So that left the desk. There was the surface, the top drawer and Sally's files in the two lower drawers on the right.

He pulled open the wide top drawer and looked through the contents. Then he decided he needed two boxes from the cellar. No, three. Trash, Goodwill and a box for her parents if he found anything they'd like to keep. He fetched the boxes and sat back down again. Pens were easy, as he liked Flair felt tips and she liked Bic ball points. All of the latter went into the trash box, along with the pencils, which he rarely used. There, that was a start. He looked at the clock. Nine-forty-five. He could stop and get ready for the math lesson. He looked instead out the window to the north and continued. Paper clips, pins, left-over pen caps, breath fresheners, thumb tacks, match books, all easily trash. Farther back into the drawer, business cards for plumbers, house cleaners and the like, gum wrappers, now-meaningless notes, some in her handwriting, some in his, some with phone numbers, some with dates. Keep the business cards and the rest was trash, except for a snapshot of Sally and her parents taken by Sam when they had once rendezvoused on the north rim of the Grand Canyon. He put the picture into the Sanderson box.

Which left a key ring, lying with his pens and the business cards in the tray at the front of the drawer, as the only thing in the drawer. The spare key to the small Toyota pickup, and what he thought was a spare key to the Honda, which was the predecessor of the small Toyota pickup, the key to the desk itself, which was, of course, unlocked. A key to the back door, which they never used. And a post office box key.

He almost tossed the entire set of keys into the trash box, but instead, when he heard Ellie come in through the front door and yell his name up the stairs—"Mr. Butler? You there?"—he put it in his pocket and walked down to greet her.

"Hi, there, cutie." She smiled; it was remarkable, he thought, she seemed always happy to see him. "What's new? Got your homework done?"

"No. Mom has me writing something about evolution." She made a face and did the gagging gesture that kids seemed to like these days.

"Evolution?"

"About the Ark and the Flood, really. And how all the animals came off the boat onto dry land and went off to populate the world. And how after a while there were white polar bears and black grizzlies and black and white pandas and everything. Like that. Mostly what I have to do is read about it in my science book and...paragram it."

"Paraphrase."

"What?"

"The word is 'paraphrase.' To write something over in your own words. Not copy, just tell the story yourself."

"Okay."

"Say it. Paraphrase."

"Para-phrase. But mostly I just copy and Mom doesn't care. She hates science class. Why don't you teach me science?"

"Oh, I don't know anything about evolution."

"We also do plants and bugs. You could do that."

"We'll see. So anyway, your math's not done?"

"I just started it this morning after prayers."

Raised in Madison County, Arkansas, David had been introduced early on to one of the various forms of "YER-GONNA-BURN" evangelism, enough to convince him, when he reached puberty, that his mind was impure and his soul condemned, as he sinned rather regularly, say three or four nights a week. He agonized over what he saw as his evil ways, an agony that, in turn, made him unattractive to the girls he knew, which thereby increased the problem, and the concomitant agony. His teenage years were not happy ones, and more than once he considered suicide.

In his early twenties, David was tossed out of his parents' home in Kingston and he put together enough money to pay too much for a run-down, two-house chicken farm near Hindsville, with a double-wide trailer and a near-oppressive mortgage. He worked hard, lived simply, went to church twice a week, and managed to scrape by. On his own, with nothing to do except work, and with no money to get the cable TV, he took to staying at home reading the Bible and listening to Christian radio. He became an admirer of Dr. James Dobson, who often spoke on his radio program of having spent many hours each day on his knees with his family, as his father, an evangelist, had prayed for relief from the various vicissitudes of having essentially no income. While Dr. Dobson (as David called him) never exactly recommended to his listeners that they do the same, David adopted the practice, often spending two to three hours at prayer, amid the chores required by the chicken houses.

When David and Cardinal were married, and David became the spiritual leader of his little family, which included Ellie and, within weeks, a child-on-the-way, he instituted the same practice of daily, hours-long prayer. Four months into the marriage, however, and through the calibrated employment of vaginal therapy, Cardinal was able to persuade her husband that wouldn't the Lord be satisfied with a half hour a day? And later, after one especially memorable night of conjugal compromise, David had consented to the use of kneeling pads on the hard linoleum of the kitchen floor, and so every morning found the three of them kneeling in a circle in the kitchen, praying.

"I only did three problems," Ellie continued. "They're hard."

"Well, spread out here and get to work. I've got to run to the post office, so I'll be back in a few minutes."

It was about five miles from Sam's farm to the post office in Hindsville. Out to the end of the dirt road, then across highway 45, onto 295 and into town. The town itself had taken a hit when the 412 by-pass had been built, leaving the crossroads a couple of miles from the passing traffic. Two antique stores had almost immediately closed up, and the Valley Café had been struggling for business ever since. Then a few years later the small bank had been robbed and there was now talk that it, too, would close soon. But, the local congressman looked after the post offices in his district, and A.T. Smith would be at his store until he died, and it was past that store, honking his horn, that Sam drove on the way to collect his mail. He dropped some bills, and a letter to his sister, into the slot, then unlocked and emptied his box, mostly of junk, plus a bank statement and a quarterly report from his pension fund.

He closed the little door and then, almost on a whim, he tried the key he had found in the desk drawer. It didn't work. "Hmmm," he spoke aloud and walked through the door from the lobby to the counter. A little bell rang in the back and the local postmaster, a pleasant young woman named Phyllis, popped around from the back, practically still exhaling smoke from her cigarette.

"Hi, Sam. What ya need?"

Sam leaned on the counter with his elbows. "What I need is for you to quit smoking."

She laughed. "Who was smoking? It's against the rules to smoke in this building."

"You reek. But I won't blow the whistle on you. Listen, I found this key at home and it belongs to you. I thought I'd return it."

"Hold on. There's a form to fill out to get your deposit back."

"Deposit?"

"Yup. Ten bucks. Just a minute; I'll get the book."

In a moment, she returned from the back room with a black loose-leaf binder and a pad of receipts. "Let's see." She read the number on the key out loud, "one-three-seven-nine-oh-four," while running her finger down the page in the notebook. "Nope. Wait. Maybe it's here." She flipped a few pages over and ran her finger down another list. Then, "Nope, it isn't mine. No refund for you. Sorry."

"Well, if it isn't yours, whose is it?"

"Who knows? Could be anywhere."

"Is there some kind of master list?"

"Not that I know of. Maybe at the main post office in Fayetteville."

"Well, it's hardly worth a drive into town for ten bucks."

Phyllis shrugged her shoulders. "Ten bucks is two packs of smokes, plus a Slim Jim. Or maybe there'll be a winning lottery ticket in the box. If you can find it."

"Maybe. I'll let you know."

"Fair's fair. Split it with me."

"Don't count on it."

Sam and the postmaster waved goodbye to each other and Sam walked to his pickup and drove home, thinking that the mystery probably would never be solved.

Back up at the house, he found Ellie staring out the kitchen window, her math book open and a blank sheet of paper in front of her.

"Well, making progress, I see. What are you thinking about?"

"Why do you think that God drowned..."—she pronounced it *drown-ded*—"...all those horses in the Flood?"

"I don't know anything about that."

"But they didn't do anything wrong."

"You'll have to ask David. He'll know. Now, get to work on your math."

She looked up at him and groaned. "Math is boring."

"Math is not boring. Whiney little girls are boring."

"I'd rather brush the horses than do math."

"Actually, it's too bad you didn't finish. I was going to suggest that we go riding." He walked behind her towards the kitchen sink.

"Can we? Today?"

"Well, it's a nice sunny day. Cool, but not too cool. No wind. Nice day for a ride. Too bad your math's not finished."

"I'll do it when we get back. Promise."

"No deal."

"*Please?*"

"No." He paused while he drew a glass of water from the tap and drank it down. She had decided to sulk, putting her chin in her hand and tossing her pencil down. "But," he continued, "here's what we'll do, if you'll stop being a brat."

"What?" She perked up.

"Go home now and do your assignment. I have to run to town, but I'll be back soon and around two o'clock I'll ride over to your place, bringing a horse with me. If your math is done—*and done correctly*—we'll ride over on your side of the highway for an hour or so. Okay?"

"Can I ride The Looker?"

"I don't want to take him on a line across the highway just yet. Pick another one."

"Daisy!"

"It's a deal. Get going. And get to work. No day-dreaming. I'll see you at about two." She packed up her books and started for the door. "Hold up; I'll walk down with you."

The drive to and from town, which Sam had made ten times a week for roughly twenty-five years, summers and breaks excepted, is pretty much a straight shot west on Highway 45, through Goshen, up Slaughter Hill and into Fayetteville proper. During the Nineties, the town had sprawled steadily eastward, subdividing up some perfectly good farm land and sprouting McMansions and gas stations, but with the bursting of the real estate bubble, that had slowed, leaving behind some wealthy ex-farmers, bankrupt developers and embarrassed bankers, some streetlights in the cow pastures and some streets looping to nowhere. The drive took about a half-hour, and at the first controlled intersection, Sam decided to turn the wrong way for the post office and treat himself to lunch at El Camino Real, over *The New York Times*, bought at Arsaga's. He liked reading the *Times*, but didn't think it was worth two-fifty a whack, and so he bought it only rarely. But today he treated himself to one and then, after too many chips and not enough salsa, iced tea and beef tamales, one of which he took away in a box, he headed north on College and east on Joyce to the main post office.

Inside there was a line of about five people, toward the front of which Sam patiently moved. Then: "Next."

"I've got a box key, but I don't remember which box it goes to," not exactly the truth, but close enough for an entrée.

"Go to that door over there," the clerk said, pointing to his right, Sam's left, "and press the door bell. Someone will help you. *Next*." The Fayetteville post office was nothing if not efficient.

A few seconds after Sam pushed the button, which caused no sound that he could hear, the top half of a set of French doors opened and a middle aged man with a grey crew cut said, "May I help you?"

Sam displayed the key. "I found this among my wife's things. She's deceased now, and the postmaster in Hindsville—that's where I live—said you might be able to tell me what box it's for, and that I might be due a small deposit back."

The man took the key, peered at the number on it through his bifocals, and said, "Just a minute." The half-door closed and Sam turned around to watch the coming and going around the busy lobby. The line to the counter was growing longer as the lunch hour approached.

The half-door opened and the man shook his head, handing the key back. "Not one of ours."

"Well, it was a long shot—it's been three years—but I thought I'd ask. Phyllis out in Hindsville—she's the postmaster—said there might be a small deposit. But thanks anyway." Sam turned to go.

Something seemed for the first time to create an actual connection between Sam and the agent, for he said, "Wait. I'm sorry about your wife. My father just lost his wife—my step-mother—this year and he's probably about your age. I know how hard it can be. How long did you say it's been?"

"Three years. Three and a half. A little more."

"My condolences."

"Thanks." Sam turned to go.

"Three and a half years. That would make it sometime in oh-nine?"

"May twelfth."

"Let me see that key again. No, instead, see that door over there?" The agent pointed to a door on the far side of the counter, off to Sam's right. "Go to that door and I'll meet you on the other side. I can't take you through here because it's a secure area. I'll let you in over there." The half door closed and by the time Sam cut through the line, the other door was open and the man was standing, waiting for him at the beginning of a long corridor. "By the way, I'm Price Danielson. I'm the postmaster here."

"Sam Butler."

"Come down this way, Mr. Butler, I want to check on something."

The office into which Sam was led was a government-issue space to the $n^{th}$ degree. There were pictures of the President and Vice President, another guy who might have been the Postmaster General, and Ben Franklin. The remainder of the space was undecorated, the bookshelves were haphazardly arranged and the only chair other than the one behind the desk was covered by a top coat, a wool cap and a briefcase on top.

"Have a seat," Danielson said, then laughed. "Where? Here, let me move those things." He put the coat, cap and case on top of a filing cabinet. "Let me have another look at that key." He then sat himself behind the desk. "I don't entertain guests back here often. In fact, I'm usually not here, out on the floor somewhere. Coffee?"

"No, thanks."

Danielson poured himself a cup out of a Mr. Coffee machine, dumped in two packets of Sweet'n Lo and stirred it with a pencil.

"The thing is that it was a bit over three years ago that we finally digitalized the post office box records and there's a chance that your wife's account fell through the cracks." He clicked and typed at the computer on his desk, then pulled a black loose-leaf binder off the shelf behind him, a binder like Phyllis's in Hindsville, but thicker. "So, see, Mr. Butler," he swiveled his monitor around so Sam could see the screen.

"I can't, really. I'll have to get in range of my reading glasses, which…" Sam felt in his shirt pocket, "…I seem to have left in the truck."

"Never mind, see?" Danielson pointed to a spot in what Sam could see was a list of numbers. "Right there is where this key should be. But maybe in here…" He paged through the notebook. "No. Hmmm…not here either." He shook his head, talking aloud. "…one-three-seven-nine-oh-four. Well, what about here?" More pages flipped, and once again a finger ran down the page. Finally Danielson sat back in his chair and shook his head. "No, I'm afraid not. I thought maybe…"

"Fall through the cracks?"

"Yup. The digitalization had to be done by the low-bidding outside contractor—regs, you know—save the taxpayer some dough—and as you can see," he gestured to the thick binder, "it wasn't a case of a simple scan. I suspect that the contractor subbed it out to Bangladesh or somewhere—I didn't say that—and what we got back…well, let's say there were some gaps. I thought your key might have been in one of them. But no. Sorry."

"And those are the records for all of Northwest Arkansas?"

"Oh, no. This is just for Fayetteville."

"I was told that you'd have a master list."

"You were misinformed. We're not nearly that organized here at the Postal Service. Well, I could give you a list of the Post Office box numbers in, say, Farmington, seven-two-seven-three-oh, but not the names, nor the key numbers. Especially not the key numbers, which is the only thing you're interested in. These are the key numbers for the boxes in seven-two-seven-oh-one through oh-four only. You'd have to check with the other offices if you want to track that one down."

"How many offices?"

"Northwest Arkansas has forty-six zip codes. And they all have at least one post office, complete with boxes. Except for two: Fayetteville oh-two and oh-four."

"That's a lot. Suppose it's just Washington and Madison Counties?"

"I'd have to look it up. More than twenty. Hardly worth ten dollars."

"I guess not. But thanks for your help."

"Here's my card." Danielson handed it across the desk. "Call me if there's anything else I can do for you." He stood up. "Again, I'm sorry about your loss." They shook hands. "Can you find your own way out? Down the hall and to your left and out the door. You'll be back in the lobby."

"Thank you. I remember the way. Goodbye."

Back in his car, heading east on Route 45, Sam pondered the fool's errand. A wasted trip, except for the tamale sitting beside him on the seat, the centerpiece for dinner sometime later in the week. What could the key mean? Anything. Nothing. He decided not to worry about it. When he got home, he put the key back into the desk drawer, telling himself that it might be worth ten bucks, threw the other old keys into the trash box and changed into his riding clothes. He then went down to the day pasture and pulled off Evening Smoke and Miss Run Run, Ellie's Daisy, leading them down to the stable, where he saddled them both and led them through the front gate, between the Toyotas. He swung his leg over Smokey, wrapped Daisy's reins around his saddle horn and squeezed his calves against the mare's sides, and she moved out at a walk. She was inclined to move ahead quickly into a trot, so he said, "Easy, Smoke," released the pressure and she dropped back to a walk, the younger mare's head just off Sam's knee.

The county road in front of Sam's place runs about three miles, more or less east and west, paralleling the highway, before turning sharply north to cross Route 45, continuing onto the north side. Just east of the crossing, the cars heading west on 45 mount a small rise, which meant that Sam's view of on-coming traffic was almost blind, so he hurried Smokey along a bit for the fifty yards before the crossing, put both horses into a trot, looked both ways and crossed quickly, no cars, as it turned out, coming in either direction. A hundred yards beyond the crossing, a driveway turned into the Quincy place, which consisted of a double-wide trailer, two aging chicken houses, and a yard cluttered with a couple of toddlers, their assorted toys, a nursing beagle, and two cats arguing over an unidentifiable but noticeably dead critter. The family's well-used F-150, with a deer rifle in the window-rack, tires going bald, was parked, backed up to one of the chicken houses.

When typical American consumers think of the raising of chickens, they think of a little girl in a blue gingham dress, feeding corn chops to a multi-colored clutch of hens, with a rooster or two crowing in the dawn. When typical American chicken farmers think of government regulation of the chicken industry, they think of dunderheaded, if not malevolent, Washington bureaucrats, black helicopters and drone strikes. As a result of this combination, a typical American chicken house is about four hundred feet long, filled with upwards of seventy-five thousand birds, and largely unregulated. The birds themselves do nothing except eat, shit and be medicated for four weeks or so before being harvested, having grown unnaturally fast from chick to pan-size, for reasons you don't need to know about. The machinery in the house is dangerous and often poorly maintained; the atmosphere inside is hot, dusty and practically unbreathable with ammonia. If these were factories of anything other than chicken, the Labor Department, the EPA and OSHA would have coordinated conniptions, but because it's chicken and because of gingham dresses and black helicopters, the government is all hands-off, and too many American farm children spend the hours of their youth working in them. "Family farms," they are called, and politicians get all gooey about them.

David Quincy's houses were worse than most, because they were more than twenty years old, held together with spit, bailing wire, and David's meager financial resources. Under the contract with Tyson's, the birds themselves belonged to the company, and he was merely growing them. Unless one died, that is, whereupon under the magic of the contract, title immediately passed to David, requiring him to collect the carcass and dispose of it. On the afternoon when Sam came calling, David was out of the houses and washing up, having just completed his afternoon walk-through, picking up the dead ones, to be composted into an odiferous mess which would be spread on the surrounding fields later in the spring.

Cardinal sat in a plastic chair with the baby in her lap, reading.

"Hey, Cardinal."

She looked up from her book and waved. "Sam. Get down and relax over here."

Instead Sam squeezed Smokey slowly forward, Daisy at her side, mindful of the toddlers, and pulled up near the porch, more of a deck, really, made of treated two-by-fours, attached to the side of their double-wide.

"I bribed Ellie with a ride this afternoon in exchange for getting her math done, but I don't know, it may be too chilly for her." High thin clouds had spread across the sky in the last hour and, while the sun was visible, the temperature must have fallen ten degrees since Sam had returned from town.

"She'd ride at twenty below if given the chance. She told me that you'd be by; she's in there now working. Sure you don't want to get down?"

"No, I'm fine. It's easier on my knee to sit here than it is to get down and back up. But where's David? There's something I want to tell him. You may want to listen in."

"He's just come in from the chickens." She raised her voice, "David. Sam's here."

When David Quincy came out of the house, Sam realized that, notwithstanding the pain in his left knee, he should get down to be greeted properly, so, on the ground and holding the two sets of reins in his left hand, he reached out his right. "David. Good to see you." David was as tall as Sam, but stockier, with large hands and the thick, broken fingernails of a farmer. Capped front teeth, and balding under his cap. Cardinal walked with the baby over to join them, with her book in her free hand. She leaned into Sam and put the arm with the book around his waist, and they exchanged one-armed hugs.

"What are you reading?"

"*Arrowsmith*. Ever read it?" Sam shook his head. "It's good. I can remember my mother reading it, back at the commune."

"How is Melissa? And your father?"

"Busy. The ministry is really taking off, and Dad could be every weekend in some city, visiting churches and giving talks. He enjoys it, but Mom doesn't like him being away so much. So, he travels about once a month and she's researching web-based events. Two-way fellowship and witnessing sessions, with Dad here in the studio and people on-line from all over participating."

"All over the world?"

"Potentially. Marketing—spreading the word—is the key to that."

"Right. Where's Ellie?"

"Inside in her room. She should be finishing up," said Cardinal.

"Okay, well, listen. Today she asked me a question about the Bible."

"What about the Bible?" David sounded immediately suspicious.

"A question from her science lesson. You're doing something about the Ark?"

Cardinal answered shortly, "Yes."

"So what was her Bible question?" David asked.

"She wanted to know why all the horses had to drown. In the Flood. Why God would do that. She was troubled. She was also, I'll admit, trying to avoid doing her math. I had to bribe her with a ride to get her back to work."

"What did you tell her about the horses?" David's suspicion was growing.

"Nothing. That I didn't know."

"Ellen should know the answer to that question; we've been over the Flood many times. You didn't make her question the Bible, did you?"

"Nope. David, I told you, she had the question and I said I didn't know. We don't talk about the Bible. Trust me. Never."

"Okay. So tell her this: God gave dominion over the animals to man, and he became their steward, and when He saw the evil of mankind..."

Sam put up his hands, palms out. "Whoa, whoa, whoa. David." He laughed the predicament off. "I meant it when I said we don't talk about religion or the Bible or God. You don't want me interpreting Bible verses for her, trust me on that, too. I won't intentionally cause her to question any of your teachings. Or your authority. I promise. But my math lessons can't be Sunday school, either. She's in good hands over here, you know I believe that. I enjoy the math lessons and her company, but I thought you'd want to know that she had some questions."

"Thank you, Sam." Cardinal spoke up before David could reply. "We trust you and we're happy you're helping her with the math, aren't we, David? And we'll answer all of her questions about the Bible, won't we, dear? That's our job, not yours."

"I'm comfortable with that. I just thought you'd want to know."

"Yes, thanks for telling us." Cardinal looked at her husband until he nodded and said, "Yes, thanks."

At which point Ellie came busting out of the house, down the steps and over to the three of them, clutching her math homework in her hand. "Hi. Hi, Smokey. Hi, Daisy." Her preference between the two horses was clear, as she merely patted the older mare on the head, then fussed over the younger one, adjusting her bridle, scratching under her chin, and talking softly and secretly to her.

"Did you ask your mother and father if you could go riding?"

"Yes. I'm ready."

"First, I have to check your homework."

"But that will take *hours*."

"I'm faster than that. Here's a leg up." He threw her into the saddle. "Walk her around in the yard here while I check your answers."

"Hurry."

"Ellie," Cardinal spoke. "Do as Mr. Butler says."

She pulled Daisy's head to the right and began leading her around behind the house, technically speaking the yard, but giving the term its broadest possible meaning.

"So, let me just sit on the steps here and check these over—can I borrow that pen in your pocket, David?—and then we'll be gone about an hour, if that's okay. I think we'll ride over to the post office. I want to tell Phyllis something."

And Sam sat with the math homework, Ellie and Daisy came at a trot from behind the house, slowing to a walk in the front, certain she was getting away with something, Cardinal returned to *Arrowsmith*, the toddlers to their mud fight, and David back inside the house. And the answers were all both tidy and correct, the ride was chilly but otherwise pleasant, with that special smell of horse and leather strong about them as they rode the back roads to Hindsville proper, where Phyllis had no help beyond what Danielson had said. They returned as the shadows were getting long and Ellie was getting hungry, to the yard in front of the double-wide and next to the chicken houses, where Ellie said goodbye to Daisy and Smokey, and ran inside to wash up for supper. And as Sam rode away, David said, "I can see trouble coming there, Cardinal, you watch. You may trust him, but I don't." When she said nothing, he turned on his heel and walked inside.

**The Last Tuesday of the Month.**

The barometer had been falling since noon, and the front moved in early in the morning, a thin wedge of Arctic air slicing under a warm cushion of moist Gulf air. Sam awoke around three to hear the beginning of the rain scratch against the south-facing windows in his bedroom. As long as the wind stayed from the south, the horses would be fine. He went back to sleep.

But around four, he sensed, more than heard, the wind swing around to the northwest, and he decided to get up early and get everyone under shelter. The crucial meteorological questions, he knew, were how cold and how thin the wedge from the north was. Not too cold, and the rain would stay rain. Cold but not too thin, and the rain would turn to snow. But a too-cold, too-thin wedge meant freezing rain, and that could be a mess—everything from unsafe footing and highway accidents to downed trees and no power, sometimes for days. The weather service was being cautious in its predictions, confidence in its model of the freeze line still low. The TV stations were hyping catastrophe, as they do, and Sam's neighbors tended to round upwards the estimates they had heard. "An inch of ice." "No, I heard an inch and a quarter." Best to get everyone in the stable, fed and back up to the safety of the pastures. He pulled himself out of bed, skipped his shower, cracked open a Coke, dressed in jeans, Wellingtons and a barn jacket over a hooded sweatshirt, and headed down to the stable. Teena, who didn't like the feel of storms, and didn't crave human company during them, would ride this one out in the feed room, curled in a nest of hay.

Forty minutes later it was still dark and, chilled to the bone, Sam was back up at the house, thinking about his own breakfast—coffee, toast, a quartered orange, along with *Morning Edition* and another cup of coffee. And a half-hour later, he was back down at the stable, trying to figure out where everyone belonged. So far, so good, weather-wise. It was staying just above freezing and the rain was still rain, but a cold, soaking rain. Maybe they could all go into the day pasture like usual. There was a large shelter in there, eighteen feet long and twelve deep, open on two sides and theoretically big enough for all five horses. But, under the unwritten rules of equine sociology, share-and-share-alike was seldom the prevailing principle. The usual pattern would be that Evening Smoke, the lead mare, would claim half of the eighteen feet for herself; The Looker, who was establishing himself as number two, would then take half of the reminder, leaving Restive and Daisy to share the last quarter, and putting Dreadnaught out in the rain. This would not do, especially on a day that promised to be this cold, wet and windy, even if the rain didn't freeze.

So, Sam put blankets on the two mares and Restive—that is to say the three thinnest horses—and sent them to the day pasture. He then led The Looker and Dreadnaught up to the night pasture and its shelter, which was plenty long enough for two, even if the geldings fussed at each other. There. Everybody should keep. He'd bring some hay out to them after lunch and see how they were doing.

Back up at the house again, Sam had his hot shower and dry clothes, and now settled himself in the study, where he had decided the miserable day would be the perfect time to stay inside and continue the desanctification of the so-called Sally shrine, tackling the thinning out of the bookshelves. It was now raining quite hard.

He established four piles: books about teaching, which would be offered to the university ed school library; children's books, which would go to the elementary school library; literature, which he would either keep for himself or sell to the Dickson Street Bookshop; and horse books, all keepers. Notwithstanding this organization, the going was slow and the memories were thick, especially when it came to literature, books over which they had debated for years. There were several copies of Jane Smiley's *Horse Heaven*, which they both admired and had read often enough that they could make each other smile, laugh or be sad just by naming a passage—the saddling of Froney's Sis; Justa Bob in the pond; Residual after the Distaff. But did he really need three copies? He kept the hardback and put two paperbacks in the Bookshop pile, then took one of the paperbacks and set it aside on the corner of the desk.

Because of the weather, he was certain that Ellie would not show for her lesson, and her usual time passed with no arrival. Around eleven, he went out to toss some hay down for the horses and, back up at the house, cold and wet for the third time in one morning, he decided it would be a perfect day for hot cornbread, so he mixed up a batch, heavy on the chili powder as he liked it, slid it into the oven, set the timer, and returned to his books in the study. And shortly after, he heard a car pull in down by the pickups, and looked out to see Ellie and Cardinal running under one umbrella across the foot-bridge over the creek and up to the house, Ellie with her backpack on and Cardinal carrying the baby and a plastic shopping bag. He hurried downstairs to let them in.

"Come in, come in out of the cold. Don't worry about your shoes. Come on in. Give me the baby, Cardinal." He took Esther from Cardinal and held her, wrapped in multiple layers, while Ellie and her mother shed their jackets and, contrary to his invitation, their shoes, and Ellie took the coats to hang, dripping, in the pantry. Cardinal then took the baby back, and Sam opened the oven door against the damp chill.

"Mmmm. Smells good," said Cardinal.

"Cornbread. It's just about done. Sit down. Please."

At the beginning of Sam's math tutorials for Ellie, David had insisted that Cardinal accompany the girl, supposedly to learn how to teach the math herself, but quietly to appraise the atmosphere at Sam's, which David demanded be compatible with their Christian beliefs, if not necessarily in advancement of them. Sam guessed at the latter purpose of Cardinal's visits, but not knowing what he could possibly do either way, he merely went about business as usual. But regarding the other supposed reason for Cardinal's presence, he soon recognized that she had no interest in any mathematics, teaching it or learning it, and was instead looking for a break from the tedium of the household.

At home with David, Cardinal assured her husband that the atmosphere across the highway was what one would expect from a good-natured, elderly gentleman, albeit a non-believing one, and that David's fears of the Anti-Christ—or, less dramatically, of a merely ungodly, left-leaning pervert—were unfounded. And, when David asked her about the math, she was able to pick up, through Ellie, enough jargon to convince him that the tutorials, both of Cardinal and Ellie, were coming right along. Soon, he stopped asking.

Sure enough, Cardinal quickly dropped all pretense of being a math student herself, and would bring a book along to read in the living room while Sam and Ellie worked at the kitchen table. Her tastes ran to classic literature and, except for Shakespeare, she did not read poetry. She read little written after 1930 or so, and she liked a good plot, well told. She was fond of the novels of Thomas Hardy and Sinclair Lewis, whom she considered to be modern writers. She had once spoken at length, when she was late in the pregnancy with Esther, of the fate of Sue Bridehead and how meaningful that story had become to her as she got older. Sam was unfamiliar with the character, but after he had read *Jude the Obscure* he thought he understood Cardinal better than before.

When Esther had been born and the weather had warmed with the late spring, Ellie had been given access to the four-wheeler, to which she took like Dan Gurney at Watkins Glen. She grew into her new-found independence, and began to stay longer at Sam's, spending roughly equal time with her math and the horses. When June came around, Sam proposed to David and Cardinal that they cut the math lessons to twice a week, it being summer and all, and that he pay Ellie five dollars a week for helping out with the horse chores. And so the summer unfolded pleasantly, Ellie complained only occasionally about math in the summer, plus she had a little pocket money, most all of which she saved, and she was much in advance of the Sonlight schedule. In the fall, they went back to daily math lessons, David insisted that the cash payments stop, and Sam saw Cardinal only rarely. It was nice to see her when she did come along, and he invariably told her so.

"It's nice to see you, Cardinal. I'm glad you came along."

"Ellie was all in her rain gear, ready to ride over, and I had to offer her a better alternative."

"We brought you lunch!" And out of the plastic bag came egg salad sandwiches, made, he was told, by Ellie herself, and out of Sam's own eggs! To which Sam added carrot and celery sticks, slices of avocado, and a square of cornbread each, with a pat of butter on the top.

"I make it spicy; I hope you like it. Drinks?"

"Coke!"

"Ask your mother." To Cardinal: "She's not usually allowed."

"I think one's okay."

"You?"

"Hot tea? I can't seem to get warmed up this winter."

Sam laid out the lunch on the table, Ellie said grace, but before he picked up his sandwich, he said, "Better let me see your homework, or I'll get mayo all over it." She pulled out her notebook, the cover of which bore a photo of Zenyatta and Z-12, her 2012 foal, which Ellie had clipped from Sam's *Blood-Horse* magazine, and handed it to him. He sat in the rocking chair, checking her work and nibbling a carrot. Ellie watched him like a hawk for signs of approval or not. "Um hmmm.... yes, right.... Hmmm," he wordlessly commented, mostly to see her reactions to the comments themselves. Cardinal held the baby and ate her sandwich and cornbread one-handed, and suppressed a yawn.

Before Sam was finished, Esther started to fuss a little and Sam looked up to see Cardinal lifting her sweater and undoing her bra. Ellie was mortified. *Sotto voce*, and in two syllables, her eyes wide, "*Mo-om*."

"What, Sweetie?" Cardinal offered her left breast to the baby.

"*Mr. Butler...*" She tightly nodded her head toward the baby, who now was clutching a left fistful of Cardinal's sweater.

"Oh, Sweetie, I suppose Mr. Butler has seen a baby being fed before."

"But..." The redness of Ellie's blush clashed with her chestnut hair. She sat back into her chair and tried to disappear, seeming to shrink in embarrassment inside her clothes.

"Forgive me, Sam." Cardinal stood up, and with her free hand turned her chair around and sat down again, now facing out the glass in the front door. "I seem to have embarrassed my grown-up little daughter." She got herself and the baby readjusted and continued to talk, partly toward the door, but occasionally looking over her shoulder at them. "Growing up on the commune—you know that story, don't you Sam?, how I was born in a tipi down near Pettigrew? My folks were hippies. Anyway, growing up on the commune, I didn't know there was any other way to feed a baby. The first time I saw a baby bottle in the grocery store, I didn't know what it was for." She chuckled. "In fact, breasts were pretty commonly on display around the commune, feeding or not. Mom says that shirtlessness was a political statement back in those days. Plus, every now and then the deputy sheriffs would come by, and I think the deal was that they wouldn't see the pot growing if they got to see a nice set of knockers, or two. I expect that wasn't all they saw. Whatever the deal was, no one ever got busted. Could you spare a paper napkin, Sam?" He handed her one over her shoulder and she blotted up a little overflow. "So, feeding a baby always seemed to me like a silly thing for people to get nervous about. But David does, so I try to plan ahead when I'm out, or find some private place."

"Will he be nervous about now?"

"I doubt that we'll mention it to him, will we Ellie?" She looked over her shoulder at the girl.

"No, ma'am."

"But, if he asked, we wouldn't lie about it either, would we?"

"No, ma'am."

"And if he'd prefer I didn't, I wouldn't. He's my husband and there's no reason to embarrass him."

Sam stood up and handed Ellie back her notebook. "One hundred percent correct. Nice job." Then to Cardinal, "I've got something I want to give you. It's upstairs, so Ellie can relax. I'll be back down in a few minutes." He left the kitchen and walked up to the study, where he knelt by the stack containing Sally's collection of children's literature. He made a little time, to allow Esther to finish her meal, by rearranging the stack more neatly, large to small, and by adding a few more from the shelves. He thought about splitting the one pile into two, but in the end carried the entire stack downstairs. Cardinal now had the baby over her shoulder, gently burping her, and Ellie was noticeably more relaxed.

"I've been clearing out the study, thinning the books out before I run out of shelf space. These are my wife's collection of children's books. You never knew Sally, but she taught second grade in Huntsville for twenty years. She had ex-students your age now, Cardinal."

"Except that I didn't start school until the fourth grade. Otherwise, I might have had her—well, no. I went to St. Paul until junior high."

"She was a good teacher, especially reading. And she collected kids' books. I was going to donate them to the library, but why don't you look through them? I'm sure Sally would have liked it if you could use some of them. Take as many as you want, or all of them. There must be..." he looked at the stack, "...thirty or so. There's still more upstairs. She only collected books written for little kids, Ellie, so there's not much for you. But I bought her this one as a present once, and maybe you'd like it." He handed her a book off the top of the stack.

"*My Friend Flika*," she read.

"They made a movie out of it, I think," said Cardinal, rearranging the baby in her lap.

"Yes, gender-switching the main character, to decent effect."

"Gender switching?" asked Ellie.

"The main character in the book is a boy about your age, but in the movie, they turned him into a girl in high school. And, in fact, a gelding played the filly called Flika in the movie, so everything was backwards. The movie is pretty true to the book, except for that, but the book's set back in the Thirties, pre-World War II. It's a nice description of life on a western ranch, pre-electricity. I hope you like it."

"Thanks." She smiled.

"You might notice, too, that the characters sometimes use the word 'colt' where we'd say 'foal,' so they'll speak of a filly colt."

"I think I've hear that around here, too," said Cardinal, "at least to the extent that sometimes people talk of a horse colt, by which they mean a male foal. I always thought that was odd."

While Sam had been upstairs, Ellie had cleared the table and stacked the dishes in the sink, and was now sipping her Coca Cola and looking through the book, which had a few black and white, pen-and-ink drawings.

"I think it's turning to snow." Cardinal was walking around the kitchen, bouncing the baby. "Maybe we'd better be going."

"It's not sticking yet. Why don't you and Esther get comfortable on the couch for a while, and Ellie and I will do the next lesson here at the table? You can read *Flika*. It's not *Jane Eyre*." Ellie handed the book to her mother, and Cardinal walked into the living room and sat down. "Put your feet up," Sam called in, without looking. And now, conspiratorially to Ellie, "Let's be real quiet and let them have a little nap. Here." he opened her math book, "See if you can figure out these on your own."

And a few minutes later, when Sam looked in, Cardinal and Esther were both asleep, the baby lying face down on her mother's chest, with Cardinal snoring quietly. Sam put a quilt over the baby and Cardinal's legs, and, back in the kitchen, he gave a thumbs-up to Ellie and then motioned that he'd be upstairs.

In the study, Sam began, again, but this time quietly, to thin out the books, pleased that he had decided on the spur of the moment to give Cardinal first choice. He sat on the floor amidst the various stacks and added a few to this one and that one, while leaving the majority of the books on the shelves. After a bit, he tired of sorting, picked up the copy of *Horse Heaven* that he had set aside, and began flipping through to some of his favorite passages, settling in the end on the scene where Tiffany claims her first Thoroughbred at the track. He read for a bit, and was not surprised some minutes later to hear Ellie tiptoe up the stairs, carrying her math book, and into the study.

"Are they still sleeping?" he whispered.

"Yes."

"Good. Sit down here, so we can talk quietly." She sat down next to him, both of them leaning against the side of the desk. "I'm sorry you were embarrassed before."

"It's okay." Recalling the embarrassment was itself embarrassing, and she turned the topic. "What are you reading?"

He showed her the cover. "*Horse Heaven. A story about racing. It's a little too old for you.*"

"Horse Heaven." She paused, seeming to consider the words of the title. "That story my mom told down there? That was before. Before my grandma knew Jesus. I don't think she'd do those things anymore."

"Neither do I."

The thought hung for a bit, then, "I can't do these problems."

"Well, let's have a look," and they worked through the way to graph straight lines, $y = mx+b$, until Sam heard Cardinal rustling downstairs. He raised his voice, "We're up here."

She walked up the stairs, with the baby still asleep on her shoulder. "Whew. How long was I asleep?"

Sam looked at the clock. "About an hour, maybe a little less. Feel better?"

"If I could do that every afternoon, it would make up for the nights. But then the housework wouldn't get done." She looked out the study window. "Now it is sticking. We'd better get home, Peanut. And Sam, I really appreciate the books, but if they were at the library in Huntsville, the whole county could use them."

"That's true."

"So maybe I'll take let's say ten, and you can give the rest to the library."

"That's fair. I'll tell you what—I'll keep the stack here and Ellie can pick out the ones she thinks the boys will like. Okay? Next time you're over? And look here—there goes the school bus, three hours early. Somebody thinks the roads are going to get bad."

He walked them downstairs, where everyone got bundled up, including Sam, and he walked with them, holding the umbrella, to Cardinal's car, through the wet-falling snow, and after they drove off, he took some hay back to the horses, who were standing dry and comfortable in their respective shelters.

Back up at the study, he thinned a few more volumes off of the shelves, until he came to the shelf where Sally's Bible stood, at which point he sat in the chair at the desk and realized that it was all a charade. That Lynda was right in calling the house his Sally shrine, and that whatever process he was engaged in now, it was not a desanctification. He looked at the Bible and thought of the little girl downstairs saying grace over egg salad and cornbread, and of her mother making it clear that she'd save her husband embarrassment, even at her own extreme inconvenience, and of David himself, looking for some impossible-to-imagine biblical principle that forbade a mother from feeding her infant in public. But mostly he thought of Sally, 255¾ days sober, reading that very book the night before she died. 255¾ days sober, but he knew her well enough to know that she was aching for a drink even as she reached up to return the Bible to its place on the shelf. He wondered what passage she had read that night, the night before she died. Perhaps the place was marked, or perhaps the book would just fall open with a clue to that night and the next day. But—*Sally shrine* indeed—he determined for now to leave the Bible where it was, last touched by Sally's hand, not reaching for a drink. Outside, the snow continued to fall, there would be no school tomorrow, and he would have ice balls to pick out of the horses' hooves. But the rain had not frozen, and in two days it was due to be back above freezing.

**The Following Thursday.**

They had set the meeting for two o'clock at the law school, but when Sam arrived five minutes late, Jonathan was not in his office. At first, Sam was going to wait in the anteroom outside in the faculty suite, but, standing in the open door to the office, he saw propped up by Jonathan's computer a large manila envelope with his name written on it in large capitals. The layout of the office was this: there were two chairs for visitors near the door where Sam stood, then Jonathan's desk, set perpendicular to the glass wall facing west. Between the desk and the credenza against the south wall was Jonathan's chair, allowing him to swivel between the writing area on his desk and the computer behind. Jonathan used the two-monitor setup that had become popular since Sam had retired: two wide-screen monitors, powered by the suitcase PC under the credenza. It was to the left of the left-hand monitor that the envelope stood, so as, it seemed to Sam, to be seen from where he was standing by the door, an invitation, he thought, to walk in and retrieve it. He decided to do so and see what it was while he waited for Jonathan.

He stepped inside the empty office, and behind the desk. The two monitors showed a screensaver: North America on the left screen and Europe on the right, daytime in London and Paris, but nighttime in Chicago and Denver. Tiny colored dots travelled what was apparently the North Atlantic airplane routes, most of the traffic heading west-to-east at this time of day, from the left hand monitor to the right, or at least at the time of the day portrayed, which was not real time, for it was wrong for two o'clock in the afternoon in the Ozarks, so Sam presumed it was an animation. Nevertheless, he was fascinated, and watched for a bit, as the dots transported themselves to and occasionally from Europe. Yes, now he could see that it was an animation, with the time speeded up; he could see the night moving west, and dawn soon to come to Budapest. Presumably, the dots were scheduled flights, not actual ones, with the colors perhaps designating the airlines.

After a few minutes watching the display, Sam reached for the envelope and nudged the credenza with his leg, enough to cause the screensaver to dissolve, revealing what Jonathan had been working on. The right-hand monitor showed gobbledygook; a screen full of things like this:

```
int main()
{int *ptr_one;
ptr_one = (int *)malloc(sizeof(int));
if (ptr_one == 0)
{
return 1;
}
*ptr_one = 25;
printf("%d\n", *ptr_one);
free(ptr_one);
return 0;
}
```

The left-hand monitor held a list of eight-letter combinations that were plainly University of Arkansas IT Services usernames. He recognized the names of several of his former colleagues, both faculty and staff. Turning away, he opened the envelope and found, as he had expected, a draft of Part Three of Jonathan's requirements contracts article, twenty-seven single-spaced pages, with footnotes, one hundred sixty-two of them. He sat in one of the chairs on the far side of the desk and looked the manuscript over.

Due to a facility with computers that Sam could only guess at, the draft looked very much like a published article, with running titles, professional fonts, footnotes below, all printed on two sides of the pages, which were the correct size for a published journal. Twenty-seven pages, and one hundred sixty-two footnotes. Very tidy and finished-looking. But, on closer examination, he could see the signs that this was still a draft: "see note zx, below"; "Write this footnote"; "RM: find a case for this proposition," this last apparently a note to Jonathan's research assistant, not fired after all.

He began to read.

He was on page sixteen when Jonathan came walking into the office. "Ah, Sam. Sorry. I'm glad you found the envelope. I got waylaid by a student and couldn't get away."

"That's okay. I was a little late. But I barged in and made myself at home. I hope you don't mind."

"Not a bit. What do you think?"

"Let me finish. Should I sit here or out there?" Sam gestured to the anteroom.

"Wherever you're comfortable. There's fine. I'll just carry on here..." with which Jonathan turned in his chair to the computer monitors on the credenza, dissolved the screensaver and began to type.

"I like your screensaver."

Jonathan stopped typing. "It's nice, isn't it? Purports to show every trans-Atlantic commercial flight there is. If you watch closely for a while, you can see the variations from weekdays to weekends."

"Seasonal variations, too?"

"I'm not *that* patient." He began to type again.

"How was Topeka?"

Without turning around: "Pleasant."

"The conference?"

Now Jonathan turned again to face Sam. "At Washburn. IT Law. A symposium for their law review."

"You presented?"

"Not really. Only in a minor way. I was on a panel that reacted to one of the presentations. Boy, were you right in directing me toward the mundane, with that." Jonathan gestured at the paper in Sam's lap. "The technology is changing so quickly that it's hard to keep up. And hard for the law to keep up."

"Which makes it hard for the law professors to keep up."

"Exactly. I was going to do Fourth Amendment password protection, and that's already passé. The new hot topic is protection of private SSL encryption keys."

"Beg pardon?"

"SSL: Secure Sockets Layer." Sam looked mystified. "Think cryptographic protocols." Sam shook his head. "Uh, email security. The company wants privacy; the government wants in. Or *vice versa*: the government wants secrecy and Fox News wants in. It's a constant battle, with the skirmish lines always changing."

"Requirements contracts, on the other hand, for all their mundaneness..."

"Not such a moving target. Just as long as it's publishable."

"Not to worry. Everything is publishable." Sam returned to his reading and Jonathan to his typing.

When Sam finished reading, he tapped the sheets back together on the corner of Jonathan's desk, but when that didn't break his concentration, Sam sat back in the chair and looked out the window, until Jonathan looked over his shoulder. "Oh. Finished? So?"

"What *is* that you're working on? I saw the monitors when I fetched the envelope and it looked like, I don't know what."

"It's programming language on this side..." Jonathan gestured to the right-hand monitor. "C-plus, it's called. The law school's IT boys and I are trying to write a program that will allow a professor to control wi-fi access by the students in class. We're going to have a trial run with the staff." He gestured toward the names on the left-hand monitor.

"Why not a switch on the wall?"

"God, a switch!" Jonathan slapped his forehead with his palm. "Why didn't we think of that?" Sarcasm filled the room. "No. Won't work. Wi-fi, short-range, goes through walls and ceilings. Like a radio signal. You'd have to black out the library to control access in the classrooms. The way to do it is to tie the students' usernames to their class schedules, so they can't log in when they're in class. Or supposed to be. The trouble is..."

"Is?"

"My much-respected colleagues, who want the system to be individually tailored to the professor's whims, which vary from office to office, allowing, for example, students to visit some, but not all, websites while in the particular professor's class. So, flexibility first. But easy to use by the digitally inept among us. And not easily frustrated by student initiative, the students, of course, being considerably more tech-savvy than most of the professors." Jonathan's expression rather quickly lengthened. "Should I be doing this?"

"Why not?"

"Will COPT think I should be concentrating only on that?" He pointed to the article.

"Law school community service. It counts. Does the dean know of the project?"

Jonathan nodded, but before Sam could complete his thought, Lynda arrived in the doorway.

"Well, hot shit," she said. "Here are my two favorite males. What's goin' on, guys?" She walked over to behind Jonathan's desk and gave him a kiss which, while not passionate, perhaps lingered somewhat longer than the typical office kiss. Then she walked around to Sam, put her left hand on his far shoulder and planted a kiss on the top of his head.

Sam was nervous from the time that Lynda had appeared, and intentionally did not lift his face to receive whatever kiss she might have had in mind. He had never in his life been in the position—or within two light years of it—where he was in the company of a woman who had said she wanted to sleep with him, while her husband sat behind the desk on the other side of the room. What would she say? What should he say? What would Jonathan say? Who would do what to whom?

But, naturally, Lynda was right at ease. Perhaps she'd been in the position before. Perhaps it was her impressive ability to take control of whatever situation she was in. Perhaps she'd planned it out. Perhaps she hadn't. Perhaps she didn't need to.

"Hello?" She broke his chain of thought. "Are you with us? Butler; Houston. Do you copy?"

"Uh. Yes. Right. I was thinking..." He looked out the window. "I was asking about Topeka."

"Which is odd because you were talking about programming the wi-fi service when I walked in."

"Were we? Right, we were."

Jonathan sat with his arms folded across his chest, seeming to enjoy the exchange. Now he spoke. "Look at you. Dressed to the nines. What's up?" To Sam: "She leaves before I awake."

Lynda smiled, spread her skirt with her hands and pivoted on her spiked heel. "Like it?" Blue skirt above the knees, slightly flared, red silk blouse, blue and white shoes with three-inch heels.

"Pretty," Sam said, recovering his wits.

"*Pretty*? For God's sake, Samuel."

"Sorry. Sharp."

"That's better. Photo session at University Relations across Maple in fifteen. Then rendezvousing..."—she pronounced the *s* like a *z*—"rendezvousing at the lab with the En-Y-Tee's photo man. Panty hose, you'll notice. I went all out." She hiked her skirt so it was half-way, or more, up her thighs.

"Well, sure," said Jonathan. "Why not display your undergarments to my officially-assigned mentor?"

"At ease, darlin'. *Panties* are undergarments; panty *hose* are not."

The exchange made Sam, once again, uncomfortable and he turned the topic. "This..." he held up Jonathan's manuscript, "...is really what we were talking about."

"Ah. Requirements contracts." She took the chair next to Sam. "I'll eavesdrop."

"You know what they are?"

"Sheesh. They are a continuous subject of conversation around the Wheeler/Stratford homestead."

"Continual," said Sam.

"Continual?"

"You're the physicist; you should know. 'Continual' when the items are discrete like, what did you say? Continual conversations. The wind blew continuously, causing the shutters to bang continually. Conversations are *continuous* only if you talk constantly and never talk about anything else."

"Who says we do?"

"So, what do you think?" Sam asked her.

"About the paper or about the topic?" Jonathan sat back in his chair and listened to the two of them.

"The paper."

"Haven't read it. That's asking too much of even the most willing spouse."

"About the topic, then?"

"I've enjoyed his explanations. I find the issues of language interpretation to be fascinating. And I like the asymmetry of it all."

"Asymmetry?"

"Over-orders being treated differently from under-orders."

Jonathan spoke up. "*Disproportionate* under-orders, please."

"Right. I like it that someone thought through the problem carefully enough to see that mindless symmetry is no virtue. There are physical analogues to that lesson, actually, but we won't go into them just now. Proportionality, too, has its mathematical analogues. And I like the fact that the law is not developed in the abstract, but in the context of the actual business world."

"She's an experimentalist, not a theorist, as you may already know."

"I do know that. And Karl Llewellyn would be proud."

"Who's Karl Llewellyn?"

"Jonathan?"

"He wrote it. The statute. He was one of the principal proponents of legal realism back in, what? The Fifties."

"And Sixties."

"What's legal realism?"

"After you," said Jonathan.

"You just defined it. The law should reflect how legitimate business is in fact carried out, and should not impose formalistic legal requirements on businessmen. Jonathan?"

"Contracts have become much easier to form in the last fifty years or so. For example, by not insisting that the precise quantity term be written. The buyer's requirements will do."

"It's reasonably fascinating," said Lynda. "And sophisticated. So, what do you think of the paper itself?"

"About which I've been waiting on the edge of my seat," said Jonathan.

"Well done, I think. I'll take it with me, make some marginal notes and get it back to you next week." Jonathan nodded. "I see you re-hired your research assistant."

"How did you know? Did she stop by while I was out and you were reading?"

"No. Let's see...." Sam flipped through the pages. "Footnote seventy-nine is addressed to RM. I guessed that to be her. She."

"Yeah. I took your advice to heart, but once I saw what you were on to, I realized that I could still use her, as long as I devised very narrow inquiries for her to pursue. Okay?"

"Fine with me. Though you still might have found something interesting, even if tangential, when you were looking for the case for footnote seventy-nine."

"I'll remember that."

"So," Lynda inserted herself back in, "what do the Big Three think?"

"Who?"

"What are their names, sweetheart?"

"Wilson, Selvig and Pryor. I haven't shown them Part Three."

"You're squirming."

"Right."

"Why them?" Sam asked.

"Because we think they're the key votes on COPT, don't we, sweetheart?"

"Well, dammit. I thought we agreed we weren't going to try to find that out. It's *confidential.*"

"Okay, so we speculate," said Lynda.

"Speculate all *you* want, but it's Jonathan who has to live in conformity to the social compact around here, not you. And the social compact says not to be curious. Not even interested."

"Right. Got it. Mark me as uninterested in COPT voting patterns. Oh, oh. Gotta go. Wish me luck."

"Good luck, Lynda."

"Just smile, Gwenie, and you'll have them in your pocket."

"Look...I don't know...*scientific,*" said Sam.

"See you at home. And you, Samuel, I'll see you around."

She was out the door and Sam and Jonathan said nothing for a moment. Then, Sam: "Trying to figure out who the three soft *noes* are could queer the whole deal."

"Gwen spoke out of turn, violating spousal confidentiality."

"I just don't want you to break the social compact."

"You do look after me." He seemed to want to go on, and Sam allowed him to collect his thoughts. When Jonathan spoke, he did so quietly, looking out the window, and with his fingertips pressed together. "You see, Sam, she's one of those incredibly smart, unbelievably talented, entirely confident people to whom the ordinary rules of human behavior don't apply."

"I'm unfamiliar with the phenomenon."

"It's ever-present, even on the periphery, at Cal Tech. Richard Feynman is the classic case. Nobel Prize winner, now dead, who did not have time, actually, to grade his exams. It's a famous story."

"What happened?"

"The dean or chairman, one, graded them."

"He was forgiven?"

"That's the point: no forgiveness was deemed necessary, as the usual rules did not apply."

"Don't apply? Or they *think* they don't?"

"Lynda certainly thinks that much the social compact is silly hypocrisy, for which she has no time. So, she ignores it. Flouts it, on occasion." Jonathan paused, reflecting again. "But I think she may have a point, even, that the usual rules in fact don't apply. I think there *are* different rules for people like her."

"She's a genius, you think?"

"Ah ha. The social compact among scientists—as opposed to law professors—is that that word is never used."

"She was once described to me as having Nobel-Prize potential."

"The compact allows plenty of Nobel speculation, but always based on past accomplishments, never on mere potential. Besides, experimentalists rarely win dynamite money, which generally goes to the theorists."

"Dynamite money?"

"Mr. Nobel's line of work. So, maybe she gets one of the lesser awards. Her talent is just so impressive, it's hard to believe that she should be treated just as part of the crowd."

"So much for democracy?"

"Oh, I'm not talking so much from a legal sense. I'm not crazy about some pie-in-the-sky libertarian so-called meritocracy. That's rubbish and always has been. No, I'm talking about your social compact. Just the way that she gets through life in relation to the rest of us. I think she believes, without really stating it, that different rules apply. I think she may have a point."

"Sounds like Karl Llewellyn and legal realism."

"Ha! Everything works together, doesn't it? Maybe so: the compact has to be formulated in relation to the actual world into which it fits. And in that world, Gwenie is crazy smart."

"You persist in calling her Gwen. Why?"

Jonathan put his hands behind his head and leaned back in his chair. "The first time I met her parents, I called her Lynda, and her father replied like he'd been chewing dry ice: 'Her name's Gwen.' I switched for the evening, and when I realized it annoyed her, I stuck with it. She pretty much ignores it unless there's someone else around. Like you."

"Your mention of her *versus* the crowd makes me think of what Cardozo said about trustees."

"'Not honesty alone, but the punctilio of an honor the most sensitive.' But I'm not sure Gwen would agree that the not-honesty-alone part would apply to her. I don't believe she thinks she has any higher obligation to tell the truth than the rest of us."

"Go on with the Cardozo quote."

"Can't. That's all I remember."

"'...Only thus has the level of conduct for fiduciaries been kept at a level higher than that trodden by the crowd.' I think that's the idea you were getting at: that she's on a path different from the one quote unquote trodden by the crowd."

"Yes, exactly. She does get through life with expectations different from Cardozo's 'crowd.' I think that *is* what I'm getting at."

"How does she feel about being talked about in her absence?"

"I never thought to be concerned about that. Should she?"

"It used to piss off Sally. My wife. I think she could sense that such a conversation was taking place from miles away. I'd hear about it later. She'd just know."

"Know what was being said?"

"It didn't matter what was being said. It was the sense merely of being spoken about. It bothered her."

"I've never known Gwen to complain. Actually, she's probably used to being talked about. It won't surprise you to hear that she was a precocious child. Well, teenager, too. Adult, actually."

"I would guess her to have been the very definition of child precocity."

"Nice word, 'precocity.' I would have said 'precociousness,' but I like yours better. And, yes, whatever it is that precocity requires, she has it. But..." the change of subject came quickly, "...enough about my wife. Anything else about the article?"

"You've thought about Part Four?"

"Needed reforms? I'm finding myself inclined to say that no reform is needed. I'm liking the way the statute stands now, and I think Posner's reasoning in the Empire Gas case to be elegant. A buyer can make a disproportionate under-order without breaching the contract if he has a valid business reason for doing so."

"I like that you're in opposition to the stereotyped law professor. We're usually so full of so-called needed reforms that they come out of our ears. But, remember to think about legal realism. Every business that under-orders thinks it's got a valid business reason for doing so. The last thing they want to do is litigate the facts and wait for Posner's test to be applied or not. They need to know what they're in for before they make the under-order."

"Good point. I'll think it through. Now, you've spent enough time with me, and I've got class to get ready for. I don't mean to chase you, but..."

"Right." Sam rose, feeling dismissed, a feeling common among the retired when dealing with the still-employed. "Like I said, I'll make some notes on this and get it back to you. I may mail it, if that's okay, rather than make the drive back into town."

Jonathan laughed. "You are a true delight to know. I'm beginning to understand why Gwenie likes to hang with you." He chuckled again. "Yeah, sure, mail it back. Or bring it on horseback."

"I'm used to being teased about my obsolete ways. Lynda, in fact, is very good at it. But really, I'll bring it back in...or we could talk on the phone, but I think it's coming along. Do you need it back right away?"

"The delivery part of the operation is a small fraction of the time from when you make your notes until I react to them. I'm just teasing. Mail it back. Please. Put real stamps on it. Send it media-rate. I'm pleased that you think it's coming along."

"I do. Okay. Bye then. I'll be in touch. You do know Morse code, right? Or semaphore?"

Jonathan swiveled back to his monitors, raising his right hand in farewell. "Get out of here or I'll never get anything done."

The snow had not melted in the two days since the storm, but the sidewalks were clear and dry as Sam walked down the hill to the small pickup, parked in the stadium lot, where piles of plowed snow remained. The sun was poking through the clouds, the breeze had shifted around to the southwest as the front had exited the region, and it was warming into a nice day. The pastures needed the moisture and the snow was short-lived enough not to cause any horse-handling difficulties, but long-staying enough so that it would soak in and not run off, all to the good.

As he walked down to the parking lot, Sam's thoughts were not on the tail end of the conversation and the good-natured ribbing he'd taken over his natural inclination to send the article back to Jonathan through the mail. He had said it without thinking, and only occasionally caught himself before suggesting what to the younger generations was an anachronism.

No, that little exchange was in good fun and he had deserved the ribbing. But what the hell was the rest about? Jonathan's long rumination on how the ordinary rules of society didn't apply to Lynda? Was that simply an explanation of her forwardness in displaying her panty-hose-clad thighs to him? If so, then it was nothing, neither the act of near-exposure nor her eagerness to flout the rules of decorum. Or was it about the fact that she was intent on speculating about who the so-called Big Three soft *no* votes were, notwithstanding the folkways of the law school, which made it impolitic even to ask around. It was entirely believable that Lynda Stratford, child genius, would find such tenure-related machinations to be utter bullshit and inapplicable to her. The first time Sam and Jonathan had met, Jonathan had called the idea that she would have trouble getting tenure almost funny, but even if one were to imagine it, Sam's guess was that she'd just plow ahead until all the cards were face-up on the felt.

But still, Jonathan might be apologizing on her behalf to Sam for her own breach of the law school's social compact. No, not apologizing. Not justifying, even. Just explaining. But Sam found the entire thing to be of no moment. The compact forbade *Jonathan's* snooping around trying to pry into COPT confidentiality, and no amount of Lynda's speculation would amount to that. Some eyebrows might rise if Lynda speculated aloud in the wrong company, an event Sam considered unlikely, and in any case, every petition for tenure raised at least one eyebrow or two.

Or maybe—and this is the one that made Sam nervous, made him stop beside the small pickup, leaning with his back on the front fender, made him stand there looking at nothing in particular—a car driving past, hunting for a parking spot, a coed running slowly by, ear-buds in, doing her afternoon run, a small jet lining up to land to the south at the muny airport, the same car driving past again, still hunting, which led Sam to raise a hand and offer his spot—maybe, he continued to wonder as he exited the parking lot, heading south on Razorback Road, maybe Jonathan's speech about Lynda and the social compact was his veiled admission that he knew of Lynda's proposal of intimacy with Sam, knew of it, or wouldn't be surprised to hear of it. Perhaps he was saying simply that this is what Lynda does. The ordinary rules don't apply to her, and she is not restricted to the path trodden by the crowd. Perhaps he was letting Sam know, not that his permission was granted, for it wouldn't be needed, but that such proposals, and their consummation, were part of the life he led with Lynda, his Gwenie, and that he was willing to accept that, to take the chaff with the wheat, if you will, the tail with the hide.

All of this made Sam nervous, as he now drove east on highway 45, and not because he intended to take Lynda up on her proposal. He had told her the truth when he said he had no interest in sleeping with her, no curiosity even, no desire. He enjoyed her company and wanted more of that, but not the other. And for exactly the reason he had told her, because he sought friendship, not sex, and guessed that they would not both survive together. Plus the fact that she really was too young to be of interest to him. So, Jonathan's acknowledgement, if that's what it was, of the proposal did not make him nervous because of what might happen between the two of them, but what it might do to the other two of them, him and Jonathan, and their working relationship. They seemed to be getting along smoothly enough and Sam didn't need Jonathan to be thinking that he was sleeping with his wife. Even if the usual rules did not apply to Lynda, they did apply to Sam, and all of this made him nervous about what Jonathan was thinking.

He pulled into the gate at his place, having sorted through the above about three times to no conclusion. He would just have to see.

# 4

## FEBRUARY

**The First Monday.**

 The fact that horses react so differently to things that move and things that don't move does not mean that they always do so immediately. Sometimes it takes a great deal of study to tell one from another. Something that appears at first, or second, or tenth glance to be stationary might just suddenly spring to life and attack. Just One Look, of course, had never in his life seen an actual predator (leaving aside a couple of trainers and vets on the backside), but something deep in his genes often warned him that even the most innocent-looking, immobile clump of something could at any moment decide to eat him.

 Consider, for instance, one cool, rainy morning in February, when Just One Look headed along the fence line that kept him out of the creek, and toward the gate that led into the eastern day pasture. As had become The Looker's practice, he had lingered behind after the others had already left the stable paddock, lingered behind to clean up the bits of hay they had not eaten, and to have a long morning's drink out of the tank in front of the easternmost stalls, which, for reasons he saw no need to enumerate, he preferred to the tank in front of his own stall. *This one*, the lead human around here, didn't seem to mind that he stayed behind, as the others were escorted toward the day pasture, an attitude that Just One Look found puzzling. The humans at the various tracks where he'd lived had never allowed him to decide for himself what he wanted to do, or when, and while he was always suspicious of change, he was beginning to think that in this instance, it was acceptable.

And so, the paddock cleaned of every bit of hay that his nose and whiskers could account for, and his thirst sated, Just One Look headed along the fence line, and toward the gate that led into the eastern day pasture. And there, just beyond the gate, it was. A clump of something. He stopped and watched it. It was not moving. His memory was keen, and he thought that this clump of something had not been there before. He studied it. No, he was certain; this clump had not been there before when he had walked through that gate. He studied it some more, his ears straight up and turned toward the clump. Still it did not move, but he was not yet certain that it would never move. He stood watching it, prepared to run, and knowing—in fact *seeing*—that the way was open behind him for a retreat, if needed.

He stood like this for three minutes, not moving a muscle, studying the situation. His ears were pricked forward. He tested the air, but the breeze was from behind him, and he could get no scent of the clump. He breathed deeply, the air vibrating his air passages. His pasture mates, he could see, were grazing quietly in the pasture beyond the clump, which comforted him, but still he stood, making sure. He took two steps toward the gate and stopped. The clump did not move. Behind him a squirrel chattered and ran noisily up a hickory tree; he turned his left ear around in the direction of the tree and examined the noise. No danger there. He turned the ear back toward the front. His eyes did not move.

A few more steps, and still the clump did not move, and Just One Look began to relax a little bit. He put his nose to the ground and nibbled at the dirt. He felt the need to defecate, and he did so. The grass on the other side of the gate tempted him, and he took a few more steps. The breeze calmed behind him and now his nose could pick up a faint, familiar scent, a scent that did not signify any danger, though it was not yet strong enough to identify. A few more steps and he was within ten feet of the clump, which still did not move. But now he could identify the scent: it was *this one*. He walked over to the clump, sniffed it deeply, then nudged it with his nose. It made a noise, though not one that was meaningful to him. But yes, now he was certain. It was *this one*. He nudged the clump again, got the same unknown sound again, so, deciding that everything was safe, he walked quickly around the clump and trotted toward his pasture mates. He stopped, looked back at the clump and began to nibble the grass where he stood, now with his ears turned backwards to monitor his rear.

An hour and a half later, Ellie arrived on her four-wheeler. Teena greeted her as usual by lying down to have her belly rubbed. Not seeing anyone one around, though both pickups were parked at the gate, nor any horses, Ellie walked up the hill to the house carrying her backpack with her book and homework in it. She opened the front door, took off her shoes, walked in, put her backpack on the kitchen table and yelled toward the stairs. "Mr. Butler? You here?" No answer. "Anybody home?" She shrugged to herself, took off her rain jacket, wet from the ride, and hung it over the back of the rocking chair. Looking out the south windows in the kitchen, down to the stable, she could not see anyone around, so she unpacked her homework and sat down at the table to get herself organized, and to finish the last few problems.

After about twenty minutes, she glanced out of the windows again and saw that Afraid of Nothing, as she now called Dreadnaught, was standing in the paddock by The Looker's round pen. This was odd, and the only way that it made sense to her was if Mr. Butler had forgotten to close the gate to the day pasture. That would be unlike him, as he was always careful about closing gates, and had insisted that she be, too. It was best, she decided, to go down and investigate, not to mention that it was always more fun to visit with the horses than to do her math. So, leaving her book and homework on the table, and grabbing her jacket, she walked down to the stable, got a halter and lead line from the tack room, haltered Dreadnaught up and led him back toward the day pasture.

By this time, Sam Butler had come to and dragged himself about thirty feet back away from the gate and toward the chicken coop, where he was now sitting on the ground, somewhat sheltered from the light mist that was falling, leaning up against the wire of the coop, figuring that before long Ellie would show up.

When she saw him, she screamed, which threatened to spook Dread-naught, who stopped in his tracks, raised his head and pulled the lead line tight. "Mr. Butler!" She started to run toward Sam, but the horse pulled back away from her, jerking the line through her fingers. The sting of the rope burn seemed to settle her and remind her to take care of first things first, so she calmed the horse down, led him through the gate into the day pasture, de-haltered him and closed the gate behind her, and now she ran to where Sam leaned against the chicken coop.

"Mr. Butler. What happened? Are you all right?" He did not look so good. He had been bleeding badly from the head and there was dried blood all down his face. One cut over his left eye was still seeping blood, his eyes were closed and he held his left arm close to his rib cage, cradling his right arm in his lap. "Are you all right?" She was afraid to touch him. She raised her voice. "Are you all right?" She had to choke back her sobs.

He opened one eye. "Hi, kiddo." His breathing was very shallow. "I got kicked." Breath. "My own damn fault." Breath. "You're going to have to help me."

"Should I call nine-one-one?"

"They'd never find us out here." Breath. "Go up to my room." Breath. "You know which one?"

She nodded. "Next to the bathroom?"

"Good." Breath. "Get my money clip, my keys and my cell phone." Breath. "Top of the dresser." Breath. "And in the left hand drawer," breath, "my Medicare card. Red, white," breath, "and blue." Breath. "Okay?"

"Okay." She rose and started to take off at a run.

"Wait." So quietly she almost didn't hear him. She turned back. "Put those things in your pockets and then ride your four-wheeler back here." Breath. "We'll use it like a wheelchair." She turned to go again. "Wait." She turned back. "And grab," breath, "a roll," breath, "of Vet-rap when you come," breath, "back. And some gauze pads." Breath. "And some HEW." Breath. "The goop we put on wounds." Breath. "Okay. Go."

Ellie left him and, still holding back her tears, ran past the stable and up the hill to the house. Her shoes were muddy and she almost stopped to take them off, before deciding to hurry up the stairs and into Mr. Butler's bedroom, where, she noticed, the bed was neatly made and there were no clothes strewn about. She found his keys, money and phone easily enough, but inside the drawer there were many cards and she had to fumble through them twice before she slowed herself down, wiped her eyes on the ball of her thumb, and looked once more, finding the Medicare one right near the top. Then she ran out of the house and down the hill to her four-wheeler. Half-way down the hill she stopped. Should she call her mother? She decided not to, not until Mr. Butler told her to. She ran the rest of the way, hopped on the four-wheeler and gunned it back toward where he lay. She was halfway to him, beyond the tack room, when she remembered about the tape and gauze and goop, so she stopped, ran back and found what he needed.

His eyes were closed again when she pulled up next to him by the chicken coop, but he opened the one that wasn't glued shut by the blood. "Good girl." He squared his shoulders and, using his left hand under his right forearm, he held it out to her. "Remember how to wrap a horse's leg?"

"Yes." She was afraid of what he was going to ask her.

"Okay, then. Wrap my right arm. I think it's broken."

"I don't know how."

"Yes, you do. Go on, now."

"I don't want to hurt you."

"It will feel better once you wrap it."

She took his right wrist in her left hand. "What about the sleeve?"

"Wrap right over it."

"I can't get the tape started." She felt helpless and began to sob again.

"Here, I'll help," he said. "I'll bet Daisy never said that to you." And she sobbed a little laugh through her tears. "Come on, Ellie. It'll be fine." So she held his wrist, he held the end of the tape against his forearm and she began unrolling the elastic tape up toward his elbow. He grimaced, and she stopped, but he said, "Tighter," and she continued to wrap. "Tight as you can. Now back down," he said before she got as far as his elbow. "Now back up. That's good. Now cut it off."

"I forgot the scissors."

"Okay, then we'll have to tear it off." Breath. "This may hurt. I'll hold it here." He took a shallow breath as he put his left hand over the tape at his elbow, "Now pull it as hard as you can." He shouted as she pulled on the tape, but it finally gave way, and he sat back and closed his eyes. "Wow."

It took him a few minutes to catch his breath, before he said, "Okay. Got enough left to do my head?" She held up the remainder of the roll of Vet-rap. "Okay. Now I can't see what has to be done, so you're on your own." Breath. "Put a gob of HEW on the gauze." He waited with his one eye open while she did so. "Okay, now just pick the spot that looks the worst and put the gauze pad on it..."

"There's a place that's still bleeding a little."

"Okay, then that's the place. Now, wrap the tape around my head to hold it on. That a girl. Now, tear it off. It won't hurt this time." She finished the job and he said, "Okay, now let's just sit here for a minute before we go. Are you all right? Sit down here. You're doing great."

They sat on the ground for about five minutes, before Sam got up energy enough to talk. "Okay. First. Get five flakes of hay from the hay room. Put them on the back of your four-wheeler. And spread them out in the day pasture."

"But it's not time for them to eat." Ellie felt calmer now, and was no longer crying.

"I don't know when I'll be home, so let's put some out now. Go ahead. I'll wait."

That took about ten minutes.

"Now, pull your machine over here by me." He waited while she ran again to the four-wheeler. He had to speak more loudly, over the sound of the engine. "Slow. Close enough so that I can reach the rack on the back with my good arm. There. Back up. A little more. Stop." Sam needed to take a deep breath, but it hurt too much. "Now, you come over here and help me under this arm. Turn the bike off and set the brake." She came around to his side as he got himself ready to stand up. "Wait. I think I need a sling. Get a piece of baling string." She ran to the hay room and came back with a piece of orange plastic twine that they made into a loop for around his neck, and through which he slipped his right wrist. "Okay, now let's get me to my knees." Steadying himself against her four-wheeler with his left hand and with her under his right arm, he pivoted and got his knees under him, then his left foot. "Now. Up. Ooo, that hurts." But he was standing now beside the machine and by shuffling his feet to the left, he got close enough to lean his butt against the seat. "Let's see. What now? Bring that cinder block over and put it under my right foot. Good. Now go behind me, and when I say so, pull me onto the seat by pulling on my belt loops. Ready? One, two, three. Now."

The pain in his ribcage was intense, but she did the job and he was now sitting side-saddle on the four-wheeler. "Okay. You drive. Walking speed. To the big pickup." Ellie swung her leg over the seat, started the engine and popped the clutch, almost putting him back on the ground.

"Sorry."

"Walking speed."

"Okay."

"No bumps."

"Okay."

It took several minutes to drive at walking speed from the scene of the accident to where the pickups were parked at the entrance to the farm, and the trip, while uneventful, was painful and took most of Sam's energy. When she stopped the four-wheeler at the pickups, and swung herself off the bike, Ellie said, "Shouldn't I call my mom?"

"Maybe you'd better."

But there was only voice mail, so Ellie said, "Mr. Butler's hurt," and then hung up. "Should we wait until she calls back? I don't know where she is. Sometimes she forgets that the phone is recharging. Should I try again? I can go get her."

"No, let's get me into the truck." With Ellie's help, Sam transferred his butt from the ATV to the front seat of the Toyota. He took a minute to catch his breath again, then said, "Okay, I'll take it from here. When you get home, tell your mother what happened and have her call my cell. What are you doing?"

She had run around to the passenger door of the pickup and was climbing in. "I'm going with you." It was not a question, and her voice held a determination that he had never heard from her regarding an adult. Sam didn't argue.

"Okay," he said, then discovered that she was going to have to start the ignition and shift gears for him in any case. "Okay. Good. Take this key and..."

When he looked across the seat at her, her eyes were closed and her hands were clasped below her chin, the fingers interlocked and gripped tightly together. Her eyelashes were still damp from before, but she was no longer crying. She did not pray silently, for he could see her lips moving, though he could only catch small bits of what she said: "Dear Jesus...Mr. Butler...protect...please...Mr. Butler...help...please."

Sam looked out the windshield of the truck, breathed shallowly against the pain in his ribs and waited, listening to Ellie's soft entreaties, and to the song of a wren busy somewhere in the branches of a lilac bush. When she went silent, he turned to her and smiled. She smiled back and wiped her eyes on her sleeve.

"Ready?" he asked.

"Ready."

"Okay, turn the key to the right for me."

She held the key too long, and the starter gears ground, a harsh counter-point to her quiet prayer, but the engine caught.

The drive from Sam's place near Hindsville to Washington Regional Medical Center would ordinarily take about a half-hour, maybe three-quarters, depending on the traffic. But before they got very far past Mayfield, Ellie said, "Why are you driving so slow? Are you all right?" and Sam knew he could be in trouble.

"Ellen," he said, and she was immediately scared again, for he never called her Ellen. "I'm feeling a little drowsy, and that's not good after you've been hit in the head, so you're going to have to help me stay awake."

"What should I do?" She was scared, which reminded Sam that he had not only to take care of the driving and not wreck the truck, but he also had to take care of the girl.

"Why don't we sing? Know any good songs? Do you know *Good Golly Miss Molly*?" Sam felt like if he stopped talking he would immediately drift off to sleep. "Here we go..." He taught her the first verse, and then made her sing it along with him. "Louder!" And then the second verse, and they shot through Goshen with the windows down, the cold air acting against the drowsiness, singing rock and roll at the top of their lungs. *Mustang Sally* got them to the top of Slaughter Hill, and *Blue Bayou* to the Fayetteville city line, at which point the traffic became busy enough to keep Sam awake and make him concentrate on his driving.

Coming from the east, as they were, the route to Washington Regional is circuitous: west on Mission, north on Crossover, west again on Joyce, south on College, west on Millsap, which turns into Futrall. Sam pulled into the emergency room portico exhausted, breathing shallowly and with his right arm throbbing. He put the truck in Park with his left hand reaching over, and, leaving the engine running, he lay his head against the steering wheel. "Go on in and see if you can find someone with a wheelchair. Hold onto my phone for me, okay?"

Ellie stepped down from the truck, holding both her own phone and Sam's, ran past the emergency call button that neither of them knew existed and through the two sets of sliding glass doors that opened for her and closed behind.

Inside, there was chaos. Ordered chaos the hospital administrator would say, but Ellie in her confusion could not see the order. Directly in front of her, two grown-ups sat behind glass windows. Above the windows, large red letters said "EMERGENCY TRIAGE," but she didn't know what that meant and, besides, there were lines three deep in front of each window—a young woman holding an ice pack to her head, and old woman in a wheelchair, looking grey and with tubes in her nose, a man holding a baby on his shoulder, wrapped in a blanket, others with nothing obvious wrong with them. To her left there was an open area with chairs, mostly occupied, a fish tank, and six flat-screen TVs, three of them showing the same news program, two playing cartoons and one with some kind of computer menu displayed. There were three people dressed all in green, with hair nets, even though one was a guy, but they seem hurried and unapproachable. To her right it was quieter and she saw a policeman standing, looking around. That seemed to be the way to go, so she walked over to the officer, but, not seeing her coming, he turned away and walked through a door which looked like a mirror when Ellie got to it, and she was afraid to walk through it because it might be for police business. She looked around the corner behind the mirrored door, hoping for another way into the police station, if that was what it was, but there was only another small waiting room, a turned-off TV and a half-dozen chairs, all empty. She saw against the far wall a line of wheelchairs, and she tried to get one to take out to the pickup, but she couldn't figure out how to get it loose from the rest. There was a long empty corridor ahead of her, and she ran to the nearest door, and the next one, but both were closed. She now ran back to the other side, where the TVs were playing, and up to one of the women dressed in green.

"Can you help me? My teacher..."

"I'm busy, honey. Talk to the people in triage." She pointed back towards the entrance, then turned and hurried through a set of swinging doors. Ellie walked back to EMERGENCY TRIAGE, but the lines were even longer now, so she went back outside to see what Mr. Butler thought she should do. The pickup, however, was gone and he was nowhere in sight. Now near panic, she ran back inside and to the right and knocked on the mirrored door. The door opened.

"Can you help me, sir?"

The officer, who was very tall and wore both a gun and a stick on his belt, knelt down to be closer to her level. "What do you need, Missy?"

"My teacher, Mr. Butler, is hurt and now I can't find him."

"Well, maybe he's in the restroom there. I'll just go have a look. Butler, you say?"

"Yes, but no. He couldn't walk so good so I don't think he's in there."

"How did you get here?"

"He drove, but I rode along to help."

"Why didn't you call nine-one-one?"

"Mr. Butler said they'd never find us out here."

"Well, where did you see him last?"

"In the pickup, outside the doors. But now the truck is gone and so is he."

"Maybe he decided he wasn't hurt so bad and went home."

"He wouldn't leave me here. Besides, I have his phone."

"Okay, come on, Missy, we'll find him." The officer stood up and Ellie followed him as he cut line at the EMERGENCY TRIAGE window. The glass slid open for him, but the officer first spoke to the woman who was first in line. "Excuse me, ma'am, but this should just take a minute." Then turning to the window, "Jill, this little girl seems to have misplaced her patient. Have you processed a Butler? What's his first name, Missy?"

But before she could answer, the woman named Jill spoke. "Right here. Samuel C. Butler. Medicare patient. Head wound, multiple contusions. Intake seven minutes ago. They took him straight inside."

"What happened to his vehicle, do you know?"

"The orderly moved it to the parking lot. I've got the keys here. Green Toyota pickup, Ark tag JRA six-seven-three."

"Okay. That's what we need. Your pardon again, ma'am." This last to the woman now moving up to the window.

The officer walked Ellie to a chair, just by the entrance. "Why don't you sit right here, Missy, and I'll be looking in on you from time to time; I'll be right on the other side of those mirrors. You can't see in, but I can see out. In a little bit, we'll check to see how your Mr. Butler is doing, but we don't want to bother the docs right now. But can you tell me your name?" He pulled a small spiral notebook out of his pocket.

"Ellen Quincy."

"Okay, Ellen, you've got a phone—maybe you should call somebody to come and help you. Now stay right here where I can watch you."

Ellie sat down where she was told and tried calling her mother again, but got only the voice mail. "Mommy, Mr. Butler is in the hospital and I'm here with him. I don't know what to do. Please turn on the phone and call me. Please. Bye." After she hung up, she sat with her eyes closed and tried not to cry. She hadn't called her mother Mommy for a couple of years, and when it sort of slipped out, it made her feel little again and she thought she couldn't do that as long as Mr. Butler needed her.

She opened her eyes and looked around. People were still milling about, coming and going, standing in line and sometimes being taken in through the swinging doors by one of the people dressed in green, whom Ellie decided must be nurses, even though some of them were guys. The TVs were still going, but hardly anyone was watching and it was hard to hear anyway. The fish were pretty, but she didn't know why there were fish in the hospital. The old woman in the wheelchair moaned softly, but seemed to be asleep.

Next to her chair there was a small table with a plastic flower, a couple of magazines and a copy of the Holy Bible. Ellie picked up the Bible and held it in both hands in her lap. She immediately relaxed, as it reminded her that God was here in the hospital with her and Mr. Butler, and everything was going to be all right. She didn't read any passages, or even open it, but just felt the comfort of holding the Book in her lap.

She dialed her mother's number again, now feeling a little better, but hung up when she got the voice mail. And it was just then, as she was closing her own little red flip-phone, that Mr. Butler's iPhone rang in her pocket. She had forgotten that she was still carrying it. She took it out and looked at the screen and it read "STRATFORD." She wasn't completely for sure what to do, as she had never answered anyone's phone before, but then she decided she should.

"Hello?"

Lynda Stratford sat at a computer screen in the control room of the advanced laser lab at the university, holding her phone to her ear with her left hand while navigating the mouse with her right.

"Who's this?" She knew she hadn't misdialed.

"My name is Ellen Quincy," the voice said.

"Where's Samuel?"

"He's in there with the doctors."

"In where? Where are you and why do you have his phone?"

"There was an accident and he got kicked and he had me help him to the big pickup and he drove here, but I came along to help. Now the policeman says he's in with the doctors, but I haven't seen him. Could you come here, please? I'm just a little kid and I don't know what to do."

"Yes, of course, I'll be right there. Where are you?"

"At the hospital."

"But which one?"

"I don't know."

"Fayetteville or Springdale?"

"Fayetteville, I think."

"Or Rogers?"

"I'm not sure. Fayetteville, I think."

"*You think.* Not good enough. Okay, so look around and tell me what you see. Somewhere it must have the name of the hospital."

"Well, there are these sliding glass windows with workers behind. It says 'emergency triage' over the top." She pronounced it *TRY-age.*

"Triage. Okay, so you're in the ER. Go up and ask them which hospital you're at."

"There's a line."

"Argh. Look around. Pick anyone who looks nice and isn't bleeding. Got someone?"

"I guess."

"Okay, go over and say 'excuse me, but which hospital is this?'"

"Okay." Ellie walked, holding the phone to her ear, until she stood before a matronly-looking woman, as old as her grandmother, wearing a red dress. "Excuse me, which hospital is this?"

"*¿Como?*"

"I don't think she speaks English."

"Christ Almighty."

"Please don't do that."

"What?"

"Use the Lord's name."

At that point, a man a couple of seats down from the Spanish-speaker said, "Little girl? This is Washington Regional."

"Thank you, sir. He says it's Washington."

"Great. Now sit down and stay put. I'll be there in ten minutes." Lynda broke the connection without waiting for a reply, and sat back in her chair. "Well, shit." If she shut down the experiment that was running she'd lose two weeks' worth of data. But she couldn't let it run unattended, and her post-doc was teaching and wouldn't be by to relieve her for a half-hour. She looked around the control room, but she was alone. "Shitshit. Fuck." She glanced again at the monitor, then got up and walked quickly to the door. The corridor was empty except for one dark-eyed coed walking toward her, her hair pulled back in a ponytail, and wearing a pink and green *ZTA* sweatshirt.

"You there. I need you in here right now."

"What?" The coed took out one ear plug. "Did you say something to me?"

"Yes. I'm Dr. Stratford and I need you in here right now." Lynda held the door to the control room open for her, trying to watch the monitor across the room.

"Uh, I've got class in ten minutes."

"What class?"

"Calc two."

"I'll cover for you, but there's been an emergency and I need to be at the hospital right now. Please, come in here."

"I don't know. The prof's got a pretty strict attendance policy and..."

"God damn it, get in here. I will take care of your Calc prof when I get back from the hospital. Trust me. I will perform oral sex on him if need be, but..."

The coed laughed. "*She*, actually. I think she's just a TA."

"Even better. *Please* come in here." The coed seemed to surrender and she walked into the control room. "Okay, sit here and all you have to do is one thing. Okay? See this read-out right here?" Lynda pointed to the screen. "If it varies more than half of one percent, then click right there..." Another point. "...on ABORT. That's it. Sit here and watch that read-out. No texting. No talking on the phone. No tweeting. No nothing. Watch that read-out. My post-doc will be here," she checked the clock on the wall, "in seventeen minutes. He's never late. His name is Chang and he looks Chinese, but he's actually from Singapore. Give him all the info about your Calc two class, and I'll cover for you. Remember: plus or minus half of a percent and shut it down."

"How much is half of one percent?"

"Jesus help me. You're in Calc two; you figure it out." Lynda grabbed her phone, her iPad and her keys and headed for the door. On the way out she stopped and said, "What's your name?"

"Gina. Gina Lucini."

"Okay. Thanks, Gina. And half of one percent is two point seven micro-Joules. More than that, plus or minus, and pull the plug. Have Chang call me when he gets a chance."

It took Lynda three minutes to run to her car, parked in a reserved spot in the Harmon Street garage, and seven minutes to drive to Washington Regional. She broke several local traffic ordinances on the way, ran through two lights very late in the yellow, and the one time she was caught dead to rights by the red, she did stop, but then jumped the green in front of the opposing left turn arrow, and pulled into the parking lot at the Washington Regional emergency room not much more than the ten minutes she had told Ellie to wait.

She walked quickly through the double sliding doors, noting both the floor mat saying "Welcome to Washington Regional Medical Center" and the young girl sitting by herself holding a Bible. That must be Ellie, but Lynda walked right past, ignoring both the girl and the triage attendants, and directly through the double swinging doors into ER treatment. Lynda had realized on the mad dash to Washington Regional that, with her lab coat, her iPad, her university ID on a lanyard around her neck, and the radiation dosimeter on her lapel, she could probably pass for a physician. A stethoscope across her shoulder would have helped but there was no time for that. What the heck, she could be a psychiatrist. Through the swinging doors, she spotted the nurse's station and presented herself there.

"I'm Dr. Stratford." She flashed the ID in the direction of the nurse. "Did you check in a Samuel Butler this morning?"

The nurse bought the role-play without question. She consulted a chart and said, "Yes, Doctor. He's in Room Three. Dr. Rose is with him."

"Room Three. Thank you." Lynda turned, quickly saw the exam room numbers and which way they ran, so that, with only a moment's hesitation, she could take the correct step in the right direction. She wasn't sure whether the protocol would be to knock or just walk into the exam room, but she was saved that difficulty as a middle-aged man in scrubs walked out of Room Three just as she approached.

"Dr. Rose?" She thought not to shake hands. "I'm Dr. Stratford. Lynda Stratford. Is Samuel Butler in there?"

Rose consulted a chart in his hand. "Butler? Yes. Sixty-eight year old white male. Are you his PCP?"

"No, just a friend. I was walking through the ER and checked the intake manifest and saw his name. What's going on?"

"Well, he's a tough old bird, I'll give him that. Says he was kicked by one of his horses. He took two blows to the body and one to the head, but I think the head wound must have come when he hit the ground. He's got a deep contusion on the right forearm and the ulna is probably bruised, but it's not fractured. The fifth and sixth ribs on the right are separated, and I think his right lung partially collapsed, but it's okay now. Mild concussion, twelve scalp sutures, couple of facial lacerations, broken nose, but no skull fracture, which is why I don't think he was kicked in the head."

"Are you going to admit him?"

"No, I don't think so. I've got him sedated right now, and he's going to think a truck hit him when he wakes up. But he'll heal and be okay. Unless he sneezes that is."

"Sneezes?"

"The ribs."

"Right. Did you wrap his chest?"

A look of confusion passed over Rose's face. "Of course not. He said something about driving himself here from Madison County and he was concerned about his neighbor girl who came along. Know anything about that?"

"She's out front. I'll take care of her."

"He won't be able to drive himself home, that's for sure. It's a miracle he got here at all. He says the girl helped him, but I don't know how she could have."

"I'll get him home as soon as you're ready to release him."

Rose looked at his watch. "Let's give him half an hour. He'll still be sedated, but I'd like to be sure about that lung. If it's okay, I'll release him to you."

"I'll be outside."

Back in the waiting room, Lynda walked over to where Ellie sat with the Bible and the two phones. "You must be Samuel's little guardian angel." She sat down in the next chair over.

"Are you the lady who called?"

"I am. My name's Lynda. You're Ellie, no?"

"Ellen Quincy."

"Nice to meet you, Ellen Quincy. They tell me in there that you're a hero." She gestured with her head toward the swinging doors.

"Are you a doctor?"

"Not the kind you mean."

"But how could you walk in there like that? I thought it was just for doctors."

"Well, I'll tell you, Ellie. I had to lie just a little bit. Or at least not tell the whole truth."

"But what if they caught you?"

"Then I get caught. But sometimes it's hard to get permission, you know what I mean?" Lynda winked, then looked up to see a police officer approaching the two of them.

"Do you know this girl, ma'am?"

"Well, actually, officer, we just now met. We have a mutual friend who's a little banged up in there."

"What was his name again?"

"Samuel Butler. You seem suspicious of me."

"I told the young lady that I'd look out for her, and that's what I'm doing. Let's start at the beginning—your name is...?" The officer extracted the little notebook from his pocket again.

"Gwendolynda Stratford. *Doctor* Stratford." She flashed her ID.

"And you don't know Dr. Stratford, Missy?"

"Not really."

"So why..." this directed to Lynda, "...why do you suppose I should surrender custody of this girl to you?"

"Well, you could trust me."

"Or not."

"Do I fit the profile of a child molester?"

"There is no profile."

Ellie spoke up. "Her name came up on Mr. Butler's phone when she called."

"Voilà," said Lynda. "The guardian angel is smart, too. Look here, officer..." She pulled out her phone and held it so he could see the screen. "Now, here in my speed dial list is..." she scrolled down, "...ta da, Samuel Butler. And...if I call it..." she pressed *call*, "...moments later..." she gestured toward Ellie with her left hand, just as Sam's phone rang. Ellie held it up so the officer could see: "STRATFORD."

"I think I'm convinced. If you'll just let me make a copy of your ID there..."

"Why?"

"When a child shows up in the ER unattended, the Fayetteville police are interested, and I opened a file on her. I'll put a copy of your ID in the file and close it. That will, I suspect, keep my captain happy. If you please..." He held out his hand for the ID and Lynda surrendered it, and watched as he walked back to the room behind the mirrored windows.

"So, where are we, now that I'm apparently off the hook as a suspected kidnapper?"

"Did you see Mr. Butler?"

"No. But his doctor said he'd be ready to go home in a little bit."

"Is he going to be all right?"

"Yes, or so says Dr. Rose. Who's coming to see us now." She nodded toward Rose walking their way. "Dr. Rose..."

"Dr.... what was it?"

"Stratford."

"Doctor of what?"

"Ouch. I'm busted. Philosophy. Physics, actually. What blew my cover?"

"We haven't wrapped separated ribs for fifty years."

"Why not?"

"Wrapping the chest restricts the depth of the breathing. The dangerous part of separated ribs is that by breathing shallow, fluid builds up in the lungs and pneumonia sets in, which, at his age, could kill him. So, he's got to keep breathing, even if it hurts. He'll heal. Here..." he handed Lynda two slips of paper. "One is for Percocet against the pain, so he'll be able to breathe deeply. No refills and don't let him take them too eagerly."

"I've heard." She raised her eyebrows.

"I'm serious."

"I know you are."

"And the other prescription is an antibiotic against infection, though the only wounds that were exposed to the air and soil are the head lacerations, and they bled themselves pretty clean. Plus, this young lady applied a nice head bandage with, I'm told, some veterinary treatment. I wish I knew what the veterinary medicine was, but we'll just have to do."

Ellie spoke up. "It's called HEW." She pronounced it *hugh*.

Rose raised his eyebrows to Lynda, who said, "I'd believe her. I've stopped being surprised by her perspicacity."

Rose looked around the emergency waiting room before raising his voice. "Hey, Barb. Got a minute?"

A nurse jotting some notes onto a chart looked up. "My shift ends in ten minutes..."

"Less than that." She walked over. "Look up a veterinary medication called Hugh and see what's in it."

The nurse pulled out her phone, touched the screen three times and then asked, "*Hugh*? How are you spelling that?"

"H-U-G-H, I suppose. Maybe it's Hughes. H-U-G-H-E-S," said Rose.

Ellie spoke up again. "H-E-W. Mr. Butler calls it the goop. But he calls lots of stuff goop. It's this greasy stuff that comes in a jar?" Her little uptalk at the end was the first indication since she had discovered the accident that she was beginning to relax.

The nurse touched the screen three more times. "Here it is. Zero point two percent nitrofurazone. 'Has been shown to cause mammary tumors in rats. For use in equids only.' I wonder why that?"

"Because we don't eat them. Okay, I guess that our sixty-eight year-old male patient doesn't have to worry much about nascent mammary tumors, but the little girl? Maybe. I don't suppose you used gloves?" Ellie shook her head. "Did you wash your hands?" Another shake. "Okay, the nurse here will take you into the back and wash you up good, just before she goes off duty, okay, Barb?" Turning back to Lynda, "Okay, so the antibiotics are just to be safe. Take them all. Starting tonight. Any questions?"

"Anything we should watch for?"

"Dizziness. Loss of balance. Shortness of breath. Blood in the urine."

"And if...?"

"Back in here. Pronto. And he should see his PCP sometime this week for a checkup. Anything else?" Lynda shook her head. "Well, I've got one more thing. Don't *ever* do that again."

"Right."

"I'll have an orderly bring him out in a few minutes. He'll still be woozy from the sedative. Good bye."

"Doctor."

As Rose walked away, Lynda bent down and whispered in Ellie's ear. "See, Angel? It's easier to get forgiveness than permission. Remember that. So, you go get washed up by the nurse, while I take care of the logistics." Ellie departed, and Lynda pulled out her phone again and dialed Jonathan's number, getting his voice mail. "Hey, listen. I'm at the Washington Regional ER. Sam Butler got himself kicked by one of his pampered equids. He's going to be okay, but I've got to get him home. He drove himself here with the neighbor girl in tow, but now he's in la-la land, and she's practically catatonic with the fright of it all. So, I'll take Sam and little Miss Jesus-loves-me back out to the home in the hills with my car, and here's what you have to do, darlin': get a ride over here and drive Sam's truck to his house, where I'll meet you. It's a green Toyota pickup with a university parking sticker. It shouldn't be hard to find. The keys are probably with the attendant at triage. They'll be expecting you. Bye. See you out there." She made kissing noises and broke the connection.

A few minutes later an orderly rolled Sam out in a wheelchair, his arm in a sling, a head bandage, a white tape across his nose, looking old, sheepish, and stoned. He blinked his eyes in confusion, then looked up at Lynda. "Where did you come from?"

"I called you, young Ellen picked up and I left a three million dollar, tax-payer-funded experiment in the care of a sorority girl to rush to your bedside. A place I've been wanting to rush to for months now."

At this point, Ellie arrived, having been scrubbed and then abandoned by the nurse to find her own way back to the waiting room. "Are you going to be okay, Mr. Butler?"

"Hey, pard. What day of the year is it?"

"I don't remember. Are you going to be okay?"

But Sam's eyes drooped and his head dropped.

"Is he going to be okay?"

"He's just sleepy. Thank you, Mr. Orderly," Lynda said. "We'll take it from here."

"My service goes all the way to curbside, ma'am. If you'll pull your car up to the doors there, I'll help him in."

Lynda's Volvo was fetched, Sam was roused enough to be installed in the front seat, covered by a blanket presumably paid for by Medicare, with Ellie in the rear. The officer showed up to return Lynda's ID, which she had forgotten. He took a cell-phone photo of the car and its tag, and off they went. A stop at Walgreen's to fill the prescriptions went smoothly enough, except that Lynda had to pay because Sam, who was now asleep, couldn't direct them to the pharmacy that kept his insurance records, and Ellie forgot that she was still carrying his Medicare card.

The ride out to Madison County was uneventful, though the car became something of a mobile communications center as one by one all of the phones in the car began to ring. Chang called to say that the test was running smoothly and that Gina Lucini had done her job perfectly. It turned out that her Calc two TA was a PhD candidate in physics whom Chang knew and there would be no problem there. He was free to stay until ten when the over-night crew would show up to relieve him. He had other work to do in the lab, so it was no inconvenience at all for him, and for Lynda to take care of her emergency, which he hoped was turning out well.

Almost simultaneously, Ellie's phone rang and it was her mother, full of remorse for having forgotten to turn the phone on, but why hadn't she called David or her grandmother? Ellie said she hadn't thought of it. Cardinal wanted to speak to Sam, but he was still asleep, but Dr. Rose said he was going to be all right, and they had stopped for his pills. Cardinal said, "Where are you?" and that she would meet them all at Sam's house in ten minutes. Lynda said, "Fifteen," but by then Cardinal had hung up.

Lynda's phone rang again and it was Jonathan, wondering how Sam was. He said that he would just drive himself to Washington Regional, find Sam's pickup, leave his car there and drive on out. He could then ride back to the hospital with Lynda and pick up his car, but that he couldn't do any of that until about three o'clock, so she could hang out with Sam until four or so, if she was free to do that. She was, see you soon.

At which point Sam's phone rang and it was Melissa Wyckoff, Ellie's grandmother, who had gotten the number from Cardinal. Sam was still asleep and Ellie was still answering Sam's phone, so she filled her grandmother in on where they were and what had happened and that Dr. Rose had said that Mr. Butler was going to be okay.

Of course, neither Lynda nor Ellie knew precisely what had happened; no one did, really. But then Sam woke up and began to speak, perfectly clearly and as if he were in the middle of a conversation. "...well and Dee just fired off and I hit the..." He looked around. "Whose car is this?"

"Mine."

He looked over at Lynda. "How did you get here?"

"I'll explain later."

"Where's Ellie?"

"I'm back here."

Sam turned to look in the back, but caught himself with a groan. "What happened to me?"

"You tell us."

"I mean what happened to me?"

"Busted ribs. Bruised ulna. Mild concussion. Why don't you just sit back and relax? We're almost there. Ellie, scoot over so he can see you just by turning his head. Your little guardian angel did good, Samuel. You owe her."

"Who?"

"Ellie."

"I think I..." but his head drooped and he slept again.

"What's 'fired off' mean, Angel?" Lynda asked.

"When a horse kicks without aiming. Like automatic."

"Um hmm. I believe our old friend Samuel Butler could have been killed this morning." They rode in silence the rest of the way into Madison County, with no more phones ringing, and Sam only waking once to say, "I don't know who Kim Kardashian is," and then falling back asleep.

"Why did he ask that?"

"He's about two sheets to the wind. Why did he ask you what day it was?"

"What day of the year. It's a game we play."

"Well, what day of the year *is* it, Angel?"

"I don't feel like playing."

"Okay. Anyway, here we are."

"If you go down there," Ellie pointed over the front seat and out the windshield, "and across the creek, you can drive up on the grass and to the house."

"Thank you. I didn't know there was any other way."

"Most people park down here with the pickups. See? There's my four-wheeler. It looks funny with the big pickup missing."

"The times I've driven out, I've always parked by the house."

"That's my mom's car. And my grandma's."

Indeed, when Lynda pulled her Volvo up to the house, Cardinal, David and Melissa were all standing on the porch, looking over the railing. Ellie was out of the backseat and shortly in her mother's arms, jabbering and finally crying, trying to tell the entire story at once. Her grandmother joined the embrace.

David gave her a pat on the head in approval, then walked down the steps and introduced himself to Lynda, not shaking hands. He peered in through the driver's side window.

"Better get him into the house."

"Which'll be impossible if he doesn't help. My husband is coming and the two of you could probably manhandle him up the stairs, but he won't be here for another hour at least. Well, hell, I guess we could just leave the old bastard sleeping there for a while."

"I'd ask you, ma'am, to watch your language around the women."

"The women folk. Please."

"The little girl, then."

"Ahhh, right. I've already been instructed in that regard by your daughter there, but…well, there it is."

"She's actually my step-daughter, not my daughter."

"I thought you had adopted her."

"I did, but I don't think that makes her my daughter."

"Actually, I think that's exactly what it makes her." The tension built for a minute before Lynda said, "Let's see if we can wake him." They could, and they got Sam standing beside the car. "His right-side ribs are busted so why don't you take the left side, David, and Samuel, lean on David."

"Are his ribs wrapped?"

"Really, David, we haven't wrapped busted ribs for fifty years."

"Oh."

"Just kidding. I didn't know it either until this afternoon. Okay, Samuel, set course for the porch stairs. Here we go." Sam's left arm was across David's shoulders and his right in a sling, supported under his right armpit by Lynda's left hand, and they got him moving in the correct direction and up the steps. Cardinal and Melissa managed the doors into the kitchen, and once inside, Lynda said, "Who knows the layout? Couch or bed, what do you think, Ellen's mom?"

Cardinal laughed. "I'm Cardinal. That's my mom, Melissa. You've met David, my husband. I think upstairs, to the bedroom. The bathroom is up there and he'll need that more than he needs the kitchen. Ellie, lead the way."

The stairs were too narrow for three-across, so Lynda fell back and David and Sam went up slowly, two steps for each riser.

"Let's see," Lynda said, "I think sit him on the side of his bed for a minute while we get organized. Angel? Did you grab the sack of pills? Why don't you run down and get them?"

"Her name's Ellen," said David.

"Term of affection." Ellie left to fetch the pills and the four adults formed a half-circle in front of Sam, who was awake, but just barely, and blinking his eyes.

"My room," he observed. "I have to pee."

"I suggest that Melissa and I see to Samuel's needs, while you and David, Cardinal, rustle him some grub."

"Thirsty."

"Hungry?" Sam shook his head. "Okay, pal, what will it be?"

"Coke."

"And ice, I think, Cardinal."

David was clearly uncomfortable with this division of labor. "I think I should help him with the bathroom, shouldn't I?" He was just as clearly uncomfortable in equal measure with the idea of helping Sam urinate.

"Get lost, Dave. I was trained as a nurse, and I'm guessing that if Melissa hasn't seen a man piss, she's read about it. We'll get him into bed, Cardinal, get him his Coke, and David, you get the pills figured out... Ah, the pills."

Ellie entered the room, having been spared the discussion of Sam's personal needs, but she immediately identified another. "What about the horses?"

Lynda whistled. "The guardian angel comes through again. She's smart as a tack. Wanna be my lab assistant, honey? So...there we are. Melissa and I will get him horizontal, Cardinal bring him his drink and whatever pills he should take now, and Dave and the angel can organize the chores. Now, give us a little privacy and we'll reconvene in the kitchen."

When the others left, Melissa asked, "How do we get this done?"

"Still have to pee, Samuel?" He nodded. "Anything else?" He shook his head. "Okay, stand up, lean on me. Prepare the way, Melissa: lid up, seat down."

In the bathroom, Sam turned toward the toilet, but Lynda said, "No, sir," and turned him the other way. "You'll sit. We don't trust your aim."

"Sit?"

"Sit."

"I just have to pee."

"Sit." Sam looked confused, but began to fumble with his belt buckle.

"Allow me." Lynda undid the belt and pulled his jeans down below his knees, then looked up at Melissa. "You okay with this? I can take it from here…"

"The up and down might be tricky," Melissa said. "I'll stay to help."

Quickly, Lynda pulled Sam's shorts down, then the two of them, one under each arm, lowered him onto the commode.

"You may begin."

"I don't need you two looking…"

"Right. We'll prepare the bed. Call us when you're finished. *Do not* try to stand up on your own."

"Shut the door."

"Leave it open. Don't flush; the doc said to watch for blood in your urine. Call us when you're ready." Lynda and Melissa exited the bathroom and heard the door being pushed shut behind them.

"I wouldn't have expected him to be a difficult patient," Melissa said.

"I would have."

"You know him better than I, I suppose. I actually just met him down in the kitchen, and he's half-stoned. But Ellie talks about him all the time. Do you think we should bathe him? I noticed he still has some blood on his face."

"I think face and arms only. The rest can wait until morning."

"It'll be easier to do where he's sitting right now. That way, it won't get the bed wet."

"Right. When he calls. What about pajamas?"

"I suppose we can find something in the dresser there."

"I'm thinking not to bother. It will be hard to get the bottoms on, and it will hurt him to get his arms in the tops. Skivvies only?"

"It might be cool tonight."

"Help!" This from the bathroom.

"We're coming. We can find an extra blanket somewhere against the cool air."

"And I'll turn up the thermostat downstairs."

Back in the bathroom, Sam was standing by the commode. He'd managed to pull his shorts up, but "It hurts to reach my pants."

Lynda looked behind Sam into the toilet. "Clear as lemonade." She flushed and put the lid down. "Sit." He did. "Now step out of your jeans; you won't be needing them. Melissa, I'll wash; you see if you can find the extra cover."

Cardinal arrived back upstairs with the Coke and the pills just as Lynda and Melissa were getting Sam into bed and covered over. "I finally found a straw in the pantry; I thought that would make it easier."

"Good work. What does the prescription say?"

"Two antibiotics right now and then one every eight hours. Repeat for five days. Pain: maximum of four in a day, no refills. I think we should hold off on the first one until he begins to complain. What do you think?"

"Perfect," said Lynda, and Melissa nodded. Lynda sat on the edge of the bed, "Okay, honey. Take your medicine. There's two; one at a time?" Sam took the pills, then drained the glass of Coke.

"Good," he said.

"Why don't you try to get some sleep, Sam?" Cardinal said.

"We'll all be down in the kitchen, Samuel. Holler if you need anything. Try and get out of bed without one of us here to help and you'll think that horse kicked you again. Hear me?"

"Go away."

"I mean it. Let's go, girls."

Downstairs, David was staring out the front door while Ellie was at work with pencil and paper.

"Whatch doin', Sweetie?" Melissa asked.

"Making a chart of the chores."

"My God, she's the perfect guardian angel. So, it's about three o'clock. Jonathan should be here pretty soon. What's next?"

"I think someone should spend the night here with him," said Cardinal.

"Natch," said Lynda. "I volunteer."

"I'm not sure that would be proper," said David, turning back to the group.

"Which hardly merits a response..."

Melissa broke in, "David, you've got your chores with the chickens. Cardinal's got the babies. Ellie's too young. So, it's either me or Lynda. She's got her work at the university during the day, but I'm free. So, Lynda takes the night shift and I'll take the day. There's no other way." She shook her head. "No, darn it, that won't work either. Stuart has a webinar scheduled for the next three days, and I've got to be on the board."

"Mom, if you take the boys home with you tonight and let them hang out at the studio tomorrow, I'll bring Esther over in the morning and look after Sam."

"The boys at the studio?" Melissa rolled her eyes ceiling-ward.

"So, maybe my husband can take the day shift. Today's Monday, so he's got no classes tomorrow. He can look after Samuel and work on their project at the same time."

"That should work, but can he do it?"

"When he gets here, we'll know."

"But what about Wednesday?"

"Do you really think he'll need help that long?" Cardinal asked. "He's not going to be an invalid, after all."

"Okay," said Lynda, "I'll spend the night, but I'm going to have to be gone by...say six-thirty. Six would be better. Either Jonathan stays during the day or... Cardinal?"

She nodded. "And David and Ellie can come over about when? To do the horse chores."

"Eight or so," said Ellie. "I wrote everything down. Feed and water in the morning. Check on them in the afternoon, and feed again at night. Mister's been getting a little extra hay and..."

"You and David can take care of the morning. What about tonight?"

"Is your husband going to spend the night?" David asked. "He could help with the evening feed."

"Depends on his schedule. We'll see. Angel, leave careful instructions that I can follow..."

"We've got one injured party upstairs in bed," said Cardinal, "kicked by a horse. We don't need two more. No way are we going to leave you two greenhorns to take care of the horses..."

"Okay, so David and Ellie do the horses, morning, noon and night, starting tonight, until Sam is up and around. Lynda stays tonight and her husband to-morrow during the day. We'll re-evaluate the situation tomorrow night." Melissa looked around the circle and everyone nodded.

"Now," said David, holding out his hands and taking Cardinal's in his right and Melissa's in his left, "we've neglected too long to say thanks to the Lord for delivering Sam from his accident. Join our circle, Ellen. Lynda."

"Well, I'll tell you what, guys. Why don't you take care of the thanksgiving and I'll check upstairs."

"It would be best if we all joined in. Please give Ellen your hand."

"I'm afraid I'd short-circuit the whole deal. Or the roof would collapse. Really. I'll just slip upstairs and check on our boy. Carry on without me. Please."

Upstairs there was little to check on. Sam was asleep on his back, snoring softly. Lynda felt his cheek for a fever, but it was cool, and she then tried to move his hair around into some order. She picked up his bloody, dirty clothes, looked around and found a laundry basket in the closet, which was full enough to justify doing a load later when she was alone. She could still hear the murmurings of David's prayer coming up the stairwell, so she sat on the end of the bed, gently massaging Sam's foot, waiting for the prayer session to end, wondering what Jonathan would think if he walked into the middle of it. He would handle it smoothly and diplomatically, of course, bless his heart; he had the ability to soothe people, even strangers, even religious strangers who were at this moment pestering the God of the Entire Universe with news of a minor concussion, a couple of separated ribs and a bruised ulna.

It became quiet down in the kitchen, but who knew what that meant? The Lord had hung up? David had run out of thanks to give? Perhaps the givings of thanks were proceeding silently? Assuming they wouldn't forget about her, but tired of sitting, Lynda stood up and looked around the upstairs, finding her way into the study. Unlike the rest of the house, it had a disheveled look about it—one desk drawer ajar, books in boxes, with gaps on the shelves. It looked like he was moving, or at least clearing out, about which Lynda knew nothing, but was vaguely interested.

She was browsing the bookshelves when Jonathan walked in behind her, crossed his arms in front of her to hold her close, and kissed her neck.

"Well, hello." She leaned back into his embrace. "I didn't hear you come in. Did the prayer meeting break up?"

"They were just finishing when I walked in."

"You were introduced around?"

"I was; did it myself. Cute girl, attractive mother, handsome grandmother. The guy—David—seems not to entirely approve of you. Likewise is my guess. Poor baby." His right hand slipped down to cup her left breast and she turned her head and opened her mouth to him.

"Ummm. The sparks flew almost immediately."

"And how's Butler? The word downstairs was that he's going to pull through."

"He was kicked, but it looks like the hooves landed a good ten inches short of being fatal. He's asleep now. I'm going to spend the night here, okay? You can stay, or come get me in the morning." She kissed him deeply again, then, "We should go down."

Back in the kitchen, Jonathan quickly nixed the plans. "No classes tomorrow, but it's advising week, and I've got a dozen impossible-to-reschedule meetings with students. Sorry. Do we have any other options?"

"Ellie and David will do the early horse chores," said Cardinal, "and I'll come over with the kids and relieve Lynda. We'll do morning prayers here, David, then you'll leave to take care of the chickens and the rest of us will hang out here, helping Sam with what he needs. Ellie can do her school work here. I'll make supper and then we'll see."

The last detail concerned the vehicles. Jonathan had left his car at the hospital and had driven Sam's pickup home, which would have been fine, but now the two of them needed separate rides back to town, and they only had the Volvo at Sam's.

"I'll just have to drive out early and pick you up." His disinterest in this prospect was unmistakable in Jonathan's voice.

"Here—this will work better," said Melissa. "Cardinal, I'll spend tonight at your place, then I'll pick Lynda up early in the morning and we'll drive in together..."

"Which means that you might as well stay here tonight, Mom, and let Lynda go home with Jonathan."

Lynda shook her head. "This is getting way too complicated. We've got the who's-staying-where-when figured out. And I accept your offer, Melissa, for a ride in tomorrow. Six, if you can do that. Six-thirty if you can't."

"Six is do-able. And it will get me into town nice and early."

And with that, the group split up, Ellie and David to return for the evening feed, Melissa to arrive early in the morning, and Cardinal somewhat later. Everyone left, the house became quiet, Sam slept comfortably, and Lynda started a load of laundry and looked around for something to prepare for dinner.

**The Next Morning.**

Melissa walked into the kitchen at six sharp to find Lynda sitting at the kitchen table with a cup of coffee, Skype-ing Chang on her iPad. She nodded at Melissa and said to the screen, "My ride's here. I'll see you in the lab in forty-five minutes or maybe an hour—I've got to fetch Jonathan's car at the hospital—it depends on how fast my ride drives." Lynda lifted an eyebrow at Melissa, who made a so-so gesture with her right hand. "Make it an hour and a quarter. You'll have to brief the team; Romero will be up against her history class at eight. So, are we straight? At one p.m. today, we'll go to protocol one-two-one-A, and maintain that for five hundred hours, then evaluate. Check?"

"One-two-one-A. One p.m. Central. Check. Take your time; we'll be fine. See you back here."

"Out." Lynda ended the call and shut down her tablet. "Ready?"

"Ready. Sam?"

"Is asleep again. He ate well at about nine last night, complaining in three equal parts about the pain, being fussed over and my choice for dinner. I gave him a Percocet and ignored the rest. He then slept through the night until about four, when he woke up to pee and was pretty sore again. This time I gave him a half-tab, and put him back to bed. I've left Cardinal a note about last night and this morning." She gestured at a sheet of paper on the table. "If you talk to her, tell her not to take any shit from him about what she fixes for breakfast. And that he hasn't had his antibiotics yet this morning."

"We should go, to get you to your meeting. Cardinal will be over shortly. I assume Sam will be all right alone until then?"

"I'm sure he will be."

In Melissa's car, the radio was set to the local Christian station that carried Stuart's program, but she quickly changed to the campus NPR affiliate.

"Steve Inskeep annoys me," Lynda said, and Melissa snapped off the radio. "I didn't mean for you to turn it off. Only that he annoys me." They rode in silence along the dirt road until Melissa turned onto the highway heading west toward Fayetteville. "It was nice to meet your family. I'm especially impressed with Samuel's guardian angel."

"Ellie asked me to ask you not to call her that."

"It's a term of affection. And admiration."

"She perceives, correctly I suspect, that you're making fun of her. She's a little girl, remember, and she takes her religion seriously."

Ellie had proposed several times in the months after Cardinal's second marriage and her own adoption, had proposed first to her mother, then to David, that she should be baptized. As much as anything, I suppose, her desire was based on a need to belong to something, anything, more than it was on a willingness to commit her life to Jesus. She was, after all, only seven years old, and the very concept of life-long commitment to any One or any Thing was suspect, which led to David's steadfast refusal even to consider her baptism. In the end, then, and as with most things in her life as it was turning out, the event occurred at Ellie's own initiation and in a way that surprised even her mother, who had come to know better than anyone else her strong-willed daughter's independent ways.

Nine months after Cardinal married Brother David Quincy, Ellie sat with her mother and her grandparents one Wednesday evening in the little church in Wesley and listened, with a group of about twenty other parishioners, while David preached the Gospel, the lesson that evening being drawn from Peter's Second Epistle, Chapter 2. Halfway through, she stood up, excused herself and walked in front of Cardinal, Melissa and Stuart to the aisle between the rows of folding chairs. But instead of turning left, to exit the sanctuary to visit the restroom, which everyone in the church including David expected, she turned to the right and faced the altar. She was dressed in jeans and a tee shirt and her hair was loose to her shoulders, and she spread her hands to her sides, palms facing forward, and stood for what must have been a count of thirty. David stopped preaching. Cardinal, who was heavily pregnant at the time, leaned across in front of Stuart and asked if she was all right. The congregation waited, wondering if she were about to speak in tongues or something, a practice that would have been most unusual in David's church. Instead she stood, saying nothing, eyes closed, arms spread, palms forward. Then, still silent, she walked forward and fell to her knees in front of her step-father.

"What do you want, Ellen?" David asked, having been put off-kilter by the unexpected interruption.

She said nothing, but remained kneeling, arms still spread.

"I think she wants to be baptized, David," Melissa said.

"Is that what you want, Ellen? We're not set up for that tonight, but we can do it some Sunday."

Cardinal rolled her eyes heavenward, suspecting that such equivocation would accomplish nothing. And, she was right, as Ellie did not respond.

"Baptism is an important and sacred step, do you understand that, Ellen? And you must be immersed in the Living Water of our Lord Jesus."

She did not respond.

"Perhaps you could just say the words, David," Stuart said. "The immersion could come later, couldn't it?"

"Is that what you want, Ellen?" David asked.

Still she did not respond.

So David, not at all sure that he was doing the right thing, but uncomfortable with the way he appeared to be at a loss in front of his flock, put his hands on the kneeling child's head, and baptized her as Ellen Christine and the congregation prayed in celebration. Ellie never said a word throughout, but as she walked back to her chair, she was smiling contentedly.

Melissa stopped talking while a car sped past her on the left, crossing a double yellow line. "I've lived here since the Seventies and still can't get used to the way people drive."

"They are *very* patient about turning left in front of on-coming traffic."

"True. And they stop dead in the traffic lane when a funeral passes in the other direction. It about cost me my life years ago, learning that lesson."

"How so?"

"I was driving along at about sixty over on the west side of town, on the way to Prairie Grove. Straight road. A couple of cars ahead of me. A hearse with its lights on was coming the other way and I see the brake lights of the car in front of me go on. I sort of back off, watching the on-coming funeral. When I look back to the car in front, I realize he isn't just slowing down for the funeral; he's at a dead stop in my lane. I climb on the brakes, but there's no way I can get stopped. There's nowhere to go on the right, so I pull into the other lane, right into the teeth of the hearse, carrying the dearly departed and about to send me to the same place."

"What happened?"

"The hearse pulled onto the shoulder to his right, and so did the two following cars. By then I had room to pull back in front of the stopped car. I'm guessing that everyone involved was cursing me, excluding the deceased, but I didn't know the damn rule."

"Is it the law?"

Melissa shrugged. "I don't know. Ask Sam Butler. But sometimes custom trumps the law, at least in the people's day-to-day lives. And speaking of custom, Ellie will be bothered that you didn't join the prayer circle. That's rarely declined in rural Arkansas."

"I'm the first non-believer she's run into? There will be others."

"You're far from the first. Cardinal and her first husband ran with a pretty rough crowd. White trash, to say it plainly. They were non-believers who were not thoughtful enough to be skeptics. But they still would have held hands and bowed their heads, just out of old habits. In a way, I admire you for not partic-ipating in a ritual that you don't respect. I'm afraid that David's explanation is unlikely to be flattering to you, but I'll do what I can."

"I think it's just short of criminal, you know, that she's being home-schooled. She seems very bright and she deserves better."

"You mean it's a shame she's being *Christian* home-schooled, don't you?" Melissa glanced over from her driving.

"I'm actually less prejudiced than you think I am. No. Any home-schooling."

"You have something against learning at home? I'm guessing you learned plenty at home. I did."

"Not math." Melissa raised a skeptical eyebrow. "Okay, sure, some math, too. But my parents supplemented the formal, structured lessons that I got at school. And that kids need."

"You have a particular admiration for the Huntsville public schools?"

"About which I know nothing."

"Imagine the worst."

"Samuel's wife taught there. How bad could it be?"

"We didn't know her. But I said *imagine* the worst; I grant you that some-times one's imagination will miss the mark. I'm sure Sam's wife was both compe-tent and caring. That would not be typical, in my opinion. Recall that Cardinal herself went through the Huntsville system. She would know, don't you think?"

The conversation lapsed for a bit, until Lynda broke the silence. "Look. A child's education requires three things if it's going to be any good: competent teachers, teaching a rigorous curriculum, and parents who are involved in the education. I'll grant you that with home-schooled kids we can presume the third. But, I don't presume the first, and my suspicion is that a Christian curriculum is anything but rigorous, at least in science and math, and probably elsewhere. Maybe it's better than having the first two requirements without the third, but parental involvement by itself is nowhere near enough."

"Which, of course, is exactly why Sam Butler is teaching Ellie math."

"It doesn't bother you that Sam...well, I don't know what he thinks about religion. He's not a church-goer, but he had a Nativity scene in the living room at Christmas."

"Ellie set it up for him."

"I've heard the story. He was touched by the painted horse."

"I don't really know much about Sam..." Melissa laughed, "...beyond the fact that he's circumcised..." Lynda joined the laughter when Melissa said, "Sort of reminds me of my college days."

"Ahhh," Lynda said. "The single-most salient fact..." More laughter. "Okay, I'll admit it: three guys about whom that is the only thing I remember, including their names."

It was some minutes before either was able to speak again. Then Melissa continued through her chuckles, "I just met him last night. But, no, I don't care about his church-going habits, or not. David may, but I don't."

"Your daughter?"

Melissa shook her head. "Don't know. But I can tell that Ellie admires Sam as much as she's ever admired anyone her whole life. He seems to care for her, and he knows his way around a math book. Perhaps I have low expectations when it comes to my fellow humans, but that seems like enough. Less than what Ellie deserves, maybe, but more than Cardinal and David have coming." They let the thought hang for the remainder of the drive until, heading out of the Futrall roundabout, Melissa said, "Any idea where Jonathan left his car?"

"Second row south at the ER parking lot. A blue BMW convertible... Ah. There."

Melissa pulled in behind the car, but both sat for a moment saying nothing, Melissa with both hands on the steering wheel, looking out the front, and Lynda, not opening the door, looking down at her iPad. Finally, Melissa said, "Thanks."

"For Sam?"

"For looking after my granddaughter in there yesterday. So far, we've only pieced together what happened after they arrived here, but you were a great help to her, we know that, and I thank you for that. We all do."

"She was a scared kid, trying to help a friend. Who wouldn't have looked after her?"

"Want a list? Take the praise; you deserve it."

"Okay, I will. And you're welcome. I won't say it was my pleasure, given the circumstances, but I'm happy the way it turned out. And I'm glad to have met you."

"Will we meet again?"

"Perhaps. Call me if you need some help with Samuel. And thanks for the lift. Sorry to get you up so early."

"Really, not a problem. Bye."

Lynda stepped out of the car, watched Melissa drive away, checked the time on her phone and realized that she could still make the meeting with Chang and the team.

**Two Weeks Hence.**

"Tough old bird," indeed. Sam had not heard Dr. Rose's appraisal and was not aware of it, but two weeks after the accident he was up and around, still sore, but off the pain meds, doing most of the chores with Ellie's help, and finally free of Cardinal's fussy ministrations. David still dropped by occasionally to move hay from the barn to the feed room, as picking up a bale was still one thing he couldn't do. Ellie could handle a wheelbarrow half-full of manure, and most of the rest, he could take care of himself.

He had spoken to Lynda regularly as he healed. She would inquire about the healing, but she wouldn't fuss over him like Cardinal did, and their phone conversations took on the casual disconnectedness they had before Sam's accident.

So, they spoke regularly, but he hadn't seen her until she arrived unannounced one morning, after Ellie had been and gone. As had happened before, he just looked up and there she was, standing behind him with her hands in her jeans' pockets, as he tried to tighten the hose so it wouldn't leak. He would probably have to replace the female connection.

"Hi. How long have you been standing there?"

"An hour?" He shook his head. "Maybe less."

"Probably."

"How're ya doin', pal?"

"Good as new. You?"

"Cranky. PMS."

"What is it the children say? Too much information? Feel free to keep news of your hormonal fluctuations to yourself."

She stuck her tongue out at him. "What the children say is TMI. And I saw you to bed, remember, if not in the manner of my dreams and desires. We have no secrets, you and me."

Just One Look was still in his round pen, watching the two of them, and Evening Smoke was prowling the near paddock, the other three having already headed up. Teena the dog was out nosing around somewhere; yesterday had been sunny and warm, with a breeze from the south, but overnight clouds moved in and the ten o'clock temperature would be the high for the day.

"What's with that one?" Lynda pointed at the mare, who was walking toward the two of them, her nostrils vibrating in a soft nicker.

"She's begging."

"For a carrot?"

"No. She likes to have her udders rubbed."

"Well, yeah. Who doesn't?"

"Behave yourself."

"At least it's nice to know that someone around here is getting a little mammarian stimulation. Lucky girl."

"Less than you'd think. My ribs are still too sore for me to help her out." He paused. "You could do the job. That is if you don't object to a little cross-species homoeroticism."

"I'm in."

"Wait a minute while I get the powder."

"You powder your horse's udders?"

"Gold Bond Medicated. Nothing but the best."

"No, your horses aren't pampered."

"If you knew her life story, you'd say she deserves it."

"How do you know her life story?"

"She's a Thoroughbred. Records are kept. Hold on." Sam disappeared around the corner into the tack room, and emerged moments later holding something behind his back. "Watch this." When he displayed the gold bottle of powder to the horse, she increased the amplitude of her quiet nickers twenty-fold, almost to a whinny. She pranced, whinnying, to the middle of the paddock and stood still. "Our usual spot," Sam said. "Okay, now look. She weighs twelve hundred pounds and is unbelievably strong. She won't hurt you on purpose, but she could kill you by accident."

"Hey, who's the one in the ER a couple of weeks ago?"

"Exactly. And I don't have time to drive you to the hospital this morning. I have to fix that hose. So remember: six feet or six inches. If you stay beyond six feet, she can't hurt you, and if you're within six inches, well, she can push on you pretty hard, but she can't kick you. And she's not a biter. Right? So, come over here on this side..." They walked to the left side of the mare, "...and first stroke her hip to show her your intentions are honorable, and you aren't going to eat her."

"Eat her? Why would I eat her?"

"Your eyes are in the front of your head, and she's programmed to recognize that such animals are predators. Plus you smell like you eat meat. Which you do. So, stroke her hip a little."

Lynda laid her hand on the mare's hip. "It's solid muscle."

"Correct. Equines do not put weight on at the hindquarters."

"To die for."

"She likes you, I can tell. So, hold the powder in your right hand, put your right arm across her hips, face forward, and quickly move in. Put your right leg in front of her left hind. That's it, but closer. Lean into her. That's it." Lynda was dwarfed by the horse, whose hip was taller than Lynda's head. "Good, now remember to stay close. If she pushes against you with her leg, your natural reaction will be to back off, but that's exactly wrong. Lean into her, push back, stay close. Okay?"

"She is the most powerful thing I've ever been around."

"And she is retired and well past her prime. You can imagine..."

"I can't, actually. Have you ever ridden a race horse in its prime, running full out?"

"Never. Nor is it on my bucket list. It would scare the shit out of me."

"What is on your bucket list?"

"None of your business. Okay, now bend over and survey the territory." Lynda did so, and studied the mare's brown belly as it sloped upwards toward the rear, and there were two thumb-sized udders hanging limp and rubbery between her legs.

"What's that flap of skin?"

"Where?"

"Between her legs, aft of the udders."

"I don't know what it's called. The other mare doesn't have one."

"What's it for?"

"Don't know."

"I want one."

"See the man. I'd like a tail myself, to flick away the flies."

"Okay, so what am I doing? Powdering those adorable little udders?"

"Fill your left palm with powder, put your right arm back across her hips, now reach under and powder everything on this side. Watch out for her reaction." Which was to spread her hind legs, reach out with her front, and stretch her neck straight out ahead. "Lean in. Here, plant your left foot farther out here so you can push against her. Okay now, rub her belly with your knuckles."

"Shouldn't I scratch her?"

"Your manicurist would have a stroke. No, use your knuckles." At that the mare stretched more, her nose far out ahead and her upper lip extended even farther. "Watch her head; she'll lower it to show you when she's about to shake, which will scare you if you don't see it coming. Look at her lip..."

"She looks like an elephant."

"The equine upper lip is prehensile. I'm certain they share a common ancestor. It's the lip that shows you if you've hit her spot. Okay, watch; she's going to shake. Be ready. Lean in."

And the mare exploded in a full-body shudder. The sound went from subsonic to low-register, dust flew, her nose almost hit the ground.

"She's going to collapse!"

"She's okay. Stay with her." The mare was stretched out again full length, tail to nose, her neck now arched around to the left.

"How long does this go on?"

"Until you stop."

"How do I stop?"

"Just stop."

"My arm's tired."

"Just stop."

"Will she shake again?"

"Probably. Watch her head."

"Okay, I'm stopping." She did, but stayed right next to the mare.

"You're only half done, of course."

"My forearm feels like Popeye the Sailor."

"Lactic acid build-up. It'll go away shortly."

"So I can just step away?"

"She's not going anywhere. She knows you're only half done." Lynda brought her hand with the powder back from across the mare's hips and stepped back. "See, with my sore ribs, I can't reach over her back, nor can I lean into her. It's plain, though, that she accepts your performance, though I'm not ready to concede that it's better than mine."

"Equine foreplay?"

"Hardly. No stallion would be allowed to put his nose in there. But if you've ever watched a foal nurse, that's exactly the spot he goes for, banging his muzzle right where you were rubbing until the mare releases. They aren't always gentle. I think it's that instinct you're touching. Of course, at that point the mare has a bag, unlike now."

"Cows have bags all the time; why not horses?"

"Cows are almost always either pregnant or nursing. Often both."

"Why don't you breed her?"

"There're too damn many horses; we don't need any more."

"You? Or the world?"

"The world."

"Okay, to the right side." Lynda switched sides. "Step back; I'm flying solo this time."

Sam retreated to the work bench between the stalls, scooted himself up, wincing at the pain in his side, and leaned back against the wall to watch. Lynda was an amazingly quick learner, and showed no fear at all of the huge animal. She stepped in, powdered her right hand and set to work. This time, with the presumption of familiarity that Sam had come to expect, she lay her cheek on the mare's near-side rump. Almost immediately, the mare shivered and shook, and this time, as Lynda kept rubbing the mare's belly with her knuckles, the mare lifted her right leg, not to kick but just to stretch out to the side. She lifted Lynda completely off the ground.

"Whooo-ee."

"Hold on," Sam yelled. "She'll put you down." And she did. "Move back in close."

This went on for another five minutes, until Lynda said, "Time's up," and removed her hand.

"Pat her on the rump, say 'you're done,' and walk away.... Come over here and sit down."

Lynda handed him the powder, sat up on the table, and pulled up the sleeve of her sweatshirt to show her swollen forearm. "Look at me. I've never felt anything so powerful in my life."

"A raging river rapids?"

"True, the river feels alive. But she *is* alive."

"You look like an Olympic gymnast." She was white with talc to above both wrists.

"Sad to say, PMS-afflicted gymnasts are rare. The good ones are either pre-pubescent, or they've starved their ovaries into submission. No, I meant look at my arms. I feel like the Man of Steel."

"You've mixed your comic-book metaphors. Jonathan says you could have been an Olympic kayaker. Surely you've worked out."

"Yes, but weight machines don't nicker. We may have revolutionized the world of fitness training this morning. Notify the kinesiology department."

They watched, saying nothing more, as the mare walked through the gate and headed up toward the day pasture. "Why don't you open up the bay's stall there and let him out? He'll want to follow her up."

"I've always wondered what a bay horse is."

"Brown body, black mane and tail, and black from the knees down. See? Whoa there, buddy." Sam stopped The Looker with a hand to his chest. "The most common Thoroughbred coloration. Look: his otherwise brown ears have just a thin tracing of black around the edges. Then there's chestnut—sorrel in Quarter Horses. Like the two mares, the one you were working on and the one already up. Then there's a bay where the brown is so dark the horse looks almost black. The two geldings that have already left are dark bays. Then there are greys, also called roan, sometime almost pure white, but I don't have one of those. That's it."

"Not much variety."

"They are hopelessly inbred. Less genetic diversity than is good for them." He released The Looker, who walked on past and up to join his pasture mates. "They are thought these days to be fragile, accident-prone beasts, but his ancestors were stalled in a small, slow boat from Cádiz to Veracruz, and then they walked to Santa Fe with Cortés, where they escaped or were stolen by the Indians, and managed to adapt themselves to an entirely foreign ecosystem. Fragile? Nonsense. It's a remarkable story, really. That plus the Indians' ability to master so quickly an animal they'd never seen before. But, we killed most of the Indians and sent the rest to the reservation, and we inbred the horses, in both cases thinking we were improving the breed. And in both cases, being wrong."

"Should I be taking notes? Is that the one who kicked you?"

"No. Dreadnaught. Dark bay. Already up. Are you staying for lunch?"

"I'll have something to drink and watch you eat. Unlike that horse, I have to manage my hindquarters."

"By skipping lunch?"

"Okay, I'll be honest. Nothing in your fridge interests me."

"Come on up. We'll find something for you. I don't think your hindquarters need managing."

"How flattering that you noticed."

"The view was unobstructed when you were at work on Smokey."

"There's hope for me yet."

Sam did not respond, but when he held the kitchen door open for her up at the house, he said, "Abandon hope, ye who enter."

"See you an aphorism and raise. Hope springs eternal."

"How about an egg and onion sandwich? The egg is three hours old. The onion is older, but it's red."

"Speaking of aphorisms: you were wrong about Shakespeare writing that hell hath no fury, and so forth. That scorned-woman bullshit."

"Who did?"

"William Congreve. Is that egg and onion going to be on rye?"

"Both impossible and the wrong choice. The right choice is sourdough."

"Got any sourdough?"

"Good choice. Mayo and horseradish, required. Sit down. Drink?"

"Just water."

Sam filled a glass with ice and added water from the tap. "Congreve? Who's he?"

"Nobody. A hundred years after Shakespeare."

"One of the cruel mysteries of old age: at the same time that you become less sharp and your memory fades, you become more and more certain that you're always right."

Lynda didn't sit, but strolled around the kitchen and living room, her hands in the back pockets of her jeans, looking at the now-familiar objects. "The vaunted wisdom of the elderly?"

"It's more stubbornness than wisdom. That's why Ellie is so good for me. She keeps me unstubborn. You should meet her."

"I did."

"She's the reason I'm helping Jonathan, you know. How long do you have?"

"You have a proposal?"

"I thought you might play something."

"Not today. I've got to be back by one. Why is the study upstairs all topsy-turvy, while everything down here is neat as a pin?"

"How do you know that?"

"I spent the night, you'll recall. Actually, you probably don't recall. You were pretty wasted."

"And you took the time to nose around in my study?"

"Not much. Jonathan and I were sort of necking up there while David led the family in group prayer for your safe deliverance from... I missed the *from-what* part."

"Where was I?"

"Zonked out in your bed. Snoring like a babe. Do they talk like that around you?"

"Sometimes."

"Doesn't it make you want to pull your hair out?"

"Not really."

"It would me. It does just knowing that it doesn't you."

"First, not that many things make me want to pull my hair out. Other than you, I mean. Second, they might be right."

"Bull."

"Always remember, please, that any god powerful enough to create the universe in six days is powerful enough to make it look like it took billions of years."

"And why would a god do that?"

"A sense of humor?"

"God has a sense of humor?"

"An excellent one, presumably. But more to the point, third: my impression is that Cardinal has been treading water for a long time, just keeping her head above water. Christianity is keeping her afloat. If you think I'm going to set about drilling holes in her life boat, you don't know me very well. I don't care if what she believes is true, and I'm sure as hell not going to try and convince her it's not."

"Do as you will. But if I get asked to join their prayer circle again, I may do more than just say 'no, thanks.'"

"I doubt you'll be asked. I never have been. Special circumstances, I guess, I mean with me being struck down in my prime and all. The study's a mess because I'm thinning out the books on the shelves, going through Sally's things. Come and eat."

"Why now?"

"The sandwiches are ready."

"I mean why sort through her things now?"

"It's time. Past time."

They sat and began to eat.

"Mmmm. Good. Could use a slice of tomato."

"I don't buy tomatoes except local ones in the summer. Not worth it."

"You're right, actually. And it's excellent just like this. Why?"

"Once you eat an egg laid today by a hen who's free to scratch her way through a barnyard looking for bugs and whatever, you'll never eat any other kind."

"Quote, unquote bugs and whatever." She made air quotes. "Perhaps I'll not pin you down on the *whatever* and choose not to think of the details of her diet. I guess that's what they mean by free-range hens."

"Wrong. So-called free-range chickens are birds grown under lights in crowded houses like all the rest of them. The farmers who want the designation are required to leave the doors open for a while every day to allow the birds to leave, which they don't, not being very adventuresome. It's all just USDA bullshit to keep consumers happy, without really telling them anything. Read Michael Pollan."

"Your chickens leave the coop."

"My chickens are smart. And there's twelve of them, not fifty thousand. It makes a difference."

"Well anyway. The sandwich is excellent."

"Go on eating. I've got to get something from upstairs." Sam stood up, washed his hands at the sink, then climbed the stairs and returned with the book that he had set aside in the study. He put it down next to her plate. "For you."

"For me? Why?"

"It's one of the thinned-out. You'll like it. Guaranteed."

Lynda picked up the paperback. "*Horse Heaven*," she read aloud, "by Jane Smiley." She turned it over and studied the back cover, then put it back down on the table. "Better keep it."

"Why? After your knack of delivering a knuckle-rub to the mare down below, you're required to read a horse book. That's the best."

"There're a lot of horse books out there, I'm told."

"The best. Ever. Period. *Horse Heaven* is so good that no one need ever write another horse book. The genre is complete."

"Better keep it. Maybe someone else?"

"You're beginning to annoy me. How hard is it to say thanks and carry it away?"

"Not hard, but I won't read it. Maybe another of your friends will."

"Maybe some quiet night, nothing on the tube, no important scientific truths to pursue, Jonathan busy with requirement contracts. You'll pick it up. The first four pages will get you. You'll thank me."

"I do thank you. It's a nice thought, even if it is part of the thinned-out. But I don't care for the cover and I don't read books whose covers turn me away."

"What are you? Some kind of living, breathing human cliché? What's next? You hang wall paper with one arm?"

"There is sense to the image. One-armed paperhangers *are* busy."

"But judging a book by its cover is stupid. *That's* the cliché. If they put a dumb cover on *Hamlet* you don't read it? Come on."

"The rule doesn't apply to well-known works, or if the author is dead."

"You're serious, aren't you?"

"Of course. When am I not?"

"And the previously unacknowledged connection between the cover and the literature is...?"

"Look: the publisher wants me to read what's inside, right? They presume to know what I'd like. They design the cover to appeal to those presumed sensibilities. If they misjudge me so substantially, they don't deserve my time. I don't need the cover to attract me, or not, to *Hamlet* or *The Great Gatsby* or *Bleak House*. Not, in the case of *Gatsby*. But if I'm handed a book I know nothing about, it makes a good deal of sense to decide based on the cover."

"But you *do* know something about *Horse Heaven*: that your admired friend Sam Butler—who just made you an admittedly excellent sandwich—said it's good and guaranteed that you'd enjoy it."

"And if the sandwich looked like that cover, I would never have taken a bite. Tell me that it's wrong to judge a sandwich by its looks."

Lynda gestured at the book still lying on the kitchen table, and Sam picked it up. The cover was a cartoonish rendering of a race horse and jockey, the horse's legs, with identical white socks, extended straight out, front and hind, his eyes showing a bit of white, his head too small for a Thoroughbred, the jockey, handlebar moustache, bow tie, ridiculous beanie and all, looking out at the audience, instead of where he's going, standing straight-legged in the stirrups, as no jockey would ride today, seemingly taking all of his weight on his testicles.

"They used to draw galloping horses like that, even in serious art, because they didn't know what they actually looked like in stop-action. The human eye is not quick enough to follow the movement of the hooves. It turns out that one of the first practical applications of photography was to settle a centuries-old question of whether a horse's hooves are all off the ground at the same time during the trot."

"Are they?"

"Yes. But the human eye isn't quick enough to see. An early photographer in the eighteen hundreds set up a series of cameras with trip wires and essentially made the first motion picture. I forget who. Whom."

"Who. It's still a stupid-looking cover, and the publisher knew it. Intended it."

"I'll bet they didn't think it is stupid."

"You're right, and that makes my point better than I did. They designed it to appeal to certain readers. I'm not one of them."

"What about the author? They are her words that you're choosing not to read, not the publisher's."

"Jane Smiley? Pulitzer Prize winner? Movie-rights seller? You don't think she had a say in the design of the cover? Wise up. I'm guessing she approved of it, or was given the chance to."

Sam was silent for a while, turning the book over and over in his hands, before placing it back on the table, front cover down. "So why do you suppose that, over centuries, to judge a book by its cover has been a metaphor for superficiality? Who's out of step here? A sandwich might actually be tasty, even though it looks a mess."

"Centuries?"

"Whatever. Appearances can be misleading: oysters on the half-shell. Gumbo. Fois gras."

"Things usually are as they appear to be. Often, anyway."

"Which strikes me as something a lawyer might say, not a scientist."

"Backwards. The way things appear to be is always the null hypothesis. The state of the climate does not depend on carbon dioxide levels. The in-coming signal is noise, not the Higgs. The opposite proposition is the one that must be proved. Only after statistically valid proof are appearances rejected. It's lawyers, on the other hand, who are so good at always seeing both sides of everything. Maybe the ugly sandwich is good, maybe not. Maybe the cover is emblematic of the writing, maybe not. I'd better try it and see. Maybe my client killed the child, maybe not. It looks like he did. I don't want to know; I'll defend him either way."

"So, would Jonathan read the book?"

"Probably."

"Then take it. A present from me."

Neither spoke for a long time, sitting, staring in different directions over each other's shoulder, Sam out the kitchen door to the west, Lynda out the far window to the east. In both directions, the sky was now solid gray, low and overcast. A crowd of slate-backed birds flew onto the fieldstone patio, outside the south-facing window where they could both watch them through the picture window.

It was she who broke the silence. "Birds of a feather seem to flock together. Who knew? Go ahead; make the point. Next thing, you're going to tell me that it's hard to make a horse take a drink, too."

"Dark-eyed juncos. I should toss some more seed out for them."

"You're pissed off, aren't you? I warned you I was in a foul mood. Combative."

"It's as if I'd introduced you to my good friend and your first reaction was that he was homely and you didn't want to get to know him."

"Wrong again, as he didn't choose his homeliness. But right, if he pierced his eyebrows or had a swastika tattooed on his cheek. And multiple piercings is a hell of a lot more like a book cover than a hooked nose or a splotchy birthmark. That's all I'm saying, Samuel: there's a price to be paid by those concerned when they put that cover on the book. Maybe I'm the only one put off, in which case the price is small, but it's not irrational for me to be put off. Or 'stupid,' as you first put it. Rather harshly, I thought." She reached across the table and squeezed his forearm. "But I forgive you. You make a heck of an egg and onion, which, if memory serves, is what Elwood P. Dowd's sister made for the orderly from the mental hospital, which won his heart and thereby changed everything."

"Memory serves, except that she was his cousin, I believe, not his sister. The daughter of his mother's sister. First cousins. And it was unclear if horseradish was part of the deal, as it should have been."

"Egg, onion and horseradish on sourdough after an equine belly rub; it's a day I won't forget. Kiss me goodbye?"

She stood up from the table, put an arm across his shoulders and kissed him on the mouth, ending by licking his lips, which remained closed. "Ummm. You're a prude, but the horseradish lingers. Don't see me out." She turned back at the kitchen door. "You keep me sharp, Samuel; you bring out the honesty in me. With anyone else I would just have declined the gift, probably by saying that I didn't care for Smiley."

"But between us there are no secrets."

"Correct. Nor any lies."

"Just a cliché or two. And you're right about getting a horse to drink if he doesn't want to." He shrugged his shoulders. "You can salt his hay."

"Gotta jet. I'll call you."

And she was gone. Sam sat at the table, still littered with their dishes, and watched her walk back to her car, which she had now begun to park down by the pickups, and drive off to the west. He then picked the book up. The trouble was, of course, that she was right about the cover. And what pissed him off was not her opposition to the cliché but that she was right about the cover, and that he knew that he himself had put off reading the book for that very reason, but would never have admitted it to anyone, including her. Especially not to her. Still and all, when he re-read the first four pages, he found them, again, to be entirely excellent.

He put the book down and looked out the window toward the stable. There was still that hose to fix. Maybe if he jammed an extra washer into the female coupling, that would stop the leak at least temporarily, and save him a trip to town. It was now spitting snow.

**Later That Day.**

Having moved the copy of *Horse Heaven* from the bookshelf to the desk in the study, having shared the title with Ellie and the cartoonish cover with Lynda, and having moved it again back to the desk in the study, Sam now returned it to the bookshelf and proclaimed the book-thinning to be over. Cardinal and Ellie had picked through the children's books and then he and Ellie had taken the others to the county library in Huntsville; three boxes of literature were behind the seat of the small pickup, waiting to be redeemed at the used bookshop on Dickson Street when he got around to it, which he was in no hurry to do. Three more boxes had been gratefully accepted by the ed school library, and so now the shelves were less crowded, and Sam had moved a ceramic pot, a Hopi kachina doll and two horse figurines from the living room up to the study to fill in the spaces. Sally's Bible he hadn't touched—literally hadn't touched—and a few inches to the right of it there was one spot yet to be filled. He had it reserved for a picture of Ellie that he had taken at last October's Chili Pepper cross country meet, with her hair in a ponytail almost matching the autumn color of the rusty-red dogwoods at the edge of the woods, in their favorite spot, a hundred meters from the finish, as the runners ran by. As soon as he found just the right frame for it.

So, the books were thinned out, the top drawer in the desk was empty except for his things and the key ring, and that left only Sally's files to go through, two drawers on the right, one marked "PERSONAL" and one "PROFESSIONAL." And oddly enough it was the professional drawer that yielded the unopened letter to the post office box.

There was little in the personal drawer of any interest. Bank statements for her checking account, the details of which they had shared every month. Newspaper clippings of up-coming—now long past—art shows in Tulsa, Dallas and Kansas City that she wanted to see. Some cross-stitch patterns that she might sew one day, but never did. An AA file, thick with tales of encouragement. Things like that.

He sat for long minutes over the personal drawer, thinking about Sally and their lives together. This, he thought, was the desantification of the so-called Sally shrine at its most acute, and he let it be for a while, while he made himself walk down to the tractor shed, ostensibly to find a box to put things in, but actually to give himself time to decide if that drawer—her *personal* files—really needed to be emptied out. He couldn't find a suitable box, but then whistled to Teena and the two of them walked slowly up to the pond, where he sat on the bench and she sniffed for squirrel sign. Scaring up nothing interesting, Teena eventually hopped over and curled up at his feet. She was not a swimmer, and Sam had given up long ago trying to coax her into the water. Instead, he asked aloud, "What do you think, old girl? Do I have to empty that drawer?" The dog looked up at him, but gave him no help with the question. "I think I do, or it will always be the Sally shrine." And so it was, back up at the house, that the entire contents of the personal drawer went into a white, drawstring plastic garbage bag. Everything. It would have been harder to do if there had been anything actually personal in the personal drawer.

The professional drawer should have been easier, and it was, with file after file of Reading Recovery materials, kiddie-lit reviews, math games for second graders, and so on, easily coming out of the drawer and into the trash bag. But a file folder marked "Disks with viruses—DO NOT USE" contained no floppy disks at all, but the letter. Unopened. Addressed by a blocky hand to Sally Sanderson, P.O. Box 3720, Fayetteville, AR 72704. No return address. A stamp featuring Acoma pottery. The postmark was smudged and illegible.

He studied the handwriting. He had graded enough anonymous law school exams to have no faith in his ability to determine a writer's gender, or anything else, from the script. This was blocky, straight up-and-down. More printed than cursive, but not all block capitals. Uppercase S,S,P,O,B,F,A, and R. The rest lowercase. The sevens were crossed as Europeans do, but nothing else about the writing looked European. The four was written with one pen-stroke, not two, and the two had no curlicue. He thought that maybe the writer was one of those left-handers who didn't write backhanded, but he couldn't be sure.

Sam turned the envelope over, but the back was blank. He held it up to the light, but it was a security style, and revealed nothing. Nor could he feel anything like folded stationery inside the envelope. By heft, he would have guessed it to be empty. Feeling more than a little nosey and violative of Sally's privacy, and at the same time afraid of what he would find, he opened the envelope along the short side and out fell a newspaper clipping, which fluttered to the floor of the study. He looked inside, but there was nothing else. He picked up the clipping and found it to be tiny—only about an inch square. It was unmarked, but he recognized the typeface of *The New York Times*. It read:

"An article on August 29 about the changing nature of the ceremonial first pitch at baseball games misidentified the type of animal represented by the dancers in skintight, metallic green body suits at a recent game at Citi Field. They were amphibians, not reptiles."

A correction. Sally's correspondent knew her well. Yes, she read the corrections in the *Times*. "Listen to this one," she'd say, and he'd lower the business section, which, here in the provinces, contained the sports pages in the back. "Due to an editing error, an article on Monday about the struggles of the tourist industry in the mountain west, gave the incorrect altitude for the town of Crestview, Colorado. It is sixty-three hundred feet, not sixty-three hundred miles." Then she'd chuckle quietly to herself, as she would turn next to the op-ed page, and he'd go back to the sports. And yes, the odd, persnickety precision of the correction in the envelope would have amused her. They had cancelled their subscription to the *Times* when the price went to one-fifty a copy, and it was perhaps then, some years before the accident, that her correspondent began to fill her in. But this envelope was unopened. Unopened and mislaid? Or unopened and saved? In a Disks with viruses—DO NOT USE file that was otherwise completely lacking of any content, and why save disks with viruses anyway?

It was difficult to know what the hell it all meant, what the hell was going on. Or had been going on. There was something sharply intimate about the correction, or rather about Sally's correspondent knowing such a minute detail of her reading habits. Even more, her quirky sense of humor. What else did this person know? Did it mean that Sally had had a lover? A lover who sent her *New York Times* corrections clippings rather than erotic poetry? Or in addition to? Or just a friend with whom she shared, for whatever reason, an affection for the paper's correction policy, and a quiet post office box? How oddly old-fashioned was a secret post office box. But why? Was the secrecy of the box one tiny exception in their otherwise shared relationship? Or one of many? And, Sam admitted to thinking, was her correspondent male or female, and what additionally would that mean, one way or another?

"Things usually are as they appear to be." Thus had been Lynda's insight, just that morning, into literary evaluation and cover art. Or more broadly, she had said, to the world in general. And, again, Sam saw that she was wrong and, again, too superficial. For how do things appear to be? Is a correction in an unopened envelope addressed to a secret post office box any more than that? A correction, an envelope, an address. The appearances are what he chose to make of them. And for the moment, he chose to make nothing of it, other than that he now had a box number, for whatever good it might do him. Maybe he'd get Sally's ten bucks back from the Postal Service. Sam dropped the clipping into the waste basket, folded the envelope in half and set it under a paperweight on the desk, and closed the now-empty professional drawer. *Desanctification, indeed*, he thought.

**The Following Weekend.**

The NCAA Indoor Nationals were to be held this year in Fayetteville, and Sam and Ellie had long had plans to attend, and with the excursion into town, and lunch at Hugo's, they had the tickets. They would spend part of Friday afternoon watching the early stages of the hept- and pentathlons, come back on Saturday for the prelims of most of the sprints and the finals in the women's high jump and the men's pole vault, and on Sunday, for the rest of the finals, and especially for the women's pole vault. On Friday, they pretty much had the arena to themselves, plus the teammates and families of the competitors, for the combined events are not to everyone's liking. The events move slowly and, to tell the truth, the competitors are not particularly good at any one event, it is only that they are spectacularly good at all of them together. On Saturday, they had seated themselves in the end zone and watched all of the prelims, Ellie keeping time with her new stopwatch and carefully recording all of the results and trying to figure out in advance what the seeding would be in the finals on Sunday.

Between the two of them, Sally had been the first one to go to a track meet. She got massages, it turned out, from a woman who also worked on the track teams, men and women's, not as a staffer, but on-call as needed, which was often. This therapist had often talked to Sally during the course of the massage about the runners, jumpers and throwers who competed for, or who once had competed for, the Razorbacks and who, therefore were some of the best in the collegiate game, with not a few of them achieving national and international recognition. Sally had been talked into attending an indoor meet in the company of this therapist, and she was hooked. Sam went along a meet or two later, and so was he.

They preferred the indoor meets, less pure though they were than the out-doors. Indoors, everything was happening right in front of you, the runners often a few feet away, and nothing was taking place more than a hundred meters or so away. And several events would be happening at once, say the men's shot put and the women's triple jump being contested as the girls ran the 5K around them. Or the sixty meter hurdlers dashing between the pole vaulters and the high jumpers. The uniforms were brightly colored, the athletes were in perfect shape, and you could hear them—you could even smell them—as they ran, jumped or threw in front of you. Sally rather wryly commented early on that for Sam the major attraction was watching flat-chested girls in ponytails run and jump in front of him (the description did not fit the throwers), and he did not waste his breath denying this. His tastes in females did run in that direction, Sally's looks to the contrary notwithstanding. He was unable to resist the sight of a tightly-packed group of middle-distance runners, ponytails swaying in unison, thin wrists with watches, lean (but not too lean) and wiry, four and a half minutes of this in the mile being the nicest four and a half minutes in sports. They were indeed lovely.

There is something very close to the basic nature of humanity to run, long or short distances either one. And to jump. And to throw. The high jump is the most basic and most difficult of all the events they watched: a human versus gravity. Here's a bar; propel your body over it. No rules, no tools, just jump. But Sam was most surprised that he became a fan of the women's pole vault, an event that he previously hadn't even known existed. The men were impressive, sure enough, but with them is was all muscles and upper body strength, the bent pole throwing them to impossible heights, accompanied by lots of grunts and explosions. But the women tended to be slenderer, less top-heavy, and they floated to the bar, rather than attacking it. Sure, the heights were lower, but somehow that didn't seem to matter; the fun was in watching them float. Then a few years ago the face-up technique was introduced, and the vaulter would do a half-twist, with one of her hands still on the pole and float over, feet first and face up, and the event became even more dance-like, followed, of course, by a fifteen foot fall onto the mattresses below.

So, they became track fans, then ardent track fans. Yes, they cheered on the Razorbacks. Sam found it to be almost disturbingly enjoyable to add his voice to the sound of a couple of thousand others inside a small building, trying to urge a young person to go faster, higher, farther. But they cheered for the others, too. The fans, even the competitors, at track meets are remarkably appreciative even of the opposition. There is little trash talk among the fans or athletes; everyone encourages everyone on. When a jumper from another team is staring down the bar at the winning height, there is no distracting hooting from the crowd. Save that for basketball games. At a track meet, the entire audience goes quiet, to allow the jumper to concentrate. The athletes urge each other on, and they all congratulate the winner at the end. Win or lose, Sam and Sally would always walk away, hand-in-hand, throats raw from cheering, feeling rather proud of humanity.

When the horses worked their way into their lives things got a little complicated. Serious track fans spend parts of two or three days at the meet, from prelims to final relays, lunch and dinner both in the stands, chatting up the parents of the competitors, welcome to Fayetteville, we hope your kid does well. But the horses needed to be fed, watered, moved from one paddock to another, checked for lameness and injury, and generally given the pampering they deserved and had come to expect. So Sam and Sally would come and go, one at a time, in and out of the meet, to attend to the chores that needed doing, each to watch his or her favorite events, meet you back here in time for the finals of the mile. It worked out well, and they'd catch up the next morning over the paper's sports section, filling each other in on what the other had missed.

Then Sally had been killed, and, of course, everything changed. That was in mid-May, the twelfth, and Sam's world was turned upside down. But in an odd way, it wasn't until the following January, when the first days-long indoor meet came around that the full impact of her death came to him. He would not be able to attend, or at least not like before, when it was both of them. Who was going to do the chores? How could he park his seat on a hard bench in front of the women's pole vault, as he liked to do, and watch for the hours that it took to contest the event, and still be home at feeding time for the horses? He became a part-time track fan.

Ellie became a fan via her math lessons. One day she was sitting at the kitchen table finishing her homework while he was looking over the detailed results of the SEC meet, which he had printed off the computer at the library. She had asked about it and he shared the pages with her; full of numbers, it seemed almost like part of the lesson. On the spur of the moment, he had introduced her to alternate numbering systems, with bases other than ten, in particular the base-sixty system on which timing is based. See? 57+5=1/2. Huh? 57 seconds plus 5 seconds equals 62 seconds, which is 1 minute and 2 seconds. 50+21=1/11. Fifty minutes plus 21 minutes equals 1 hour and 11 minutes. So what is 45+30?

Unfortunately, David saw Ellie working on some problems that Sam had given her, and, through Cardinal, had put the kibosh on the whole base-sixty idea. He had once heard Phyllis Schlafly say on Eagle Forum that such alternative numbering systems were a waste of time and vaguely unbiblical and besides they were not in the Sonlight curriculum, so instead Sam set Ellie to work translating the metric results of the long jump into feet and inches and before long she, too, was a fan. And then the deal was cemented once when they went to see Wallace Spearman, Jr. and he ran one of the fastest two hundreds ever run indoors. He was tall and slender, started the race right in front of where they were sitting in the end zone, and he glided around the track without seeming to disturb the air through which he was running. And thereafter, they paid attention to every race he ran and attended races together when they could.

And so, on Sunday, Sam pulled into the yard of the Quincy home, discovered he was early and sat on their porch reading their Sunday paper for a few minutes until the family pulled in, having come from church, of course. Ellie was the first out of the truck and ran up the steps, yelling "hi just a minute I'll be right out the service lasted too long" before blasting through the front door. At a more leisurely pace, Cardinal, carrying Esther and holding Joshua by the hand, and David, carrying Isaiah, walked up to the porch.

"Nice service?"

"Of course," said Cardinal. "You should come sometime."

"I've been invited."

"So, next week?" This was David.

"My standard answer to Ellie's invitation is 'we'll see.'"

"We'd like to have you," said David.

"You'd be very welcome," said Cardinal. "And Ellie would be pleased."

"Seek and ye shall find," said David.

"Knock and the door shall be opened," Sam said, completing the thought.

"Amen," said Cardinal. "Listen to *you*, quoting Scripture."

"I've heard the song. Thanks for the invitation. We'll see...but probably not."

"Will you at least stay for coffee, Sam?" Cardinal asked.

"I have a feeling that that would disappoint Ellie," Sam said. "I think she's anxious to get going."

Confirming this appraisal, Ellie came bursting back through the front door, now decked out in Razorback gear, including a cap, with her stopwatch on a Razorback lanyard that Sam had bought for her birthday. "Let's go."

"Slow down. I'm talking to Cardinal and David."

"No, let's go. We'll be late for the first final."

"'We'll be late for the first final,' she says. We'd better go. We'll be home sometime after nine."

"What about your evening horse feeding? Do you want me to do it for you?" Cardinal asked.

"No, thanks. I've left them on the day pasture and they'll be fine until we get home. I'll drop Ellie off here and then go switch pastures and probably put out some hay for them besides. They'll be okay without grain one night, though I'll be lectured to in the morning by Smokey."

"Come *on*. Let's go. Bye, Mom," she kissed her mother on the cheek, then Esther. "Bye, David; bye, boys. *Let's go.*"

The national championships would be well-attended, a full house being about four thousand fans, but this early in the day the crowd was thin. They parked a nice walk away from the Tyson Center to avoid the exit-rush, and then, even with tickets, waited in a short line to get in. They passed a lengthy list of rules and regulations for the arena, the first of which—"No exit and re-entry"—was completely unenforced. This had initially caused Ellie a little concern: "Why is that the rule if they still let you come and go?"—a question for which Sam had no good answer, except to say that someone had not thought carefully when making the sign. The rule against outside food was another one that was poorly enforced and they were equipped to violate it, for his backpack contained sandwiches and chips for their dinner, though they would buy over-priced drinks to go along with the food, which he thought made up for the technical violation of the no-outside-food rule. The bag-checker apparently thought so, too, for she made no complaint when she looked inside. And practically winked at them when she said, "Enjoy the meet."

Inside, they made their way across the lobby and into the arena itself, and immediately were at the running track, the entire setup being jammed and non-commodious, the better for the intense crowd participation that was to come. When the track cleared, they walked in front of the reserved seating at the finish line, toward which they turned up their unreserved-seat noses, and then they stopped at a small stand in the end zone, where he had Ellie pick out an Indoor Nationals tee shirt for herself.

"For me? Thanks!," she said.

"Why don't you put it on right now?"

"Here? I'd have to go to the restroom."

"No, just pull it on over the one you already have on. I've got something else for you. Here, give me your cap." She pulled her ponytail out of the hole in the back of the cap, pulled the new white tee shirt with the NCAA insignia over her red Razorback one, and squirmed to make them fit together. She replaced her cap and re-did her ponytail. Sam then produced a felt-tip pen and handed it to her. "Okay. Here. Now that's for getting the autographs of the national champs."

"Where?"

"On the tee shirt."

"Right on the tee shirt?"

"Sure. Back, front, sleeves, sides. Fill it up."

"Would they do that?"

"Most will. You'll have to ask them when they walk off." They found their way to the far side and to seats up about twenty rows, right in front of the pole vault runway. Perfect. They settled in. "Okay, here are today's events. Clip that on to your clipboard there and get yourself organized. Actually, there's your first autograph there."

"Who?"

He pointed across the infield. "Over there. Number one-thirty-seven. The girl from the Razorbacks that tied for second in the pentathlon yesterday. She's in the high jump today, and warm ups should begin pretty soon."

"You said national champs."

"Tied for second is pretty good. And she's one of ours."

"Will she do it?"

"Go ask her."

"What should I say?"

"Congratulations on the pent. Would you sign my tee shirt? See what she says. Go on, now, before she gets seriously into her warm-ups. She's from St. Lucia in the Caribbean, remember, so she'll speak with an interesting accent."

"How do I get there?"

"The same way we came in. Around behind the bank in the track and over to where she's standing."

"Are you coming?"

"I'll watch you from here."

Off Ellie went, a little girl in a crowd of adults, a white kid who had never been around so many black people in her life, an American about to meet her first St. Lucian, a fan about to ask for her first autograph. Sam had actually heard an interview with the girl on the radio and she seemed very open and modest, and he thought that it would be a good place for Ellie to begin asking, even if she'd tied for second, and not won. He watched as she found her way around, waved to the jumper from as close as she could get and then he could practically read her lips as she made her request and when the jumper plainly asked her where she wanted her to sign, Ellie turned her back and pointed over her shoulder, and the signature was added. Sam zoomed in with his smart phone and snapped a picture. Several kids roughly Ellie's age watched the process and apparently got up their nerves from Ellie's example and made a line, most holding out programs and one other presenting his tee shirt to be signed on the back. A few more words were exchanged between the jumper and the kids, and then with a wave she walked over to begin the serious business of getting ready for her event.

Ellie stayed where she was for a few minutes and Sam could see that introductions were being made, some giggling was involved and then Ellie pointed across the infield to Sam. He stood up and waved, and before long Ellie and two young girls were running up the steps to where he was sitting. More introductions, and Sam made room for the newcomers, who were at the meet by themselves, their parents to come along later. Ellie showed them her clipboard and how she had organized the finals, after having watched the prelims yesterday, and she showed off her stopwatch, though she kept the lanyard around her neck while they used it. Then she asked Sam who she should get to autograph her shirt because one of her new friends knew where the entire Razorback women's team was sitting, at least the ones not competing right now or soon, and maybe it would be fun to get their autographs, too, if it was all right with him.

"Whatever you want. Just check in with me every now and then." And off they went.

The afternoon and evening unfolded in an entirely pleasant fashion. Sam had gotten to chatting with a young African-American assistant coach of some kind from the University of South Carolina whose job it was to record the women's pole vault, concentrating on Carolina's entry, but also recording the vaults of others from the SEC, including two quite good Razorbacks. The Carolina vaulter appeared to be an Asian-American named Petra Olsen, but she turned out actually to be from Sweden. She was a good vaulter; after all this was the Indoor Nationals. But she didn't place, and everyone encouraged her over the bar, and cheered supportively when she went out. And as she waved regretfully to acknowledge the cheers, Sam thought that it perhaps said quite a lot about the new century and so forth that an Asian-Swede named Petra Olsen was competing in the women's pole vault for the University of South Carolina, but when he mentioned it to his new friend, the African-American assistant coach, who within Sam's memory could not even have attended the University of South Carolina, she didn't seem to find it remarkable at all.

Sam was actually not disappointed that Ellie spent as much time with her new friends as she did with him, even if it meant that she did not time each race down to the hundredth of a second with her new stopwatch. He was also pleased that he'd had the foresight to make twice as many sandwiches as the two of them could ever eat, so she could invite the two girls, whose names it turned out were Blair and Molly, to join them when they got hungry, at about three in the afternoon. It was difficult for Sam to judge the ages of the girls. Twelve, to Ellie's eleven, was his guess, but maybe it was their public-schooling in the city, against Ellie's rural, home-schooled ways. They acted more grown-up than she did, their speech was slangier, if less precise, than hers, and Molly wore a loose-fitting top that revealed no figure, but allowed a bra strap to show. As the three of them chattered away, ate their sandwiches, and watched the meet, Sam came to realize that, while he thought of Ellie as a little girl, "young girl" was probably the better term, and even that would soon be obsolete, even in these post-feminist times when it had become acceptable in conversation (though not in the papers) to refer to the grown women performing in front of them as "girls."

The only intrusion of the outside world into the Tyson Center was at about four, as the men's mile, the only remaining vestige of the non-metric world, was being contested, when Sam's smart phone gave a burp and the screen said "Text message in-coming." He had never, in fact, received a text message in his life, and he was inclined to ignore this one, and in any case would need Ellie's help to figure out how to retrieve it, and when she returned with Blair and Molly from an autograph-hunting trip—her shirt now filling up with names—she showed him how to read it. It said:

"finished. want to see it before i submit? jonathan."

Ellie showed him how to reply, but the lingering soreness of his right arm translated to his hand and made it difficult to do the thumb-typing that is common with phones. She teased him when he tried to use his fingers, so instead he handed her the phone and dictated while she typed:

"Congratulations."

Molly interrupted. "You're supposed to *abreeve!*"
"Totally," said Blair.

"Drop it on me," said Molly, and they touched index fingertips. Sam watched Ellie absorb the tweener lingo. But he said "No, go ahead and spell it out," and she did, while her new friends watched, shaking their heads at the dorkiness of it all. She typed:

"I'd like to see it, but go ahead and submit without waiting for me. Hay to L. Too bad you're not at the track meet. Looks like the R'back men will win; women maybe. SCB"

The first reply came directly from Lynda:

"Bor-ing. "hay"??!! Xs, L"

Followed by:

"if u like it, i like it. b there soon, Jonathan"

But he never showed.

In the end, the Razorback men already had an insurmountable lead for the title when they won the 4X400, the final event. The Arkansas women ran their hearts out and won the final heat, supposedly the fastest, but Oregon had a better time by a few hundredths, quite an accomplishment as they were running against the clock only, out of a slower heat, and the Razorbacks ended up in fourth place, two points out of second. Sam and Ellie called the Hogs with the home crowd, and drove home, tired, happy, but tracked-out and sore-throated from yelling like crazy, bringing the women's relay team home just that much short of being national champions.

# 5

## MARCH

**The First Saturday.**

A few years ago, a group of Swedish scientists concocted a delightful experiment. They set out a course for horse and rider, put heart monitors on both, and gave precise instructions to the rider. Something like this: Walk here, trot there, do a loop around that barrel, stop and turn around at that point, then canter through this figure eight. That kind of thing. And they warned the rider that there would be a man with a folded-up umbrella standing beside the track near the end, and the third time around the course, the man would suddenly open the umbrella, trying to spook the horse. Be ready. Third time around. The rider took the horse through the course, and the third time around the man with the umbrella stood exactly as he had the first two times. He did not open the umbrella.

But the horse's heart rate went up.

Okay, so they can read your mind. Remember that.

Maybe not. Maybe they were reading the rider's muscles flinching in anticipation of the umbrella's opening. Maybe they were smelling the rider's nervous anticipatory aromas. Maybe they could feel the rider's hands tighten just a bit on the reins as they approached the man with the umbrella. Believe those things if you want. Or believe that they can read your mind. If you're nervous, they know it, and understandably think that whatever it is that's making you nervous is something that could attack them.

Clint Eastwood learned this lesson on the set of *Rawhide*. The director would say "Action" and the horses would spook. Horses, of course, know the meaning of "Action" no more than they know "That's a wrap" or "Where's the damn SAG rep?," but the actors knew what the word meant, so the horses knew, too. Eastwood the director starts filming a scene with a very low-key "Whenever you're ready."

Sam Butler knew that horses could read human minds, and had tried to explain it to a friend who was convinced that his horse was afraid of yellow school buses. Something about the color. Wrong. It's the rider, Sam explained, who expected the horse to spook when a school bus was on the road, expectation fulfilled. So Sam should not have had to re-learn the Swedish-Eastwood-yellow-school-bus lesson on vaccination day with Ellie, a Saturday, no math lesson. But he was. Sam had put out on the work table between the stalls ten syringes and hypodermic needles, and the bottles of vaccine, plus alcohol, cotton and an emergency kit in case something went wrong. Now, he was inside Just One Look's stall, holding one syringe in his hand, another between his teeth, and Ellie, assisting, held two balls of cotton soaked in alcohol. He would give the shots, Ellie would hold the goods, and The Looker was outside his skin in fright. He paced quickly back and forth within the confines of his stall. He expelled a few biscuits, as they are called, paced some more and then defecated again. He showed the whites of his eyes and his ears were turning every whichaway.

Sam, shielding Ellie with his left arm extended, watched him, mystified. Just One Look had been stuck with more needles at the track than anyone, Sam Butler in particular, wanted to think about. Steroids and pain killers, mostly, but also Salix against bleeding in the lungs and antibiotics against infection were common. Aminocaproic acid, conjugated estrogens, prednisolone sodium succinate, carbazochrome, the list goes on. Cobra venom is not unknown. Plus vaccines and assorted other medications. The Looker, like most Thoroughbreds, was more used to needles than a strung-out junkie in Echo Park. So what the hell was going on? He watched the poor animal pace and tried to figure it out.

Of course. It was Ellie. She had been nervous coming into the stall, nervous about sticking The Looker, and the horse had sensed that and decided that if *the other one* had something to be nervous about, so did he. His nervousness then made Ellie worse, and so on, spiraling upwards until someone, maybe all three of them, got hurt.

"Let's leave him alone for a while to let him simmer down, okay? Keep your eye on him and just back out of the stall." When she was safely outside, he said, "Put those things down and go into the tack room and get me...a towel. Oh, and a right-handed hoof knife. And the big jar of Vaseline. No, the small one." The errand he sent her on was meaningless, but he wanted her out of The Looker's sight and occupied doing something to get her own mind elsewhere. She disappeared around the corner and Sam raised his hands to the frightened horse. "Easy, boy. It's all right. Easy." He held out his hand and the horse stopped pacing and sniffed it. "Thataboy. Okay. I'll be back." And he turned and walked quickly out of the stall, put all but one of the syringes back into the vet's paper sack and sat himself on the table.

When Ellie came around the corner carrying the items he had sent her to fetch, he said, "Put that here on the table, and let's go check on the chickens."

"The chickens?"

"Yeah. Walk with me." They passed by the stalls, the horses watching them go, with little in the way of interest, and Sam said nothing until they were well away from the stable. Then, "Why do you think The Looker is acting so funny?"

"Because he doesn't want the shot?"

"No. I don't think so. He's been at the track, remember, and he's gotten more shots in his six years than the two of us have in our combined...let's see, seventy-nine. No, he's not worried about a little vaccination."

"Then what?"

"He's acting funny because *you* don't want him to have the shot."

"Me?"

"You. He sees that you're nervous about the shot so he thinks, 'hey, this must be some different kind of shot if Ellie's nervous. So I guess I'd better be nervous, too.'"

"He's afraid of me?"

"No, that's not what I said. He senses that you're afraid of something about the shot. He doesn't know what, but if you're afraid of it, then he thinks maybe he should be, too. That's pretty good horse-thinking, really. He knows that you're much smarter than he is. Here, hold this, please." He handed her the six cc syringe, with the inch-and-a-half needle attached. "Do you think it looks scary?"

"Yeah."

"So, you see? He's not afraid of the needle. He's seen needles. He's afraid of your fear."

"What should I do?"

"Would you want to be stuck with that needle?"

"No!"

"Me, neither. But here's the trick. Think you can fool him into thinking you're not afraid?"

"Fool him?"

"Sure."

"Isn't that like lying?"

"A little bit. But I think you're allowed to lie to a horse."

"I'm not sure."

"Well, you're allowed to pretend, no?"

"I guess."

"Then, that's what we'll do. He's not as smart as you are, remember. So all you have to do is pretend you're not afraid, then he'll be okay. Wanta bet?"

"But how?"

"Easy. See that bag of hen scratch over there? Think it would hurt to stick this needle into the bag?"

"No."

"Go do it."

"Really?"

"Really." She walked over to where the fifty pound bag of scratch was leaning against the coop, waiting to be carried inside. She looked over her shoulder at Sam and he nodded. "Go ahead. Stick it." She did. "Did the bag flinch?"

"No."

"Did you hear it say 'ouch'?"

She giggled. "No."

"All right, then. Come back over here. Think you can treat a horse like a bag of corn?"

"No."

"Me neither. But we don't have to. We just have to fake it. Walk into a stall just like you walked over to that bag of scratch. Just like you did. That ought to fool him, don't you think?"

"Maybe."

"Oh oh. *Maybe* won't do. The Looker will see *maybe* in your eyes and feel *maybe* in your hands, and he'll freak out again. It's got to be 'yes, I can pretend. I can fool him.' I'm not asking you not to be scared. Just pretend you're brave, just enough to fool him. Will you give that a try?"

"I guess." Sam looked at her over his glasses, until she nodded and said, "Yes."

"Good. So, who do you think would be the easiest to fool?"

"I think Mister." Restive.

"Good choice. I think so, too. He's older; he's calmer; he's not too bright. So let's do him first. I'll get the medicine and you go into his stall..."

"...and tell him it's going to be okay?"

"Tell him that you're not afraid. That you get shots all the time at the doctor and they hardly hurt at all and it's over in about a second. But wait. First get a handful of grain from the feed room and put it in your pocket. Then you can give him a treat at the end. Okay? I'll meet you in Restive's stall."

Sam had to replace the needle that she had stuck into the bag of scratch, and he took his time doing it to give her a chance to be alone with the horse. And when he turned the corner, holding the syringes, the vaccine bottles and two balls of alcohol-soaked cotton, he liked what he saw. Ellie was calmly talking to the horse who was standing there apparently half asleep.

"Good. Okay, you hold the cotton. We've got to put one shot in this side and one in the other."

"Where?"

"In his neck."

"When I get a shot it's in my arm or my bottom."

"Well, he doesn't have arms and if we stick him in the butt he's liable to kick us into Crawford County. Here's a nice strong muscle right here." Sam put his left hand on the horse's neck just ahead of his shoulder. "See? There's his scapula and we want to stay away from that, and down here's the big vein back to his heart, and we want to stay away from that, too. How're ya doing?"

"Okay."

"Good. So pick the spot, anywhere in this triangle." Sam outlined the area with his forefinger.

"*I* should pick the spot?"

"Yup. Anywhere in there." She hesitatingly pointed out a spot on Restive's neck. "Perfect. Rub some alcohol right there." She did, while Sam loaded the syringe with vaccine. "How's he doing?"

Ellie looked around Sam's back at the horse's head and shrugged her shoulders. "Okay, I guess. He's just standing there."

"Know why?"

"Why?"

"Because you're so calm. Now rub the spot again with alcohol. Good."

"Will it hurt?"

"We'll ask him when we're done. He might flinch a bit at the sting. Here goes." Sam stuck the needle in, but the horse did not flinch, and he pulled the syringe back a touch. "See? First you have to pull back on the syringe, to make sure you didn't hit an artery or vein. Can you see? No blood came out. So now..." Sam began to depress the syringe. "Not too fast and not too slow. There. Now, give me your left hand and here, you hold the syringe. With your other hand, put the cotton right at the base of the needle. Good. Now, pull out." She did. "Rub the spot good with the cotton...and we're done on this side."

"Did I do okay?"

"You were great."

They switched sides to repeat the process as before, the horse standing totally without concern. Sam loaded up the second syringe. "See? I keep the rabies vaccine in my right pocket—*R* is for rabies and for right—so I don't get them mixed up. I'm ready. Ready Restive? Okay, pick the spot." He stuck the needle in, pulled back, then depressed the plunger, and then again had Ellie pull the needle out.

"There. Now give him a bit of grain and tell him he was a good boy." She did both. "Who's next?"

"Daisy, I think."

"Good. But she's taller, so you'll need the stool from the tack room. I'll meet you in her stall."

Standing on the stool, Ellie was at eye-level with the point of the injection and she seemed to become immediately unsqueamish about the process. For the second injection, Sam let her push the syringe in to get the feel of the medicine being administered, and so it was for the next two horses, with Sam loading and inserting the needles, Ellie administering the dosage and pulling out. He wondered how it was going to be when they finally got back to The Looker, but Ellie seemed hardly to remember how antsy he had been at the beginning, and if she didn't remember, neither did the horse, and he stood quietly for the entire process, just like the veteran he was.

"Nice job."

"It wasn't so bad. And I don't think I lied to anyone, do you?"

"Not a word. Let's get cleaned up."

It took fifteen minutes or so to get everything put away, and the used syringes into the milk carton that Sam used for sharps, which needed special attention as hazardous waste when he went to the transfer station. Ellie jabbered on about how much fun giving the shots had been and that she wondered how a person got to be a vet. "We'll have to look into that," Sam said, and as they were walking back toward the house, they noticed a car parked behind the pickups. Sam didn't recognize it, but Ellie did.

"It's my grandma."

"It'll be nice to meet her."

They walked over to the car, where Melissa was already out, paying attention to the dog. Ellie ran the last ten yards, gave her grandmother a hug, and said, "Come say hello to Mr. Butler."

Sam stuck out his hand. "Nice to meet you. I've heard a lot about you."

"Professor Butler. Not as much as I've heard about you."

"Sam. Please."

Melissa smiled, but said nothing, while turning to Ellie. "Did you forget what's happening this afternoon, young lady?"

"Ummm. I think so."

Melissa turned back to Sam. "Some of the other home-schooling moms have put together a field trip for the kids..." back to Ellie, "...*now* do you remember?" Ellie shook her head slowly, looking much more like someone choosing to forget than someone trying to remember. Back to Sam, "Crystal Bridges. The Norman Rockwell exhibit."

"I hear that it's very nice," said Sam. "I haven't been."

"It is nice," said Melissa, "and you should go. And you, Miss Ellen Christine, should have been home from the Professor's a half hour ago. Get on your four-wheeler and scoot. You smell like a horse and need to change before they come to pick you up. They're going in the church's van," this last to Sam.

"We were giving the horses their shots," Ellie said, "and I got to help. At first The Looker was afraid, but then we figured out it was because I..."

"You can tell me all about it later. Now, get going, or you'll keep the van waiting."

"But we're not done here."

"Yes, we are," said Sam. "You go on and do as your grandmother says. You did really well. Go on, now."

And she was on her four-wheeler and gone.

Melissa watched her go and shook her head. "She *is* a whirlwind."

"She actually did quite well today. At first, she was nervous about sticking the horses—me, I mean...." Melissa seemed to be listening with only half an ear, looking around the farm. Confused by her apparent inattention, he went on. "I wasn't going to have her do it, but she didn't like the idea. And they were picking up on her fear and practically jumping out of their shoes. But we had a talk, and I convinced her that if she would pretend not to be scared, then the horses wouldn't be either. I wasn't sure it would make a difference to the equines, but it did. At first she was hesitant, because she thought it was going to involve lying to the horses. I guess I convinced her that pretending wasn't exactly the same as lying."

"Ellie tells me there's a fishing pond that you two sometimes visit."

"Back there a short walk." Sam pointed up a hill to the southeast. "Want to see it?"

Melissa smiled, but said nothing and started walking in the direction indicated. They walked in silence for a while, uphill, that shortly had her breathing through her mouth, not exactly panting, but her breath laboring. "I don't walk as much as I should. Do you have to do something with the horses? After the vaccinations?"

"They should stand in their stalls for a half hour or so, just to make sure there's no reaction to the vaccines."

"I've heard of anaphylactic shock."

"If it were that, they would have been dead thirty seconds after the shot. No, that's more likely a problem with penicillin, and it's rare. But not with vaccines. More like swelling—a big mosquito bite—and not that serious. Just some anti-itch oil, vet goop, something like that. We'll check on them when we get back."

They walked through a gate into the day pasture, then through another and into a largely wooded area, and then through a grove of mixed hardwoods and cedar trees to a small, round pond.

Sam spread his hands. "It's not much. It used to be bigger, but it leaks. You can see where the water level once was." He pointed to a change in vegetation about two feet above the present water level.

"Why does it leak?"

"Because I let the trees grow up on the downhill side. When we first moved in, the county agent warned me that those tree roots would cause it to leak, but we didn't care, as we liked the trees and we weren't sure the agent knew what he was talking about. It's spring fed, so it always has some water in it. Turns out the agent was right, but I still like the trees. My wife and I used to come up here to fish. One time, she caught twenty-three blue gills in one hour. Probably one blue gill twenty-three times. After that she stopped baiting the hook and just sat holding the pole and reading. I don't seem to have the time to fish anymore since she died." He looked up at the trees on the downhill side. "Some day, the wind will topple one of those trees, probably that tall maple right there, and it will uproot and breach the dike and that will be that."

"Will you be able to fix it?"

"Probably not. It will be nice to have a little brook running through the breach down into the pasture."

"Professor Butler," Melissa said, "I've been wanting to talk to you for some time. We've met before, you know."

"We have?"

"Yes, up at your home. The day you were hurt."

"Ahhh. The night of the walking wounded."

"How are you feeling now?"

"My arm aches, but there are no sharp pains any longer." He took a slow, deep breath. "See? As long as I take it slowly."

"Can you ride?"

"Yes, at a walk. I have to use a mounting block to get on, which seems odd."

"You were kind of out of it that night, Professor."

"Won't you please call me Sam? I haven't had anything to profess for many years."

"You're an Emeritus Professor, aren't you?"

"Oh, *Emeritus* is just Latin for 'old fool.'"

Melissa laughed, then said through her chuckles, "I doubt you're much older than I am, and as for being a fool..."

"Sixty-eight."

"Well, okay. Somewhat older than I am. I'll be fifty-eight next year."

"You carry your years lightly."

"Why, how nice of you. My hair was once the color of Ellie's, but it went grey almost overnight shortly after Cardinal was born, before I was thirty. Some hormone deal, the doctor said. Rare, but more common with redheads. My weight's about the same as it was back then, but its distribution has changed. I guess I don't feel fifty-eight. I think I'm supposed to."

"There's a bench just over there where we can sit if you like. I don't feel much like a professor anymore. I just look after the horses and teach Ellie her math. And how to give shots."

"Okay. 'Sam.' But know that you are always 'Professor Butler' around Ellie and her mother. And David. She must not forget who you are." Sam didn't respond and Melissa said nothing for a long while, as they walked around the pond to a wooden bench, very homemade-looking, sitting under a tall pine tree.

"I planted that loblolly pine as a seedling, when we first moved here. This tall." Sam spread his index fingers six inches apart. "And now it's what?" They both bent back to look at the top of the tree. "Thirty feet? Forty, maybe." He now looked down at Melissa. "Why mustn't she forget?"

"Because you represent the possibilities of life. She hasn't seen much of them so far."

"Her possibilities are rich. She said earlier that maybe she'd like to be a vet. She's very bright. I love having her around, you know."

"I can see that. Well, I knew it before I arrived. It comes through when she talks about you. It came through the night you were hurt. Even though you were pretty spacey from the drugs. It's very important, Sam, that you remain in her life."

"Why me? There's lots of horsey math tutors around. Well, maybe not so many, I guess."

"It's not because of the math. Or the horses. It's because you're not a true believer."

Sam chuckled. "Excuse me for laughing, but you surprised me. I thought that you and your husband—forgive me, but I've forgotten his name."

"Stuart."

"I thought that you and Stuart were true believers. I know that Cardinal and David are. Ellie, too, for that matter."

Melissa was quiet for a moment, then bent down, picked up a small stone and tossed it into the pond. They watched the ripples expand, then reflect from the shore closest to them. She did not speak until the last movement of the water had died away. "My husband is a good businessman who enjoys the sound of his own voice." She picked up a second stone, but noticed that it contained the fossil of a shell. The stone itself was small, about the size of a golf ball, and on one side quite ordinary: dirty white and black, contoured with pits and bumps. Underneath, though, it was pure white, and in the center, a red-orange convex impression of a shell, as big as her little fingernail, perfect, the striations of the shell clearly visible. She held it in her hand for Sam to see.

"I know. They're everywhere around here. Turned up when they dug the pond, I imagine."

"I don't mean to say, understand me, that Stuart doesn't believe what he preaches. He does. But if things had turned out differently, he could have become a radio sports-talk guy and he would have been perfectly happy. Or some kind of self-help motivational speaker. Or had a TV cooking show. Religion is not at his core; talking is."

"And you?"

"Me?" She turned the fossil over and over in her hand. "Me. I had a teen-age daughter who had one abortion, one child and three shop-lifting arrests, married to a pot head, on his way to being a meth addict. I had to do something or she would have been gone. Ruined. When Stuart found Jesus, I saw it as a way to save Cardinal's life, not my own."

"Did it?"

"I think so. Cardinal is smart, and she's a rather pragmatic Christian. She knows her life is better now than it was, say, eight years ago. Far from perfect, sure. But she's learning how to make it better, manage David. I expect that the babies will stop soon. She'll use Jesus to keep things moving in the right direction."

"You sound like something of a pragmatic Christian yourself."

She smiled. "The Lord and I have come to an accommodation."

"Accommodation?"

"That's between Him and me."

"So what about David?"

"David." She sighed. "David scares the shit out of me."

"Why?"

"Because he's dumb as a brick. I love my daughter to death, but I'll swear: she attracts losers like a magnet attracts iron filings. James Austin—that's her first husband—was worse. But David... Christianity has something of a bad history in the hands of the ignorant, you know. Maybe, just maybe, Stuart's ministry is doing something about that in a small way. I like to think so."

"But David's just a part-time preacher at a small church in Wesley. And a chicken farmer. How much trouble could he get into?"

"It's Ellie. Oh, I love the others just as much. But Ellie's been through a lot, and I hate to see David work his ignorant come-to-Jesus ways on her." They sat quietly for some minutes. "May I keep this fossil?"

He smiled. "Sure. So I'm the David antidote?"

"Did I make it sound like that?"

"It's a little more than I signed up for. A little bit too much to ask of a lapsed Presbyterian."

"David thinks you're Jewish."

Sam shrugged. "It's a common misconception in the county."

"Why?"

"Early on after I moved here, someone asked me if I was a Christian and I said 'no,' thinking the question meant the usual born-again-Jesus-is-my-personal-Savior thing. Turned out that the question was more cultural than religious and my 'no' was taken to mean I was Jewish."

"But you never corrected the record?"

"Nah. To do so would have fed into the Madison County attitude that it matters. Like 'Hell no, I hain't no Jew.' So I let people think what they want. I don't think it matters much."

"You're an atheist?"

"Oh, no. I'm not smart enough to be an atheist."

"Smart enough?"

"It takes a certain quality of mind, I think, for a person to say 'I know there's no God.' A massive confidence in one's own intelligence. I don't have that kind of sureness about anything, really."

"So, what are you?"

"I hear that these days I'm called a None. N-O-N-E. None of the above. I read somewhere that an agnostic doesn't know if there's a god, but a meta-agnostic doesn't even know if he knows if there's a god. That's about where I am." He waited for a response, but Melissa was silent. "In any event, I told Cardinal, and David, too, that I couldn't be part of her religious training, but that I wouldn't question any of their teaching, either. There it stands."

"Professor." He looked over at her. "But you're good for her, Sam, you are. Just by being you. Just by being intelligent, and a *professor*. By talking to Ellie about the horses and the farm and the spring and her math. By taking her to track meets and to lunch in town, and by letting her ride the horses. By teaching her how to vaccinate and how to fool the horses. By being very quietly and non-outspokenly someone without a biblical world view. Someone who cares for her and shows her that there's a world out there."

"A world outside of Norman Rockwell's?"

"Actually, I found the art quite nicely done. And his world more complex than people imagine."

"My grandmother was a Rosie the Riveter. Ruby the Riveter, actually, building tail assemblies for B-seventeens at Goodyear in Akron during the war. The Big One. Double-ewe-double-ewe-two. When the boys came home, she quietly went back to work as a clerk at Polski's. A department store—Fourth floor. Ladies' apparel. Going up, please." He stood to go. "I should go check on the horses and let them out."

"Someday, ten years from now, we'll have to tell Ellie about this conversation."

"It's a deal. Right here, the three of us on a bench. I'll be near eighty, she'll be twenty-one and the pine tree will be marginally taller."

"In ten years, Ellie will be in college, if I have anything to do with it, and I'll be..."

"And you'll be just fine."

"But the pond will be gone? I think I'll miss its presence."

Sam stuck his hands in the rear pockets of his jeans and contemplated the pond. "The Second Law is a cruel master."

"Second Law?"

"Of Thermodynamics."

"Which is?"

Sam shrugged. "Things fall apart. The universe is winding down. Eventually that dike will fail and the water will head downhill. If you want to be precise, entropy is on the increase."

"What was that word?"

"Entropy."

"Which is...?"

"A measure of the disorder around us. Which is increasing. Everything tends toward confusion and collapse. Every crystal vase on the Earth is destined by the Second Law eventually to break."

"You don't split infinitives, even when you talk, do you?"

"A lifetime of dealing with OCD editors. A colleague once asked me whether anal-retentive has a hyphen, and I said 'yes' without even getting the joke."

"This entropy thing is a little depressing."

"The First Law—Conservation of Energy—says that, in a transaction with nature, you can never come out ahead. The Second Law says you can't break even, either, not in the long run."

"I never cared much for science. Or math. Which leads directly through Cardinal to you. When she was young and we lived at the commune, I discouraged, I'm afraid, any interest she might have had in math or science. So now she and David want to home-school the kids and there's a hole in the home curriculum that you're filling. If I had done my job years ago ...," she left the thought incomplete.

"You do what you do," Sam said.

"I had several failings as a parent. That was one of the little ones."

An uncomfortable silence followed that thought, and Sam, at a loss for what to say, turned the topic back. "I'm a little surprised that you don't know the Second Law. Many evangelicals use it to refute Darwinian evolution, which has species tending toward the more-complex. They've got it wrong; all the Second Law says is that eventually all of this," he spread his arms, "will be ground to dust. More grandly, the sun will collapse and blow the Earth to smithereens. Thereby increasing entropy and advancing the interests of the Second Law. Before then, a little increased complexity is tolerable. The Second Law says all milk bottles will eventually break; it doesn't say you can't turn some disorganized sand into a glass bottle."

"Stuart handles evolution with care, but it's not a big part of his ministry. David thinks the Earth is six thousand years old."

"You?"

She looked again at the fossil in her hand. "I see God's touch in this shell, but it's not a mere six thousand years old. And only an idiot would think it is."

"I agree. I've seen some old things—the Pyramids, the Parthenon—and that shell looks much older to me, even conceding that things are not always as they appear."

"You've traveled some?"

"Long time ago."

He gave her his hand to help her up. "Looked at one way, the spring that feeds the pond is one of the sources of the Mississippi. Not as famous as Itasca up in Minnesota, or Yellowstone in Wyoming, or San Isabel over in Colorado, but still. From here to an unnamed creek down below, to Brush Creek and into the White. Two years ago, during the big flood, the pond overflowed and filled the pasture where we're going with a couple hundred small silver fish. Upon which the crows had a feast. The irony, of course, was that the extra pressure on the dike from the flood made it leak more, so now it's lower than ever. Here, come this way. We'll walk back through the day pasture."

They took their time, of which they both had plenty that morning, getting back to the stable, a pleasant walk through the woods and pastures, Sam pointing out the sights, such as they were, along the way: a stag-horn oak that probably wouldn't last through another summer, two flirtatious red-tails, passing time high up in a sycamore, he squatted down to show her the early signs of the daisies and buttercups that would come along later, the former he would let be, but the latter to be eradicated before they took over. Melissa was mostly silent, listening with a faint smile on her face.

Back at the stable, the horses were restless, past ready to be on the pasture. Not to be hurried, he checked them all for signs of reaction to the vaccinations and found one swelling requiring attention.

"You treat your animals well."

"My neighbors say I pamper them." He made his voice a singsong. "'They're farm animals, Sam.' It's a detriment of my suburban youth. We grew up without rural sensibilities, and never were really very good at acquiring them."

"What's to acquire?"

"You have to start young. Four-H, for example, is where rural kids learn that it's okay to eat your pets. We never caught up with that, and our chickens, I'm embarrassed to say, die of old age. *My* chickens. Changing pronouns is as hard as anything. Just a minute." Sam walked into the tack room and came out with two halters and lead lines, haltered up Evening Smoke and Just One Look, the two dominant ones, and handed one line to Melissa. "You okay with this? You take Smokey and I'll follow. We'll just walk them back the way we came. The others will come along, and The Looker will make sure they don't come around."

"Do you have to do this every morning? How do you manage alone?"

"Normally, they put themselves up, but I thought you might like to walk up with them. Most of the hospitality I can offer around the place has to do with the horses. It's a pretty equine-centered little farm. I'm out of practice with visitors, if you want to know the truth."

"You're doing just fine."

"Here we go."

The transportation of the five animals—six including Teena, who had now joined the procession, lagging behind out of hind-kick distance at the rear—went smoothly enough, the two haltered horses were released, and all five took off across the pasture and up the hill, prancing and bucking, manes and tails flying.

"They run just because they like to run," said Melissa. Sam said nothing, but smiled at her and nodded, coiling up the lead lines. "Sometimes I feel like that."

"You're a runner?"

"No. I meant it more broadly."

"Restive, the dark one there with the narrow blaze, is a bit off on the right hind. Can you see the way he short-steps it?"

"Why?"

"Hard to know. I'll have to watch it. Sally could spot lameness a day and a half before I could, but I'm getting a little better."

"Your wife?"

"Yes. Tonight I'll rub him down with some Absorbine and see how he is in the morning. Maybe he has a little muscle pull. Or it could be in his hoof." He turned to look at Melissa. "Have you ever seen your granddaughter ride?"

"No."

"You're in for a treat." Without apparent signal, all five horses stopped running simultaneously and began to graze. Melissa and Sam watched them for a while, until Sam spoke. "I guess the show is over."

"Have you ever owned a mule?"

"A mule? Why do you ask?"

"A friend of ours owns one. Named Mike, for the governor."

"I'm told that it's required that if you're going to own mules, one of them must be named for the governor. There are still a few Bills around the county, I'm told."

"I think their ears are cute."

"They say a mule'll be your friend for ten years just waiting for the chance to kick you in the head. I've got enough trouble."

"But you *were* kicked by a horse. Which one?"

"Dreadnaught. The dark one there. The last one through the gate when we walked up."

"I like his name."

"Ellie used to call him Naughty, but lately she's switched to Afraid of Nothing. I think she thinks it sounds more grown-up, for her, I mean, not for the horse."

"Why is he always the last one through the gate?"

"Pecking order, if you'll accept a mixed-species metaphor. Dreadnaught is number five in a five horse herd. He's a little pushy because he's always looking around for someone to make number six, and he'd like it to be you. They were all walking up to the day pasture the day of the accident, and I was behind Dee."

"Who was the last one through."

"Good for you. And it had turned rainy and drizzly and they were all feeling pretty feisty and rarin' to go. And without even thinking about what I was doing, I clapped my hands to encourage them to get going, which they didn't need, and *boom!* Dreadnaught fired off, double-barreled, and I woke up on the ground, bleeding. Which is where I was when Ellie found me. I knew better, but I'm an old fool. I may have mentioned that."

"*Emeritus*, in Latin."

"Exactly. I deserved worse than I got. I keep forgetting that you were there that evening. You saw me at my most ridiculous."

"And in your Fruit-of-the-Looms."

Sam laughed. "Ha! Now I *am* embarrassed."

"Your friend Lynda Stratford and I helped you use the toilet and got you into bed, while David, Cardinal and Ellie divided up the chores."

"Gadzooks, it gets worse and worse." Sam covered his face with his hand.

"Relax. Actually, Lynda took care of most of the really personal things. She said she'd been trained as a nurse."

"I doubt it, but I guess there's no reason to sort that out now. Anyway, a very belated thank you for that day. To the whole family."

"My pleasure. Ours." They watched the horses graze for a few minutes. "What now?"

"Clean up the stalls. Top off the water tanks. Move some hay into the feed room. Couple of other things. What about you?"

"I'm meeting Stuart at the studio at one. Some techie is coming by to peddle a new software package, which we don't need and can't afford, but Stuart says we should listen to him so we can keep up."

"Keeping up. It must be a big job."

"Endless. Hopeless, really. Things change so fast it makes my head spin. I was just getting used to Facebook and Twitter and now everyone is migrating to Tumblr and Instagram. And, they say, if Yahoo! buys Tumblr, everyone will leave there, for I forget where. It all seems so, I don't know, petty. Pointless. Which is the last thing a Christian ministry should be. I think I'd rather help you clean the stalls."

"If the world were properly programmed, Restive there..." Sam pointed at the horse nearest the fence line, "...would walk over right now and stick his head between the wires to get to the grass on the other side."

Melissa laughed pleasantly, then shook her head. "Good for you, Sam, good for you. Listen. Forget all that David-antidote talk. Pretend I never said it. Just stay in her life, okay, Professor? That's all I ask."

"I can do that."

"Thanks. Now, get to work. I'll find my way back to my car."

"Come anytime. Come riding sometime."

It wasn't until hours later that Sam noticed the paper stuck under the windshield wiper of the large pickup. "Thanks for the lovely morning. My cell is 595-3174. Call me if you need anything. (I have yours already from Cardinal.)— Melissa."

## The Next Thursday.

It had been back in February when Sam had discovered the unopened envelope in Sally's files, but during the following weeks he had thought little about it, and had analyzed the possibilities that it represented not at all. Of all the things that the envelope—indeed the post office box itself—might suggest, he had rather stubbornly refused to see anything beyond the ten dollar deposit that might be coming to him. Some day, but why make a special trip to town for ten bucks, a third of which he would spend on gas getting to and from?

Today, however, he had come across Postmaster Danielson's card while looking for something else, there were no pressing chores to do, and he fancied a steak from Country Meats for dinner, maybe with some sautéed mushrooms, maybe the left-over rice, onion and mushrooms all sautéed together. Greens. A slice or two of sourdough and a Moosehead. Maybe two. Yes, he thought, that would do nicely for a Thursday evening dinner at home. So, some shopping, maybe *The New York Times* to splurge, and he'd stop in on Mr. Danielson on the way home.

It took him longer than it might have to do the shopping, as he knew several of the young clerks and cutters at the butcher shop, and he enjoyed catching up on what was new in their lives. But he came away in good order with a nice-looking T-bone and all the trimmings, picked up a copy of the paper at the drugstore, and pulled into the post office parking lot on Joyce Street at about three o'clock.

Inside the lobby, he went directly to the door to the left of the counters, rang the doorbell, displayed the card, and asked for Mr. Danielson of the woman who opened the door. He was directed to the other door to the right, and then ushered down the corridor to Danielson's still-messy office. Sam knocked on the doorframe and Danielson looked up from his work.

"Excuse me, Mr. Danielson. Remember me? I'm Sam Butler." He displayed the card again, "I stopped in some time ago about..."

"Ah, yes, the man with the unknown box key. I remember, except..." he got up from his desk, walked to the door and held out his hand, "...your name again?"

"Sam Butler." They shook.

"What can I do for you this time, Mr. Butler? I trust you've been well?"

"Very well. Except that I got on the wrong end of an excited horse. A little of this and that bruised, most notably my ego, but no permanent harm done. Listen, I think I've discovered the box number and I thought maybe I could get the deposit on the key. I just bought myself a steak for dinner, and maybe you'll end up paying for it. Box thirty-seven-twenty. Seven-two-seven-oh-four?"

"That's us. I think I can take care of that." He retreated to behind his desk, moved and clicked his mouse, while talking to himself, as computer users do. "Um hmm. Sit down, won't you? Here. Let's see. Scroll down. Hmmm. That's odd. Let me check here. Well, now," he looked up from the monitor. "Box thir-ty-seven-twenty is still active."

"Active? But what about the rental fee? Who's been paying that?"

Danielson shrugged. "What's your wife's name?"

"Sally Sanderson. Sarah, actually."

"Not Butler?"

Sam shook his head. "Sanderson."

Danielson turned back to his computer and typed. "No one, apparently."

"But the box is still active. How can that be?"

"Officially, it can't. Don't tell the boss." Danielson nodded in the direction of the president's picture. "Sometimes things just—like I said the other day—fall through the cracks. That account never made it from hard copy to digital, and after that..." he spread his hands, "...there it sat. Somebody should have caught it; probably me."

"Neither rain nor snow nor dark of night..."

"Yes, so they say."

"So the box is still active, but as best I know it hasn't been visited for almost four years. What happens to the mail that goes into it?"

"Of course, there could be a second key. Lemme check that...Hmmm. Nope. So, putting that aside, regs say we're supposed to return to sender anything not retrieved from a box within thirty days. But," he gestured toward the pictures on the wall again, "...but we're a pretty small zip code in a nice roomy building, and so we usually throw out the fourth class and save the remainder."

"Forever?"

"Theoretically. Or until a postal inspector stops by, whichever comes first."

"So, can I get what's in the box?"

"Well, sure. You have the key. In order to give you what's been held back here, I'm supposed to ask to see the letters of administration of your wife's estate, but know why I'm not going to?"

"Why?"

"Because you said her name was Sanderson and yours is Butler. If you'd been trying to be dishonest, you wouldn't have. Box thirty-seven-twenty. Go see if the key works. I'll see what we held back, if anything, and meet you out front, by the box."

"Right. Thanks."

Sam walked down the corridor, waved as Danielson branched off to a side hallway, and let himself out the door into the public area of the facility. Box 3720 was far down the bank of boxes, near the exit, the smallest size, roughly three-by-three inches square and a foot deep. The key worked but the box was empty.

Some minutes later, Danielson appeared from a door Sam hadn't noticed. Sam had expected to see him lugging a plastic box full of mail, but instead he had only one envelope in his hand. "This is all we've got." He opened the envelope and pulled out two pieces of paper. He handed a three-by-five piece of light peach-colored paper to Sam. "Sorry we missed you" was printed across the top.

"What is it?" Sam asked.

"Someone tried to send—no, *did* send a certified letter to thirty-seven-twenty. For whatever reason, your wife didn't retrieve it, and it was returned to the sender."

"The reason is plain: she'd been dead for two weeks. May twenty-six, oh-nine." Sam pointed to the date on the form.

"Right. I'm sorry for the reminder. Now." Danielson handed Sam the other piece of paper from the envelope, a standard sheet of letter-sized paper. "I stopped back at my office and looked up the tracking number; it's there on the form you're holding. That's what took so long for me to get over here. It—whatever it was—the certified letter was returned to five-eight-two-oh-two where it was retrieved by the person who signed for it there. I printed you a copy of the image of the signature there."

Sam looked at the scrawl, hardly identifiable as a signature at all, in fact. No actual letters were apparent, only three loops and a line, with a dot above the line. "Five-eight-two-oh-two. Where's that?"

"Grand Forks, North Dakota. I had to look it up."

"North Dakota?"

"North of here." Danielson tightly laughed, clearly a bit uncomfortable with the situation.

"That scrawl doesn't look at all like the writing on the other envelope I found."

Danielson shrugged. "Sometimes people are neater addressing envelopes than they are with their signatures. Thank God. Or maybe one person addressed the envelope and someone else picked it up when it was returned. There are a hundred possible explanations."

"Sender's Name?" Sam pointed to a spot on the form, where was written 58202-0017.

Another shrug, which seemed to be Postmaster Danielson's favorite gesture. "We fill that in with whatever we can get from the return address on the envelope. Most letters don't have to have a return address, but certified letters do, so there's for sure someplace to return them to. I'm guessing there was no name."

"'Final Notice,'" Sam read, "Article will be returned to sender on May 31.'"

"That's clearly what happened. That's all that's left here. Up in North Dakota, the original sender would have gotten the letter back, with a similar form, now marked 'RTS-UNC' in that spot. Return to sender—unclaimed."

"Right." Sam refolded the paper. "Can you tell when the item first appeared in this box here?"

"Fifteen days before it was returned, whatever that would be."

"May sixteenth. Four days after she died. May I keep the envelope?"

Danielson handed it over; it turned out to be an official USPS business envelope. "Sure. I got it for you." After a pause, "Want to know what I'd do next? If you want to do anything at all, that is. I'd email the postmaster up at five-eight-two-oh-two. There's a chance that she'll remember something. I wrote her name and email down for you."

"But I don't have the sender's address, only a zip code."

"Yeah, but a nine-digit zip code."

"Which is?"

"Could be a particular set of houses on a street, or an entire apartment complex. With those two zeros at the beginning, it's most likely a unique post office box: box number seventeen up at five-eight-two-oh-two. The postmaster will know. She won't give you a precise street address, but if it's a box in her office, she'll tell you that. Maybe she'll remember whoever sent it or re-claimed it."

"Four years, nearly..." Sam shook his head.

"Yeah, that's a long time."

"It doesn't seem so long ago."

"No. I suppose not. Now, Mr. Butler, you're going to have to excuse me. Why don't you stop by sometime, and let's get thirty-seven-twenty back on the books, okay? Or, if you'd like, I'll process the deposit return right now."

"Thanks. But I think I'll hold onto the key for a while. You'll put the box rental fee into the box for me?" Danielson nodded. "Thanks. I've used up enough of your time. Goodbye. And thanks again for your help and for the information."

"Have a nice day."

**That Evening.**

The steak was done to perfection, at least to Sam's tastes, meaning pink on the inside and burned from the fire on the out-. He had cooked it over the fire in the hearth, a practice of which Sally disapproved, complaining of grease splatters on the fieldstone hearth, but he cooked it there anyway, as he would do, occasionally, even when she was still alive. It was March, so soon the last fire of the spring would have been built, and his grilling would move to the outdoors, but tonight, indoors was just fine. He then laid out the meal, tablecloth and all, on the kitchen table, opened the beer and poured it into a glass, and sat for a minute, looking out the window into the darkness. He then ate slowly, neither reading nor listening to the radio, just savoring the steak and beer, the quiet and the dark.

When he finished, he cleared the table, put water on the stove for his coffee and walked upstairs to the study, where he picked up the envelope addressed to Box 3720, Fayetteville, and then looked through the wastebasket for the newspaper correction that had been inside. Back in the kitchen, he measured out the Nescafé, added milk and then the hot water, and sat down, looking at the envelope, the Sorry-we-missed-you form and Danielson's print-out of the signed receipt by the sender, re-accepting the certified letter. There was, of course, no reason that the sender of the correction necessarily had to be the same person as the sender of the certified letter. There was no return address on the envelope in his hand, as there had been on the certified letter, Danielson said. He looked again at the smudged postmark on the envelope. Only the year was discernible:

2008. The correction itself, of course, gave him a hint of the date. It referred to the paper of August 29th, year not given, but presumably the year of the postmark. Clearly it had arrived before Sally had died, because she had filed it away. Not necessarily in '08, though, for it was not certain that it was sent immediately after her correspondent had clipped it from the paper. But still, he guessed that the correction had appeared in the paper shortly after August 29th, '08, and had arrived in P.O. Box 3720, Fayetteville, shortly thereafter, nine months, more or less, before Sally's accident.

Inside the postmark's circle was what he supposed was the originating zip code. The first, third and fourth numbers were impossible to read, the second was either an eight or a six, and the last digit was probably a two. Thus it could be 58202, the zip code of the certified letter, but it could equally as well be 16972, wherever the hell that was. He looked at the tidy printing on the envelope and at the looping scrawl on the return receipt. Maybe; maybe not. Probably not. No, he thought, not the same. He put the original envelope, the clipping, the peach-colored form and the print-out of the signature, he put them all into the USPS official-business envelope and laid it aside, picked up the *Times* and began to read, sipping his coffee.

And it was entirely appropriate, of course, that one of the corrections in that day's paper would have caught Sally's eye:

"A picture caption on Saturday with an article about a showdown between Scottsdale and Cave Creek, Ariz., over the right to use the motto 'the West's most Western town' misstated, in some copies, part of the name of a buffalo being shown off in Cave Creek. The buffalo is Harley Wallbanger, not Harvey Walganger."

There was something almost charmingly twentieth-century about the entire post office box matter, Sally's possession of it, Sam's ignorance of it, the correspondence that went on via it, the envelopes that had presumably arrived in it, the corrections, the poems, the photos, whatever, the unopened envelope, the certified letter, everything. Not to mention the possibility, even the likelihood, that Sally had a quiet email account as well, which had contained—might still contain—who knows what? But it was far beyond his e-skills, to track such an account down, let alone to try to figure out what the password might have been. It bordered, he thought, on the creepy for him to be snooping around for, or in, Sally's emails, even if he knew where to begin, which he didn't. He had one foot sufficiently in the digital age to know how to find the original article in the *Times* which had been corrected by the clipping in the unopened envelope, and he knew he could Google P.O. Box 17, 58202 to see if anyone's name popped up, but what would he do with the name anyway? He could use the address that Danielson had given him to email the North Dakota postmaster, but how would anyone remember who had claimed a returned letter from four years ago? And who knew how many times the box's owners might have changed in the years since the certified letter was returned? And the looping signature could be anyone's. Or no one's, actually, as the sender might have wanted to disguise his name. Or hers.

All he had that was at all definite was the clipping in the unopened envelope and the Sorry-we-missed-you form, sending the unclaimed letter back to North Dakota. North Dakota? Sam had never been to North Dakota, and as best he knew, neither had Sally, but of course, that meant nothing. Almost on a whim, and thinking himself very foolish for doing so, he wrote on the outside of the envelope the following column of figures:

| Aug | 2 |
| Sept | 30 |
| Oct | 31 |
| Nov | 30 |
| Dec | 31 |
| Jan | 31 |
| Feb | . . . |

He had to pause. Was 2009 a leap year? No. Leap years were always even-numbered.

| Feb | 28 |
| Mar | 31 |
| Apr | 30 |
| May | 12 |

And, of course, it was in keeping with his mood that night that the sum was 256. Two to the eighth; four to the fourth.

Which, equally of course, meant nothing. The starting point of his calculation was the date of the original article, not the correction, nor when it was sent to Sally, nor when she retrieved the envelope from her post office box, but chose not to open it. And the ending date was the date of her accident, not of the arrival of the unclaimed certified letter. So, on a day in August 2008, an article in the *Times* confuses faux amphibians for reptiles, frogs for lizards, and on the same day, they buy a game chestnut mare named Miss Run Run, with a bowed tendon and a star on her forehead, and Sally stops drinking. Shortly afterwards, the *Times* discovers the mistake and publicizes its embarrassment, Sally's unknown correspondent clips and sends the correction to her, but she doesn't open the envelope, nor does she throw it away. And 256 days from the beginning, she takes a drink, and another, puts Tommy Greene's life at risk, and dies, too soon to read the North Dakotan's certified letter wondering, presumably, where are you, are you okay and why aren't you writing?

So there he was: nowhere. With the dinner dishes waiting to be cleaned and the horses needing to be put up for the night. Teena got the T-bone bone, the chickens would get the table scraps in the morning, and Sam would go to sleep wondering what had been going on and for how long. And, of course, this: what was the connection, if any, between the unopened envelope, Sally's 256 days of sobriety, the accident, and the certified letter?

**The Following Tuesday.**

The question remained with him long after she had asked it: "Do you know how easy it is to hack into a listserve of which you, yourself, are a member?"

They had been sitting several weeks earlier—two weeks after they had sparred over the cover of *Horse Heaven*—had been sitting in the Valley Café, on one of what had become their irregular afternoons over pie and coffee, irregular because Lynda, outside of her lab, acted on whim and impulse, not on schedule. She would call, he would protest, and they would meet. She never spoke of her work or her experiments, nor was she the least bit interested in the politics of the Physics Department. (Once, when he'd observed that physicists were probably above petty campus politics, she'd rolled her eyes and said "Don't kid yourself," but nothing more.) But she was interested in Sam and Jonathan's working arrangement, Jonathan's article, his tenure and how were things going? Part Four was complete, the article was finished and sent out for review, and Jonathan was beginning to think about a second article. And Sam had stressed again, as always, that Jonathan should not be asking around to identify those that Lynda persisted in calling The Big Three: Wilson, Selvig and Pryor, speculated to be the soft *no* votes. And this time she had looked up from her pie and across the table at him and asked, "Do you know how easy it is to hack into a listserve of which you, yourself, are a member?"

"No. Do you?" She had lifted a small bite of pie to her lips, looked at him through her eyebrows and said nothing. "You'd enjoy these little meetings more if you'd have something other than coconut crème."

"I'd enjoy these meetings more if we'd go out to my car and you'd rearrange my clothing."

"Quit. You're telling me that Jonathan's read COPT emails and knows that Wilson, Selvig and Pryor are the *noes* willing to switch their votes?"

"I didn't *tell* you anything. I *asked* you a question. You know: a bunch of words with one of those curvy things at the end. With a dot?"

"'Do you know how to hack into a listserve?' is a question. 'Do you know how easy it is to hack into a listserve?' is a statement. Notwithstanding the punctuation."

"In my opinion, lawyers use the word 'notwithstanding' too often."

She had refused to elaborate on the non-question question, and he had dropped the matter, but the question remained with him in the several weeks since, not exactly haunting him, or eating away at him, rather nagging, pestering him, itching at his brain, until he'd arranged to have coffee with Johnson Reynolds, the chair of COPT who had initially proposed that he work with Jonathan. They met, between Reynolds' two classes, in the coffee shop which occupied a corner of the library on the second floor of the law building. They danced around the COPT deliberations for a bit:

"How's Jonathan's article coming?"

"Finished. Submitted. Two acceptances in hand. Hawaii and St. John's."

"Congratulations."

"I didn't do much."

"Except to get someone who had written nothing to have an article submitted and accepted."

"I'm convinced that COPT will be unanimously impressed."

"Unanimity we don't need. Have you met Gwen?"

"Yes. You? Probably not, or you'd know that she goes by Lynda."

"Lynda? I thought it was Gwendolyn. The *Times* called her Gwendolyn."

"Gwendolynda, to be precise. Jonathan and her father call her Gwen; she and the rest of the world, Lynda. With a *y*."

"Did you see the article?"

"Yes. They called her Stratford, after one initial Gwendolynda. I thought the article was very flattering."

"To her and to us. The provost is post-coital."

Then: "Suppose I were to tell you that Jonathan is curious about the identity of the three *noes* who were willing to change?"

"I'd tell you that COPT deliberations are confidential. I'd tell you to tell Jonathan not to wonder about that. I'd especially tell you to tell Jonathan not to be asking around about that. It's considered to be in bad taste."

"I've told him all of that. He says he's curious but insists he hasn't asked."

"Well, okay then. Are you curious? Does their identity affect your job?"

"No, not at all. But his curiosity has, for unknown reasons, made me curious. I'm not sure why. I've never been outside looking in before. Not since I first arrived, that is."

"You sailed through, I'm told."

"The committee was asleep. Suppose I were to ask you flat out?"

"No confirm; no deny."

Sam sipped his coffee, stronger than he made it at home, then pulled the science section out of *The New York Times*. "There's a picture in here," he said, "taken by the Cassini spacecraft, looking up through the rings of Saturn, with one of the moons in the foreground, I forget which one, the one with the volcanoes. Volcanoes on the moons of Saturn. It got me thinking, the picture did. When I was a sophomore in college, I took an astronomy course, and the TA took an hour one week to show us the project he was working on for his Master's. He was taking pictures of a certain crater on the moon, through the university's telescope, some crater off to the right as you look at the moon, as I recall. Then he'd make slides of the pictures and project them onto a white ball, big, like say a beach ball. Then he'd set up a camera perpendicular to his image of the crater on the ball and reshoot the photo, so now he had a picture, twice removed from reality, which showed his crater as a true circle. He'd then repeat the process several times during the month and, by carefully measuring the shadows of the crater walls, he could calculate how deep the crater was. No one had ever seen the crater looking straight down from above. No one had ever seen the far side of the moon. And now..." he gestured at the paper, "the far side of a moon of Saturn. It's remarkable, I think. I remember thinking that my grandmother, who had been born during the Indian wars and lived to see Neil Armstrong walk, that she had lived through unimaginable changes. But it's happening again, isn't it?"

"Imagine how your grandmother would react to today's world: from the Indian wars to the war on terror."

"But that's time-travel science fiction. In the real world, we live our own generation and two more, give or take. Every generation, I think, is shocked by what its grandchildren are doing, good and bad. Kids sexting naked photos is shocking to me. Imaginable, but shocking. So is three-D printing. But beyond those two generations, it's unimaginable, but that's of only theoretical concern, because no one lives that long. The rate of change is accelerating, the second derivative is positive, but each new generation is taught to accept that increasing rate of change, so it's a wash."

Reynolds thought for a minute. "Wasn't it Virginia Woolf who said the world changed in nineteen-ten? Your grandmother would have been how old?"

"In her twenties, I guess."

"And think of the unimaginable things that she was due to see: airplanes, rock 'n' roll, women voting."

"TV."

"Modern art, the rise of communism."

"The end of colonialism, social security, space flight."

"Antibiotics, the state of Israel, prohibition and the end of prohibition."

"A British queen. Negroes in the big leagues. Actually, you may be convincing me that the second derivative is *not* positive. I'm not sure that our generation has seen as much change as that, or the next one as much as we've seen. Still and all, I think you'd have to go back a long way to find a society in which the grandparents were not shocked by the lives of their grandkids."

"Pre-industrial."

"Or pre-contact America. It's computers that are the most puzzling to me." Sam took a pen out of his pocket and wrote "Wilson, Selvig & Pryor" in the margin of the *Times*, next to the picture from Saturn, and slid it across the table. "Suppose I were to ask you what you thought of that?"

Reynolds picked it up, looked at the writing and slid it back to Sam. He thought for a minute, pulling at his beard, spreading his moustache. "There's a certain faculty member, who will remain unidentified, but if he—or she—were to see that picture, he—or she—would go postal."

Sam picked up the paper, refolded the science section and put it back on the table. He dabbed his lips with a napkin and said, "That's a slur, you know, on the fine federal workers who deliver the mail. My own personal postmaster, a young woman named Phyllis, is a valuable, if underpaid, public servant, and an entirely well-adjusted individual, who wouldn't think of shooting her fellow valuable, but underpaid, public servants." He sipped his coffee and dabbed his lips again. "How's Bill Lindsay doing?"

"About as you remember him. Last time we chatted, his list of reasons for the impending collapse of American higher education in general, and this fine university in particular, numbered a mere eight."

"Let's keep it at eight," Sam said, re-assembling the day's paper and placing it on the floor at his feet. "How're your kids?"

Grace, it turned out, had completed her PhD in the classics from Columbia, and was now on the post-doc carousel, this year at Colorado, wishing that she was on the escalator instead, heading up toward one of the tenure-track jobs that might open up in the future. "You know how the market is for professors of the classics."

"No, but I can guess. And Jimmy?"

"Please. *James*. He's decided he's an entrepreneur, and has opened a business, manufacturing green insulation."

"Who cares what color insulation is?"

"Green as in environmentally-correct insulation. The business is due to take off, I'm told, as soon as the climate warms a bit more. It would help if you'd cut down a few trees."

"I'll see what I can do. It's a growth industry, is it?"

"His motto is 'The climate is changing; be glad you're old.'"

"Cheery. But then, I *am* old. Are you invested?"

"What do you think? And you?"

"I'm retired, remember? Living on a four-oh-one-kay."

"How is that?"

"Fine, just so's I don't live too long."

"By the way. I looked up the origins of the word 'dreadnought.' There was a British warship, First World War vintage, of that name. H.M.S. Dreadnought, O-U-G-H-T. But Webster's finds A-U-G-H-T an acceptable variation, though perhaps archaic. I thought you'd want to know."

"I'll inform Dee, who will be totally unconcerned. Anyway, Ellie doesn't call him Naughty anymore. I think it's begun to sound like baby talk to her."

"Where do they come up with these horse names, anyway?"

"It's considered an art form. The new horse is named after a Linda Ronstadt song."

"*You're No Good*?"

"Very funny. *Just One Look.*"

"...that's all it took?"

"Yeah." They lifted and touched cups. "We call him The Looker."

"We?"

"Ellie and I."

"Is he? A looker, I mean."

"Very much so, if you'll forgive my bias: bright bay, with a crooked blaze. A big guy; sixteen-two."

"Which means?"

"Sixteen hands and two inches at the withers."

"Which means?"

"He's five-six—about your height—measured just above his shoulders. I can just see over his back, but you couldn't."

"Nice word, withers. How old?"

"The girl is eleven, just turned; the horse is six."

"I remember our kids at eleven. It's a nice age, watching them figure out who they are, after which, look out, their hormones explode."

"I don't myself remember being eleven." Sam shook his head. "Not a single event. I mean, I suppose I remember events that happened when I was that age, but I don't remember actually being eleven."

"I do. I won a county-wide spelling bee. Went to state, but didn't make the finals."

"What tripped you up?"

"Prairie."

"A hard word for eleven, I guess."

"I missed the first *i*. It was nerves, really, more than spelling; I knew it was wrong as soon as it was out of my mouth."

"You just needed a hit of Ritalin to sharpen your focus."

"I actually heard somewhere that that's about to become an issue. Think of it: PEDs in the National Spelling Bee."

"I always thought that if there were a performance-enhancing drug for professors, the students would have wanted me to take it."

"And would you have?"

Their conversation went on like this for a bit more until Reynolds left to get ready for class, leaving Sam alone at the table. He refilled his cup, opened up his newspaper to the photo of Saturn and Enceladus with its marginal note, and sat back to ponder what he now thought he knew and what he should do about it. He lingered for a half-hour, reading what he wanted out of the paper, occasionally interrupted as one or another of his former colleagues stopped by on their ways in for, or out with, coffee. Then, just before taking down the dregs in his cup, he checked the Corrections column and was rewarded with one that Sally would have appreciated. It read:

"The Personal Health column last Tuesday, about CPR, rendered incorrectly the title of a song by the BeeGees that provides a good rhythm for administering chest compressions. It is 'Stayin' Alive,' not 'Staying Alive.'"

And what was it about that correction, or maybe his remembrance of Sally's amusement, that made him decide for now that Wilson, Selvig and Pryor were just Jonathan's lucky guess? And maybe by suggesting otherwise, Lynda was just fooling with his sensibilities, as she enjoyed doing? For now, he would do nothing, other than fold and refold the science section so that it would fit in the hip pocket of his jeans, leave the rest of the paper behind for whoever came next to the table, and head home to whatever needed to be done there.

**The Following Tuesday.**

It was 9:45 in the morning and the Quincy family was at prayer. The baby, having been fed, was asleep in her crib, and the boys were watching a Bible-story video turned low in the living room, so only three of them were actually, literally, praying—David, Cardinal and Ellie—kneeling in a small triangle on the kitchen floor, close enough together so they could join hands in a circle, which is what they did when they prayed aloud, but now each had hands folded under chin, in silent prayer. They knelt on small squares of remnant carpet that Cardinal had found in the thrift shop. As was customary, they had first prayed aloud—David, then Cardinal, and then Ellie, she seeking blessings for David, her mother and the babies, as well as for the soul of James Austin, whom she still thought of as her father, even though her DNA knew, and the state of Arkansas had decreed, otherwise. And she had ended asking for blessings for Mr. Butler, for Teena the dog, and for each of the horses, whom she called by their official registered names, not the nicknames she had for them, because she was addressing the Lord.

Now they prayed silently, David with his brow creased in concentration, Cardinal with her face blank and peaceful but, internally at least, with one ear cocked for noises from the baby's room, and Ellie with her eyes tightly shut and her lips moving, her quiet words inaudible over the hum of the refrigerator. They would remain like this until the timer on the stove went off, at which time David would attend to his chores outside, Cardinal would see to the children and the house, and Ellie would leave for her math lesson at Sam Butler's place across the highway.

Ellie's eyes opened and she spoke. "Will Mr. Butler go to heaven when he dies?"

Cardinal opened one eye. "We're at prayer, Ellie."

"I know, but will he? He should. It's not fair." David took a deep breath and then exhaled. Cardinal held her own breath, and Ellie looked back and forth between the two. "Will he?"

"Ellen." David's voice was flat and quiet, and his pause lingered on. "This is our time for silent prayer. You may pray that Mr. Butler accepts the Lord and is saved. Jesus Christ: born of a Virgin, died on the Cross, rose from the Tomb, and will come again. Amen."

"Amen," said Cardinal.

"It's not fair." Ellie was adamant. "He's such a good person and he's so kind to the horses. And he helps me with math and riding and tending the hens and all kinds of stuff. And he's helping a teacher at the university who's in trouble. It's just not fair."

David more im- than ex-ploded. His voice was calm, but his eyes were dark. He breathed deeply and Cardinal almost spoke, until she saw that her husband was going to.

"Ellen, you know as well as I do that we get to heaven by the Lord's salvation, not by doing good works. We get to heaven by what we believe, not by what we do. If you could earn your way into heaven by doing good things, then some Jew or Arab or anyone could get in. *I* am the way, the truth and the life. No man cometh unto the Father, but by me."

"It's *not* fair."

David's hand snaked out and slapped her across the face. Her head rocked with the blow, and a red imprint appeared on her cheek. "You will pray silently, Ellen, and ask the Lord's forgiveness for your blasphemy—Cardinal..." He had detected her slight movement toward her daughter. "Leave her be."

And Ellie closed her eyes, squeezing tears out of the corners, and prayed in silence, but what she prayed for was not for David to know. And when the timer buzzed, she was off her knees, out the door and onto her four-wheeler before David and Cardinal could react.

**A Few Minutes Later.**

When Ellie's four-wheeler spun through the gates at Sam's farm, he was cleaning out the stock tank in the isolation paddock about fifty yards south of the stable, where a new horse spent his or her time after arriving on the place from elsewhere, free from any nose-to-nose contact with the residents for a period of time long enough to be sure that no unwelcome microbes had tagged along. Say, two weeks or so. The last resident of the isolation paddock had been Just One Look, now some months ago, during which time the tank had become green with algae. Sam was thinking about dismantling the entire isolation paddock, thereby making it that much more difficult for him to commit to another horse *in extremis*, of which there were thousands.

When Ellie pulled in and killed the engine, Sam raised in greeting his hand holding the scrub brush, thereby causing bleachy water to run down his arm, under his sleeve and into his armpit. "Dammit," he said, tossing the brush into the bucket, and when he looked back she was already by him, running toward the stable. He had expected her to come over and ask what he was doing. Well, maybe she hadn't seen him.

A few minutes later she still hadn't appeared, so he thought no more about it and went back to his scrubbing, and when he was ready for the rinse, he called down to her, "Hey. Turn on the water."

No answer.

He cupped his hands to his mouth. "Turn on the hose."

No answer, and when enough time had passed for the water to have run through the hose, no water.

He walked back to the stable, bothered, actually, not at all at the extra steps. He found her in the third stall, just where the water hydrant was, brushing Daisy's coat.

"Hi. Gone deaf? Good morning."

She did not turn to look at him and continued brushing.

"You okay?"

Still she did not turn, but he heard what might have been "Good morning," spoken quietly into the horse's shoulder. He turned on the water and walked back along the hose to the scrubbed-out tank.

With no children of his own, and hence no grandchildren either, and having spent his entire career teaching adults, Sam knew essentially nothing about how children thought or acted. He had never seen Ellie get either moody or mad, but then what child didn't? He understood that, in an odd way, she was becoming his best friend—and he wasn't sure what that said about either his retirement or his widowhood—but he still knew little about what she thought or why she acted in the ways she did. She seemed consistently happy to see him and the animals, but now he had no idea of what to do or say.

He stood with the hose for the ten minutes that it took to fill the tank, then walked back to the stable and turned off the water. She was still brushing the same horse in the same spot.

"You're going to wear out her hide if you keep brushing her there, you know."

He heard a muffled "Sorry," and she moved her hand with the brush onto the horse's withers.

"Mind if I help?"

She shook her head and he walked behind her, into the tack room and picked up one of the stiff brushes used on tails and manes. Back in the stall, Sam lifted the horse's tail and began drawing the brush through its length, which was almost to the ground.

"We'll have to trim her or she'll be stepping on it soon."

Again she said nothing, and they stood for some minutes, continuing to brush. The horse, sensing the strange mood between them looked first over her left shoulder at Ellie, then over her right at Sam.

Finally, "Ellie, look at me. I need to know that you're okay."

She turned her head so he could see her right eye and now he knew that she had been—still was—crying.

"Hey, what's the matter?" He walked over to her and put his left arm across her back. He had touched her very rarely since she had been coming over, and he was surprised by the feel of the boniness of her shoulder. "Are you okay?"

Now she began sobbing, but instead of turning her head into his embrace, she leaned forward and buried her face in the horse's mane, her arms hanging to her side, her shoulders heaving with her sobs. She was speaking now, but with the sobs, and her running nose, and her voice muffled into the horse's neck, he could not understand a word.

He let her cry for a minute, then stepped behind her and put one hand on each shoulder, not pulling her away from the comfort of the animal's side, but just holding her two shoulders, clumsily, he was aware.

"Can you tell me what's wrong?"

She shook her head.

"What happened?"

Words, but not understandable ones.

"Ellie, I can't hear you."

"I said something."

"Said something to whom?"

"David."

"What did you say?"

"It was bad."

"What?"

"I don't want to tell you."

"You can tell me."

She shook her head again and this time he turned her toward him by the shoulders. And when she faced him, he could see not only the streaming tears, but the red welt still plain on the left side of her face.

"Did David hit you?"

She nodded her head and said something he couldn't catch.

"What?"

"I deserved it."

"What did you say?"

"It was a bad thing."

"No child deserves to be hit in the face."

"I spoke against God." She looked up at him for the first time, and now the words began to tumble out. "I shouldn't have, I know. I didn't mean it. I mean, yes I did at the time but I shouldn't have said it and I'm sorry. I didn't mean it. But..."

"But what?"

"Nothing. I deserved it."

"Let me look." Sam turned her face to the right to get a better look at the welt, which was clearly from an open-handed blow, so there was at least that. "Should we put some cream on it? Does it sting?"

"No," she said, shaking her head. "I've got to go."

"Go where?"

"Home. To say I'm sorry."

"Will you be okay? Do you want me to go with you?"

She shook her head.

"What about your homework?"

"I didn't bring it. I gotta go."

"Wait. First, blow your nose." He handed her his handkerchief. "And hold on. Let's splash some water on your face." She did so, out of the tank in front of Daisy's stall, and he handed her a towel from the tack room. "Feel better?"

She nodded. "But I gotta go and talk to him. Tell him I'm sorry. Ask him to forgive me."

"You'll call me if there's trouble?" The question sounded overly dramatic. *She's eleven,* he thought. *How could she do that?* But he walked with her back to her four-wheeler, no longer touching her and neither of them speaking, and watched while she started the engine, pulled away and accelerated up the hill toward the highway and her home.

The dog looked at him as she drove away, and he walked over to her, squatted down and scratched her ears. "I didn't know what to do," Sam said, more to himself than to Teena. She listened carefully for words she recognized, but hearing none, she lifted her hind leg, exposing her belly for a rub. "You always do, don't cha, old girl? Without even thinking." Then he walked back to the stable, sent the horses up to the day pasture and coiled up the hose, already missing the math lesson.

**Simultaneously with the Foregoing.**

As Ellie rushed through the kitchen door and rode off on her four-wheeler, Cardinal and David at first looked at each other, Cardinal expecting an explosion. But David was oddly constrained, fuming inside perhaps, but almost as if he were waiting for Cardinal to light the fuse. She only sighed, stood up, dusted off her knees and turned to see to the boys in the living room.

"Turn around, please." Perhaps her determination to go about the morning chores as usual was exactly the spark that David needed. "Where are you going?"

She kept her voice flat. "To check on the boys."

"Do as you will, but I'm going to go and get Ellen. I'll drag her back by her collar if I have to." He turned to go.

"Don't."

He turned back and took a step toward her. "What!"

"Don't go. If you go over there now, you'll bring Sam Butler into it. And that's not fair to him. Wait. She'll be home soon."

"You coddle her, Cardinal. I won't do it, and I won't have it. I never thought I'd hear such a thing said in my house."

"I don't want you to hit her across the face like that again."

"I'll punish her anyway I want to. And you'll remember who the head of this family is."

"James used to hit her on the face. It was terrible that I stood around, stoned and drunk, and let him do that, and I'll never..." She paused, looking for the words and struggling to keep her composure, "...I'll never forget that. If you hit her, she'll put the two of you together in her mind, and you don't want that. Neither do I. And I won't let that happen. Hear me? Now, you have chores in the houses, and I'll see that she is punished when she comes back."

"Send her to her room, then. I don't want to see her." He left, slamming the back door while Cardinal walked into the living room.

About twenty minutes passed, during which Cardinal checked on Esther, sent the boys outside to play in the yard, and picked up their bedroom, before she heard the sound of Ellie's four-wheeler, clearly too early for the usual math lesson to be over. The front door opened, with Cardinal now in the kitchen, putting away the breakfast dishes.

"Ellie. You'll come back here, young lady." When Ellie walked into the kitchen, Cardinal knew immediately that she did not have a rebellious pre-teen on her hands. Her expression was contrite and her tears were not of anger but something else. Embarrassment? Sorrow? What? "What do you have to say?"

"I have to say it to David."

"You'll say it to me first."

"Just that I'm sorry. I should not have spoken against the Lord. I should not have spoken against David. I won't do it again. I promise."

"Did Mr. Butler tell you to come back and apologize?"

"No, ma'am. He didn't tell me to do anything. Just to blow my nose and splash water on my face."

"Did he see the mark?"

"Yes, ma'am."

"What did you tell him happened?"

"Nothing."

"What did you tell him you were going to do?"

"Come back and apologize to David."

"What about your math lesson?"

"I said I didn't have it done."

"And what did he say?"

"Nothing."

"Well, David doesn't want to see you now, and said that you should go to your room."

"But..."

"But, if you're going to apologize, you may go and do that. He's in one of the houses." Ellie turned to go. "But wait. Let me see your face." Cardinal sat down on one of the kitchen chairs and pulled Ellie over to her, the better to see the mark. Her hand was cool and when she touched the girl's cheek it was still hot, and she jumped, almost as if she'd touched a hot stove. She put her cheek to Ellie's face. "Do you remember being hit before, Sweetie?"

"Yes."

"Do you remember when I was hit?"

"Yes."

"This isn't like that."

"It isn't?"

"No. James would get drunk and angry and he'd want to hurt us. I should never have let him do that to you and someday maybe you'll forgive me. But David doesn't want to hurt you. You mustn't say things that question the Lord's truth. There's nothing that David and I want more than for you to be a good Christian girl. Do you know that?"

"Yes, ma'am."

"And you are. I know you are. But be careful, okay?"

"Yes, ma'am."

"Okay. Now go find David and say you're sorry."

"Yes, ma'am."

It was cool as Ellie walked across the yard, but it was hot when she walked into the chicken house. The propane heaters were roaring, as the young birds needed it to be in the nineties. The air was stifling, the dirt and ammonia made it almost too thick to breathe, and Ellie could not see the end of the house, five hundred feet away, through the dust. Her eyes began to water, but this time not from her tears, and she wiped them on her sleeve, then held her arm up to her face, to breathe more easily through her sweatshirt.

David was about fifty feet in front of her, with his back to her, picking up dead birds with a hook and placing them in a black plastic bag. She walked twenty feet toward him when, sensing her presence, or perhaps noticing the movement of the birds in reaction to her presence, he turned, saw her and yelled something at her that was lost in the roar of the propane, the din of the feeders, and the noise of the birds. He pointed back toward the trailer.

Not knowing what else to do, she dropped to her knees in the sawdust, which sent the birds scurrying away from her, folded her hands together and bowed her head. Her eyes were closed and she waited. After a minute, she cracked her eyelids and saw David's feet standing in front of her. She looked up at him, afraid he might strike her again, but ready to accept it if he did. His lips were moving, but she still couldn't hear what he said, though he seemed less angry and was no longer pointing. She broke her clasped hands and cupped her right ear. She said nothing.

He knelt down in front of her. "Pray with me. Our Father, Which art in Heaven, hallowed by Thy Name..."

Ellie matched his rhythm, which was slow, and said the words with him. "Thy kingdom come, Thy will be done, on Earth as it is in Heaven. Give us this day our daily bread and forgive us our trespasses. As we forgive those who trespass against us. Lead us not into temptation, but deliver us from evil. For Thy is the kingdom and the power and the glory. Forever. Amen."

Ellie opened her eyes and looked into his. "I'm sorry, David. I didn't mean it and I shouldn't have said it. I'm sorry. I deserved what you did. I won't ever say it again."

"Go to your room now, Ellen, and I want you to copy out the fourteenth chapter of John completely." She stood up and turned to go. "Twice."

"Yes, sir."

"And stay in your room until I come to check your work. Understand?"

"Yes, sir."

Ellie walked out of the chicken house and did as she was told. Cardinal stood at the kitchen sink and watched her walk across the yard and up the front steps, tremendously sad for what she had, over the years, put her daughter through.

**That Night.**

The boys were asleep and Ellie was in bed, though she was allowed to read for another half hour before lights out. She was two-thirds of the way through Sam's *My Friend Flicka*, and was enjoying the story, though the events of earlier in the day kept distracting her attention. She had written out the chapter of the Gospel of St. John, twice as David had required, and she had seen its significance, because it contained the Lord's admonition that David had quoted to her that morning, on their knees in the kitchen. To show him that she understood, she had used a red highlighter to draw a tidy box around the key passage, and as an additional act of contrition (though she didn't know the word), she had copied out the next two chapters of John as well. She had then stayed in her room until she presented her work to him at supper, where he had looked at it, said nothing, but nodded her to her place at the table, and then required her to say grace over the meal, while the rest of the family sat more than usually silent, knowing that Ellie had been punished. Now she was reading in bed, trying not to think about having been struck, or about crying at Mr. Butler's and how comforting his arm had felt around her shoulders and how she had wanted to crawl into his lap but had been too embarrassed and besides they were standing up and there was no place in the stall to sit down except on the ground.

Now in the evening, David sat on the couch reading the local paper, while Cardinal paced the floor in a circle with Esther, who was fussy, on her shoulder. She sang quietly to the baby, an unidentifiable tune, and patted her on the back and tried to ignore how tired her feet were. In ten minutes or so, Stuart's evening broadcast would be on Channel 51 and they would watch it together.

David looked up from the paper, his face stern, as if he had been preparing a speech, not reading the sports. "I'm going to ask on Sunday if anyone knows another math tutor."

Cardinal stopped pacing and turned to face him. "Why would you do that?"

"Are you ready to do the math? That was the agreement, you know. That you'd learn from Butler."

She started walking again, which put her back to him. "And you know that I'll never be as good as he is."

"Look at me."

"Esther needs to walk. I can hear you. I'm listening."

"Then we'll have to find someone else. I told you, I don't like having her over there all the time. It's not good for her, and you saw that this morning."

"Come on, David. You'd be cutting off your nose to spite your face."

"What's that mean? I don't know why you can't speak plain English."

Now she turned to face him, walking to and fro in front of him with the baby. "It means we'd be doing something to make a point and end up hurting ourselves."

"Then why didn't you just say that? It drives me crazy when you do that."

"I'm sorry, dear." She shifted the baby to her front side and went over to sit next to him on the couch, their thighs touching. She took his thumb in her hand.

"But I don't think we can find a better math tutor than Sam. I talk to the other home-schoolers, and they're jealous."

"Jealous? Well, they can have him, for all I care."

"I don't think he'd do it for anyone but us. I think we're lucky. So do the other moms."

"Why just us?"

She shrugged, then laid her head on his shoulder. She smiled, though he couldn't see it. "We're special, I guess."

"Well, I'm tired of his crap."

"What crap, David? He teaches her math and about horses. That's all."

"He's not a believer."

"We knew that at the beginning. And he hasn't done anything wrong. He doesn't talk to her about religion, he told us that." She looked up at him. "And he doesn't question you."

"What happened this morning then? Who put that idea into her head if Butler didn't?"

"She *likes* him, David, that's all. And he's an old man. It's natural that she'd be worried about what happens when he dies. She wouldn't be Christian if she didn't. She forgot a Bible lesson, that's all. I do that sometimes." She bounced their hands on her leg and lay her head back on his shoulder. "So do you."

He softened. "We'll see. But I'm keeping an eye on him. And her."

"And me?" Her voice became lower. "Are you keeping an eye on me?" She lifted his hand to her lips, then returned it, this time into her lap. She spread her knees slightly and turned her face for a kiss, which he gave her with only a bit of reluctance. The kiss became long and deep, and by the end of it David's hand was buried deep into the crotch of her jeans. "I think Esther's ready for bed. I'll be right in."

"You father will be on in a couple of minutes."

"I think Daddy can get along without us tonight. You go on in. I'll be right there."

Cardinal walked first to the nursery and got Esther settled on her back, now asleep and sucking her thumb. She then checked the boys' room and found them both asleep in the bottom bunk, as was common. She disengaged them, and moved Joshua to the top and tucked them both in. Ellie, when she looked in her room, was asleep with the bedside light still on, and *My Friend Flicka* open on the bedspread where it had slipped out of her hand. Cardinal marked the place in the book, turned off the lamp, kissed the girl on the forehead and left the room. She locked the front and back doors, measured the coffee into the machine for the morning, turned off the lights in the living room, and then opened the bedroom door.

"Well my goodness, David Quincy," she said, leaning against the door jam and crossing her arms across her chest. "Look at you." She snapped off the overhead light and closed the door behind her.

**Two Days Later.**

The pre-stamped postcard appeared in the Hindsville post office, *Poste Restante*, and hence into Sam's box eight days after they had met for pie, conversation and the question that had remained with Sam. It had no signature, but was in Lynda's hand, with two words written on the back: "Child's play."

That night, he called her cell. "Child's play?"

"Beg pardon?"

"Child's play."

"What is child's play?"

"You tell me; you wrote it."

"I wrote what?"

"Child's play. Presumably a reference to how easy it is to hack into a list-serve."

"Is it?"

"You wrote it. I got the postcard."

"Why would anyone write a postcard anymore when you can send an email?"

"I don't always read my email."

"It's not that hard. Maybe that's what the postcard means."

"Has he?"

"What?"

"Hacked the listserve."

"How would I know?"

"You probably told him to."

"Who?"

"Jonathan."

"Why would I do that?"

"Would you? Did you?"

"What do you think?"

"I never know what to think about you."

"Speaking of that book you wanted to give me..."

"Don't change the subject."

"Speaking of that book..."

"Which we weren't."

"...and the cover thereof. Margaret Atwood's *The Year of the Flood* has a typo on the back cover. I was browsing at the library and I thought of you when I noticed it."

"What's the book about?"

"How would *I* know?"

"You aren't reading it?"

"Hell, no. Have you not been paying attention? The sloppiness on the outside is suggestive, you'll concede, of sloppiness on the in-?"

"The thing I'll concede is that an author of her stature deserves more than ten seconds worth of contemplation of her work."

"Ten seconds is usually enough. If she wants more, then let her proof the damn cover. Not that the cover was particularly inviting, even putting the typo aside. Apparently there are honey bees involved in the story. How not original."

"What was the typo?"

"Leaving the word 'not' out of one of the In-praise-of squibs.'"

"Ouch."

"Indeed."

"Maybe I'll give it a try. Just to irritate you. It might be worth it. What's the title again?"

"*The Year of the Flood*. Post-Apocalypsical, I believe."

"Well, never mind then. Not to my tastes."

There was a pause on her end of the line. Then, "Incoming from Chang. Gotta go. See you soon."

"No more postcards." But she was gone.

# 6

## APRIL

**The First Friday.**

Horses have no muscles below the knee. Bones, ligaments, tendons. Skin, hair, hoof. Lots of blood. No muscles. You may imagine, if you like, that a horse is standing on his middle finger, with his knee really being the next to the last knuckle, and, if you'll check on your own hand, you have no muscles below that knuckle either. So, twelve hundred pounds, resting on four finger bones, sixty per cent of the weight on the front. Additionally, if a horse suffers a leg injury, because of his quirky digestive system, he cannot lie down for long without colicking, so he cannot convalesce in the human sense, and must remain on his feet. And, if one foot bears an undue share of the weight, the laminae that hold the hoof together tend to collapse, the horse founders and death soon follows, the sooner the better.

All that is why horses with broken legs were shot. Then and now.

On the inside of each leg—above the knee in the front and below the hock in the rear—is a spot of horny hoof material about as big around as a circle made by your thumb and forefinger. This is called the chestnut and is thought by believers in evolution to be a vestigial toe, left behind when the modern horse's ancestors specialized the one bone in the foot into a leg. Behind the fetlock is another horny protrusion called an *ergot*—French for spur, and almost unde-tectable in many horses—and within the sole of the hoof is the frog, so called, thus making three vestigial toes, plus the one that survived as the horse's leg. So, four toes, one of which bears the horse's weight. Times four.

One might think that non-believers in evolution would have a hard time accounting for the chestnut, but one would be wrong about that. The explanation normally goes something like this: "He's God. I'm not. How would I know why He put the chestnut there?" This explanation, of course, can be used to explain practically everything, leaving time for non-believers in evolution to study on more difficult questions like why the Bible never mentions the Arctic and how the snake managed the phonemes of Hebrew. Or as Ellie had wondered, why God drownded all those horses, drowning being an especially cruel death for horses, who will swim until exhaustion. Other more humane manners of death were surely available. Okay, so God doesn't belong to PETA. But you'd think He could have managed membership in one of the less-radical humaneness organizations. Why not? The answer normally goes: "He's God. I'm not" and *et cetera* and so forth.

Mid-morning, on one bright April day, Sam and Ellie were studying The Looker's left front chestnut, without its origins, secular or divine, on their minds. Rather, Sam was showing Ellie how the horse had been trained to pick up his foot when his chestnut was squeezed.

"You try."

He was on one knee, his right, and she was on both, to his right, so she had to reach in front of him to grab the chestnut. She did, squeezed gently, and the horse picked up his left hoof. Sam caught the hoof with his left hand and laid it on his raised left knee, where it rested for a few moments before Sam pushed it off and the horse set his hoof down.

"Now the other one."

"Walk around?"

"No, just reach under. But first, turn your cap around."

"Why?"

"So you don't tickle his belly with the bill." He waited while she pulled her hair through, then turned the cap backwards, catcher-style, tucking her hair behind her ears. "Good. Now, reach under."

She did, the horse lifted his right hoof, but then replaced it when no one was there to hold it up.

"Now this one again." She did, and this time Sam held the hoof on his raised knee. "Hoof pick." She handed him the tool. "See? This vee is the frog and we have to clean out the dirt that gets in there." He dug for a minute; she watched intently; the horse stood still, his ears listening behind. "Brush." She handed him a blue-bristled stiff brush, about as big as her shoe. "So, we brush the sole clean, and look to see if the shoe is loose. How's it look?"

"Pretty tight. How come he only has shoes on the front and not the back?"

"That's where he carries most of his weight. Look how big his head is, and the front feet have to hold it up. See any nails he might have stepped on?"

"No."

"Me neither. Remember to listen when you're using the hoof pick; sometimes you'll hear something you can't see. Now, rub your hand across the sole. Nice and strong, hear?" He rapped the hoof pick against the bottom of the hoof. "Now, bend over here and give it a sniff."

She did. "It stinks!"

"It does? Let me take a whiff." Sam inhaled deeply. "No. That smells sweet to me. Strong but sweet. When a horse gets thrushy, the smell turns rotten and then..."

"What?"

"There's some goop in the tack room to cure thrush. Actually, Smokey's a little thrushy now; I'll let you smell her feet when we're done here, so you can tell the difference. Now, switch sides. You make him lift his foot and I'll hold it, and you pick it out and brush it off."

"What about the back ones?"

"They're harder and you have to be stronger to hold a back one up. I'll do them this time and you can watch, okay?"

"Okay."

Five horses, twenty hooves, of which Sam did the ten hinds and the two of them split the tasks on the ten fronts, finishing up an hour later in Restive's stall, her cap still backwards, and his knees stiff from the squatting.

Out of the blue: "Do you think there are horses in heaven?"

"What?"

"You know. That book you showed me."

"*Horse Heaven*?"

"Yeah. Do you think there are?"

Sam shrugged. "Why not?"

"I hope so. What do you think heaven is like?"

"Better ask David."

"He'll just tell me I should already know, if I studied the Bible."

"Then ask Cardinal."

"But I want to know what *you* think."

Sam paused, thinking, putting the various tools and ointments into the carrying bucket. "Well, I know what heaven would be like for Teena." Sam nodded towards the dog, curled up out of horse-harm's way. She lifted her head at the mention of her name.

"What?"

"A place where she'd have four legs. Slow, fat squirrels. A place without thunder."

"Why not thunder?"

"Low frequency sounds make her nervous."

"Low what?"

"Frequency."

"What's that?"

"Well," Sam sketched a sine wave in the air, "a sound wave looks like this and..."

"What?"

"Wait. Come out here." They left the stall, closed Restive in, and Sam knelt in the dirt outside, where he drew a sine wave in the dust. "A sound wave looks like this."

"It does? Really?"

"Well, no. Not *really*. This is just a graphical representation of sound. The height of the humps, see?, represents the amplitude, or how loud the sound is. High humps..." he raised his voice, "...for a loud noise, and low humps..." he lowered his voice to a whisper, "...for quiet noises. And this distance is called the wave length. If the wave length is short..." he drew the picture and raised his voice to a falsetto, "...the pitch is high..." She giggled. "...and if the wave length is long..." he lowered his register, "...the pitch is low. Got it?"

"Is that really what sound looks like?" She tilted her head and looked doubtfully at the sketches on the ground.

"No, like I said, this is just a graph. So, you try. Draw the graph of a soft, high note." She looked confused. "Soft..." he pointed to the second graph, still visible in the dirt, "...and high." He pointed again, and spoke in a high, near-whisper, "...put them together." He watched her struggle with the combination, and then saw it click.

"Like this?"

"Very good. Now, loud but low." She thought for a bit and then drew the right picture. "Good, good. See why we study graphs in math class?" Her smile was broad, her eyes bright, and goose bumps rose on his arms. "Now, back to frequency. If the wave length is short, and the sound is high-pitched, like this... then lots of cycles fit into a second, so we say the *frequency* is high. And if the pitch is low, like this... then there are fewer cycles per second, and we say the *frequency* is low. I forgot to tell you: this..." he framed one sine wave with his two hands, "...is called a cycle. See, beginning and back to the beginning. So, a wind chime is high frequency, and thunder is low. And there's something about low frequency sounds that bugs Teena and makes her want to hide out in the feed room until the storm's over."

"I don't like lightning."

"Which causes thunder, but that's a lesson for another day. You can tell how far away the storm is by counting the seconds between the lightning and the thunder."

"How?"

"Another day. Next time there's a storm, we'll get together and I'll show you."

"Why not now?"

"Blue sky. And homework to check up at the house. I'll put the tools away and you lead the horses up, okay? Meet you back here."

As he waited for her to return, Sam looked at their graphs, traced in the dust outside Restive's stall, and thought how entirely pleasant it was to spend time teaching Ellie. But, he knew, the lesson wouldn't stick unless he went back to it in a few days, and on the way up to the house with her he thought about how he might merge the sound graphs and the graph lesson from her math book into one. That would require him to push the curriculum a bit to get her more quickly into the graphing of curves.

## The Following Day, a Saturday.

Postal regs had changed, with some fanfare, requiring the little Hindsville post office to close every day at eleven-thirty, except Saturday, when it was open until noon. This was only a minor inconvenience to Sam. Access to the boxes was still 24/7 and so it was only if he needed stamps or if he had a package waiting for him in the back, that he needed counter service. He saw Phyllis, the postmaster, less often, and he missed catching up with what was new with her and the Hindsville news in general, but still it was better than putting a box out on the road, where all manner of mischief could be done. But today he wanted to mail a package to his niece for her birthday, meaning he needed counter service, so he drove over before lunch, and leaned on the counter for a long chat with Phyllis, who was mostly out of sight in the back, multi-tasking her chores.

He was not surprised, on driving home, to find Lynda's Volvo parked in the spot reserved for the small pickup, causing him to park up by the isolation paddock. It was not that he had expected her, for they had set up nothing, but he had come not to be surprised by her unexpectedness. It was, though, unusual to find her sitting at the kitchen table, which she had covered with blue books. She had made herself coffee, apparently stooping to Nescafé, and on the counter was a grease-stained paper bag, contents unknown.

He closed the door behind him and she looked up from her work. "Made myself at home. Hope you don't mind. Can't get a damn thing done at our place or the lab, and should have had these graded ten days ago. Brought burgers."

"You short of pronouns today? Where's Jonathan?"

"Home. Buzzing around. Pestering me."

"You work. I'll be down at the stable. Take your time."

There's never nothing to do: his retirement mantra. There were three wooden fence posts that needed replacing. Somewhere there was a way into the chicken coop for an opossum, which he had surprised after dark two nights ago; the birds were safe at night, locked into their house, but he should find the way-in and patch it. It was time to service the tractor, and either before or after that there was a pile of manure that needed to be spread on a pasture. The lawn needed mowing. And so forth. Nevertheless, he thought he might saddle up Smokey for a little ride, just because it was a nice spring day and he felt like taking it easy. It took ten minutes to walk the mare back from the day pasture—where, she made it plain to him, she was quite content to stay with her buddies—and another ten minutes to tack her up. He then walked her to below the porch, and when Lynda came out he said, "You okay for a while? I think I'll take a ride up the road."

"I'm fine. Have a nice ride."

"See you in about an hour. I thought you had a TA to grade exams for you."

"I do, for the undergrads. But this is a grad-level course in non-linear optics, so I've got to do it myself. In fact, my TA is in the class."

"I'm all for being non-linear. See you in a bit." He turned, walked back to the road, swung his leg over the mare and let her set the pace at a slow trot as they headed east. His ribs were still a little sore, just enough to remind him of the accident, but Smokey's gait was an easy one to cushion as he posted with his knees.

Winston Churchill is said to have said that the outside of a horse is good for the inside of a man, or some such platitude, but Sam, who was not especially an admirer of Churchill or his politics, was of a mind to reject the insight, so-called. Churchill is also said to have called Gandhi a half-naked fakir, and had rejected Roosevelt's Atlantic Charter because, while he thought self-determination was good for Europeans, it was not so good for the far-reaches of the glorious Empire, democracy, after all, being a restricted commodity when it comes to the pigmented classes. Sam, not to say FDR, had no stomach either for colonialism or its principal apologist, thinking it to be one of the four really bad ideas of the last couple of centuries, the others being communism, fascism and inter-league play, with colonialism having the most long-lingering unhappy effects.

Sir Winston did, on the other hand, have a nice appreciation for the English language, which Sam grudgingly admired.

Politics and literacy aside, Tories and Labour, the-sun-never-sets, *Rule Britannia*, none of which was particularly on Sam's mind as he set out, he did enjoy riding. He thought it true, though, as someone less famous but more insightful than Churchill had once said to him, that horses know more about humans than humans know about horses, because one learns more by being ridden than one learns by riding, an observation that might equally apply to colonialism.

But the day was bright and cool, spring green and budding, Smokey's breath showing and her exertion sending her aroma up to Sam. She preferred the soft berm to the hard-packed dirt, but the branches along the side caused

Sam to have to duck, so they worked at cross-purposes for a while, until a heel in her flank won the argument for Sam, proving the prior point. His ride took more than the hour he had told Lynda, as he stopped to chat with a neighbor, then rode through that neighbor's pastures, and another's, finally linking up with the south end of his own property, and through the back gate to the day pasture, where he let Smokey loose to rejoin her mates, she not having gotten sweaty enough to need rubbing down. He then lugged the saddle on his shoulder, his ribs complaining, a hundred yards or so to the tack room.

Back up at the house, Lynda had cleared the kitchen table, her blue books stacked a foot high on the floor. "You're late."

"Get them done?"

"Fifteen minutes ago. I've warmed the fries in the oven, which will do them no harm, but the burgers had to be disassembled so as not to cook the condiments."

"How'd they do? The class, I mean."

"They're grad students. A is average, B is bad. Seventeen As and eight Bs. Five of the Bs are on their way out of the program, and the other three ought to be worried about exiting. They'll all be given Master's degrees for good attendance, denied access to the PhD program and sent off to teach high school physics. Some of them will be good at it. The foreign students will be sent home to do whatever, though, true to form, some will overstay their visas and settle in. My TA, I'm pleased to say, got the top score. Otherwise, I'd have broken a lab table over his head."

"I forget that you know whose exam you're grading. At the law school..."

She waved off the rest of his sentence as if she were aborting a landing on a carrier. "Oh, please," she said, now moving the fries to the table. "Spare me the usual gushing over the law school's sacred anonymous grading system. It's total bullshit."

"Meaning what?" He flipped the re-warmed burgers once in the pan, then placed them on a platter containing the buns and salvaged condiments. "I always found it quite liberating to grade without knowing whose paper I was reading."

"You didn't care?" They sat and began to reassemble the burgers.

"Of course, I cared. Cheese?"

"No, thanks."

"There were students I liked and ones who annoyed me. Students who were in class every day and ones I never saw after Labor Day. Ones who would come by with questions and ones who would buy some study guide, or worse, had last year's notes. Secret exam numbers allowed me to put a grade on a paper uninfluenced by any of those."

"Why on Earth should you be uninfluenced by those things? Someone who cuts class ought to suffer."

"Even if he aces the exam?"

"You bet. Besides, if my TA goes from step one directly to step six in some problem, I know he knows what goes in between, and it would be pedestrian to make him spell it out. One of the others, I know equally well, is shooting in the dark. Why deprive myself of that insight?"

"Jonathan told me about some prof at Cal Tech who never graded his own exams anyway. Drink?"

"Beer. Feynman. Yes, that story is told."

"It's not true?"

"Hey. It's in Gleick's biography of Feynman, so it's true, now, anyway, even if it wasn't true before it was inserted into Gleick's biography of Feynman." She bit into a burger and followed it with a swallow of beer. "Pretty good burger. That was Princeton, anyway, and I think it's more of a comment on the Forties *versus* today, than it is on Feynman *versus*, say, me. I would not trust anyone else to grade my exams, and I wouldn't even think about not grading them."

"Though tardily?" He glanced at the pile of bluebooks on the floor.

"Give me a freaking break; they're done. And I also wouldn't artificially close my eyes to what I know about the students. Nor, I trust, would Jonathan."

"Meaning what? He rages against the system?"

"Or more."

"More?" She raised an eyebrow but said nothing. "I don't believe you."

"Believe what you want."

"It's totally against the rules."

"The rules are stupid."

"I disagree, but, in any case, it's impossible. You wouldn't believe how tightly access to the secret numbers is controlled."

"You've tried?"

"Once. Inadvertently. Totally innocently." Sam sipped at his beer and thought for a moment to get the recollection in order. "There was one exam one semester that was particularly well done and I wanted to say so in a note to the student."

"How thoughtful."

"Thanks. But all I had was the number. So I asked my secretary for a name, after I had turned my grades in to her, thinking they had been processed, when they hadn't. First my secretary refused, and it isn't easy for a secretary to refuse her professor. And then within minutes I was on the carpet in the associate dean's office, being reminded of what the rules were and how the integrity of the entire grading process depended on the students trusting in their anonymity. And the way to do what I wanted to do was to address the note to the exam number and deliver it to my secretary. She'd take it from there." He took another drink of beer. "Just for asking. Forget it. Can't be done. An unbreachable wall."

"If you say so."

"I say so. The dean says so."

"Right."

"Where are these burgers from? They're good, even warmed over."

"They'd be better if you had a microwave. Burger Shack. On MLK." She considered a fry, which drooped when she held it up in her fingers.

"I've seen the place, but haven't been in. Why do I need a microwave? Just so I can hurry up? I like the pace at which I live. Hurrying up to eat is like hurrying up to ride. Both are bad for the digestion."

"I think it's a statement. 'I, Samuel C. Butler, do not have a microwave.' 'I, Samuel C. Butler, do not have voice mail.' 'I, Samuel C. Butler do not have catsup in the house.'" She pronounce it CAT-sup. "For Christ's sake, *everyone* has catsup in the house. Which would have improved the fries, while we're at it."

"Excellent fries. I have mustard, don't I? And mayo? And red hot sauce? I don't care for ketchup, that's all. And it's ketchup, not catsup."

"Which is why, next time, I'm bringing my own. I'm sure you have an explanation for why you like instant coffee, which, I guess, doesn't hurry your life up."

"Want another beer?" She shook her head. "Nescafé makes breakfast easier to fix, not faster. And I've grown to like the taste. Leave me alone."

"Why don't you take me riding sometime?"

"Gladly. Now?"

"I'm still eating."

"When you're finished."

"You've just gotten back." Sam shrugged. "Anyway, I can't. I have to go."

"Ellie and I have a trip planned for next weekend. Around Withrow Springs. Why don't you come along? The trailer holds three horses."

"Pass. I had in mind an adult outing."

"She's a better rider than either of us. She won't hold us back, but *vice versa*."

"I was thinking more about the level of the conversation, not the speed of the gait. Communing with nature, not the Holy Ghost." She crossed herself.

"You really are a shit. She's a little kid who loves to ride. We don't talk religion and besides, it's harder to ride and carry on a conversation than you might think. Have you ridden?"

"A few times. Nothing memorable. I'm thinking with your company it might be. But not with the little angel."

"Ellie."

"Ellie. Right. St. Eleanor of the Stables."

"You're beginning to annoy me. Drop it. Pick your day. No advance reservations required, as long as the weather is fair. Stop by and we'll just ride the back roads around here. Just the two of us."

"Sorry. I shouldn't tease you about your guardian angel. But I'd much prefer having you to myself."

"Anytime. I have in mind putting you on one of the boys on a bad day."

"I'll be ready. Oh, by the way, Jonathan and I are having some people over to watch the Kentucky Derby, I forget exactly when."

"First Saturday in May."

"Right. Come on over. Eat some guacamole. Drink some bourbon. Regale us with Thoroughbred stories."

"Maybe I will. You'll permit a little proselytizing for Old Friends?"

"Which old friends?"

"Capital *Old*, capital *Friends*. It's a Thoroughbred retirement charity. One of the best. I'll put in a pitch for them."

"Well, hell, we'll pass the hat. Or sell the juleps at five bucks a hit. All proceeds to blah, blah, blah."

"I'm convinced. You may earn your way back into my good graces, notwithstanding your anti-social ways."

"Anti-social?"

"Mocking a small child. Blaspheming the religions of the world. Thumbing your nose at the law school's grading system. Overall failure to show proper respect to your elders. Refusing to read *Horse Heaven*. Generalized abuse of the norms of society."

"Only when they've earned such abuse. And I have great respect for one particular elder. Enough to surrender my virginity to him."

"Virginity?"

"Well, I *would* have. It's a date, then."

"First Saturday in May. Post parade: five Central, approximately."

"Any advice about where to lay my money?"

"Bet the grey."

And soon after, Lynda packed up her blue books and headed home, leaving the dishes for Sam to clean up, which was fair because she brought the burgers.

**Three Days Later.**

Perhaps, given the way things were to turn out, it was important that Sam and Melissa would run into each other a few days following Lynda's suggestion that Jonathan had breached the law school's anonymous grading system. The chance encounter was at the used bookstore on Dickson Street, Sam selling and Melissa buying. Sam's visit required three trips, carrying heavy boxes full of books, from a NO PARKING zone, uphill a half block to the front door of the store. On his second trip, he noticed Melissa browsing the trade paperback section, but he didn't speak to her then, needing to get the boxes into the store and his truck moved before the parking authorities wrote him up. He then moved the truck two blocks uphill from the used bookstore to the parking lot at Nightbird, the indie bookstore. Sticking his head in the door, he told the clerk that he had just a minute's business to do at the used bookstore, and he'd be back to buy something here, he didn't know what.

Back then down the hill, he arranged for one of the owners to look through his boxes, calculate his credit and he'd be back in, in a day or two, but maybe not until next week, you know how things go. By then, Melissa had recognized his voice and looked up, but went on with her browsing until he walked up the short flight of stairs and over to her.

"Science fiction?" he asked, his tone indicating more surprise than disapproval.

"An old fancy for me. Got any recommendations?"

"Not really. Not my genre. Are you free for coffee? I'm parked up at Nightbird and owe them some commerce in exchange for the privilege."

She checked her watch. "Sure. Let me buy these and I'll walk up with you."

"Where's your car?"

"Parked around the corner."

"You pay to park?"

"You don't?"

"I'm an objector."

"Ah, one of those." Paid parking on Dickson Street was a relatively new phenomenon, and had been intensely controversial when the city imposed it. "It's been, what? Three years? Time to give it up?"

"Never."

She put one more book into her green canvas Wyckoff Ministries International bag, and headed to the counter in front, Sam a few steps behind. She paid in cash, The Dickson Street Bookshop being one of the last businesses extant that operates out of a computerless cash box. The walk up the street was pleasant on the sunny spring day and neither felt the need to speak. Inside Nightbird, they placed their orders at the front counter, hot tea for her and cold coffee for him.

"Iced coffee?" she asked. "It's not summer."

"People drink iced tea and cold beer and scotch on the rocks and cold martinis even when it's cool. Why not coffee?"

"Why not?"

"And besides, I'll show you the main attraction in a minute."

When the woman behind the counter made change for them—they bought their own—Melissa displayed her bag and said to her, "I've been shopping at the competition down the street; I hope that's okay." But the woman replied, "The used store? They're not the competition; they're our partners in literacy. Thanks for coming up here; maybe you'll see something new you like."

At the condiments table, Sam added cream to his coffee and they watched as the white cascaded around the ice, down through the black. "That's worth the price right there," he said. "The money's for the show; the coffee's free."

"It is pretty," she said.

At the table, he took a sip, then slouched back in his chair. "So. Science fiction?"

"Yeah, lately. I seem drawn back to it. What writers do you like?"

"I'm not really very well read; surely not compared to Cardinal, and probably not you."

"I didn't so much mean the classics. How can one talk about the classics having just been caught shopping for science fiction? What's your genre?"

"I'm not sure I have one. I read le Carré, but not spy novels generally. I like the Hornblower stories, but not Jack Aubrey. I don't read detective novels, except for Mickey Spillane."

"Spillane? Why does that surprise me?"

"At the beginning, it was pure contrarianism: my freshman English teacher ridiculed Spillane in class one day, and just to show him, the next day I brought one with me. After a while, I developed a taste for him."

"So, a man without a genre, so to speak."

"Genre-less in Giza."

"I think that should be *Gaza*."

"Just testing. May I see?" He nodded towards her bag.

"Sure." She emptied the bag onto the table, and out with the books came several other items. One, a small red and white package, slid off the table and onto the floor, and Sam picked it up.

"Books, plus a sink stopper. And, let's see, a hose nozzle, a light switch, and a box of assorted nuts and washers. You've been to the hardware store."

"Stuart gave me a list."

"This would appear to be everything one could ask for in a sink stopper." He turned the package over and read the back, then laughed aloud. "There are step-by-step instructions for using it. I find that funny." He handed the package to her. "Who would have thought that instructions were needed."

"I bought it without noticing that feature." She read. "'One. Before turning water on insert stopper into drain. Two. Turn water on. Three. Pull stopper up to drain water.' I like number two the best."

"I think there's something very astonishing about life in the twenty-first century."

Melissa sorted through the books on the table, turning them right-side up. "Maybe that's why I read old science fiction." There were six books, which she sorted through, placing them facing toward him in some kind of order, which she quickly explained. "I think I'll read them in this order." She pointed, his left to right.

"They're new to you, or re-reads?"

"Some of each. Seventies-era, mostly. Sci-fi was popular at the commune. I read it, because it was around, but I looked down my nose at it at the time. In favor of the classics."

"Hence Cardinal's tastes in reading."

"Precisely. Parents, most of us anyway, have no idea how we're going to influence our children's lives. We'd be more careful if we did. Wait to have them. Maybe never do." She took a sip of tea. "Do you regret never having?"

"Practically speaking, no. Partly because of what you just said. But theoretically, sometimes it feels like I—*we*—sat out life's most noteworthy dance. But no, not really. You're reading what the younger you scorned."

"*Scorned* is too strong, but in a way, yes."

"Trying to regain the magic of your salad days?"

"Maybe it's that." Her voice was flat, indicating pretty clearly that that was *not* it. "And you're selling. Is that something that you do often?"

"Not for quite a spell. Actually, I'm mostly selling some of my wife's books, thinning out the shelves in the study. I offered Cardinal all the children's books, but she generously only took a couple and said the rest should go to the library."

"She told me about the kids' books; in fact, I've already read a couple to the boys. They like them, and they're rather unlike the usual biblical fare they get. But I didn't know that was all part of a larger project."

"Lynda Stratford calls my house the Sally shrine."

Melissa interrupted. "What a terribly cruel thing to say."

Sam thought for a moment, looking not at Melissa, but down at her books on the table. "Actually, I think she may have a point. When I look around, I see that I've changed almost nothing since Sally died. It's almost as if she had just run out to the store on the weekend. Back in time for lunch. Want anything?"

"Just because you have a valid point to make, doesn't give you license to be cruel. There would have been plenty of ways to say it other than that way."

"Lynda, I have found, is entirely without artifice or social convention; she always says, I think, exactly what's on her mind. At least to me she does. Or seems to. How is one to know? In its own way, I find it refreshing. Jonathan, her husband, is more diplomatic, but she has little time for diplomacy. He's the lawyer; she's the scientist: the cultural stereotypes are intact."

"I'll admit that I didn't warm to her the night of your accident. Even less, the next day. Even less, now."

"The next day?"

"I gave her a lift back into Fayetteville, after she had spent the night at your place. I was driving in, and it saved her husband a trip out and back. We chatted a little bit, had a disagreement about home-schooling, then changed the subject. I had to ask her not to use her little nickname for Ellie, but I also told her that I appreciated the way she looked after Ellie at the hospital. And I meant it. We parted cordially enough, but not really as friends. I haven't seen her since."

"Nickname?"

"When she and Ellie drove in with you on the passenger side, she was calling Ellie Angel. Short for Guardian Angel, I think. It made Ellie nervous, so I asked her not to. She sort of agreed, but only sort of."

"She did call Ellie Angel once in my presence. I didn't object because, you know, she may be as accurate calling Ellie my guardian angel as she is calling my house the Sally shrine. Someone seems to be looking after me, and I'd soon it was Ellie as anyone."

"Lynda may think that Ellie looks after you, but Ellie thinks she uses the nickname because she asked her not to use the Lord's name in vain. Sometime the afternoon of your accident. I suspect that Lynda isn't used to being asked such a thing by a child, but Ellie's like that. But anyway, you like her. She's your friend. I'll admit that we met under rather unusual circumstances."

"I do like her, which doesn't mean that I don't want to wring her neck now and then. I enjoy her visits, which are usually spontaneous, unplanned. Which took some getting used to. She doesn't call ahead, but just arrives. She plays the piano beautifully, and I've enjoyed sitting by the fire this winter, just listening to her play, or reading while she does. She pops in during the day sometimes and pokes around the stable. Horse care is one of the few things she's not an expert at, but give her time. And our conversations are enjoyable; I find her stimulating. She's incredibly smart—perhaps the smartest person I've ever known. And as with a lot of very smart people, she does not suffer fools gladly."

"It's my impression that she doesn't much suffer non-fools gladly, either."

Sam laughed at this. "No, I suppose she doesn't." He sipped his coffee, then picked up one of her books, still spread out in front of him. "*Ringworld*," he read aloud, then turned the book over and read the blurb on the back. And another. "*The City and the Stars*, Arthur C. Clarke. I've actually heard of him, though not the book. *The Moon Is a Harsh Mistress*. So, is there a theme here? Some pattern that I would see if I knew the genre? *A Canticle for Leibowitz*. Interesting title, that one. And this one: *Where Late the Sweet Birds Sang*. Kate Wilhelm. What a wonderful title. Where late the sweet birds sang. Is the rest of the book that good?"

"How could it be? It's Shakespeare. Sonnet seventy-three. 'Bare ruin'd choirs, where late the sweet birds sang.'"

"Impressive. You quote Shakespearean sonnets."

"I recognized it, but not with that precision, I'm embarrassed to say. So I looked it up in the used bookstore."

"I'm not sure I've ever read a sonnet, his or anyone's."

Melissa gestured around the book store. "You're probably within twenty feet of dozens. Hundreds?"

"You'll have to recommend one sometime." He gestured at the books on the table. "Is there a theme?"

"Not really. Post-Apocalypse, Wilhelm and Leibowitz. But not all of them. *Mistress* is said to be one of the top ten libertarian tracts of all time. Up there with Ayn Rand, if that's your taste."

"She isn't. Unreadable. Which is why I've never actually read any."

"Me, neither. *Leibowitz* is an interesting read, about the era between the first nuclear world war and the second one. Civilization is pretty much wiped out by the first war, and a group of Catholic monks save what documents they can, holding them for thousands of years, until the documents—called 'The Memorabilia'—until they no longer know their meanings; they just treasure them as sacred artifacts. Of course, civilization catches up with them, the Memorabilia play a role in the reinvention of nuclear weapons, and everything goes kaplooie again."

"Cheerful."

"Well-written, though. There's an exchange near the end, as the second war approaches, an exchange between a priest and a scientist, in which the scientist doubts that he has a soul. 'You *are* a soul,' the priest says. 'You *have* a body.' It's a classic, in its own way. In the end, Miller wrote little else of note, then killed himself."

"Cheerful again."

"Yeah." It seemed as though she was going to continue, so Sam said nothing, inspecting the cover of the book. "Just junk."

"You didn't give me that synopsis as if it were junk."

"No, you're right. They aren't junk. And it's important that they aren't." She sipped her tea, put the mug down, then paused a moment or two again. Then, "I'm reading them instead of Bible study. I haven't told anyone else that and I'm not sure why I'm telling you."

"The passage you quoted a minute ago sounded like it was Bible study."

"Atypical, in this selection. I don't know. Bible study is seeming to be increasingly beside the point."

Her phone, lying on the table, beeped and she looked at the screen.

"Call?"

"Text. From Stuart. We're doing a Spanish-language broadcast today and he's letting me know that it went okay."

"I didn't know he preached in Spanish."

"We have a native-speaking associate who does most of it, but Stuart is getting better. He still reads his Spanish messages, but he's beginning to be able to deal with call-in questions on our Spanish broadcasts. It's the future of the business, you know. English-speaking America is pretty saturated with Christian messages."

"I never feel so poorly educated as I do when I'm around bi-lingual people. I envy his abilities."

"He learned his Spanish selling used cars in Huntsville, which a skeptic would say is entirely appropriate. The gutsy move comes next month."

"Gutsy?"

"A Hindi language program."

"Over the air?"

"On-line at first. We'll see how it goes. A preacher from up in Bentonville."

"Hindi. Huh. Ever think of trying Cherokee? The symbolism would be exquisite." The conversation lapsed while Melissa seemed to think about the Cherokee/Christian possibilities.

"We wouldn't exactly be breaking new ground, would we? Europeans have been trying to peddle Christianity to the Cherokees from the beginning. The methods have not always been exemplary."

"A decent point. So why is Hindi particularly gutsy, more so than Spanish?"

"Things will appear on the website not only in a language I don't understand, but in letters I don't even recognize. Know what 'Jesus Christ' looks like in Hindi?" He shook his head. "Neither do I. It seems a little beyond my abilities to manage. Maybe I should be learning Hindi instead of reading sci-fi."

Sam was reluctant to return to the matter of her delicate choice of old science fiction over the Bible. Or over studying the Bible, at least. But she returned to it, showing that her mind was not entirely on electronic evangelism. "There are two kinds of Bible study: individual reading and prayer for understanding, and group discussions. About six months ago, I switched my alone time to this," she gestured at the books on the table. "And for the past month, I've been making excuses to the group I study with. At some point they'll begin to wonder—maybe they already do—but for now..." She left the thought unfinished.

"A few days ago," Sam said, "well, that night the moon was nearly full, and it will be new tomorrow night, so it was about two weeks ago—I realized that I had forgotten to open the gate up to the night pasture, so at about ten o'clock, I walked back to do it. Three horses were waiting, wondering—if horses wonder—why I was late. The moon, as I said, was nearly full, and high in the sky. It was very beautiful, in that colorless, moonlit way." He paused, organizing his thoughts. "There's a point to be made here; bear with me." She smiled, but said nothing, her chin in her hand, her elbow on the table between them. "The grass is coming on, now that the nights are warmer, enough to give the land a contour, which my mind knew was green, though the color was missing in the moonlight. The horses surprised me by not rushing through the gate. I'd say that they sensed the quiet beauty of the moment, but that would be ridiculous. For whatever reason, they calmly walked through the gate and wandered up the hillside, in and out of the moon shadows made by the trees and the few clouds that drifted along. I couldn't look away. Twice, I turned to walk back to the house, but turned back just to watch. It was entirely peaceful, with the moon, the horses, the shadows, the grass. It added to the beauty somehow that I knew the ways of the horses and, even though it was quickly too dark to identify them by their markings, I knew who would be in the lead and who would follow. Who would stop walking right away and begin grazing, and who would hunt out the perfect little patch of grass. Who would stop and look back over his shoulder at me." He looked across the table at her.

"It's a lovely scene, lovingly told. Thanks. But..."

"But?"

"Somehow, I thought you were about to qualify that."

"If I were less transparent, I would've been a better lawyer. But I found myself thinking of a quotation I once heard, from some Eastern text, the Gita maybe. Something about there being no joy in the finite."

"It's from the Upanishads. There were several devotees at the commune. Jesus said something quite similar in the Sermon on the Mount. Lay up for yourself not treasures upon the Earth, but lay up treasures in heaven, for where your treasure is, there will your heart be. That's a paraphrase. Same idea, though, I guess. That what's here around us isn't enough. Even half-and-half, cascading down ice cubes in the coffee is not enough."

"There was a time when I would have thought it important to debate you and to figure out what passages like those meant. No joy? None? How can that be? Maybe he meant something different from the ordinary meaning of joy. No treasures on Earth? Why not? Did he mean only tangible treasures, or visual ones, too? How could such an experience not be treasured? Why shouldn't it be? And so on. But standing by the gate the other night, watching the horses walk up the hillside, in and out of the moon shadows, it seemed to me that the passage—or passages, you tell me—were entirely beside the point. I didn't care—I still don't—what Jesus meant, what those Eastern mystics meant. I lost that night all desire to figure out what they meant, to parse out the words, to wonder about the translations, to construe their meanings. To be a lawyer about it all. It was gone. The hillside, the horses, the moon shadows, the night, the bats overhead, the armadillo rooting about, it was all, I don't know, enough." He looked at her. "What's here around us, you called it. It's enough."

"But maybe..."

"No, really. I don't want to debate it. Or figure it out. Or convince you of anything. The only reason I told you the story—I've told no one else—is to say that you'll get no criticism from me if you're playing hooky from Bible-study class. It's not that I want you *not* to study the Bible, but I'd understand if you don't. That's all. I'd understand." He sipped his coffee, looking over the glass at her, her expression hard to read. "You're inscrutable. Just now, or always?"

"I was thinking that, while you envy Stuart's ability to speak Spanish, I envy Lynda her friendship with you."

He left the compliment unanswered, while he moved her books from a horizontal line in front of him, to a vertical line across the table, maintaining their order. "We should meet again for coffee and tea. I've come upon an ethical dilemma. Maybe you can help."

"You dismiss the relevance of the Bible, but still want ethical advice? Do I sense a contradiction?" She chuckled.

"I dismissed the relevance of heaven, an afterlife, whatever it is that makes people say that all of this..." he gestured around the bookstore, "...is...whatever. Unjoyful. Unworthy of being treasured. Less than satisfying. Less than enough. It's a little like standing on the rim of the Grand Canyon and having someone say 'Boy, you think this is spectacular, you ought to see it stoned.'"

Melissa smiled. "St. Augustine was very much of that mind: as amazing as the natural world is, it's even more amazing—I suppose he would have said *infinitely* more amazing—with a toke of spirituality. Attitudes around the commune were much like that, with considerable emphasis on the *toke*, and without Augustine's preference for Christianity. But I certainly see your point. It goes back to your *enough*. Christians, of course, are never allowed to think that all this is enough."

Sam leaned closer, his elbows on the table between them. "The Sermon on the Mount made sense, probably, where and when it was said, but would He have said it standing next to me watching the horses walk in the moonlight? I'm guessing not. Actually, I'm hoping not. I'm hoping He would have just stood there, wearing jeans, maybe, and work boots, watching the horses in the moonlight, saying nothing, not preaching, performing no miracles. Just watching. Quietly. Maybe He would have. Do you suppose anyone ever told Jesus to be still? Not to teach or preach or pray; just to watch? Probably not. Still and all, I'll admit that spiritual writings are useful as books of rules for human behavior. Everyone needs rules. You have them, more than I do."

"What's your dilemma?"

"I'm not ready to share it just yet. Maybe next time we meet. Let's see...I'm worried that someone I know has done something that I'm pretty sure is wrong, but which I'm also pretty sure will injure no one at all. Do I tell the authorities? That's it in a nutshell, with no details."

"It's wrong but no one will be hurt? How's that work?"

"Crossing against the light at three in the morning? No, it's more serious than that. But I think that no individual person will be hurt, though an institution might be."

"But institutions are just collections of individual people, aren't they?"

"You're right, but I still don't know what *I* should do."

"Well, there is always the Golden Rule."

"Do unto others... Okay, would I want somebody to turn me in if I were the wrong doer? Surely not."

"But, if you were the authorities, would you want to be told? Probably."

Sam considered this. "Hmmm. Does the Golden Rule lead to a broad no-snitching rule? That seems unlikely to me. I've always thought it odd that the Golden Rule tells the boys who drive by my house and toss their beer cans in my yard that that's a legitimate practice just because it's okay with them if I toss *my* beer cans in *their* yards. Shouldn't the Rule be 'do unto others as they would wish to be done unto'? Or something like that."

"But that leads just as surely to a no-snitch rule."

"Not necessarily, because as you say, the authorities would wish for me to snitch. And there are lots of *must-snitch* rules around. Lawyers have one, actually. So does West Point. Police forces, I think."

"But priests do not. Doesn't that end the inquiry right there? Priests above all must follow the Golden Rule, no? And if they're not required to go to the authorities, then who is? Unless maybe some higher commandment requires their silence."

"We're within inches of talking about priestly sex abuse, aren't we? It seems that now it goes almost without saying that if a bishop, say, knows that a priest is abusing children, he has to tell the police."

"But that's different from a priest hearing confession."

"Okay, so suppose a bishop takes confession from a priest who admits that he's been putting his hand in some altar boy's pants. Must the bishop inform?"

"I vote 'yes.'"

"Me, too, though I don't know what either canon or secular law has to say on the matter."

"What about government whistle-blowers. Are they required to blow their whistles?"

"Don't know. Maybe, or be liable themselves for the transgressions that they see? Does this count as Bible study? So that you don't have to feel guilty?"

"Who said I feel guilty? But you're right; I think it does. If Stuart asks, I'll say I've been studying the Golden Rule. Not that he asks anymore."

"Would he be offended that I was picturing Jesus a few minutes ago, leaning against my fence, dressed in jeans and work boots, watching the horses in the moonlight? More to the point, were you?"

"I'm not, and I doubt he would be."

"David?" A look of concern passed across her face, which Sam took as affirmation. "I suppose he would be."

Melissa was silent for a minute. "Probably, though that's largely irrelevant to anything important. But, maybe this is. I think I should tell you, even if he wouldn't want me to: Cardinal says that he's on the look-out for a new math tutor."

Sam was stunned. "Really? I'll miss the lessons."

"Of course it's not the math."

"So, what is it?"

"Oh, all of this. Jesus in jeans at the gate to the night pasture. The Golden Rule as a must-snitch rule. It's you, and everything that I've come to love about you. It's your scrupulousness about keeping religion out of math class, when David thinks it should be at the center of it. He probably also thinks that you're too smart. Too well-educated. A Northerner. A professor. Admired by Ellie more than she admires him. Everything."

"What can I do about any of that? I really will miss the lessons."

"The thing is that Cardinal likes you and wants you to do it. And she knows that you don't talk religion with Ellie. A battle over those kinds of things with David is one that she will win, and he knows it. So she thinks he's waiting for an excuse to go to someone else. Maybe if you ever say you're tired of it…"

"Which I wouldn't do. I'm not."

"I know. Just something like that. Too much horsey stuff. More riding than equations. Trips to town, cancelled classes. Too many track meets. Something that he can hang his hat on, instead of taking on Cardinal over the true issue. I don't know. Just be careful; keep your eyes open. Like I said at the pond: it's important that you stay in her life. If David would just loosen the reins a bit. But that's unlikely."

"If bullfrogs had wings…" He cocked his head, trying to look ironic. "So, we won't miss a lesson. Thanks for the tip." He stood up to go. "Are you walking back down to your car? I'll walk with you, but I've got to head back out to the country."

"I think I'll just sit here for now, have another cup of tea and start reading one of these." Melissa stayed seated and picked up one of the science fiction books, but looked across the table at Sam, seemingly unwilling to let their conversation end. She fanned the pages slowly with her thumb. "Old science fiction. Say what you want, but it's such a relief to see quotation marks."

"I'm afraid I don't follow you."

"Oh, it's just one of those things that irks me about so much modern fiction."

"I'm still not with you."

"It has become very fashionable in modern literature to present dialogue without using quotation marks."

"I guess I don't read enough to have noticed. Why don't they?"

"Presumably to irritate me. To make a punctuational statement. To make the book harder to read. To show that the author is hip. To show that the author is not only hip, but is a serious writer. Because it's the flavor of the month. To show that one aspires to be Cormac McCarthy. Last year the previously-sensible Louise Erdrich dropped her quotation marks and won the National Book Award, thereby cementing the practice as the flavor of the decade. I once asked a local lit prof what she thought was the reason, but I couldn't understand her answer. Something about breaking down the separation between internal and external speech." She shook her head and put the book back on the table. "I think it's just to annoy me personally. You have to go. In a half hour or so I've got to head back to the studio, so there's no sense in driving home now. I can walk up from here."

"Still paying to park?"

"Still paying to park."

"I've enjoyed this, Melissa."

She smiled up at him. "In spite of my punctuation tirade?"

"Maybe because of it. We'll have to do it again."

And walking back to his pickup, Sam popped into the used bookstore and bought himself a volume of Shakespearean sonnets.

## The Following Saturday.

Sam and Sally would often load up two horses and take off for a day of trail-riding. Their trailer, even, had a small and very basic living quarters in with the tack room, which allowed them to take overnight camping trips, though they rarely did that, as it required finding someone to take care of the other horses while they were gone. After Sally's accident, Sam lost most of his desire to take such trips, and was content to ride the roads and pastures around the farm. (About which Sally would have said, "Oh, what fun is that?") So, except for trips to the vet's, the trailer mostly sat behind the isolation paddock, unused. As with most bits of machinery, of course, it was better for it to be used than not, so Sam was looking forward to the trip with Ellie to Withrow Springs for a variety of reasons.

The horses watched suspiciously as he pulled the big pickup through the front gates and around to the trailer, nervous because a trip in the trailer was at the very least a break in their comfortable routine, and at worst, a trip to a place that held needles, dental drills and other unpleasant tools. He ignored them, which helped, and attached the gooseneck to the ball in the bed of the pickup, checked that the lights were working properly, put new wood chips down in the back where the horses would stand, and laid out the tack for Smokey and The Looker. He hadn't yet told Ellie that she would be riding the new horse, but she would certainly be excited at the prospect of taking him on a trip. They could either tack up here at the farm, or take the tack along and do it at the park; he thought the latter, to give the horses a chance just to stand around and do something they knew well—accept the saddle and bit—before they set out along a trail that they didn't.

All of this took only a quarter of an hour or so, and then he had to wait another twenty minutes before Ellie arrived, not on her four-wheeler, as he had expected, but in her grandmother's car. She exploded out of the front seat of the car and ran across the paddock to where he was waiting, sitting on the wood chips at the open back of the trailer.

"Sorry I'm late is it too late to go I couldn't get the four-wheeler to start and David was busy and my mom with the baby and I tried to call but you didn't answer, can we still go?"

"Slow down, slow down. If you're late, I hardly even noticed. Sit down here and calm down. You can't get The Looker if you're going sixty miles an hour."

"The Looker? Are we taking him?"

"I thought we might. Any objection to riding him?"

"*I* get to ride him? Really? Grandma!" Melissa had just arrived, walking up the hill. "I get to ride The Looker! Well, I've ridden him before lots of times, but just here at the farm, not out on a trail. It'll be great."

"Hi." Sam did not get up, but held out his right hand for Melissa to shake. Instead, she took it with her own left hand and squeezed. "I didn't expect to see you again so soon."

"ATV trouble, I'm told. It's a good thing I was on my way out or the ants in her pants would have exploded. You might say she's looking forward to this little trip, aren't you, Peanut?"

Somehow Ellie got the message in her grandmother's tone, and slowed herself down, losing some of her little-girl-isms and aging about two years on the spot. "It's going to be fun. And Mr. Butler says I can ride The Looker. He's the new horse. Who are you going to ride?"

"Oh, ol' Smoke and me; we're a team. Why don't you come along with us, Melissa? You can ride the one Ellie calls Daisy."

"Grandma, you should. She's real gentle and she'll be nice for you to ride. Come on. It'll be fun."

"My riding days are over, I'm afraid. My hips are sore as it is. No, I think I'll pass. You two go along."

"You could just ride along with us in the truck and sit at the park while we ride. It's a nice day, it should be quiet in the park and that way Teena can come along, too, if you'll look after her and keep her on a rope."

"Yeah, c'mon, Grandma."

"Got a book to read? It'll be nice."

"I do have a book to read; one of the ones that you watched me buy yesterday."

"Which one did you decide on?"

"*Leibowitz. A Canticle for...* Not the one I said I'd start with."

"Have you got it with you?"

"In the car. I was going to try and find some time to read at Cardinal and David's."

"You've got babysitting or something to do over there. I shouldn't take you away from that."

"No. Just visiting. Stuart will be out later, in a couple of hours."

"Well, please. Feel free to join us. Ellie's right; it should be fun."

"I think I will. Let me get the book and call Cardinal from the car."

"Good. I'll get the dog and then we'll load the horses and be off."

They sat three-across in the front seat, with Ellie in the middle, and when Sam got in, he handed her a loose-leaf notebook. "Hold this, okay?" To Melissa: "When you take a horse off the farm, you've got to take his medical records along, in case there's some trouble." Sam started the truck, pulled the rig out through the front gate, got out to close it behind him, and then they set off east down the county road. Behind them, they could hear the left-behind horses, calling from the pasture to the two in the trailer. Up on the pavement, they continued east. Withrow Springs is north of Huntsville on Highway 28, an easy half-hour drive. "Why don't you show your grandmother The Looker's past-performances chart?"

Ellie opened the notebook and found the section for The Looker. "Mr. Butler taught me how to read this chart. It's for the races. See? Here's his official name. Just One Look, but Mr. Butler and I call him The Looker. And here..." She pointed. "...this means he's a bay gelding, see? 'b g.' Bay gelding. And that's his dad and that's his mom, and that's his grandfather, and here's his birthday. February 21, 2007. And then..." She ran her finger down the list. "...here are all of his races. I forget what these letters mean."

"Those are the tracks he ran at," Sam said, his eyes on the road. "OP is Oaklawn, down in Hot Springs. CD is Churchill, where they run the Derby. MNR is Mountaineer, over in West Virginia. There's a couple of others, until he ends up at EHD which is Eastern Hills Downs, over in Claremore, which is where I found him."

"And so these are the details of all of his races." Ellie ran her finger horizontally along the numbers beside each entry. "And the times and stuff. These numbers show where he was during the race, and these little tiny numbers show how far behind he was."

"Six?"

"Six lengths behind," Sam said.

"The winner?"

"The next horse ahead of him."

"And here's the names of his jockeys. See? Mike Smith rode him, and *he* rode Zenyatta. These are the names of the horses that finished in front, so you can see he was third in this race here, at...what was MNR?"

"Mountaineer."

"And he was second in this one."

"He had heart, but he was slow."

"*I* don't think he's slow!"

"Well, no. Not for you. You should have been his jockey."

"Don't give her any ideas."

"The races are listed old to recent," Sam said, "reading from the bottom. And you can see the course of his career by seeing the decline in the quality of the tracks where he ran, starting with Oaklawn and Churchill and ending at Blue Ribbon and Eastern Hills.

"'Tired' it says. And 'tired' again. 'Through after half.' 'Weakened.' 'All done three-sixteenth.'"

"Those are the racing secretary's comments, as concise a form of the English language as you'll ever see. 'All done three-sixteenths' means that he ran out of steam a furlong and a half from the finish line. How long's a furlong, Ellie?"

"An eighth of a mile."

"What's three-sixteenths in yards?"

She thought for a few seconds. "I can't do it in my head."

"Yes, you can. How many yards in a furlong?"

"Two hundred and twenty."

"Which is very close to two hundred meters, over which who is the best runner in the world?"

"Wallace Spearman, Jr.!"

"Correct, leaving aside a Jamaican or two. Okay, so a furlong is two hundred and twenty yards, and three-sixteenths of a mile is how many furlongs, again?"

"One and a half."

"So?" He paused. "Two twenty plus one ten is?"

"Three hundred thirty?"

"Correct. So, Melissa, our friend Just One Look was done with three hundred yards or so to go."

Melissa went back to reading the secretary's comments. "'Stopped'? 'Eased'? 'DNF'?"

"'Did not finish,' that last one. He was a front-runner without the legs to hold on. 'Eased' means that the jockey saw he was done and let him just gallop out. 'Stopped' means what it says and he just didn't want to run that day, and quit. Most likely because he was sore. His career probably should have ended right there, but you can see they thought they might get a few more bucks out of him at a cheaper track. It's a tough business. But, if they hadn't run him at Claremore, we never would have known him, would we, Ellie?"

"We love him, don't we, Mr. Butler?"

"We surely do."

"Why do you think he didn't win?" asked Melissa.

"Well, he's a little over in the knee, which probably led to some pain for him in the forelegs."

"Over in the knee?" asked Ellie.

"His conformation. Looked at from the side, his legs aren't straight up and down, but his knees bend over a little, toward the front. It's a lot better than being under in the knee, but it's not good conformation."

"What about his pedigree?" Melissa again.

"Decent. I don't know much about pedigrees, really. Or genetics. It leads too quickly to eugenics."

"What's you- what was that?"

"Eugenics. Like breeding. You want to take this one?"

"Go ahead," said Melissa. "You're doing fine."

"Eugenics is the theory that people should be bred the way horses are. That certain moms should not be allowed to have babies with certain dads."

"Even if they love each other and get married and everything? That doesn't seem fair."

"No, it doesn't, does it? So anyway, it's pretty discredited these days."

"Discredited?"

The road was straight and uncrowded, and Sam glanced over at the two of them. "No one much believes in it any more. For people, anyway. For horses it's still in full sway. There are people who make lots of money deciding which mares should be bred by which stallions. That's why that second chart is there, the one that was available the last time he was up for auction, at Keeneland in Kentucky.

It goes into detail about what other foals his mother had and how well they ran, and then for his second dam and so on."

"What's a second dam?"

"His mother's mother. Like Melissa is to you. We say 'maternal grandmother' for people. You should see a complete pedigree analysis sometime. I can't even read them, full of jargon like 'a three-by-two Devil's Bag cross.'"

"What's that?"

"Jargon. I couldn't even tell you what it means, except that a horse named Devil's Bag appears more than once in the pedigree."

"What's jargon?"

"Specialized language that only the experts understand."

The front-seat conversation lapsed while Ellie and Melissa paged through the notebook, looking at the past-performances chart for Sam's other Thoroughbreds.

"Where's Smokey's chart?"

"She never ran at the track, so she doesn't have one. For some reason, her first owners decided to make her a broodmare instead of racing her. Those owners are listed in her papers, so I could ask them why, but I never did."

"Why?" Ellie asked.

"Because I don't care."

The Forest Trail at Withrow Springs follows an abandoned roadway roughly northeast to southwest along the western edge of the state park. Sam parked the pickup and trailer in a lot across from the main camping area, not far from the springs after which the park was named, which was less a spring in the sense of the one at Sam's place, a small cistern which filled with water seeping out of the ground. Withrow Springs was more of a good-sized brook running out of a shallow cave in the side of a hill, presented nicely by the tenders of the park, with fieldstone walkways leading up to perches where visitors could peer into the cave and watch the spring water flow past their feet. In the parking lot, Sam and Ellie unloaded the horses, all ears-pricked and nostrils-wide as they surveyed the new—and, it turned out, otherwise horse-less—surroundings. They then brushed the two horses to let them know that everything was okay, that this place was safe and not to be frightened of, tacked them up, left Melissa with a book and the dog, who was tied with a long rope to a picnic table near the springs, and set out on the trail.

The first part of the trail was rather steep, running along the right side of a deep depression in the ground, one that in the west would be called a box canyon and back east a ravine, but here in the Ozarks a hollow, or more commonly, a holler. They could see to the bottom, but a hiker would have had to crawl on all fours to get up the sides. To their right, the land was flatter, and less overgrown than the woods around Sam's farm, as his had been timbered back in the Seventies and there had not been enough time for the underbrush to thin out. It takes a while. After the steep climb, which took about ten minutes and had the horses breathing hard, unused as they were to workouts, the slope turned to a gentle rise, and Sam and Ellie rode side-by-side, not really talking, but pointing to the things they saw: an old dead oak tree, left to stand by the park authorities, and having lost all of its branches, leaving a twenty-foot tall stump; a bald eagle, sitting on a branch far on the other side of the hollow; a doe, swollen in pregnancy, but still weightless on her hooves. The redbuds were past their prime and leafing out, but the dogwoods were numerous and lovely, bursts of white with their tiny green leaves coming on behind the flowers.

At the top of the rise, the trail flattened out and Sam put Smokey into a trot, Ellie following suit. But The Looker was the larger, younger horse and his trot was bigger and faster than the mare's, so quickly Ellie was ahead of him.

"Wait for me when you get to the road," he yelled at her back, and she waved in response, not looking around.

After a few minutes, Sam put the mare into a slow lope, just enough so that he could keep an eye on the girl and the big horse, and they rode like this until she reached the parking lot at the end of the trail, about two miles from where they'd begun. She waited while Sam and Smokey caught up.

"Which way?"

"I don't think we want to ride back along the road the whole way, but if we go down this way just a bit we'll come to the trailhead for the War Eagle Trail, and we can take that back to hook up with the Dogwood Trail and that will take us back to where Melissa is waiting, okay?"

"Okay."

"Single file along the side of the road, on the right side. Keep checking over your shoulder for traffic, but remember, The Looker will know what's behind him before you do. You go first."

The War Eagle trail runs along a high bluff first above a small creek, then above the river it is named after and about half-way along it crosses Highway 28. They got down and walked the horses across the highway, then re-mounted and rode almost to the springs, then turned onto the Dogwood Trail, a loop that brought them back to the trailer and Melissa. Her book lay open on the picnic table, but she was off looking at the springs, Teena on a leash, hopping and nosing about.

"Grandma!" Melissa turned and waved. "Next time we're bringing a horse for you! Daisy!" They walked the horses over to where she was standing. "Let's go again."

"I'm tired. Let's just sit here with your grandmother and rest for a bit."

"I'm not tired. And The Looker isn't tired. We'll go around again."

"No, that's too long for you to ride alone. We can stay longer next time."

"Please? Just once more around? Please?"

"I'll tell you what: one lap around the Dogwood Trail." To Melissa: "It's less than a mile; she'll be okay." To Ellie: "Be careful. No cantering, okay?"

"I'll be okay."

"No cantering, *okay*?"

"Okay. No cantering."

"Wait here." Sam tied Evening Smoke to the side of the trailer, then ducked into the tack room and came out with a whistle on a lanyard. "Here. Put this around your neck, and if anything happens, blow the whistle."

"I'll be all right. I'm not a baby, you know."

"This is the way they do it in the Forest Service. You have to be grown-up to ride alone, and this is part of being grown-up. Bend down here." She did, and he looped the lanyard over her head. "Off you go. No cantering."

She rode off and Sam and Melissa walked over to the picnic table and sat down on the same side. "Hi," she said, and nudged his near arm with her shoulder. "Have a nice ride?"

"Wonderful. She should be all right alone around that trail, it's only about a mile long, and pretty flat. Made for birdwatchers and dogwood-lovers." He turned to face her. "I didn't expect to see you so soon after Nightbird. Will there be talk? Will eyebrows be raised?"

"Should they be? Coming along to watch my granddaughter ride her favorite horse with her math tutor is hardly worth a raised eyebrow."

"It's nice to see you. Did you get the sink stopper to work?"

"Third try. I kept forgetting the second step."

"Which was?"

"Fill up the sink with water."

"How's the book?"

"It's good. I'd forgotten how well written it is, even if one is not given to books about the end of civilization."

"While she's gone: I've been thinking about what you said. About David looking for another math tutor. You know, Ellie told me once that she wished she could go to public school. Maybe that's an option? I'd miss the lessons, but we could still do the horses together."

"Cardinal isn't crazy about the Huntsville school system. Which she went through."

"Fayetteville? You and Stuart live in town, don't you? If they gave your address as hers, they'd probably get away with it. The Fayetteville school bus turns around about a mile from their place."

"*Left wing socialist drug addicts.* That would be David speaking. Which is not to say that Huntsville High is exactly drug-free."

"But short on socialists, I'm guessing. Well, how about a religious school? Shiloh Christian has a pretty good reputation. So does St. Joseph's."

"Shiloh's too expensive. And St. Joe's? Catholic? Among the Romans? Egads. No, seriously. I think David has in mind that the boys will go to Shiloh, probably because of the sports. But he feels differently about girls than boys, sad to say. And about Ellen differently than his own kids, even sadder. For her, he's committed to the idea of home-schooling. You're it, I'm afraid."

"I never thought it would be so much fun. Really."

"It's not exactly law teaching."

"It's teaching a bright, hard-working kid something she knows nothing about. When you look at it that way, it shares those characteristics with the teaching of the first-year Contracts class. Which just happens to be the very best job in the world. If you want to read your book, go ahead, I'll be quiet. I just wanted to mention that while she was gone."

"I was just thinking I wish I had a thermos of some kind of nice tea." She had a small smile on her face, looking across at the springs. "That would be pleasant: a hot cup of tea, Ellie riding her favorite horse, or one of them, a stream running out of the mountain, and you sitting here talking about having had the best job in the world. Perfect."

"I'd prefer a beer maybe, if that'd be all right."

"That means cooler, ice..."

"No, room temp would be fine. I should keep some in the trailer, but to tell you the truth, I don't use the trailer much anymore. This is the first time in a while. Once or twice since Sally died, not counting trips to the vet's. This has really been fun. I'm going to suggest to Cardinal that we let a couple of weeks go by and do it again. Maybe to Steele Creek, over on the Buffalo."

"I'm sure it'll be all right."

"Will you join us?" Sam made the invitation without looking at her. "That would make it even nicer. You don't have to ride; just bring a book. Watch after Teena."

"And the tea?"

"And the tea." They let the thought rest for a moment. "Want to know what I'd *really* like to do? Take her camping. Some of the folks in the little riding club in Hindsville go every summer. Two or three trailers, a half-dozen kids with assorted parents and grandparents. Horses for everyone. They make a convoy out of it. They get on four-twelve right here in Hindsville, and follow it through the Oklahoma panhandle. They stop for the night at a motel across the border in New Mexico, a place with pens for the horses. Four-twelve dead-ends into Interstate twenty-five at Springer and from there they drive up into the Rockies. There's an outfitter that backs up to some wilderness area up there, I forget which one, where they can stable and feed the horses, and buy food and supplies for themselves, and they spend a week camping and riding in the park. I've never gone with them, because it's pretty much a kids' event, but I think it would be fun to take Ellie. It would give her a different group of kids to be around for a while."

"Expensive?"

"Not to worry."

"You do too much for her. Tell you what: let Stuart pitch in. He does too little."

"Trouble is, there's some details to work out first."

"Details?"

"I have to find someone to look after the animals while I'm gone. It's a pain in the ass and one of the reasons I don't go anywhere much anymore. Teena and the chickens have to be fed, but mostly it's the horses that need looking after. There's a couple of neighbor kids who are okay for an hour or two at a time, but not for a week or more."

"I suppose I could do it, with a little instruction from you. Well, detailed instructions, actually."

"You and Stuart? It would be a long drive out and back, a couple times a day, for a week or more."

"Probably just me; Stuart couldn't get away that much."

"Could you do it by yourself? It's a lot of work. Besides, there's still all the driving."

"I could stay at Cardinal and David's, instead of driving out and back."

"For that matter, you could stay in my guest room. It doesn't get much use these days. But what about your work?"

"I can do most of it remotely, if I can get internet access."

"Can't help you there."

"Sure you can. The morning after your accident, Lynda Stratford was Skyping some Asian gentleman from your kitchen table; I was there."

"I don't know how that's done. I've never actually Skyped. Nor tweeted, for that matter. I don't think I can get wi-fi from my house."

"Maybe she was using a cell-phone connection. More expensive, but do-able. Or maybe you're wrong about the wireless possibilities."

"I like the whole idea. Let's think about it. I think the trip is usually in June, after the kids are out of school, and it warms up in the Rockies."

"Here's a piece of advice: Don't mention it to Ellie until you clear it with Cardinal, or she won't be able to sleep between now and June. But if it will make it work, I'd love to help out."

"Are you sure? It'll be a lot of work. The chickens need to have their eggs picked up, and be put up at night, plus feeding and checking on the equines."

"They'll be someone to call in the event of emergency, right?"

"Yes, but emergencies are not permitted."

"I'll remember that."

"Teena seems to enjoy your company. And she's not much trouble."

"She's a nice girl. I enjoy hers, too."

"She's so different from the horses, so much more affiliative."

"Affiliative?"

"Maybe that's a word I made up. Dogs in general and Teena in particular affiliate themselves with humans much more than horses do."

"Why, do you think?"

"Oh, because we both eat meat. Dogs seem to know that if we just all stick together there'll be more to eat for all of us. But horses have always been among the eaten, and they never quite trust that we won't revert to our carnivorous natures."

"We don't eat horses. Not in the US anyway."

"But we used to. It takes evolution a long time to adjust. It's like why you see so many road-kill armadillos."

"Possum on the half-shell."

"What?"

"That's what they were called at the commune. Hippie-speak. Possum on the half-shell."

"I hadn't heard that. Possum on the half-shell. It's very clever. So anyway, for like a million years armadillos lived in a world in which nothing that could hurt them moved at more than about twenty miles an hour. Now there are cars that go sixty. Cars have been around for a while, but not long enough—like one second's worth of their entire existence. They never expect that car to get here so fast. Check back in ten thousand years; they'll have learned. Ditto horses and humans. But we're in it together, aren't we Teena? Well, here she comes."

"Bet she wants to take another lap?"

"No bet."

The girl rode over to them. "Can I go around once more?"

"You," said Sam.

"No, it's getting late."

After The Looker was tied up next to Smokey on the side of the trailer, Ellie joined them at the picnic table and they listened while she described her last circuit around the Dogwood Trail, just she and the horse, and what they saw and how she didn't canter at all, except for one little bit up a hill on the trail because it seemed hard for The Looker to trot uphill. And they decided to leave the horses tacked up until they got home, so they loaded up, pulled out and Sam and Melissa sat quietly all the way home listening to Ellie talk about everything that was on her mind.

Sam decided to stop at the post office in Hindsville, but pulling the trailer into the small parking lot threatened to clog everything up, so he gave the key to Ellie to run in and grab the mail, while he and Melissa sat with the rig on the road out front, still quiet, watching as the girl climbed over Melissa and out of the truck, looked both ways then ran across the road and into the lobby to fetch the mail. She brought out two hands full, folded over, with Sam's copy of *The Blood-Horse* on the outside, which she leafed through, showing her grandmother the pictures while Sam drove the rest of the way home.

It was not, then, until after Teena had hopped out of the tack room, the horses had been backed out of the trailer, de-tacked and led up to the eastern day pasture, the trailer had been parked and cleaned out and the tack put away, and after Ellie and Melissa had left, that Sam first had a chance to look through the mail that Ellie had collected from the post office box. The envelope was not addressed to *Poste Restante* this time, nor was the address in Lynda's handwriting, but typewritten directly to his Hindsville post office box. Inside, a single sheet of paper. The column on the left, twenty-seven names, all unknown to Sam, five groups of five, plus two. Across from each, a three-digit number, all less than five hundred. No note. No annotations. No explanation.

None was needed. He was plainly sitting at his kitchen table looking at a list of law school secret exam numbers.

The list itself proved nothing. It could be entirely fictitious, names and all, a prank by Lynda to get his goat. But he was certain it was not. More likely, it was last semester's exam numbers, which became accessible by the professors after grades had been turned in and posted, with new numbers issued the following semester. Or it could be a list pulled at random, Jonathan the IT man doing it just because he could, with no intent ever to use it. That Sam reckoned to be the most likely explanation: Lynda asks Jonathan if he could hack the secret exam number list. Jonathan says "sure." Lynda says "do it." Jonathan asks "why?" Lynda says "to show me you can." A short time later, Jonathan says "here." Lynda says "impressive," and a short time after that, Lynda mails the list, or a copy of it, to Sam.

The issue was, what should Sam do with the list? Blow the whistle on Jonathan? Tell the dean or Johnson Reynolds? Counsel Jonathan to destroy the list, cover his tracks—whatever that meant in the digital context—and never use the breach for any purpose, enhancing the worthy students being as distasteful as punishing the unworthy. Or—what Sam ached to do—ignore it. Throw the damn thing away. It could be batting averages of twenty-seven minor league ball players, couldn't it be?

For now, nothing. Sam put the paper back in the envelope, the envelope into the top drawer of the desk upstairs in the study, and went out to do the chores. The theoretical ethics discussion he had had with Melissa at the bookstore had just become rather more immediate, and his life had become more complicated than it had been in a long time, more complicated than he wanted it to be.

### The Last Wednesday in April.

Lynda Stratford arrived at her lab at 6:45 in the morning, as was usual, and called the meeting of her team to order at seven sharp, which was more an iron-clad practice than merely usual. And, as was always strictly enforced, they all turned off their phones, not just to vibrate, but *off*, so that she missed Sam's call at 7:07, which rolled over to her voice mail.

At the meeting, besides her and Chang, her post-doc, were two PhD candidates, three advanced science and math undergrads and two sophomore work-study students, one of whom was a math major and one business. That one, Romero—Lynda insisted that they all be professionally on a last-name basis, including her—not Dr., not Prof., not Ms., not Lynda—rather Stratford—anyway, that one, Romero, the business major, Lynda thought to be the smartest, the hardest working, the most careful, the most reliable of the bunch. This opinion was part truth, part contrarianism, and part a ploy to keep the scientists and mathematicians in the group from becoming smug. Romero was, in fact, very reliable, she had an equal seat at the conference table, her opinions on the parts of the experiments in which she was involved equally sought after and equally valuable, and her European history class at eight served as a fixed end to the meetings.

"All right, gang," Lynda said to close the meeting, "steady as she goes. The schedule remains the same. We meet again a week from Friday morning, at which time Sebastian will have a spread sheet of the preliminary figures for one-twenty-one-B," she glanced at Sebastian, who nodded, "which Westphal will crunch by a week hence." A glance at Westphal and another nod. "Fine. Anything else?"

Westphal spoke up. "Long and I are swapping sessions day after tomorrow so he can take his girlfriend out to dinner on her birthday, okay?"

"Where to, Long?" asked Kerr.

"A Pakistani place she likes up in Bentonville. Aroma."

"Hot?"

"Which? The food or Long's girlfriend?"

"Both," said Long with a smile. His girlfriend, who actually was very attractive, called herself, with some bitterness, a laser-lab widow and she did not care for the amount of time Long had to spend with Stratford's team. She had a particular dislike for Stratford herself, whom she had met at this and that physics department function, and about whom Long often spoke, reminding her of the great advantage to his career and to their future plans that Stratford had agreed to be his dissertation advisor. Long also felt her slipping away from him, and hoped that this birthday evening would help and c'mon, Jenny, two more years and I'll be finished.

"Happy birthday from all of us, Long," Lynda said, "and as much as we'd like to join you, I'm afraid we can't." A ripple of laughter went around those at the table, three of whom, of both sexes, also had laser-lab widows who felt roughly the same as Long's girlfriend did about Lynda. (Romero, on the other hand, had caused Kerr to know, two weeks prior, that if he wanted to ask her out, she'd say 'yes,' and since they both worked for Stratford, there'd be no laser-lab widow problem. But Kerr thought that Stratford wouldn't approve, and so had not, though he was tempted.) "Okay, Westphal for Long on Friday evening, and *vice versa* Friday afternoon?" Nods. "Got that, Romero? Revise and post the schedule, but this week only, right?" Nods. "All right. Friday the third of May. Seven. No late-night celebration, Long; you're due back in the lab on Saturday morning. Adjourned. Chang, stick around." The meeting broke up, Romero to her history class, Kerr to the control room for immediate monitoring duty, the others to their various cubbyholes in the building, and Lynda and Chang together down the hall and up two floors to Lynda's office, where for an hour she got a report on a method of optical squeezing that he was working on.

So, it wasn't until nearly nine when Lynda thought to check her voice mail and came across Sam's message from nearly two hours before. "I need you." Nothing more. She dialed his cell but got the voice-mail-not-set-up message. She tried the land line. No answer. She looked at the clock. Half an hour out there. Nine-thirty. A couple of hours there and a half-hour back. Noon. It was do-able if it was not an emergency like the accident. But if it was, then she *had* to go. She was pissed that he hadn't told her more in the message and that now he wasn't answering, but maybe he did, really, need her as the message said. She called Chang, said that she'd be back at noon unless he heard from her, left word with Jonathan that she was driving out to Samuel's, and went to get her car.

The scene that Lynda entered when she walked up to the house could have been composed by one of the lesser surrealists of the early twentieth century: Sam sat on the fieldstone of the patio, leaning against the side of the house, with his legs out in front of him, his Forest Service cap pulled low over his eyes and his chin drooping onto his chest. At his side sat a whiskey bottle a third down, and a paperback book, front cover down. And stretched out straight in front of him lay five feet of copperhead, with a splotch of blood where the snake's head should have been. The only movement was the spastic twitching of the snake's tail, and the only sound was the rattling of the cicadas in the sycamores.

Lynda squatted on her heels and lightly touched the toe of Sam's boot. He lifted his head, opened one eye, and said, "You took your goddam time."

"I just got the message. What happened?"

His second eye, the right one, opened. "When I got up here after last night's feed, Teena was sitting there with that..." he nodded toward the snake, "...at her feet. She had a lopsided grin and the side of her face was swollen to the size of a softball, with blood seeping out of the fang marks." He closed his eyes again and let his chin descend to his chest. "You will never convince me that that isn't the same snake who bit her on the leg years ago."

"Where's the head?"

He shrugged his shoulders.

"What did you do?"

"What could I do? Splashed the wound with whiskey, shoved three Benadryl down her throat, put her head in my lap and read her a Mickey Spillane mystery while I tipped the bottle all night."

Lynda moved her hand from his boot to rest affectionately on his shin, then reached under the cuff of his jeans and gave his bare skin a squeeze. "Oh, Samuel, I'm so sorry."

"I kept thinking all night that checking out to the words of Mickey Spillane, having just bested your oldest and worst enemy in tooth-to-tooth combat is not a bad way to go."

"*She* killed the snake?"

He wiped his nose on his sleeve. "Her finest hour."

Neither of them spoke for a while, she gently stroking his shin.

"Where is she?"

"Who?"

"The dog."

"Around here somewhere. Probably down at the stable waiting to be fed. God, I'd forgotten how much I hate the taste of whiskey. Excuse me." He spat over the edge of the patio.

Lynda removed her hand. "She's not dead?"

"Oh, she's fine. Credit Benadryl." Still with his eyes closed, he said, "I, on the other hand, have been sitting on these cold stones all night, sipping the whiskey and thinking. About what was and what will be, about life and death, dogs and snakes, horses and what it's like hardly ever to sleep. About what you sent me and what the hell I should do about it. About Sally and Cardinal, about Ellie and about you. World without end, amen. I'm cold and I'm stiff, I'm not sure I can move and I need to be in bed." Here he opened one eye again, picked up the whiskey bottle, and looked at the label. "Old Overholt rye. It's all there was in the house. I'm not the epicure I once was."

Lynda stood up, looked at her wristwatch, then offered him her hand. "Success at last. And who said romance was futile? I always knew you were one personal tragedy away from surrender. Come on old man; I'll get you upstairs."

Sam pulled himself unsteadily to his feet. "I can put myself to bed, thank you. I'm not about to be molested by some horny physicist half my age." He turned and, with one hand for balance on the side of the house, began to walk toward the door.

"Then why the hell am I here?"

Without turning back, Sam said, "Ellie will be by at ten-thirty for her math lesson. Factoring second degree binomials. Take it for me, okay? Check her homework, answer her questions and give her a new assignment."

"Holy Name of Jesus. Factoring binomials with Little Orphan Annie. I'd rather eat the damn snake."

Arriving at the door, he opened the screen and walked inside, heading for the stairs. "Six $A$ squared plus twelve $A$ equals six $A$ times the quantity $A$ plus two. You can do it." Now in the kitchen, he raised his voice to be heard. "And she's not an orphan." Through the kitchen. "And watch your language. Ellie takes abuses of the Lord's name very seriously." Now at the steps upstairs. "If you find the snake's head, leave it alone; it can still bite you." Half-way up the stairs, his voice fading to obscurity. "And feed the dog; she's had a long night."

**Four Hours Later.**

Sam awoke to the sound of two phones ringing. He'd been having one of those dreams into which reality intrudes: he and Sally were at breakfast, talking about something. Organizing the weekend, maybe. Or school-board politics, maybe. He couldn't remember. The kitchen phone rang, but when Sally picked it up, it continued to ring. She kept on talking, both to him and into the phone, but the conversations were so mixed up, he couldn't understand either, and meanwhile the damn phone kept ringing.

Then he was awake and the dream vanished, except the phone was actually ringing. Two phones. The land line in the kitchen, and his cell phone, which he now remembered he'd kept with him when he was nursing Teena, just in case, and, he remembered, too, putting it on the table at the top of the stairs, after he'd said "Feed the dog; she's had a long night" to Lynda and headed for his bedroom. Apparently he had left it on. He sat up on the edge of the bed, discovered that he was still dressed, and shook his head to clear the cobwebs. More than just cobwebs: his stomach was very uncertain, what with the whiskey, with food neither before, during nor after. He was stiff all over, his ribs aching more than they had since the accident, and the lack of sleep, coupled with the too-rapid awakening, made the parts of his body feel as if they were not properly connected. The cell phone stopped ringing, probably rolling over to the voice-mail-not-set-up message. But the land line kept ringing, so he stood up and walked downstairs, rubbing his eyes and trying to come together, to wake up.

"Hello?"

"What happened?" It was Melissa.

"About what? The dog and the snake? How did you hear about that so quick?"

"About Ellie?"

"What about Ellie?"

"Something happened. At your place."

"Like an accident? With the horses? The four-wheeler? Is she okay?" His heart jumped with a jolt of adrenalin, and immediately he was awake, the grogginess gone.

"Nothing like that. I don't know much, and it's hard to piece together. She called me on her cell phone from her room at home, crying and it was hard to get the story straight. She was scared, mostly I think because Cardinal and David were shouting so loud at each other, but I don't know about what. She'd been sent to her room, I don't know why. But you must know. What happened?"

"I've got no idea. I was up all night nursing the dog, so this morning I called Lynda Stratford and asked her to take the math lesson. I didn't want to miss, but I was exhausted, and went to bed when she got here at about nine this morning. No, later. Anyway, I was asleep until your call woke me up. Hold on. My cell is ringing."

"Take it. Call me back. I'll call Cardinal."

Sam had to walk back upstairs to get the cell phone. It was Cardinal. "Sam, what happened?"

"I don't know. I was just talking to Melissa and she said Ellie called her from her room on her cell, and she was scared because you and David were shouting at each other. She—Melissa—was going to call you, but here you are."

"I hear her in-coming beeping at me now. But what happened at your place? Ellie came home about two hours ago, clearly upset, but mostly she just clammed up and sat on the deck, staring out. It was so unlike her. When David came out after his chores he saw her and thought the worst, but I said you wouldn't ever. Ellie seemed to get the drift of what he was worried about, and she said no, it wasn't that, it was something Lynda Stratford said. That's when David sent her to her room and started shouting at me. David's coming out of her room now. Call you back."

The connection broke. Sam called Melissa, but got voice mail and in the meantime his land line rang again.

"It's Cardinal. Oh, Sam, David's on his way over to your place and he's as mad as I've ever seen him."

"About what?"

"I guess about what Ellie just told him. He ran out of here without saying anything to me except 'I told you, damn it.' And 'I'm gonna shoot the son of a bitch.' He should be there in a few minutes. Be careful, Sam. There's a gun in the truck."

"Cardinal, I'm not going to get shot over a missed math class. I'll talk to him and see if I can calm him down. You talk to Ellie and see if you can figure out what's going on. And call your mother."

"Call you back."

The confrontation should occur...where? Down where he parked the pickups. Then, after a bit maybe he could get David to walk up to the house and sit down and have something to drink. Sam cracked himself a Coke and headed outside. His mouth tasted like shit, his head was foggy from lack of sleep, and he didn't know what the hell was going on. On the way out the door, he saw a note on the kitchen table: "Orphan Annie's a decent mathematician, but she left in an eight-cylinder huff. Call me, L."

*Later*, thought Sam. He could now hear a vehicle, undoubtedly David's, coming too fast down the road from the west.

David's truck pulled in behind Sam's pickups, blocking both of them in, while Sam was halfway down the hill. Cardinal's description of David's anger had made Sam anticipate that he would storm out of the truck, spit and piss flying, voice raised, demanding...what? Instead, Sam could see David sitting in the truck, both hands on the steering wheel, seeming to collect himself. Praying, maybe. He finally opened the car door and stood out, when Sam was about ten yards away.

"David. Cardinal called to say you wanted to see me. What's going on?" If David had taken a moment to collect himself in the truck, it was to collect himself into a state of chilling, unnatural calm. His face was white, not red, his hands were loose, not clenched. He was sweating through his shirt under his arms, but somehow Sam knew it was cold, nervous sweat. Sam repeated himself. "What's going on? Do you want to come up to the house?" Sam felt off-kilter from sleep-deprivation, the disconnectedness of his body parts, the too-sudden shift from asleep to awake, and the rush of adrenalin when he had thought Ellie was hurt, clashing with the whiskey of the night. And now this: David's chilling calm.

When David spoke, his voice was even, if pitched unnaturally high. "Let's cut all the crap. She's never to come over here again. Ever. Hear me? I don't want her here ever again."

"What? Why?" Sam's mind refused to focus, to comprehend.

"You poison her mind. You pollute her soul. Stay away from her."

"David, come on. I do no such things. I teach her math. Come up to the house where we can sit down and talk." Sam wished he had not opened the Coke, which had soured his stomach.

David took a step closer, but still raised neither his hands nor his voice. "You are a heathen, a lying son of a bitch and a blasphemer. You lead Satan into a little girl's life and give him access to her heart. You will burn in Hell, but you will not take my family with you. Hear me? You will not take my family with you."

"I teach her about fractions and graphing. We take care of the horses together. I never talk to her about religion, and I refer all of her biblical questions back to you. What do you want me to do? I've never lied to you or to Cardinal. If you think otherwise, then you don't know what you're talking about."

"From your ungodly whore then."

"What? My what?"

"That Stratford."

Sam wiped his hand across his face and groaned. "Oh, God. What did she say?"

"What a sick joke—you asking for God's help. It doesn't matter what she said. That bitch and whore is your way of creeping into Ellen's soul, and I won't have it."

"Lynda Stratford is neither a bitch nor a whore. She's my friend, and I won't have you talking like that about her to me. But..." David began to speak. "Shut up and listen to me. But, she doesn't speak for me either, and if she said something that you find offensive, I'm sorry. I'm sure we can get it straightened out. What was it? Why don't you come up to the house and we can talk about it?"

"I'm not here to debate with you. You're slippery with all your college words and you can talk me around in circles and tie me all in knots. It doesn't matter what she said. She said it, and you and her and Satan are after Ellen's soul and I'm telling you that it stops now. *Now!* And if she ever comes over here again..."

"David, you can't tell me who I can invite as a guest to my house. But, I'll make sure..."

"Not Stratford, dammit. Ellen. If *she* ever comes over to this farm again, I'll..."

"You'll what?"

"I'll beat her bloody."

"The hell you will. You lay a hand on that child in anger and I'll have the sheriff at your place in ten minutes."

"No, you won't."

"Don't wager your freedom on it. You'll spend a month in jail, I'll see to it. The Madison County prosecutor is a former student of mine."

David spat on the ground at Sam's feet, then wiped his lips on the back of his hand. "You think you're so all-powerful, a big-deal university professor who can throw his former students up to me. Well, mister professor bullshit, you're not as smart as you think you are. And I know you won't call the sheriff neither."

"You're crazy, you know that? I will not allow that child to be brutalized by you. Lay a hand on her and you'll be in handcuffs, led away. I'll see to it. I swear I will."

"No you won't. Because I know you, see? And you can picture your little pet right now, can't you? After I've had at her. I'll black her eyes and I'll loose her teeth. She'll bleed, hear me? Bleed from her nose and her split lips." He nodded his head, daring Sam to deny the image. "You can see her, can't you, you bastard? You can see her spitting up blood. You bastard. You can see the welts across her backside from my strap. You can see it, I know you can."

"You'd do that to her?"

"You're damn right I would, Butler, to save her soul from you and that..." He paused, as if catching himself before using a vulgarity. Then, "...that ungodly woman. And I know you, see? I know that putting me in jail for a month wouldn't pay you for seeing her like that. Not by half it wouldn't pay you. You won't let that happen to her, and you know I'd do it. You know I will. If she ever sets foot on this land again, I'll do that."

"But David, I can't keep her away."

"You tell her to go and she'll go."

"Cardinal will never put up with this. She'll take the children and leave you."

"She won't. She's my wife. The Lord called us to each other, and she won't let you separate us. And she won't because it will be your idea. If it's my idea, Cardinal will work her ways on me. But if I tell her that you sent Ellen away, she won't know what's happening. So, keep her away from here or I'll beat her until she bleeds."

"David. I can't...You wouldn't..."

"To save her soul, I would. And you know that. But I won't have to because of that picture you're thinking right now. Leave her alone and stay away from my family or you'll hear it in your sleep. You'll hear screams at night and you'll know it's her."

And with that it was over and David was back in his truck, leaving Sam standing on the dirt road with the grass strip down the middle, knowing that David had him perfectly figured out.

Halfway back up to the house, Sam was taken ill, and he stood, one hand on a tree for support, emptying the whiskey out of his stomach down the front of his shirt. His head was light, and he gasped for breath through the vomit, and his ribs caught sharply. He could see the picture that David had painted, he could hear Ellie's screams, he could smell her blood. He could hear her sobs as she begged David to stop. And the image, the sounds and the smells would not go away.

From up at the house, he heard a phone ringing, but he could not imagine talking to anyone. Or calling anyone. Or doing anything. The only thing he could imagine was driving. Driving to nowhere.

## Two Hours Later.

They say, scientists do, that one can drive a car while technically asleep. That the brain can continue performing routine tasks, like keeping the car going straight, while an EEG shows brain waves characteristic of sleep, not deep sleep, but sleep. Cruise control helps, but is not necessary. Trouble comes when the sleep deepens, or when something non-routine occurs, at which point one either wakes up or dies. Owners of horses have no difficulty believing this brain science, because every one of us has seen a horse loafing in a pasture or stall, one hind leg cocked, tail still swishing at the flies, eyes wide open, but asleep. Sometimes they lie down, sometimes even flat, but usually not. Their knees lock so they don't fall down and they sleep, standing up, eyes open.

Sam Butler was not asleep as he drove west on US 412, through Springdale and Siloam Springs and across the state line into Oklahoma, but his brain had largely shut down, unable to deal otherwise with the image that David had put into his head, the image of Ellie being beaten, of her blood and her screams. He stopped for red lights, roughly observed the speed limit, usually driving well under it, even paid the toll on the Cherokee Turnpike, and once he stopped to be sick again along the side of the highway, though there was nothing left in his stomach other than bitter slime. Yet he did all of this while being largely unaware of what he was doing. He was trying to drive away from what he had seen, but what he had seen he had seen only in his mind's eye, and it could not be driven away from.

Thus, it would not be an exaggeration to say that Sam came to his senses at the intersection of highways 412 and 69, the exit for Pryor, his senses having been not shut down, exactly, but occupied almost entirely in his flight from what David had promised he would do. He saw and heard little, smelled, tasted and felt nothing until he came to his senses and took the route that led to Claremore and the track. The parking lot he pulled into held a few cars and pickups, and several trailers, and it actually took him a minute sitting there stopped, with both hands on the wheel, to figure out where he was. He looked around. The sky was overcast, the land flat, and he was horribly tired, though he couldn't quite remember why. He thought he'd lie back in the seat and close his eyes for a bit, but as soon as he did the image of Ellie bloody and begging David to stop re-formed and he snapped awake. He couldn't let himself go to sleep, so he got out of the pickup and walked across the parking lot and up the ramp into the grandstand, overlooking the track.

The grandstand was empty, as there were no races that day. The track itself was empty, too, as it was much too late in the day for horses to be working. He took a seat half-way up the rows, put his elbows on his knees, his head in his hands and tried to figure out what to do. His head throbbed, his stomach was sour, and he had an adrenalin and whiskey hangover that made his skin feel empty.

Would David do it? Probably not. He was not, Sam thought, an evil person, nor one, Sam thought, who could convince himself that Ellie had to be beaten bloody to save her soul. He had said it just that plainly to Sam, but he probably hadn't meant it. He had for sure once slapped Ellie with his open hand, but that was far short of this threat. He probably wouldn't really do it.

Would Cardinal permit it? Certainly not. If she saw it coming in advance, she'd keep it from happening; Sam was confident she could and she would. And if it happened before she knew about it, and before she could prevent it, she would take Ellie, the baby and the boys and leave, Sam had been right about that. They'd go to Melissa and Stuart's and they'd be safe there. Or Melissa would stop it herself. She had no respect for either David or his preferred form of Christianity, and would use his threat as an excuse to take Ellie away from him. She may not be fond of Lynda and her aggressive atheism, but she would surely not permit David to beat Ellie in the name of Christ.

But, even as Sam lay out these reasons, almost visualized the arguments lying out on the grass of the infield, almost saw them spelled out in the lights of the tote board, he knew that they were insufficient. David *probably* wouldn't do it. Cardinal would prevent it *if* she saw it coming. But neither was good enough; both allowed for the possibility that Ellie ends up broken and bleeding, with Sam and Cardinal and Melissa and Stuart trying haplessly to repair her body and her spirit after the fact. The possibility was small perhaps, but not small enough to ignore. Small, but large enough to plan in the event of, and any such planning turned his stomach and made him want to weep. Everything that any of them could do after the fact seemed almost pitiful in the face of what it would do to Ellie to be beaten like that. David in handcuffs? David had understated it: it would not pay one-tenth of the toll. Not one-hundredth. Nothing would, and Sam had known it the instant after David had made the threat. He would not risk the smallest possibility of the event if there was a way to prevent it.

And was there? A way to prevent it? Nothing that the sheriff could do in advance, nothing that Child Welfare could do, nothing that Cardinal or Melissa or Stuart, or even Ellie herself, could do in advance would foreclose the possibility, not to Sam's satisfaction.

Except. Except if he did as David said and sent her away. Could he trust David? Could he trust him not to beat Ellie if he sent her away? Sam felt sick to his stomach again as he realized that the answer was yes. He practically gagged at the thought, but yes, if he did as David said, he could trust him not to beat her. Sam alone had in his power the pathway to protect Ellie, to ensure that she would never suffer the punishment he had been imagining. All he had to do was to give up that which had become his most valuable possession: the hours he spent with Ellie, her math problems and the horses.

This logical progression stopped there. Sam had not known what to do the day she'd been slapped, but now, yes, he thought he did. For the next half-hour, he did nothing except stare across the infield at the backside in the distance, where the horses, the trainers, the vets, the jockeys, the hot walkers, the grooms, the farriers and their friends and families would be working through the slow part of a day without racing. He thought of nothing, but the image he'd been driving away from was gone, with his knowledge that he could prevent it. He thought of nothing more. He stank of the vomit on his shirt but he didn't notice it. He had to urinate, but he was more inclined to wet himself than find the energy it would take to move. He sat, considering nothing. He sat.

He would, of course, eventually lose her. He knew that even before the thought came around to him. To a boyfriend, eventually. To the girls' soccer team, maybe. The track team. To college. To the church. A mission. To adulthood. The time would come, as it had to. As the time had come four years ago and he had lost Sally. From where he sat now, he could see the place she stood that day, along the rail, and said she wanted a Coke and Miss Run Run, the horse that Ellie called Daisy. And maybe even that day he had known that he would eventually lose Sally. Just as he now knew that he would eventually lose Ellie. He was not ready for that time to be here yet, but he suspected that he would not be ready for it later, either. He considered this thought for another silent half-hour, and then walked back to his pickup where he had left his phone and, leaning against the fender and looking back in the direction of Arkansas, the Ozarks and home, he called Cardinal, never wanting so much to get voice mail, which he did. "Cardinal, it's Sam. I talked to David, and I think it's best if Ellie doesn't come over anymore. I'm sure you can find another math tutor. You'll tell her for me, won't you? I'm sorry, but it's for the best. That's the way it needs to be." He broke the connection, placed the phone on the ground under the rear wheel of the pickup, got in and drove home. He had chores to do.

**That Evening.**

Without preamble: "What did you say to her?"

"Samuel. Thanks for calling. I thought I'd hear from you before now. Did you recover? The dog seemed to have. I've been calling you, but of course..."

"What did you say to her?"

"Well, let's see. Here's the recap: First I said we should get rid of the snake, which we interred with some ceremony in the garden by the springhouse. Ellie's a trouper, I'll say that for her. I like her. She did all of the handling of the reptile; I dug the hole. She said a few appropriate words over the headless departed, though I thought the idea of praying over a snake raised serious theological difficulties, which I didn't share with her. Then, let's see, we saw to the horses, which she introduced to me in turn. Sorry. *Who* were introduced to me. She told me who went where and why, and we fed the dog, Teena. Then, up at the house, we did the math lesson. I said that factoring was just like picking all of the oranges out of a basket full of apples, oranges and plums, which I thought was a nearly brilliant pedagogic device, though she didn't, probably because *you* didn't say it. But she got all the answers right, and that was that. So we chatted about this and that until I had to get back to work."

"Your note said she left in a huff."

"Oh, that. Yeah, an eight-cylinder huff. It's an expression that I read somewhere and I've been waiting about ten years for the opportunity to use it. I think it's from the Fifties."

"About what?"

"What about what?"

"What was she in a huff about?"

"Oh, I don't know. Out of the blue she asked me if I thought you were going to go to heaven, a question that's rarely been asked of me about anyone. I said 'no.' She looked crestfallen, and said that that was what David said, so I was now in the position of being in agreement with that asshole, so I said that our mutual friend Samuel Butler was a good man, the best, but you wouldn't be going to heaven because there is no such place. Which is all right, because there's no life after this one anyway. And while we're at it, there's no God either, and everything she reads in the Bible is nothing but a big fairy tale, and she is too smart and too grown up to still be believing in fairy tales. I think that was about it."

"Oh, Lord. Why did you have to say that to her?"

"Well, it's the truth, to start with."

"You don't know that."

"I know it, and so do you. Actually, the harsher version is that it's not a fairy tale at all, but a book written long ago by a bunch of guys with an agenda, and edited over the years by different bunches of guys with different agendas. At best, it's got some decent poetry, some entertaining stories, some slanted history, and a couple of charming attempts by some primitive simpletons to explain, for example, the multiplicity of human languages. At worst, it's a grand and devious lie. The Word of God, it ain't. You know it and I know it. It's time she knew it."

"Not now. Not this afternoon. It's too soon."

"This morning, it still was. And at that, it was past time. Be pleased that I gave her the gentler version."

"It was not your job."

"No. It was yours. I did it for you. You're invited to thank me."

"You know what you did was wrong. You were never so equivocal in your life as you were a minute ago when I asked you what happened. You knew what I was asking about, but you danced around, talking about the damn snake and the horses and the math. I may not know you very well, but I know when you're avoiding the subject, which you never do. You knew what I wanted to know and you were afraid to admit it. You knew it was wrong."

"Wrong? I knew it was the *right* thing to do, but I also knew that you'd object, and I didn't want to pick a fight with you. I still don't. Why don't I come out and I'll play for you and we can talk it out?"

"I'm busy."

"Be that way. But what I told that girl will serve her well in the end. Just be patient. She's got to grow up, grow into herself. She still has a ways to go, but today was a start. She'll thank me one day, you'll see."

"You didn't do it with her in mind. You did it to amuse yourself, that's all. Just like with that damn list of numbers."

"What list?"

"Shut up. You did it for your own benefit, not for hers, and you did it without any thought about what it would do to her in the long run. You used her, Lynda. She's a child and you used her for your own selfish purposes."

There was a pause on the other end of the line. Then, "Are we talking about me or about you?"

"You have no idea what you've done."

"Yes, I do, and she'll be better for it."

"You have no idea what you've done."

He hung up, wondering if she'd call right back. But no, of course not. She doesn't call back. She doesn't ask permission, she had told him that first night.

She doesn't call ahead, and she wouldn't call back. Which was all right with Sam, as he was too exhausted to explain anything to her, to ask anything of her. His head throbbed with fatigue; it hurt to breathe; his stomach was sour and empty, his body parts refused to reunite themselves. His legs were too weak to climb the stairs, so he sat in the rocking chair in the kitchen and stared at the phone hanging on the wall, wondering what was to become of him.

The moon was full that night, rising yellow at sunset, only a little south of due east. By midnight, it was pure white, a square of moonlight on the floor of the kitchen, where Sam still sat, still awake, still too scared and fatigued to sleep, still too sleep-deprived to think straight. Except to know that it was too late to undo what had happened, too late to change what had been said, too late to go back to before.

**The Next Morning.**

Of course, there was one last scene that had to play out. Surely Ellie would drive her four-wheeler over to find out what was going on. Even when David forbade it, she would find a chance to slip away unnoticed and drive over to Sam's to find out what was going on. And, when Sam awoke in the morning, painfully stiff and unrested from his night in the chair and the previous one on the patio, he knew that he could tell her none of the things that he wanted to say. That it was all Lynda's fault. That Sam knew that he should never have left her alone with Lynda. That he didn't believe any of those things Lynda had said. That if they let a few weeks go by, David might soften and relent.

No, he could tell her nothing that would make the separation easier, for anything he said like that would eventually get back to David, harden him, and make things worse. Anything he said like that would only encourage her to defy David and be beaten. Even to say that he was sorry and would miss her and that he loved her could have repercussions he couldn't stomach. For her own safety, he had to make her unwelcome, and he had to make her believe it.

So he steeled himself and when she rode up in the morning and ran back to where he was doing the chores, he made his face a mask and spoke so sharply to her that it caused her to stop in her tracks ten yards away. "Go home. You're not to come over here anymore." She stood and stared at him, her eyes round with fear. His voice had so frightened her that she could neither speak nor cry.

"Wha...?"

"Go home. Don't come back."

"But, I'll help with the horses, even if you don't want to teach me. I..." When his face did not break from its mask, she stopped talking and stood looking at him.

After a moment that stretched to hours for him, he raised his voice. "God damn it, can't you hear? I said go home." And then he spoke the only lie he ever told her, but it was an excellent one: "I don't want you here anymore."

# CODA

## NOVEMBER 2013

**The Second Tuesday.**

She had been wrong, of course. They had been wrong about almost everything. That was before they knew.

They stood at the fence line for fifteen minutes, maybe, without speaking. They knew each other so well by now that oftentimes speech seemed superfluous. Sometimes distracting even. They finished each other's thoughts; they spoke in code. And often they were silent.

The pasture they looked into was not theirs. Maybe they knew the owner, but they didn't know that they knew the owner. They were five miles or so from home, a slow, two-hour walk. He guessed that they would soon turn back, but there was no hurry. The afternoon was bright, and warm for February, and they had nothing in particular to hurry home to.

In the pasture were a dozen horses. No, more. Two dozen. Mares, probably. Pregnant, probably. Tails swishing the early-spring flies away, they walked here and there through ankle-high fescue. Later they would learn to say fetlock-high. They were Quarter Horses—small, stocky, short ears—and probably due to foal soon.

Sam and Sally liked watching the little ones when they arrived, but today they were too early.

"Horses grazing," she said at last.

He said nothing for a bit. Then, "Yup."

"I meant more than that."

"More how?"

"My favorite sight."

"Horses grazing?"

"They seem perfectly content." She said nothing more for a long spell. Then, "At peace." For the first time now she turned and looked at him. "You?"

He thought. "Sunrise in October..." A long pause, during which she nodded. Then "Venus fading into the morning sky. Frost on the fields, to burn off later. The leaves just having turned." Another long pause. "Deer leaping the fence line. Squirrels carrying walnuts. Crows walking..."

"You're greedy. You want it all."

"Okay. No squirrels." A long pause. "Rain."

A pause while she got his drift.

"Distant thunder," she said, "promising rain."

"You always were the subtle one. Patient." Pause. "Burgers frying."

She chuckled. "The grass after you cut it. No. I changed my mind. Clean sheets, just off the line."

He smiled down at her. "Ready?"

And a few minutes later, they started walking slowly home.

She had been wrong, of course.

Sam Butler sat with his back to a white oak tree in the day pasture on a cool November morning, a mist falling, the chores done, the horses grazing, nearing the hour when Ellie used to arrive.

She had been wrong, of course, Sally had. About horses grazing. That had been long ago, before they knew, before they had owned their own. Before they had bought the broken-down, scrawny Thoroughbred mare, who had run thirty-two races and won her various owners twelve thousand dollars, more or less, who had been juiced with steroids, had her cycles suppressed, and had been blocked so she would run through the pain. She had been whipped beyond the finish line until she lost the will to run. And when she had proved herself to be worthless as a broodmare—"failure to settle" is the jargon, no doubt caused by the pharmacopeia that had been dumped into her veins—she had been put into a dry lot in Oklahoma and ignored, until Sally had heard of her and had said "we are doing this," and they had brought her home. She had quietly given them their first lessons in horses, and had been a patient teacher with them, as they slowly learned her equine ways. She had quietly accepted her hay and her feed, or a sweet carrot or apple, or a lingering soft brush, or a stroke on her flank, but she never seemed to expect such. And she had quietly accepted the arrival of other horses on the farm, who found it necessary to exert their dominance over her. And finally, she had quietly died, and they had found her lying in the paddock one morning, and she had taught them her last lesson.

And so, now, years later, Sam sat in the November mist watching five—no four—horses grazing, Dreadnaught having wandered over a height of land and was now out of his sight. Ellie had called him Naughty at first, then Afraid of Nothing. Sam watched them and knew that Sally had been wrong. Yes, there was peaceful contentedness to horses grazing, but there was an obsessiveness about it, too. They are not like cows, who will lie down to chew the cud and contemplate (or not) the intricacies of bovine existence. Horses will graze twenty hours a day, if given the chance. They will go without sleeping. During a drought, they will nibble the grass down to the nub. They will paw at the winter turf to expose the roots, then graze on the roots. (I may have mentioned: they do not think ahead.) They will graze themselves sick, if given the chance, foundering on the spring fescue and colicking in the fall clover, if given the chance.

Nor do they always graze peacefully. They had seen nervous grazing, he and Sally had, when a new horse joined the herd and the priorities were yet to be established, the horse's muzzle in the grass, but his ears cautiously surveying the surroundings. And angry grazing, when one was separated from his buddies and forced to be alone. A chomp of grass, chewed defiantly. And they had seen a colicking horse nibble, then trot aimlessly around the pasture, bite at her flanks, lie down, get up, nibble some more, a horse that needed tending *now*.

So, Sally had been wrong back then, back before they knew.

But just now she was right, and he watched the four horses he could see, grazing with the equine contentedness that she had envied on that Saturday

afternoon in February, years ago. The mist collected on the oak leaves, still cling-
ing to the branches above his head, and dripped to the ground around him, not
exactly the rain of his favorite sound that day, but pleasant enough. He pulled up
the hood of his sweatshirt against the falling drops and the breeze from the west,
and watched them.

Sam was acutely aware that it was the second Tuesday of November, by one
measure precisely a year since Dreadnaught, who had now wandered back into
view, had gotten himself tangled up and busted the gate, when Ellie had been full
of concern that he was bleeding, and when Johnson Reynolds had driven out to
tell him about the dean's proposal and had changed his life. A year.

A year ago, he remembered, a dry summer and an early frost had taken
the leaves off the trees by now, but this year the frost was late and hadn't yet been
hard. A wet and mild summer had made for a bumper crop of walnuts, acorns
and hickories, and the squirrels would be fat through the winter. The first frost
when it gently came had turned the leaves stunningly beautiful, especially the
yellow hickories and sassafras and the red sumacs and tupelo. The cedars were
so full of berries that their limbs looked blue-green and drooped. The front that
was bringing this rain, though, would have clear skies and a hard freeze behind
it, moon-less and cold, with Jupiter rising in Gemini, and, if the wind was light,
as was forecast, the leaves of the mulberries, already yellow and heavy, would
fall straight down in the morning, a yellow cloud settling not quite silently onto
the ground. But for now, for another day at least, there was this heavy mist on a
breeze from the west, and drops falling from the leaves.

A year had passed. A year. He had seen Ellie only twice in the six months
since the separation. Once he had walked into the Huntsville Harp's, a place he
rarely shopped, but he'd been at the farm supply place in town and had ducked
into Harp's to grab a half-gallon of milk, and he'd seen their backs, Cardinal's
and Ellie's, Cardinal looking over the produce, Ellie carrying Esther, the boys
apparently at home. He quickly left the store, without the milk. And then, just
last month, he had seen her at the Chili Pepper cross-country meet. He had been
looking forward to the races, without even thinking that he might run into her.
The men were reported to be quite good this year, in the running to be the national
champs, and there was that girl from Elkins, whose name he didn't remember,
who was said to be quite a 6K runner. But as he pulled into the parking lot near

the start/finish line, with the athletes jogging or stretching their impossibly fit bodies, he saw, already heading for their—his and her—favorite spot inside the loop, one hundred meters before the finish, he saw Ellie walking with Cardinal and Molly and Blair, her two new track-fan friends from the Indoor Nationals. Not so new anymore, actually. Ellie was dressed in her Razorback gear, with her clipboard and stopwatch, and she was talking with animation to her friends, maybe about what the prospects were for a double Razorback victory. Perhaps Cardinal had glanced his way and recognized the small pickup, but if she did, her glance did not linger, and she quickly turned to herd the kids along and to pay attention to where you're going. Sam had watched from his pickup for a while and then had driven away before the races began and the next morning had read the results in the paper with no particular interest.

Beyond those two times, nothing. Six months. He had called Cardinal's cell once, and she had answered.

"Is she safe?"

"Safe from what?"

"You know from what."

"Yes, she's safe." A pause, then, quietly, "I don't know why you did it, Sam, but I'll never forgive you. Don't call again."

There was a brutal ambiguity in what Cardinal had said, and he had puzzled over it in the days and weeks to follow. *It*. What had she meant by *it*? That Sam had sent Ellie away? Did she think that David had threatened to beat him, not the girl, and that Sam had sent her away instead of fighting for her? That he was an egghead coward and had buckled in the face of David's bullying? Or had *it* meant that Sam had let Lynda teach the math lesson? Or had David reconstructed the events so as to make Sam, not Lynda, the culprit who had caused the girl to question her faith? An ambiguous word, *it*. But, alas, there was no ambiguity at all in Cardinal's final thoughts. She would not forgive him, and he had not called again.

Melissa he saw occasionally, always at his place, always in the evening, while Stuart was traveling, he suspected, though she never said it and he didn't ask. She would call ahead on the afternoon of her visits to make sure he was free, and she would arrive after dinner, drive through the gates and park up behind the isolation paddock, where her car couldn't be seen from the road, though that was not something he had suggested that she do. They did not go out and he never offered an invitation. It was understood that she would come over when she could.

From the beginning, there was a wistfulness to their meetings. On her first visit, he told her at length what had happened, starting with Lynda's arrival that morning and ending with his call to Cardinal from the track. He wept during the telling, and she let him, listening without interrupting, looking down at her hands folded in her lap. When he ran out of words, she remained silent until he spoke again.

"Will you tell Ellie for me? Will you tell her why?"

And she was silent still, until finally she said, "When she needs to know, she will. Perhaps she already does."

"But will she be all right? Will David beat her?"

"No."

"Will she be all right?"

"Yes."

After that first night, they never spoke of those events again. He would ask her first thing when she came in the door, "How is she?"

And Melissa might say, "She's fine." Or "She has a little cold." Or "She stepped on a nail and had to get a tetanus shot." And after that they would drink tea and play slow cribbage, but they did not keep score game-to-game. Or they would divide a beer and watch a movie, some DVD that she had brought with her. Or they would sit in the living room, now in the fall before a fire, each with a book, their thoughts elsewhere. They talked about little that was important, and they were not intimate. They did not talk about Sally or Stuart, or Lynda or David, or family life either in general or in particular. He never asked for details of Ellie's life beyond what Melissa told him. And she never mentioned that he had failed to do the one thing that she had told him was most important, and he had not stayed a presence in Ellie's life.

They did not talk about the past or the future or ethics or religion, or the war in Syria or global climate change, or the last election or the next one. He would tell her about his day and the animals; she'd tell him about her day and the book she was reading. They would talk pleasantly enough about the movie or how the cards were falling, or about the weather or the birds or the trees, the bald eagle he had seen circling the day pasture, the skunk walking delicately along a log by the pond, as if afraid to get his feet wet in the grass, the hen he hadn't even known was missing who showed up trailing ten chicks of various colors, or the adjoining landowner who needed to do something about the thistles. And they both shared one thought, though neither ever spoke it: that, in a different world, she would leave Stuart and move in with Sam and perhaps marry him or perhaps not, but that in this world, after the separation, to do so would cause her, too, to lose Ellie, and that, they both knew without either saying it, that she would not risk. And so, they saw each other occasionally, and he heard a little about Ellie, but that was all.

Of Lynda Stratford and Jonathan Wheeler he saw nothing. Lynda had called him a few days after the separation, acting as if they had not had cross words the previous time they had spoken, and she had cheerily asked about the Derby-watch party, but he had been cool on the phone and she had ended the conversation entirely without drama, and had never called again. The next time Sam was in the law school, he had asked his secretary how many were enrolled in Professor Wheeler's IT Law class and when Donna had said "twenty-seven," he had exited the building with no additional comments to anyone, either then or later. He eventually heard through the university grapevine that they both—The Streelers, Johnson Reynolds had called them—had resigned in May, so late as to require considerable scrambling by their respective departments to cover their classes for the fall. She, he learned, had been offered a position full of prestige, cash and limited exam-grading at Lawrence-Livermore and Berkeley, and it was certain that negotiations over such a move had been under way for months, during which she had spoken not a word of it to Sam. Jonathan. No one seemed to know if Jonathan was going to try to find a teaching job or go back into law practice. His resignation had mooted out the tenure decision, of course, and had rendered forever irrelevant the question of whether Wilson, Selvig and Pryor were the soft *no* votes, and if so whether they would have been satisfied with the requirements contracts article. Nor was the hacking, or not, into the law school's anonymous exam numbers of any remaining local concern, except to the extent that Sam's knowledge of it was something that ate away at him, which it did. The dean still offered Sam his stipend for mentoring Jonathan, and Sam took it, inwardly embarrassed by what he knew about the hack but wasn't saying. And with it, he set up a small trust account in Ellie's name, with one of his former students as trustee, and payable when Ellie turned eighteen, but he told no one about it. In due course, the trustee would inform Ellie.

Of Sally's unknown correspondent, Sam knew little more than he had known the moment he discovered that the post office box key in the drawer of the desk in the study didn't open their box in Hindsville: that she had a secret correspondent with whom she shared an affection that probably did not end with corrections from the *Times*. And that perhaps those letters were somehow related to Sally's pulling herself onto the wagon the day they bought Miss Run Run, and to her falling off of it during the afternoon with Tommy Greene. But that he would never know for sure. After months of silent debate—debate surely between himself and the absent Sally—he had decided to write to the unknown North Dakotan at the mail box up there. It had then taken him another two weeks to decide what to say. Finally, in June, he sent a letter addressed to Box-holder, P.O. Box 17, Grand Forks, North Dakota 58202, with inside a single sheet of yellow lined legal paper saying "I'd like to contact you, /s/ Samuel Butler." He thought of adding "Sally is dead," but did not.

Of course, he never heard back. He had hoped for a note. Or at the very least a "RETURN TO SENDER," perhaps written on the envelope in the same blocky hand, or perhaps not. But, no. Nothing. Probably what happened was exactly what happened when Sam, or almost anyone else for that matter, received a letter addressed to Boxholder. Or maybe Sally's correspondent no longer owned the box. Or perhaps... Perhaps the boxholder opened the envelope outside in the post office parking lot, on a North Dakota summer day, hot and with the on-rush of summer that is common in the north, with thunder clouds moving in from the west. Perhaps it would have been around lunch time, and the boxholder had ducked out of the office, or whatever, and visited the box just on the chance. A chance. Even after all these years. And perhaps the boxholder knew exactly who Samuel Butler was, and had surmised, perhaps correctly, perhaps not, what had happened and why Sam was writing now. And perhaps the boxholder sat in the car in the parking lot and thought whatever thoughts there were to be thought before returning to work, dropping Sam's note in the trash on the way in.

So. A year. The mystery of Sally's post office box had become part of his life. As had his ethical lapse, or not, regarding the hack. But Ellie was gone, and that he could hardly stand. The ache of that deprivation ran deep and constant. Somehow it all had to do with Lynda Stratford, who played his piano, rubbed his mare's belly, and offered to take him to bed. *Had* taken him to bed, once, the night of the accident, when he woke up late at night in the dark and found her sleeping quietly beside him, on Sally's side of the bed, not touching. Lynda, who called him Samuel and his home the Sally shrine, who wanted him to enlighten Ellie, and who, in the end, changed everything.

Why had she done it? Sam had asked himself that a thousand times in six months. He had come to know, over the months she had been here, had come to know her ways, but rarely her reasons. Why had she wanted to sleep with him? He couldn't imagine. Why had she toyed with him over Jonathan's hacking? Because she thought the rules were silly, breaking them sport? Had she been trying to sabotage Jonathan's career, setting up her move to loftier academic environs, to Berkeley and who knows where next? But that seemed more devious than he knew her to be, and hardly necessary, as he knew Jonathan to be. Why had she said what she had said to Ellie? To amuse herself? To punish him? To enlighten Ellie?

No. Lynda, he knew, was largely imperturbable. She had few triggers, few pushable buttons. But Ellie had unerringly found her way to one of the few, one that worked, and she had innocently pushed it in: she had compared Lynda to David. Lynda might have let anything else pass by, in deference to the girl's age, to Sam's peaceful life. But not that. *That* needed a response, a rebuttal. *That* she'd never let lie, never. Not for the sake of peace. Not to patronize a child. Not even to please her friend Samuel Butler. Somehow it made her seem more understandably human to have once lost that much control.

Sam had told her, there at the end, that she didn't know what she'd done, but he had been wrong. She knew, and was entirely unapologetic about it. What she didn't know is what *he* had done. What David had threatened and how Sam had collapsed under the weight of the threat. She would ridicule him for it if she ever found out, for she herself would surely have called David's bluff. She would have challenged David to play out his hand, to act on his threat if he dared, and then would have dropped a ton of brick on his head if he had. She would have played the odds, bet the smart money, and crushed David if the loss came to pass.

"Bridge jumpers," they call them at the track: take a heavy, heavy favorite, a sure thing to win, and bet a bundle on him to show, that is to finish third or better. If he does, you get a nice little return on your bundle, say five percent. If he stumbles and comes up lame, he'll be vanned off, probably to die, and you'll lose the bundle and want to jump off a bridge. Sam thought they were crazy, bridge jumpers. The likelihood of winning was not worth the two minutes of agony as the race played out. But Lynda would make the bet in a heartbeat. She would have taken ten seconds to look the situation over, standing in the road with David, and then sent him home to do it or not, and then to see. While Sam had taken two hours in his unslept exhaustion and then declined to make the bet. She had not been standing there in the road with him, had not had to decide, as he had, but somehow, like everything else that had happened to him in the last year, even that event seemed to have something to do with her. Lynda Stratford, the book-by-the-cover judger, who walked a path higher than that trodden by the crowd, and who would consider her own centrality to this story a part of the natural order of things.

But no, maybe she was wrong; maybe it was Just One Look who was the central figure in all of this. He had been the new horse then, a year ago when all of this began, put up in his round pen at night, with Evening Smoke his reluctant company. Sam had begun to send him and Smokey up to the night pasture with the others back in July, which had, in turn, changed the dynamics of the morning feed. Perhaps the key to the entire puzzle was The Looker, and perhaps if he hadn't been kept up overnight a year ago, perhaps that morning Dreadnaught would have been just enough more patient not to get tangled in the gate and hurt himself. Johnson Reynolds would still have arrived with the dean's proposal, but without Dreadnaught hurt, Ellie would not have been so upset, and she might not have asked him to help Jonathan write the article, which he remembered he had not been inclined to do until she asked him to. And if he'd declined, he would not have met Lynda, would never have found the key, and when the dog killed the snake, would simply have cancelled math class, or pulled himself together and taught the class himself. If only...

"If, if, if, if and if," Sally used to say to dismiss this kind of what-if-ing. "If, if, if, if and if," her index fingers plugging her ears. "If, if, if, if and if," mixing herself another drink. "If, if, if, if and if. Shut up."

The rain was falling more heavily now, causing three of the horses to retreat to the shelter. But Miss Run Run, about whom Sally had said "She's mine" as she took the Coke, and whom Ellie called Daisy after the star on her forehead, and whose image, minus the Nativity scene, still stood on the table with the lamp by the hearth, the mare moved toward the stock tank for a drink. Sam watched with interest as Dreadnaught walked over to the tank himself, pinned his ears and pointed his nose at her hindquarters, and Sam watched with even more interest as the mare retreated and left the water to the gelding. It appeared that Dee intended to move up the priority ladder and establish himself as the new number four. Maybe he had seen some signal from the mare, some hesitancy in her eyes, some sign that she was not going to put up a fight, that it was not a fight she felt like having. A few more such encounters during the next few days and it would be over. Daisy would submit and that would be that. Life was not set, he saw. Not for the horses in his little herd, anyway. And not for his own life, which had been up-ended in the last year. Perhaps—who was to say?—perhaps he would live to see the old order return, to hear the sound of Ellie's four-wheeler coming too quickly down the road from the west, to watch her greet the dog and the horses, toss scratch to the hens, and ride The Looker as if they were flying. There was always that hope.

There was always that hope. "When she needs to know, she will," Melissa had told him. She was a strong-willed and independent girl, growing up, soon to be a teenager. Perhaps one day she would pin her ears like Dreadnaught (so to speak) and point her nose at David, and say "I'm going over to Mr. Butler's now," and leave. And when she arrived, in the midst of the morning chores, he'd say "Hey, kiddo." And she'd say, "I can't do these problems." And he'd say, "We'll look at them in a bit, but Daisy's mane's a little tangled," not making a big deal of it, and continue filling up the stock tanks. And Ellie would still know where the brushes and curry combs were in the tack room, on the shelf above the one where Sam kept the goop to treat wounds, and that would be that.

Perhaps.

Someday.

But not yet. And not today.

At last he surrendered to the rain, stood up and walked over to where Daisy was waiting her turn for a drink. He scratched behind her right ear and she bumped his chest with her nose. He spoke aloud. "I know." And he stood there with her, waiting for Dreadnaught, Afraid of Nothing, to finish his drink.

Horses grazing, Sally had said, was her favorite sight. And rain, he had said, his favorite sound. They had not done favorite touch that day, but he thought of it now. The touch of a woman's breast. The weight of a horse's head, resting in the crook of your arm. A graduation-day handshake. The feel of Thai silk. His grip on a small bony shoulder as he tried clumsily to comfort a young girl, crying into a horse's neck.

And that led to the image that he couldn't shake, of the same girl, sobbing in her mother's arms because she hadn't even been allowed to say goodbye to the horses she loved. "Why, Mom?" And Cardinal's only possible answer: "Shhhh." That, he was now certain, on this day a year after it all began, that had been Cardinal's *it*. And she had been right: it was unpardonable. She had told him, he remembered, while Ellie rode The Looker through his flying lead changes on that cool January afternoon, she had told him, Cardinal had, that she was unable to forgive her own self for the circumstances of Ellie's conception. He had brushed off her concern that afternoon, but he now knew that her worldview was the right one. Some wrongs could be neither fixed nor forgotten. And his own sin in sending Ellie away without her goodbye was unpardonable, no matter how necessary it had seemed at the time. He felt sad beyond description, and he knew that no god worth worshipping would ever forgive such cruelty.

The mare now moved away from him and approached the water tank. She found the surface of the water with her lips, and drank. He watched her, then called to the dog and walked slowly, at Teena's pace, back up to the house. For the horses, today was today, without anticipation of tomorrow, but the days stretched out in front of Sam Butler like infinity.

# Acknowledgements

Andy Albertson, Will Foster, Emily Grant, the late Michael Lea, Ginny Masullo and Steve Smith gave the manuscript more time and thought than any writer has cause to expect. Their suggestions were smart and insightful, even those that I did not take. Thanks—belatedly with respect to Michael—to them all. Errors, indiscretions and infelicities, of course, are mine.

Thanks and then some to the artist and the quintet for keeping my life full and worthwhile.

And thanks to the farrier (unnamed here) who said, "I need a friend a good deal more than I need a lover," and got me thinking about this story.

# Readers Guide

1. The Math Tutor is set in the Ozarks, an area of the country ripe for stereotyping, whether as Dogpatch, Branson or Winter's Bone. To what extent did the story cause you to revise your image of the region? To what extent were your pre-conceptions reinforced?

2. At the end of the story, Sam is thinking that he has no idea why Lynda acted as she did. What do you think? Was her proposal of intimacy believable, or was she teasing him? Why did she hint about Jonathan's hacking of the listserve? And, most importantly, why did she say what she did to Ellie?

3. Was Lynda right in saying that Sam should have challenged David's religious teaching? Should he have tried, in the midst of the math lessons, to re-shape Ellie's beliefs? Or did he?

4. Was Melissa losing her Christian faith at the end, or do you suspect she never had it?

5. Sam imagines at the end what it would be like if Ellie ever comes back. Will she, do you think? If so, what do you think it will be like? Or do you read the story to tell the reader exactly what will happen when she comes back?

6. There are horses and allusions to horses throughout the story, but it's not really a story about horses. Or is it?

7. What do you make of Sally's secret correspondence? What do you make of Sally? She seems to be a major presence in the story, without ever being present, doesn't she? Why? Sam seems to think, on very thin evidence, that something happened in Sally's secret relationship (if that's what it was) that led, indirectly at least, to her accident. Is there enough there? And if not, why does Sam seem to reach that conclusion?

8. At what point in the story, if at all, did you have the feeling that things were going to take a turn for the worse? And were you right about what was going to happen?

9. Should Sam have called David's bluff? He seems to think that Lynda would have. Would you have?

10. At the end, Sam tries to figure out what Cardinal meant when she said "I don't know why you did it." What do you think she meant?

11. Was it cruel, do you think, for Lynda to call Sam's house the Sally shrine? Was it accurate, even if cruel? Why do those widowed often leave their missing partner's things untouched? Should they? Did (or will) you?

12. In their last phone conversation, Sam and Lynda both accuse the other of using Ellie for selfish purposes. Who's right?

www.ingramcontent.com/pod-product-compliance
Lightning Source LLC
Chambersburg PA
CBHW031154050726
47495CB00019B/1731